Ashes of the Red Heifer and the Final Battle

by

Steve Anderson

Ashes of the Red Heifer and the Final Battle
Copyright © 2004 by Steve Anderson
All rights reserved

This is a work of fiction. All characters are fictional and any resemblance to persons living or dead is purely coincidental.

No part of this book may be reproduced in any form whatsoever, whether by graphic, visual, electronic, filming, microfilming, tape recording, or any other means, without the written permission of the author, except in the case of brief passages embodied in critical reviews and articles where the title, author and ISBN accompany such review or article.

Published and Distributed by:

Granite Publishing and Distribution, LLC
868 North 1430 West
Orem, Utah 84057
(801) 229-9023 • Toll Free (800) 574-5779
Fax (801) 229-1924

Cover Design by Steve Gray
Cover Art by Steve Gray
Page Layout and Design by Myrna Varga

(This is a modified and expanded version of *The Enoch Scroll and the Final Battle* published in 1997 by Fletcher and Anderson Publishing, ISBN 0-966202-90-2)

ISBN: 1-932280-49-9

Library of Congress Control Number: 2004105967

First Printing May 2004

10 9 8 7 6 5 4 3 2 1

Printed in the United States of America

Dedication

To my mother and wife whose encouragement inspired the book, and to Jim and Susan who would not let the project die.

I

Fragments from the Past

Kyle Shepherd leaned against a slight outcropping of a rock wall and stretched out his legs. Gathering a pebble from his side, he tossed it in front of him, letting it careen down the face of the cliff, following its progress until it disappeared onto the desert floor. The cliff looked steeper from this height than it did from the ground. His feet confirmed that observation, for they were throbbing within his leather boots. He had stood too long on the steep rock face. He would have to rest them if he was going to continue searching for the scroll.

Looking eastward over the Dead Sea, he saw the sky was a flawless blue without the slightest vestige of the clouds that had brought in the thunderstorm. For two days conditions had been thus—hot, no breeze—suggesting a change wasn't in the offing. But even if another storm blew in, the chances were slim that it would be anything like the last one. Since modern-day Israel had kept meteorological records, no storm had ever produced so much water.

He took his straw hat off and placed it in his lap, and his eyes squinted. Looking southward, he saw the first wisp of a cloud forming near the edge of the sea, floating over Masada, The Stronghold, where Jewish patriots had held off the Romans for so long.

"A little rain would be nice," he thought. "Just enough to take some of the bite out of this heat."

Kyle ran his fingers through his black hair and yawned. It was a shame he had dropped that Chap Stick while crouching on the face of the cliff, but he was not about to go down for it. It would take him less than a minute to back down the rope that he was using for support and find it somewhere on the ground around his tent, but he couldn't bear the thought of making the eighty-foot climb back to where he was. His lips would have to crack a little more before he would do that.

His skin was well tanned, and he was handsome, handsome enough to be pitching a new cologne for an outdoor magazine—for mountain climbers or lumberjacks, perhaps. Kyle had his father's good looks, and his father had once moonlighted as a model while going to college. Kyle had the same strong jaw and blue eyes with dark eyebrows. His mouth was small with very little lower lip. His hair was naturally wavy and black. When he was a youngster, his curls had been a source of embarrassment. He was harassed by the older boys, but the girls had always liked them. When he hit the growth spurt that eventually took him to over six feet two inches, the cutesy comments had disappeared well along the way.

He moved his tongue around inside his mouth to find some spit then transferred it to his lips. Turning his straw hat over, he examined the leather sweatband now dark brown from perspiration. Something tugged at his pant leg, and his foot recoiled in panic, while he instinctively grabbed one of the rocks lying at his side. It was a black desert beetle—a large one—but it was harmless. He exhaled loudly. When would rationality replace his paranoia about scorpions? Perched this high off the ground, he had to be safe from them.

Since being stung by one two years earlier, only two kilometers northeast of these ruins of Qumran, he had allowed his fears to turn into a full-fledged phobia. But then again, he had been terribly sick, more than most, after such a sting. He discovered he was allergic to scorpions, so it was not as if he didn't have some justification. But now, whenever anything brushed against his pant leg, he reacted fearfully and quickly. That fear had surfaced often during the last few hours as he moved among the rocks on this cliff—a condition that was perhaps aggravated by the heat and the solitude.

The beetle crawled laboriously over a rock shaped like a semi-deflated football, and then stepped fully into the sun's rays, causing it to veer back into the shade, where it sought seclusion and the coolness of the shadows.

Kyle looked around for any other crawlers—the word he used for all bugs. Many of his fellow archaeologists knew all the varieties of insects throughout the Middle East by name, but he had never joined in their fascination for crawlers, considering them a nuisance pure and simple in his archaeological quests. He had been to remote spots—Egypt, Tikal in South America, the Congo—and enjoyed the variety of plant and animal life in the rain forests and deserts. Even the water buffalo that nearly trampled him off the Ivory Coast was quickly forgotten, but not the scorpion.

His college buddy, David Andreone, who caught for him when he pitched at USC, had summed up the ridiculous nature of his fear: "For an archaeologist to be afraid of insects is kind of like a doctor being queasy at the sight of blood."

He knew his phobia stemmed from an incident on his grandmother's farm in Illinois when his older sister tricked him into entering an abandoned outhouse, then locked him in for over an hour. The place was spider infested and their webs caught at his face and his hair, covering him like a shroud, until he sank shakily onto his haunches, shivering in terror. His mother eventually found him an hour later, but for years the sight of a spider gave him the cold sweats. He and his sister were reconciled, but his loathing of spiders had never lessened.

Taking his water jug from his knapsack, he downed a long drink.

"Strange," he thought, "that such a cool looking sky could make me feel so hot."

Perhaps he was wasting his time in this area. Other archaeologists had tried to dissuade him from this hunt. "You're going to spend your time around Qumran?" one exclaimed upon hearing of Kyle's plans to return to the area on the northwestern corner of the Dead Sea. "Kyle," he said sardonically, "how long has it been since the Dead Sea scrolls were found in that area?"

"You know as well as I do," Kyle answered.

"They were found in 1947, my friend, and the land has been scrutinized so thoroughly since then by thousands of Bedouins, archaeologists, explorers, politicians, den mothers, and anyone else who could drag themselves to that spot, that there's no chance something has been overlooked. Look, they've done aerial reconnaissance, infrared photography, satellite images—the whole bit—and the area has yielded everything that it's going to yield. Now, if you want to go back to that place where that scorpion got you, your chances of finding something will go up dramatically."

Kyle knew that the area around the city of Qumran had been thoroughly searched since a young shepherd from a Bedouin tribe, MuhanMad adh-Dhib—Muhammad the Wolf—had followed a stray animal to a small circular opening in the face of the cliff and discovered the Dead Sea scrolls inside, but Kyle liked to play hunches.

Wasn't it a hunch that had led him to an unopened burial tomb in the ancient city of Tikal in South America? His friends had criticized his judgment there, too, but he and his men had excavated just the same, and within two days the entrance to the tomb had been found.

So he was playing a hunch again. As in most of his hunches, he had some justification for searching in this area. Two weeks ago it had rained so hard for three days that many places in Syria, Lebanon, and Israel were inundated. The swollen Jordan River gouged out deep crevasses in its serpentine banks. One radio announcer in Tel Aviv joked that God might have forgotten his promise to Noah, not to flood the world again, which brought charges of blasphemy from the Jewish far right. But that rain uncovered some things that made Kyle feel Qumran was the right place to be.

The incident that led him here had occurred three days earlier in Jerusalem. While picking up supplies for a planned dig around Jericho, he went to a shop on the Via Dolorosa, the street where Jesus had supposedly carried his cross. There, a Jewish girl of twelve recognized him. She grabbed him by the arm, pulling him to a cardboard box of pottery that had been excavated near Qumran.

"I know you," she said while moving him toward her wares. "You are an archaeologist, and I have some things you would be interested in."

"How do you know me?" he asked as he looked inside the box. He was surprised to see several whole jars and two dozen broken pieces, all apparently of ancient origin.

"Mister Shepherd, do you not remember me? My father worked for you a few times. You said he was one of the best workers you'd ever known," she said proudly and smiled splendidly.

"What is your father's name?"

"Daniel Muir," she answered.

He looked closely at the girl and saw the father's brown, round eyes. "I remember him very well, and you're right—he was a very sensitive worker at our dig. Some have no feel for it and destroy much before they realize what they have done, but your father was quite good. What have you got here?"

Kyle knelt next to the cardboard box that had once held oranges, as a deep stain attested, and there was a trace of citric acid that mixed with the earthy, musty smells of the old pottery.

"You may be interested in some of these pieces, Mr. Shepherd. You see this one here has no cracks at all and is in mint condition."

He smiled at the way the girl had picked up the American expressions, which her father had probably passed along. Life for this girl was undoubtedly rough. Her father, Daniel, was an honest, hardworking man who had come from Russia some years ago, and because he was uneducated, he was left to do the menial tasks in Israel. Eventually, he fell into working for archaeologists because it had been fairly steady work. Unfortunately, one day he awoke to find his vision had clouded over. By the end of the week his sight had vanished altogether. Kyle had done what he could by seeking medical help for his worker, but the doctors were powerless to stop the disease that they had labeled acute bilateral blindness. Now his daughter was doing what she had seen her father do so that she might add to the family income. Kyle removed the 35-mm camera, which dangled from around his neck and set it down, knowing that he would buy something from her, even if he wasn't interested in her objects.

"This jar is in good condition. How much are you asking for it?"

"Five hundred and fifty American dollars," she stated unequivocally.

"You ask the same price that the merchants do in their fancy shops," he said.

"I have been in their stores. I know what the going-rate is, but this is a better deal," she replied confidently.

"Why?" he asked as he picked up another jar which must have once been a drinking mug. The rim was jagged, but it too was uncracked.

"Because in the stores, those men can't always be trusted. They have enough money to hire artists who are capable of making an antique jar like this and then they sell it as though it were real."

"Do they do that kind of thing?" He was baiting her.

"Surely, Mr. Shepherd, you must know of these things. If I, an ignorant girl of twelve, am aware of such things—you too must know."

He stopped looking at the mug and turned toward his precocious entrepreneur. "You are wiser than your years. What is your name?"

"Tabitha Muir."

"You are right, Tabitha. There are those who are constantly making new works of art and selling them as if they were old. But how did you learn about such deception?" A man driving three loaded donkeys passed, pushing other people into Kyle and Tabitha. Kyle lifted the box and carried it closer to the wall where he and the girl huddled until the chaos subsided.

"These streets are too narrow," she said disgustedly. "They should widen them."

"That would destroy a very old street. For a girl who knows so much about the value of old things, I would think that you would know that."

"Streets and pottery are two different things," she countered. "The streets must serve the people who are alive, not the ones who made them."

"So how did you learn about the forgeries?" he asked again.

"Many artists like to drink, and when they do, they are quick to tell how they were skillful enough to trick the rich tourists. They take great pride in it. Of course they have told the business men who bought their fakes that they will not speak of such things, but they can't hold their tongues once alcohol is in their brains."

"You know a lot at your tender age," he said.

"In the Middle East, there is no tender age . . ." She raised her eyebrows as if to say, "Isn't that so?" and Kyle nodded his head.

"I know that you are interested in shards of pottery if they have writing on them. There is one piece here that has some. Maybe you would like to buy it?"

"How much do you ask for your shards?"

"Twenty-five or thirty dollars," she said.

She stuck her head closer to the box and carefully rummaged through her artifacts.

Kyle smiled at her seriousness as her brows knit together in a furrow of dissatisfaction at not locating the piece she was after, afraid that the shard was gone just at the moment when she had the right customer to buy it. But, when she saw it hiding in the recesses of her box, she pulled it out with a triumphant smile and held it in front of his eyes. His smile dissolved.

"Where did you get this?" Kyle asked without ceasing to study the markings on the outside of the jagged piece.

"My sister found it outside Qumran," she said somewhat nervously, sensing his sudden solemnity, "but she wasn't actually inside of the old city. The government has ruled the area off limits. We were both searching for artifacts together, and we were separated for a while. When she came looking for me, that was one of the pieces she had found. What is it Mr. Shepherd? Do you want that piece?"

"Yes, I believe I do. I'll give you $350 for it."

"It's yours!"

"On one condition."

"What is that?" she asked as though expecting something dreadful.

"That you get your sister to show me exactly where she found it."

"That will be no problem, Mr. Shepherd, except my sister is a student at the Hebrew University campus and is not always free, but tomorrow is Friday and I know she has no classes in the afternoon. If you want we can meet you at your hotel at 1:00 P.M.?"

"That would be fine. Here, I'll give you a hundred dollars now and the rest tomorrow after we return from Qumran. I have a jeep, so you needn't worry about transportation."

For several minutes Kyle studied all of the pieces that were in the box. "Do you wish to buy anymore?" she asked.

"No. This piece with the Aramaic writing is all I'm interested in."

Tabitha stepped away for a moment and retrieved a rusty wagon, which she had placed in an alcove in the old wall. The hub of one wheel was red while the other three were a dirty white. The wagon was a treasure she had found in the garbage, which suited her business well.

She lifted the box with the pottery inside. Smiling her appreciation, she said thank you in Hebrew, for she knew he spoke it, and he answered in her tongue. She had heard Kyle converse with her father in her own language and knew that this man loved her people—it was in his eyes.

"Would you tell me, Mr. Shepherd, what it is about the shard that interests you? Unless my sister knows what your intentions are, she will not show you where she found the shard."

"Tell your sister that I will tell her what I'm looking for."

"All right. I'll be anxious to learn why any archaeologist who can find so many broken pieces of pottery is willing to pay $350 for such a piece and then spend half the day looking for the ground where it was uncovered."

"I will tell you." He paused, and then, "Tabitha?"

"Yes?"

"What does your sister study at the university?"

"She is in her senior year in archaeology. My father has taught her so much about these things that she took it up in school," Tabitha said with pride. "But school for all of us is very expensive." He understood her meaning and knew where the profits from her pottery sales would go.

"Yes, and my family is big with four sisters and two boys, but my parents are determined that we shall all go. We all help to save money for our educations. That is why I sell old pottery."

"You have very wise parents who put such importance on getting an education."

She smiled and nodded, then looked to him nervously and said, "You will do me one favor before I can bring my sister here?"

"What is it?"

"Please, you will not mention that I was trying to sell any artifacts to you. She has very definite feelings about anything leaving the country, even if it is so small and unimportant as these few pieces of pottery," she said sheepishly.

Shepherd raised an eyebrow and said, "She would be angry with you?"

"Very. My sister is a good person, but she is not always as practical as someone should be when she comes from a large family like ours. She does not know that it is I who gives much of the money that is paying for her education. I make the money selling pieces of pottery and occasionally a piece of pottery that is not broken—which would really make her upset—and I give the money to my mother who passes it on to her. She does not say that she has made the money selling the vases that she paints by hand, for she will not lie, but she does say something like, 'I had a good day today,' which is true, because good fortune for me is also her good fortune. My father wouldn't approve of my selling the unbroken vases, but I do not tell him. He and my sister are alike in many ways, but I must do what I can to help them. You won't tell her that I was selling these pieces?"

"I won't say a thing. Are you sure she won't miss this shard with the writing when you ask her to show me where you found it?"

"For $350 I will take the chance," she said.

"There is no reason for you to risk upsetting your family. I am more interested in knowing where she found it than having the piece. You take it, but first let me take a picture." Kyle grabbed his camera and reeled off three quick pictures of the shard, and then put it carefully back into her box. She smiled again, turned her wagon around and disappeared into the crush of people, but her presence in the crowd was apparent for some time as people moved away to give her wagon space.

Spinning on his heels, Kyle hurried to his favorite restaurant where he ate a meal of shrimp, barely tasting the food. He was too excited thinking about the morrow to concentrate on anything else.

The next day Tabitha and Elisheba were waiting in the lobby of Kyle's hotel when he returned from lunch. They sat on a circular sofa, which placed the older daughter's back to Kyle as he approached her smiling. She arose with Tabitha and when she turned, he was so surprised at her beauty that he stumbled slightly on the carpet. He stopped his forward movement, but it was short of the girls, and he could not reach her outstretched hand, forcing him to take another step closer.

"Mr. Shepherd, I'm happy to meet you. My father always spoke highly of you, and I'm honored to be able to work with you, too."

Her voice was soothing, similar to a woman disc jockey he used to listen to in Los Angeles when he had insomnia during the baseball season. There was a look in her eye that let him know that she would not utter nonsense or compliments if she did not feel them. Her hair was dark, which heightened the appeal of her eyes, and her skin was tanner than usual from her recent outings near Qumran. At first he thought she was wearing mascara, but a closer look revealed no makeup at all. She had a small, delicate nose, which bore no resemblance to her father's aquiline profile. Her lips were dry from the heat, and he noticed her licking them.

In recent years Kyle had grown somewhat smug when it came to women, believing that he had become the archetypal scientist who was capable of putting his work beyond all of his emotions, but in the first moments of encounter with this striking girl, he was aware that he still had an Achilles heel when it came to women who were this gorgeous. They left the hotel and got in his jeep.

"Tabitha tells me that you study archaeology?" he asked after they had maneuvered their way through the heavy Jerusalem traffic and emerged onto the road heading southeast to Qumran.

"Yes, I love it!" she said over the din of the wind.

"Why archaeology?"

"I like the detective work," she said with a smile.

"The mystery of it," he added.

"That's right. I always worked with my father as I was growing up and my interest began there. It wasn't just my father, though. I think I would have found archaeology on my own if he had done something else, because I always enjoyed Agatha Christie novels and plays while I was growing up, and to me, archaeology is just one series of fascinating cases after another."

"So you're a woman who likes suspense?"

"I thrive on it. And this is the most suspenseful land anywhere. Every inch of it has a story to tell . . . Isn't suspense part of the draw for you, Mr. Shepherd?"

"First names, please."

"All right."

"You're right—the suspense keeps it interesting. But there are other reasons why I like archaeology," he said.

"Which are?"

"There's money in it." It wasn't an answer that pleased her. He saw her smile wilt.

"What's wrong?" he asked.

She paused and then said," I don't think people should be in this business to make money."

"Oh? Why's that?"

Tabitha knew her sister well, and this conversation might not end pleasantly. "This is a subject I wish we wouldn't talk about," she said.

"No, Tabitha," Kyle said, "I'm interested in your sister's point of view. Surely she must realize that most of us are in this game for fame and fortune."

"Not the good ones," Elisheba shot back.

"Oooooh!" he said and then laughed. "That's clear enough. Now don't hold back, Elisheba. They say you can get ulcers if you beat around the bush."

"That pretty well sums it up. I know there are those who look for a country's historical treasures in order to make themselves rich, but the good ones, the ones who are really concerned about civilization, and history—and people!—look at archaeology as a higher calling."

"You need to be very careful before you lump all archaeologists in the same opportunistic mold. There's money to be made in this business, but I hope you don't think I'm going to try and take anything out of the country that the law won't allow."

"I hope you won't try," Elisheba said testily.

"Believe me, I won't," he said.

"Because I won't show you anything if I think you're going to take advantage of our country. I will be watching very closely."

"You do that, Elisheba. By all means you keep a close eye on me."

For Tabitha the desert was hot, but the exchange between her sister and Shepherd had a sizzle all its own. The car seemed several degrees warmer from when they started. Tabitha changed the subject. "Are you going to tell us what was on that shard that interested you so much?" she asked.

"Since your older sister likes suspense so much, maybe I should keep you in the dark a little longer," he said with a smile.

"But I don't like being in the dark," Tabitha whined.

"I am willing to tell you of some of my hunches if I can extract a promise from both of you?"

"What is the promise?" Elisheba asked.

"If I tell you of a possible finding of some importance, that you won't try to beat me to the punch."

"Beat you to the punch?" Elisheba said in bewilderment. Then Elisheba's eyes narrowed, and she answered with some bitterness: "You have worked with my father for years. You know what kind of family we come from. There is no reason to doubt us."

"I know your father. His integrity is without question, but while we're speaking candidly today, I must tell you of my own concerns—I don't know you. You've already told me of your opinion of those who do this kind of work to make money. I don't want you to try and interfere with me. If you'll promise me that you won't, I'll accept your word just as I would from your father."

"Before I make such a pledge, Mr. Shepherd, you must make a return pledge to us."

"What is it?" he asked as his eyes turned repeatedly from the road to her.

"If you make a discovery of any consequence, you will not take the materials out of Palestine."

"It's against the law to take artifacts out of the country," he said.

"Oh, please," she said sarcastically. "You know as well as I do that there are artifacts lost every month from Palestine by those who smuggle them out in hopes of finding a higher market value than they could get from one of our museums or universities."

"I give you my word that I will take nothing of any consequence out of Israel."

"So now tell us. What is it you are looking for?" Elisheba asked.

"I'm looking for the Revelation of Enoch," he replied.

"I don't know what you mean," Elisheba said.

"You don't know who Enoch is?" he asked skeptically.

"Well, of course I've heard of Enoch, but I've never heard about any revelation of his," she said.

"It's referred to in the New Testament, but no one has found it. I think the ancient citizens of Qumran had it. The Old Testament says Enoch walked and talked with God. Certainly a man with that kind of rapport with the Almighty might have some interesting things to say, don't you think?" he said with a smirk.

Kyle reached again into his shirt pocket and withdrew a photograph. "I took this picture of the shard that Tabitha showed me, and after developing it, I did a little research. The language seems altered a bit from the evolved Aramaic that has come down to us, so I, too, spent some time at your university today, Elisheba, talking with one of my friends, Dr. Samuel Bernstein, who is an expert in ancient languages. His specialty is Coptic, but he knew enough that we were able to arrive at this translation."

From his other shirt pocket he withdrew a folded paper. Elisheba's fingers snapped open the paper and she saw the following: "Protector of Enoch." Tabitha could not see it clearly, so she jerked the paper out of her sister's hands.

"What does this mean? Is it talking about the writings of Enoch?" Tabitha said.

"I don't know for sure, but I think it is," Kyle said. "It's possible the original writings of Enoch are still around, and maybe even buried near Qumran. The people who lived in this desolate spot tried to preserve holy writings—the Dead Sea scrolls prove that. They might have done the same with the writings of Enoch."

Kyle maneuvered around a rock that had rolled into the road, split from one of the ledges above them. It was a large stone, perhaps a thousand pounds in weight, which he did not see until the moment he rounded the bend in the road. He was not going fast and there was never a doubt that he would miss it. In the last few days since the record-breaking rain of a few weeks back, he had noticed many signs of geographical disturbance: huge rocks, some many tons, lying in the roads and the valleys; ancient fissures had been widened, and in some cases, entirely new cracks gaped wide in the rock where before there had been no opening.

"Elisheba," Kyle asked, "when you found the shard, was there a considerable amount of dirt on top of it, or was it pretty much lying on the surface?"

"That's the unusual part," she said. "I've never found pottery under these kinds of conditions before. It was lying on the surface, as you said, so that I could clearly make out its outline. It was not buried. It seemed more like it had been discovered earlier by someone else and then left there on the ground."

He could not restrain the slight dance at the corners of his mouth. There was an element of excitement in his voice, which he couldn't suppress though Elisheba sensed he was trying to do just that, perhaps to avoid raising false expectations.

"I hoped that would be your answer," he said.

The excitement transferred to his foot, and the pedal moved closer to the floorboard, and there was a noticeable lurch in the movement of the jeep. He leaned forward and drove onward with renewed intensity.

Within five minutes he pulled the vehicle to an abrupt halt near the base of the hill that held the ruins of Qumran. Directly above them the walls of the deserted city jutted upward and were easily visible. Kyle stepped from the jeep and stared upward at the dead city's skeletal outline—the brownish rock the builders used was tied together in one continuous series of walls like the remnants of an ancient condominium.

Qumran was once a community of deeply religious people, begun by a man whose name was so revered among his followers that it was never directly recorded, and he was simply referred to as "the teacher of righteousness." It was 200 B.C. when he began gathering disciples to this forlorn spot for the purpose of preparing a people to receive the coming Messiah.

Elisheba pointed to the west and said, "I found the pottery over here," and then set off in that direction with Tabitha and Kyle.

Minutes later they stood at the base of a slanted sandstone wall that rose sharply from the valley floor to over two hundred feet above them. Elisheba pointed to the ground at her feet. "Right here is where I found them. You can see there has been a heavy runoff from the storm down the rock walls."

She picked up a gnarled stick, washed to that spot by the rain, and used it to dig at the earth. The top layer of soil was dried and cracked, but underneath a darker earth appeared, ladened with moisture.

Kyle knelt and studied the ground a moment. "May I see that stick?" Taking it from her, he dug awhile himself.

"Do you think there is some more pottery buried in here, Mr. Shepherd?" Tabitha asked.

"No, I don't think there's a thing under this ground," he answered.

"Then your trip has been a wasted one?" Elisheba asked.

"It's too early to tell yet," he said.

"I don't understand," she said as she squatted next to him, so she might be able to see his eyes more clearly.

"I think there might be something near here, but it isn't in this ground. You yourself said the shards were lying on top."

"Somebody left the pieces then?" Elisheba said.

"Maybe . . . but I don't think so. I think they came from overhead. From this slanted cliff wall. I was hoping the rock face next to the area you found them would be slanted, and it is. If I'm right, this pottery came from somewhere on the face of this rock wall."

"But how did it come to be here?" Tabitha asked while gazing at the rock wall.

"I think the storm washed it out of its hiding place."

"But to have come down the side of this wall, even if it is slanted," Elisheba said skeptically, "would surely have broken that piece we found to bits."

"Maybe . . . but it was small, remember? Making it fairly tough. Maybe even tough enough to survive a waterslide ride to this area. I'm going to search this wall, but first of all, I'll take you back to Jerusalem."

With that, he arose and reached into his pocket and extracted his billfold, from which he pulled the remainder of the money they had agreed upon.

"You don't have to take us back to Jerusalem," Elisheba said determinedly. We'll be glad to help you search."

"I'm sorry," he said firmly, "I prefer to work alone." He returned to the jeep as they followed. Returning to Jerusalem, he dropped them off in front of their home, just south of the Biblical Zoo.

Elisheba remained silent the whole trip, obviously slighted at not being invited to participate further in the search. When she stepped from the jeep, she did so without looking back.

Kyle went to his hotel room to pick up an extra flashlight, and took the opportunity to change into some hiking boots. Then he drove back to Qumran and began searching the cliff face. When the light faded, he set up his tent near the spot where Elisheba had found the shard. He unrolled his sleeping bag within the tent and climbed inside with his head near the tent's opening. He left the flap open, so he could look at the sky.

In the distance he heard the rumbling of another thunderstorm coming from the southwest, and he remembered hearing on the radio that the Sinai Peninsula had caught some rain earlier. Never had he seen such rain in this part of the world. One of the effects of the last big storm was right next to him, for several opportunistic, white desert flowers were growing near his head. He had put his tent up carefully and arranged his sleeping bag so they would be near him. He reached his head forward and enjoyed the fragrance.

Several quick lightning flashes lit the ground, illuminating the white flowers. He recalled something from the Old Testament about the desert one day blossoming as a rose, but his thoughts were jarred seconds later when three loud claps of thunder broke around him, the sandstone walls intensifying the sound.

As of yet, there was no rain, so he rolled on his back and looked upward at the cliff as it lit up under the flashes. The ancient walls of Qumran above him were revealed briefly like the Gothic set of a Hollywood movie. For a half an hour he watched the city and the canyon walls surrounding them, wondering if this ominous heavenly show was sent for any meaning—to encourage him or perhaps to warn him.

"I've been working too long by myself," he said aloud before retreating further within his sleeping bag. Pulling at the zipper until his cocoon was complete, he fell asleep quickly, lying as motionless as the walls of Qumran above him.

II

A SECRET FROM QUMRAN

Now three days had passed since he had come to the cliffs with the girls, and his legs ached badly from standing on a slant on the steep rock face. He took off his shoes and rubbed his blistered feet.

Resting on the warm rock, he looked downward at his tent, lying unruffled in the still air. He was using it as a marker as he climbed higher to keep from drifting to the right or left from the place where the shards had been discovered. If the pieces of pottery had indeed been washed out of some crevice on this rock face, the opening must be in line with the spot where he found them, and yet he was becoming more and more skeptical that the pottery—even in their fragmented state—could have survived such a long cascade down the rock face. True, a layer of water would have cushioned them, but how could the fragments have slid so far and remained intact?

No . . . the longer he considered the matter, the more certain he felt that the shards of pottery could not have been dislodged from some higher location. He had missed the cave opening—if there was one—and he would have to begin making his way downward. His feet were stinging like an aborigine who had failed the walk-on-hot-coals test. The skin on several toes was worn away, and he dreaded renewing his search, but he had no choice. He sat a while longer, collecting his energy. At the cuff of his pants he felt movement and fought the old insect phobia. Once again something hooked his fabric, and he casually turned his head to see a scorpion trying to use his pant leg as a tunnel.

He kicked his leg violently, then rolled to his side and scrambled to his feet; the scorpion scurried toward him in what seemed an attack, but was only confusion at being jettisoned onto its back.

Clawing at the face of the rock, Kyle frantically sought a finger hold to remove his body from danger. He found a small indentation and took hold with both hands, lifting his feet off the ground; the rock loosened and slid to one side, jarring loose a fist-sized piece of yellow sandstone that fell with a splat onto the scorpion. Though dead, its nervous system sent out sporadic signals, causing its tail to strike the rock that pinned it. Then it quivered spasmodically and relaxed.

Kyle lowered his feet to the ground. When he was convinced that the scorpion would not suddenly attack, he turned to scrutinize the rock face.

A jagged opening blew its pent-up breath into his face. There was a chamber beyond. The rock that had momentarily suspended his weight was actually a door, and he had broken the seal. He could now see its general outline—why hadn't he seen it before? It was two feet in width and four and a half feet high, and yet thin enough that he could move it as he placed his shoulder and hands against it and shoved. A four-inch crack appeared down the length of the slab. Kyle's heart beat rapidly, but it was not from exertion.

He shoved at the slab again and again. When his shoulders could pass through the opening, he stooped and felt in his knapsack until he found his large chrome flashlight. His foot was very close to the carcass of the scorpion, and although he knew it was dead, he tapped twice on the rock with his foot—just to be sure—then pivoted and squeezed himself inside.

His foot immediately found water and that, coupled with his own fear of the unknown, caused him to shudder. He switched on the flashlight and shone it into the murky water. There was no dry spot, so he trudged slowly, forward.

Entering through an opening in the floor was sunlight, slightly to the left of the entrance doorway. He knew that could be the opening to the outside through which the pottery had been flushed.

He touched the wall of the cave and felt its rough, wet texture, like sandpaper soaked in water. It reminded him of the back of a shark he had felt in an open-air market in Naples.

Ordinarily there would be no moisture in this cave at all, but the torrential downpour, which had gouged out the fissures in the road, had also provided the water, which now filled the cave. There were large cracks in the ceiling, through which water was dripping even then. The air felt refreshingly cool to him after standing in direct sunlight for the last several hours.

Here the cave's wall was notched out and it was not a natural occurrence. It was a recess made by human hands that had carved the rock in the shape of an eye, two feet across. It was not a human eye—perhaps a tiger's. The lids around it pulled upward, menacingly. Maybe it was there to intimidate the superstitious.

He turned his beam on the ceiling and gasped—above him were a thousand or more carved fangs, nine inches in length, each one just like the other, jutting wickedly downward where they had been fastened or cemented into place. It was a startling sight, like the final resting place for the incisors of saber tooth tigers.

His feet sloshed forward three paces where a rock altar rose from the water. It was a three-tiered affair made with white marble, giving it the appearance of three stoves of increasing sizes, fused together. This was more than a cave then. It was a temple or a sanctuary that had been embellished with some frightening elements—perhaps to intimidate the intruder, maybe to sober the worshipper.

The smell was pungent like grass clippings that had been stacked and forgotten and were now emanating the rank odor of their deterioration. "There must be some kind of fungi growing on the walls," he thought.

At the back of the cave, only several feet away, a large urn-shaped container, whose top had been broken away, stood ominously. Even broken, the jar rose five feet from the floor's bottom. Its diameter was nearly two feet, and as Kyle sloshed towards it, he saw why the jar had been built so massively—inside was another jar; this one, though, seemed to be entirely intact.

There were markings on the outward jar, and he hurriedly examined them. At the top, the writings were less legible than others nearer the base, so he squatted on his heels, forgetting momentarily about the water in the cave, and for an instant his seat dipped into the water, dampening his pants and causing a shiver to ripple up his spine. He raised himself on his haunches like a baseball catcher and scrutinized the black writing upon the brownish surface of the pottery.

The markings were Aramaic—the same as the shard that Tabitha had shown him, except there were some additional words. Frantically he studied them with the intensity of a munitions expert defusing a rapidly ticking bomb. His eyes widened and his eyebrows arched, and then he laughed excitedly and spoke the words aloud: "The Protector of the Revelation of Enoch," he said haltingly, tentatively. Then he repeated the words more emotionally, "The Protector of the Revelation of Enoch!" and the cave reverberated with his booming voice.

Quickly Kyle arose and looked within the jar. Inside rested another jar of the same color with black markings running from its unbroken top downward as far as he could see. In lettering that stood out from the many other markings he read, "The Revelation of Enoch."

His hand touched the inner jar delicately, and he was overcome with emotion. For an instant, he wondered if he were delirious from the scorpion's sting, and he squeezed his hands around the jar to remove his doubts.

He jumped when a flashlight shone on him from behind. The light was bright—or his fear made it seem so—and it lit up the hundred fangs above him, causing them to quiver as though the mouth were beginning to shut. He half turned, trying to make out the intruder, while he covered his face with his arm, to shield his eyes from the light. The cold water at his feet seemed to suck into his legs and pump upward into his chest, rushing icily into his arms. Robbers who stole artifacts were not known for their compassion, and this would be a perfect place for a homicide. He waited, expecting the explosion of a gun, and in his anxiety he lost his footing and nearly went down.

His sudden gyration in the water forced a startled shriek from Elisheba, which echoed rapidly in the dampness. "It's me, Shepherd," she said. "What did you find?"

He put his flashlight on her, as he struggled to recover his composure. He said nothing for a long time, and breathed deeply like a marathon runner struggling for breath after crossing the finish line. "You nearly scared me to death, and the only thing you can say is, 'What did you find?'"

"Sorry."

"Oh, please," he said sarcastically, "you're making me feel guilty for snapping at you like that when you give such an emotional apology . . . What are you doing here anyway?"

"I thought you might need some help."

"Oh, really? You know that I said I work alone. I intentionally took you back to Jerusalem, so I could be alone to work out here. I think it's more than just wanting to be helpful, isn't it Elisheba?"

"What do you mean?"

"You're checking up on me, aren't you?" She gave no response. "I told you before that I wasn't going to steal any artifacts, but you don't believe me, do you?"

"I told you before, I worry about my country and its treasures. I have a duty to protect it."

"Oh really? What are you—the self-appointed Ministry of Antiquities? Where are your papers? Show me where you have the right to barge in on my find."

"It is my find, too," she said defiantly. "Remember, I was the one who found the pieces that led you here."

"I know what you found, and I think I've paid you according to our agreement. You've got three hundred bucks of my money, which should entitle me to continue this search unimpeded." He turned again to the pottery, hoping the anger in his voice would frighten her off, but her feet splashed through the water till she stood next to him.

"You don't seem to understand, Elisheba. I don't need you here. To be absolutely blunt—I don't want you here. But before you leave, please remember your promise of yesterday—that you wouldn't reveal anything that you learned. I'm holding you to that on the honor of your family name."

"Have you found the Revelation of Enoch?"

He gently wiped away a light dirt film that obscured part of the writing.

"You, too, made some promises. You said you would not take anything out of our country."

"Yes I did."

"I don't wish to be insulting, but many men have integrity when there's little money involved. A big find like this could mean a lot of money."

"Then you don't know me very well, or you wouldn't doubt me."

"You are right—I don't know you very well. I do know that the other day you were very anxious to have me return to Jerusalem. Now you have found something, but you say you don't need any help."

"That's right."

"You're going to remove all this by yourself?"

"Maybe. I haven't decided yet."

"It's impossible. You can't take these jars out by yourself."

"I'm not worried about the jars at the moment. I'm worried about one of your ancient patriarch's writings that I believe are inside here. In fact, in a matter of a minute or so, I'm going to lift this jar and see if anybody got to this find before I did. I think I can tell if it's empty or not."

"Why can't I help you?"

He turned around to face her. "Since we're being honest with one another, let me tell you something. I don't trust you."

"I'm a student studying archaeology at the university who has been taught all the laws involving a find . . ."

"Which isn't worth a camel's dung. Some of the biggest crooks I know learned their skills at a university." He said this as he surveyed the lid that covered the inner vessel.

"Before you do anything else," she said firmly, "you should contact the authorities at the Ministry of Historical Relics and tell them what you have."

"Can't do that."

"Why not?"

"Because they'll come in here, set up their camp with twenty-four stuffed shirts and completely take over the operation. Somewhere in their process as they exercise their authority, the fact that, I, an American, made the discovery will be conveniently forgotten—right around the time they slip the story to the press, and some Jewish archaeologist will get the credit. They might even pick you, but I suppose that devious little thought never crossed your mind, right?"

"It hasn't."

"Well then, you're wetter behind the ears than your feet are right now, because I know how these things are done, and I intend to protect my own interests, or this find will completely get away from me."

She turned to leave. "I'm going to the ministry right now." Moving as quickly as the scorpion's tail, his hand reached out and grabbed her arm, whirling her around.

"You're not going anywhere! If I have to, I'll tie you up and carry you back to the outskirts of Jerusalem in my jeep—after I've got everything I want, of course."

"You are going to take this find out of Israel, aren't you?" she asked bitterly.

"Not at all. It will stay here, just as I promised you, but I will handle it in my own way with my own friends and without interference from the Israeli government. Red tape and archaeological successes don't mix."

"How can I trust you?"

"You don't have much choice. Nevertheless, Elisheba, I think you have an honest face. I have been wrong about faces, but I'm going to include you in on this, because you're either very sincere about your patriotism, or a very good actress, and I'd like to learn which it is. It will be a good chance to restore a little of my faith in humanity. Shall we see if we've really got anything? The lid is sealed, so I'm going to lift the jar. If there's something in there, I can tell."

He grasped the inner jar, bent his knees to eliminate the strain from his back, gave her a wry smile, and lifted.

"Bingo," he said, as he set it down again. "There's definitely something in there. Maybe aging cheese, but there is something. I would say it weighs about seventy pounds. Do you think you could lift that much onto my back, and tie it there so I can carry it down?"

"I can," she said without hesitating. "I'm in very good shape. Where will you take the jar afterwards?"

"To Russia," he said with a straight face. She was not amused, and he burst out laughing. "C'mon, Elisheba, lighten up. I'm taking it to your own Hebrew University. I have a friend who teaches there. He's an expert in old documents, and he'll help us. Afterwards, he'll report the find to the authorities that you've been so anxious to involve in this operation. I'm not taking it anywhere. Are you satisfied?"

She nodded her approval.

"Let's lift it out of there."

Together they put their arms around the jar, and in so doing he was brought close to her face. Even in the musty room, she smelled good.

"On three. One, two, three." They strained together, and the inner jar rose from its encasement. "OK," he shouted when the bottom cleared, still intact with no sign of damage. Not wishing to take a chance that the base was cracked, he didn't set it in the water, but held it in his arms, while Elisheba examined it with her flashlight.

"Kyle, I can't find any cracks, and the top seems to be well-sealed, with a wax of some kind, I would say. It doesn't seem to have been tampered with," she said.

"There's definitely something inside here. Let's take it outside," he puffed.

She stepped through the opening before him, set her flashlight down and then took hold of the jar as he handed it through.

"I can't hold it myself," she yelled.

"I'm not going to let go of it. Just help me with the weight until I can get my body through."

"Maybe we should leave it here, and get some more professional help. We've got to go down this rock face, and how will you do it without dropping it?"

"We're not going to drop it if we're careful." Then she saw the rear end of the scorpion protruding from the rock and jumped.

"Don't worry, it's dead," he said. "Now, I'm going to have you tie this onto my back; that will leave my hands free to hold the support rope."

She looked worried. "How can I hold it up behind you and tie it at the same time?"

"I'll hold it in my arms while you tie ropes around it and over my shoulders, and then you can slide it in back of me once it's secure."

The jar was soon dangling in back of him. He watched her as she tied a rope around a rock. When he was satisfied the rope would hold him, he saluted her briskly and began his descent.

In less than two minutes he was standing by his campsite, and fifteen minutes later they were in his jeep, bouncing over the rocky road to Jerusalem.

Dr. Samuel Bernstein, professor of ancient languages, recognized Kyle's voice the moment he heard it on the other end of the telephone. They had spoken only a month earlier at a seminar held at the Rockefeller Museum, a display area for archaeological finds, located just north of the old wall of Jerusalem.

The thrust of the seminar was preventing foreign archaeologists from slipping artifacts out of the country. There was the usual discussion on how to best prevent that kind of pilfering, and more money was set aside to pay for additional security. But it was at the luncheon when Kyle was randomly seated next to Samuel that their interests in one another were piqued. Samuel was complaining about the minuscule portions of food and it was obvious the small salad would not long sustain the energies of a man who weighed 260 pounds.

"I think we should give a little less money to the security people and put a bit more into the luncheon menu. I don't think I've ever seen a salad this small. One tablespoon of salad dressing should not cover an entire salad—smother it, actually."

"Of course," he continued, "I wouldn't be so hungry if I weren't such a big man, but my size comes with the way I do my job. I read a lot of old manuscripts, and it's very difficult to keep myself from nibbling on something while reading the food list some pharaoh provided during one of his orgies—all in exact detail! I saw one the other day: roasted pheasants, 500 baked lambs, 1100 flasks of rum—of course they didn't call it rum, but that's what it was—and when I read about those things, it gets me nibbling."

Though he was in his sixties, his hair—what there was of it—was glossy black. It lay abundantly only on the sides of his head, then stopped abruptly at the crown as though tonsured for the ministry. His wide nose reddened as his body temperature rose, and when he was really hot, it glowed like an alcoholic's. At the luncheon that day as he talked to Kyle, his nose had a slightly pinkish hue because he was cooling down after a malfunction of the air-conditioning system in the main auditorium where he had just lectured.

"You know, Kyle," he said as he wiped his mouth with a cloth napkin, "so many people have given up on the cliffs around Qumran, but I personally believe there are discoveries yet to be made. Yes, I know how exhaustively they've scoured those rocks, but I believe it's not only a matter of how much time is put into the search, but also of the right kind of time for the search."

Kyle pulled the tender white meat away from a perch that a waiter had earlier boasted had come from the Sea of Galilee. "The right time?"

"I believe that God has a certain time table in the affairs of men. Discoveries are made at the moment He wishes. That is my belief—be careful of those little fish bones. They're not deadly, but if they get trapped in your throat, they're hard to wash down."

"I have always believed that the finding of the Dead Sea Scrolls in 1948 was not a matter of coincidence for several reasons. The war was recently over and as is typical with nearly all wars, when so much evil has occurred, many people begin to doubt a divine presence—certainly those returning from the concentration camps had, for the most part, lost their faith; theirs was a rising wave of atheism, and then what happens—a young shepherd discovers ancient, holy writings.

"Don't misunderstand me—I am not a religious fanatic, but a place like Qumran should never be overlooked. These people in this room feel that area has been thoroughly searched, but who knows when the time may come that another shepherd will be following a lost sheep and discover another opening in a cave."

Having just found the scroll at Qumran, Kyle was anxious to validate the old man's prediction.

"So you have been looking near Qumran?" Samuel's booming voice resounded in the telephone receiver. "I suppose you're upset with me for having suggested the place and wasting your time?"

"Not at all," Kyle said. "In fact I called to thank you for your suggestion." There was a moment of silence.

"You were successful then?" Bernstein said with unconcealed excitement. "That's good! That's terrific! What did you find? Some good pottery?" He said pottery because he didn't want to raise his expectations.

"Some pottery, yes ... And an old manuscript." During this pause, Kyle felt as though he could see the rotund professor's eyes widening.

"What kind of a manuscript?" came the terse, impassioned reply.

"I think we're looking at some writings from the Old Testament ... Oh, perhaps from the prophet Enoch."

"When can I see it?" he almost shouted, so loudly in fact that his wife Ellen, who was just donning a cultured pearl necklace in honor of their fortieth wedding anniversary, dropped it with a clatter onto her nightstand.

"I thought we'd bring it to your lab at your convenience. Tomorrow would be fine." Actually, Kyle had hoped to study the find tonight, but he was counting on Samuel's curiosity to make the offer.

"There's no need to wait so long! We'll go there tonight. You take it to my lab right away, while I call the university and have the janitor open my room for you."

"I hope we're not disrupting your evening, Samuel."

"Not at all! We were just going to celebrate our anniversary, which we'll still be able to do, after I have a look at your find. My wife is always asking me to take her on a little drive. This will be the perfect opportunity. I'll be there in about twenty minutes," he said and then hung up the receiver.

III

The Translation Begins

The janitor who met them at the loading dock looked like a young man. Kyle estimated him to be in his thirties, but he was completely bald. Whether he shaved his head, or had lost his hair through chemotherapy, or simply was the victim of an unfortunate gene pool, Kyle didn't know. If it was chemotherapy, the man seemed energetic enough as he helped lift the jar onto a dolly at the loading dock, a dolly that was especially padded to protect delicate objects. He also insisted on wheeling it to the elevator, though Kyle kept a steadying hand on the jar, lest the man prove to be careless.

"The Professor is a great guy," said the janitor. "A lot of these intellectuals look down on the hired help, you know, but not Dr. Bernstein. Do you know what he did once? He let me take home the tooth of a Tyrannosaurus Rex, so my boy could use it in his school's science fair! That's right! How many scientists do you know that would do that?"

"Not many," Kyle said.

"You're darn right, but the Doctor, he's got a feeling that things ought to be seen. You know he's involved with ancient languages, but he collects all kinds of stuff. His lab has got some better stuff in it than what we have in Tel Aviv's best museum. It's true. I've been there and the Doc's got a bunch of things I find a whole lot more interesting. My name's Omar, by the way. Omar White."

Some people's heads are not particularly attractive without a covering of hair. Omar's head fell in this category. There was a ridge along the line where the main segments of the skull joined together, as though nature, in welding those portions, had laid down too heavy a bead. His skull was a perfect anatomical lesson for anyone interested in the bone structure of the cranium.

"You got something inside of this jar?" he asked. Kyle nodded his head. "I don't think I've ever seen one with something in it," he said as he turned the key for the double wooden doors that led into the lab and swung the doors open simultaneously. The fossilized jaws of a huge crocodile gaped wide at them. Elisheba didn't see it until she had taken a step inside the room, and then she let out a gasp.

"I'm sorry," she said. "I don't know why that surprised me so. I guess I'm on edge."

"You aren't the first to be startled by Pharaoh," Omar chuckled. "Some people have accused the professor of intentionally opening Pharaoh's mouth just to frighten people, but you can see if you look at the joint there—where its mouth hinges, that it's hardened rock—fossilized. That's the way he found that animal along the banks of the Nile River, and he's just set it here on this table because it was closest to the sink. I helped him give it its first sponge bath in over 100 million years," he said with a grin.

Elisheba stopped at Pharaoh's head. By slightly crouching, she could lean inside the massive jaws with so many teeth still intact. "I wonder how many primitive deer had this same view just before they were killed?" she asked.

Inside she noticed a small, stuffed chipmunk that one of Samuel's undergraduate assistants had added as a final touch to the Pharaoh's exhibit. The tawny rodent was originally taken from the zoology building where it was supposed to have been used in a desert diorama. Sitting on its haunches with its front paws extended outward to ward off an attacking owl, it would have remained for years behind a glass wall had it not been spirited here. Now in its new home, its rigid form was creatively displayed—its open paws clutched the largest tooth on the lower jaw of the crocodile, as though it were involved in the most terrifying ride of its life.

Carefully pushing the vase, the three wound their way through the lab, which seemed more like the natural history wing of the Smithsonian Institute rather than a place for studying ancient languages. Though Samuel was not a hunter he had collected a variety of stuffed animals and birds, and they were posed everywhere.

Following the janitor, Kyle and Elisheba circled the magnificent, white form of a Kodiak bear, which stood upon its hind legs in a combative position, and at its feet, attacking with its mouth open, was the huge killer lizard that lives on four of the Sunda Islands of Indonesia, the Komodo Dragon. The Kodiak's powerful right paw was drawn backward, readying a bone-crushing blow, while the Komodo seemed to be launching a futile attack at the bear's hindquarters.

"How did Dr. Bernstein get a Komodo dragon? Aren't they on the endangered species list?" Elisheba asked.

"You're right, Miss. It is against the law to trap them. Many things in here are on that list. The doctor didn't do it. But once they've been killed and stuffed, they might as well be displayed somewhere, and the doctor has friends in the customs office who send him animals like that," Omar said. "Of course they could send these animals to the museum, but you know, those plans backfire sometimes. A museum gets a stuffed dragon, or one of those endangered storks there, and the first thing you know, they've got a picket line outside complaining that the museum is involved in the killing of endangered animals. That's not the way it is, of course, but the public gets the wrong idea, and the publicity hurts. The professor gets a lot of animals that might have been donated to some museum but the authorities don't want the hassles."

It was clear that Samuel gave free reign to his imagination when it came to the displaying of the animals. In one corner of the room a Bengal tiger was paired off against a large grayish gorilla, a six hundred pound male that held an uprooted sapling for defense like a baseball bat.

Hanging from the ceiling were hundreds of bats of various types: there were tiny mouse-tailed bats, found from Egypt to Burma; sheath-tailed bats with special membranes covering most of their tails; hare-lipped bats from America with the unusual marking of a cleft upper lip; the large flying foxes of the East Indies, which seemed almost naked for their lack of fur—bats of all sizes and shapes with their over abundance of devilish eyes, ghoulish noses and triangular ears—all hovering around the tremendous wingspan of an African Condor with its powerful beak open in a mute cry of terror. The condor's eyes bulged, and its skin sagged around its neck and face. The bats were dive-bombing the condor, desperately trying to drive it from their sanctuary.

Lifting the jar ever so gently from the dolly, they set it without a sound onto the floor. Kyle thanked Omar, who half bowed his head in acknowledgment and then excused himself, looking somewhat disappointed at not being invited to stay.

As much as Kyle enjoyed the talkative custodian, he was aware that his gregarious disposition might lead him to blab the vase's contents to the rest of the professors in the building. The time for that was not yet at hand.

Twenty minutes later Samuel Bernstein burst through the double doors and stopped. So startled was he at seeing the unmarred beauty of the jar even from across the room, that he lurched toward Pharaoh, placing his hand on the great snout of the behemoth for support. He looked like a young child, expecting to find a toy horse under the Christmas tree only to discover a living pony.

Samuel removed his coat, and then undid his bow tie. "There are no breaks in the jar?"

"None whatsoever," Kyle answered.

Still shocked that the jar could be in such pristine condition, Samuel approached it, again steadying himself, this time on the paw of the great polar bear. When it became clear to him how perfectly preserved it was, he circled the artifact with his feet shuffling along the drop cloth Kyle had thrown down to collect any loose pieces of the jar that might fall unnoticed. Samuel was astonished to read some of the symbols so easily from seven feet away.

"It is true. And the markings indicate the jar contains the writings of Enoch," he said.

Kyle smiled at the excitement of his old friend. Samuel was so engrossed in studying the writing on the jar that he gently pushed Elisheba out of the way without saying a word to her.

"This, by the way, is Elisheba Muir," Kyle said. "Elisheba, meet Dr. Samuel Bernstein."

"I'm pleased to meet you, Elisheba. I didn't know you had taken on a research partner, Kyle."

Kyle explained briefly the history of the find and Bernstein listened, but his eyes rarely left the jar.

"I wouldn't say this is the real world of archaeology, Elisheba." He turned and really looked at her now. "This isn't representative of what goes on in our business. We spend years looking and sometimes collect a few things, generally broken, and we consider ourselves fortunate. You must be a lucky girl, and it looks as though her luck has rubbed off on you, Kyle."

"Yes. I suppose it has," Kyle said, and he smiled at her.

Stepping through the double doors at that moment, wearing a silver fox fur over a white-sequined evening gown, was Mrs. Bernstein. She was sixty years old, with the slim body of a ballerina, and at the moment was slightly irritated at having her evening interrupted. Forty years of marriage, however, had taught her flexibility where her husband's work was involved. She saw now how excited he was, and her tightened lips parted in a smile. If he was happy, she was happy, and if he could really keep this visit as short as he had hoped, there would still be plenty of time for their favorite restaurant and some Latin American dancing.

"Samantha," Samuel said to his wife, "look what my friend Kyle Shepherd has found in the cliffs of Qumran."

"Is there a scroll with it?" she said as she removed her wrap and draped it over Pharaoh's snout.

"I think so, Mrs. Bernstein," Kyle responded.

"I'm very happy for you, Samuel—and you too Mr. Shepherd—but please don't tell me, dear, that you're going to break your promise about taking a quick look? Oh, I see you have your heart set on it. You might as well take it into your special room, and put all your gear on, but I'm going to join you. I'm not going to leave you tonight."

"You are such a dear!" Samuel said. "I couldn't be more excited. All right everybody, get into your robes and masks and we'll take it into the control room. The air we have to breathe out here is not good enough for our little find."

"But Samuel," Mrs. Bernstein said, "you know if I eat after 9 o'clock, I have heartburn, so give it some kind of a deadline."

At that moment Elisheba caught Mrs. Bernstein's eye. The Kodiak had blocked her form. Mrs. Bernstein walked to her quickly and offered her hand.

"Well, I didn't know there was a woman here. You may take a little longer, dear. If I have someone who will talk to me a bit, the wait won't seem nearly so long. I'm Samantha Bernstein."

"Elisheba Muir."

"Do you live in Jerusalem?"

"Yes."

"Oh good! Tell me a little about yourself. You're a student, aren't you?"

Mrs. Bernstein kept the conversation going even while all of them donned their white masks and gloves, and when the men carried the vase into the control room, she continued to chatter, as she followed after Elisheba. So many nights alone had rendered her desperate for conversation.

Samuel walked to the control panel and flipped a switch that set a video camera going above them. "We must document all of this," he said.

For over an hour the men labored to prepare the vase for opening, while Samantha and Elisheba sat nearby. Elisheba divided her time between helping the men and listening to Samantha, although there were times when she could not remember what Samantha had just said.

Finally, Samuel drew a chair up next to the jar and began examining the blackish wax sealing the outer lid. It was so dark, in fact, that at first he took it to be a kind of pitch, but after scratching with his pen-knife, his opinion changed.

"Even if there should be nothing of significance inside, having a jar as beautifully preserved as this one is, with the writing still so legible, is wonderful in and of itself."

He put his hands under the clear, plastic wrap that surrounded the vase, which was meant to collect the ancient air trapped within, and began to work on the seal. He cut carefully but quickly and within five minutes felt the lid to the jar release with a slight suction, and the air that had been caught was drawn into a stainless steel cylinder where the computers whirred, in analyzing its contents.

Samuel looked at Kyle in astonishment. "There was a vacuum! Whoever sealed this container knew the value of a vacuum!"

Elisheba stood up. "I hope you'll excuse me, Mrs. Bernstein. I . . ."

"You needn't explain, dear. I understand perfectly. Let's both get closer. Go ahead. I'll stand by you."

After giving the pump ample time to draw out all of the air within the vase, Samuel removed the plastic cover and the lid that had stopped the opening. Slowly, almost fearfully, he leaned over the vase to inspect its contents. Inside, standing on end, was a large leather scroll, dark brown in color like the husky, severed limb of an oak tree, and it seemed to bear none of the ill effects of age.

"This is the point, Samantha, where I thought we would be leaving," Samuel said, "but this scroll is in such good shape, I'm tempted to see if we can get it out of the jar."

"Oh, go ahead, Samuel. You're having such a good time. I couldn't bear to pull you away. I just hope there's a restaurant still open before we go home."

"Ordinarily, we couldn't do much more than stare at the outer portion of the scroll until we had made some preparation for unrolling it, but I have never seen a writing in this good a condition before. We must take it out of the jar and have a better look at it," Samuel said.

Kyle winked at him, let out a long breath, and took hold of the jar, and turned it upside down, while Samuel and Elisheba knelt on the ground to receive its contents, steadying the vase until the scroll was clear.

"Wait for me," Kyle said after the jar cleared the top. Setting the jar down, he placed his gloved hands around the scroll to give it additional support, so it wouldn't break under its own weight; then carefully, like three priests approaching the Holy of Holies in Solomon's temple, they walked to the long table and set it down.

The scroll was nearly three and a half feet long, and six inches in diameter. It was brown, but not nearly so dark as it had appeared within the shaded confines of the jar. Around each end was a golden band, twelve inches wide, that kept the manuscript tightly wound.

The four people hovered over it for a moment, and their labored breathing filled the old laboratory, adding point and counterpoint to each other in a symphony of respiration. When they became aware of their sounds, they laughed, easing the moment's tension.

"Can we try to read it now?" Elisheba asked.

Samuel did not answer her immediately, but examined the golden bands a moment longer. "Generally, such works of antiquity must be prepared chemically before they can be unrolled or they can disintegrate under one's touch . . . However, I've never seen anything like it. Have you, Kyle?"

"Never. I don't know how they learned the benefits of vacuum or even how they did it, but this leather remains incredibly supple." He touched the scroll at its corner and moved it gently back and forth.

"What do you say, Kyle?" Samuel asked. "Let's see how far we can go with it." Even Samantha was excited. For years Samuel had talked about the big find that he hoped would come to him before he died, and each of his expeditions around the Holy Land always started with the same optimism—like a prospector searching for that elusive vein of gold—and yet, he had never had the distinction he sought; he had never been a part of any significant find. Samantha realized that he might have found his golden vein.

Elisheba joined Kyle on one side of the table, but did not touch the scroll as the two men began unrolling it, so slowly at first that several minutes elapsed before the first inch appeared. Intensely they scrutinized the scroll, looking for cracks, or any sign that the leather was disintegrating.

"How is it looking, Sam?" asked Kyle.

"It looks very good." And they continued to talk rapidly back and forth as more and more of the scroll was revealed.

By the time they had unrolled three feet, they no longer talked, for it was not necessary. The scroll was unwinding as smoothly as a freshly tanned deer hide. As they executed the final turn of the scroll and the last Aramaic characters were revealed, as excellently preserved as were the first, they stood up and smiled. The scroll measured over thirty feet long.

"I would say, Doctor, that we have set a new world scroll-rolling record," Kyle said, which made Elisheba laugh and immediately they were all laughing, including Samantha, who for the first time in her life really understood her husband's fascination with antiquities. They were tipsy with excitement, like partygoers who had drunk deeply, but their intoxication was the thrill of the unknown. "If you don't mind, Samuel," Kyle said, "we'll pull up some chairs and simply allow you to read to us. I haven't had a really good bedtime story for a long time, but tonight, Samuel my friend, I think you'll change my routine." Kyle placed three chairs in a row opposite the place where Samuel stood, so they would be able to see his face as he read.

It was true that Samuel could read Aramaic nearly as well as he could English, and he was silently glad that no one would be looking over his shoulder as he began the translation.

"You don't care if I use the 'thou' and 'thine' pronouns?" he asked. "I've always been a fan of the King James translation of the Bible. It seems to lend an air of dignity to an old script."

"By all means. Use all the Quaker language you want on us. I think it adds a nice dramatic flair," Kyle said. "Thou art at liberty to continue."

Samuel stood over the table, his spine arching, as he leaned closer to the parchment. "'The Lord maketh his arm bare and revealeth that which will proceed his Mighty Day. He who knows the beginning from the end hath revealed it. I, Enoch, have been called to declare it through this record, which was written by my own hand.

"'I have witnessed the Lord's dealings with men to the end of the world. The veil has been removed, and my spiritual eyes have pierced futurity, and I see what will come to pass. Yea, and great are the works of God, and great will they be, even more than man is able to comprehend, till eventually all will stand at his judgment bar, quickened by his glory.

"'I was born slow of speech, but the Almighty had a purpose in my limitations, and I learned patience through the scorn I suffered. When I was sufficiently humbled, the spirit of prophecy settled upon me.

"'In my eightieth year, a vision opened before me and I was commanded to write clearly and without ambiguity for when this writing is manifested unto the world, the end of the wicked—which is the end of the world—will be close at hand.'"

Samuel's voice was clear and piercing; he seemed to be endowed with tremendous energy. His concentration was fearful as though he were speaking in the voice of Enoch himself, and yet his voice had not changed; it remained a deep resonating bass that filled every recess of the laboratory. Frightened, Samantha once began to rise, but restrained herself.

Kyle was enthralled by the reading, and his hands turned clammy with sweat, for the obvious change in Samuel's countenance was affecting him, and he knew that this moment would permanently change his life.

"'When my record shall be recovered from its hiding place near the great city of Jerusalem, know ye that the day of the Lord is nigh at hand. For centuries it will have lain, awaiting that moment when . . .'" and Samuel's voice stopped, and yet it was clear that his eyes had raced on, seeing something which took the breath from his throat, so his lips moved, but his voice was silent.

Samantha was especially alarmed at the way he looked. "Samuel, what's wrong?" she shouted as she raced around the table and stared into her husband's face, while Samuel's eyes searched the scroll. "What do you see?" she yelled. Kyle and Elisheba rose from their chairs at the same time. Without turning his eyes toward her, Samuel read again, laboriously—his face taut with suspense; as though the mysteries of Jerusalem, the tensions of the Holy City had suddenly been condensed into the words of the scroll and were now before him: "A chosen man and a woman will be called forth from the sheath of the Lord to find my revelation after it has lain for centuries in the side of the cliff near a city, which will be known as Qumran."

"You should sit down," Samantha said firmly as she tried to take him by the arm, but Samuel would not budge.

"I think Samantha is right," Kyle said as he joined the old man on his side of the table. "We've all had a lot of excitement today. Perhaps it would be best to postpone the reading until tomorrow."

"No. Can there be any doubt as to the authenticity of this record? I must see more. It's too wonderful to leave. I wouldn't be able to sleep anyway."

He returned to the parchment, while Samantha stood at his side steadying him; Kyle and Elisheba leaned slightly forward in anticipation of his words.

"'And though this interpreter is loved of God, it is not his calling to read my revelation, for that has been assigned to another. So this man will see my revelation, and know that it is, and then be called home to the Lord who gave him life as a witness that the book is all that I have said it is.'"

Samuel finished these words, stood erect and turned his head slowly toward the ceiling as if looking into the depths of heaven, then clasped his right hand over his heart and fell dead into Samantha's arms as Kyle grabbed him, guiding him gently to the floor.

IV

THE SCROLL OF ENOCH

At the foot of the Mount of Olives lies some of the most holy land for burial in all of Palestine, and Jews for centuries have sought to have their bodies interred there, because it was on that spot that the Messiah would someday stand.

It was to this place that Samuel's body was carried only a stone's throw from the tombs of the prophets Haggai and Malachi. Hundreds of students and friends, wearing the black garb of mourning, gathered on the western slope of the Kidron Valley, giving a blackish hue to the hillside.

The day began with a sky full of puffy, cumulus clouds, but as the procession approached the tomb, a large thunderhead, rising ominously towards the heavens, drifted directly over the mourners.

Elisheba stood by Kyle who said nothing during the ceremony except for a whisper to Samantha as she passed by him. "I'm sorry," she heard him say.

Those standing around him would not have understood his

meaning, for they were similar to the general expressions of sympathy, but Samantha understood, and she lifted some of the load from Kyle's shoulders when she whispered back, "Don't be sorry. Sam was so happy that night. The excitement was just too much for his heart. He died doing the work he loved . . . It was his time to go," she said as she squeezed his hand, and then moved on among the other mourners.

The rabbi explained the honor extended to Samuel for bringing his body to this valley. His voice was clear and piercing: "Our friend has spent his life searching for the truth of our ancestors. No man has traveled more over Palestine looking for archaeological sites that could shed light on our history as a people. Museums throughout Israel bear the hundreds of artifacts that he uncovered and identified. We are even told that on the night of his death, he was again examining a recent find.

"For his great contributions to the Jewish people, special permission has been given to bury Samuel here, near the tombs of the men he researched for so long."

Other thunderclouds rapidly formed as the sun soaked up the moisture still in the ground from the big rain, and before they had made their way back to the cars, the sky was completely clouded over.

TWO WEEKS PASSED. Although Elisheba made several attempts to see Kyle again, he could not be found. Shortly after the funeral he checked out of his hotel, leaving no forwarding address. The U.S. Embassy had no knowledge of his whereabouts, nor did any of the archaeologists working on digs near Jerusalem. On a borrowed motorcycle she traveled to three digs to talk with them, but no one could help her. She was beginning to believe that she had seen the last of him until he called on a Monday morning: "Elisheba? This is Kyle. I need to talk to you."

"Sure. Where have you been? I've been worried about you," she said so emotionally that the moment the words left her mouth, she was embarrassed.

"I'll tell you everything . . . or at least everything I can. How about if I pick you up in a half hour?"

"I'll be ready," she said.

For the next twenty minutes, she waited nervously at the window of her home. Suddenly she thought about her appearance and stood up to check out her jeans, which passed inspection, and then she tucked in her white blouse. Stepping to the mirror over the mantelpiece, she fussed with her hair, finally taking a brush from her purse and arranging it.

She looked at her lips and returned to her purse to pull out the first lipstick she had bought in over two years. It was the slightest of reds, and she applied it quickly before Tabitha could enter the room and begin to make fun of her.

She heard his jeep screech to a halt in front of her house, and she ran out of the front door and down the fitted rock sidewalk to him. She paused outside his jeep for a moment and stared at him, as he flashed a weary smile at her. His hair was disheveled from the ride, but he seemed to have grown even more handsome than she remembered. He smiled and opened the door from inside, and she hopped in. She saw a slight tremble in her hand, as she reached to close the door, and she folded her hands in her lap, so he wouldn't notice, then he gunned the jeep away from the curb.

"Where have you been? They said you checked out of your hotel."

"That's right. I've been staying in the home of a friend. His name is David Andreone. He's an American who has a home here and one in the states, too. I told him I needed to hole up for a few weeks, and he let me have his place. It's very nice."

A woman wearing skimpy, white shorts stepped off the curb a block in front of them, pushing a pink baby carriage. She noticed Kyle's speed and retreated to the safety of the curb.

"I've been worried about you, Kyle. What have you been doing?"

"I've been working hard," he said with a smile. "I don't suppose you can guess what's been occupying my attention?"

"The scroll?"

"Bingo. I've made some real headway with the language. It's been something of a cram course the last while, but I've gotten to the point that I can read it fairly rapidly. I've studied Aramaic, but I was pretty rusty. I think I've been getting some help." And he pointed heavenward with his finger.

"Did you have any problem removing the scroll from the lab?" she asked.

"No. I found the janitor who let us in. He let me have it."

They drove past the parliament building where the security outside indicated the Knesset was in session. He watched the building briefly, then concentrated on the road again as he negotiated a maneuver around a creeping tour bus.

"Would it surprise you to know that you and I are involved in something that will have greater repercussions on your country than what's going on right now in the Knesset?"

"Kyle, I've been thinking a lot about what happened," she said as the wind played havoc with her hair, forcing her to continually remove it from her eyes and mouth as she turned to look at him. "Isn't it possible that what happened with Samuel was just a coincidence?"

He looked at her with some surprise. "You were there. Have you forgotten what you saw?"

"I know—but I'm also trying to look at this in a logical light. Kyle, I believe that the scroll is ancient—yes, I was there to see it in the cave—but the fact that it mentions a man and a woman finding it sometime in the future does not prove that we fulfilled a prophecy. Whoever wrote the book said that a man and a woman would find it, but that's so general that it's the perfect example of the kind of prophecies that are constantly being pawned off on the world. Suppose a Bedouin family stumbled into that cave. As long as there was a combination of a man and a woman, it would fulfill the prophecy. Nostradamus was a whiz at that sort of thing."

"It's more than that," he said with determination. "I'll explain when we arrive at David's place."

"All right . . . Who is this David?"

"He's a great guy. We played baseball in college. He was a catcher and I pitched. He was very good and probably could have played—he had some offers—but he wanted to join the military. He had a dream to be in the SEALS and he made it."

"The SEALS?"

"The Navy's elite combat group. They're experts in underwater work—planting explosives and that kind of thing. They train them in everything, of course, hand-to-hand combat, weapons, picking locks. You might be surprised to know that he's taught me a lot of those things, too."

"So why is he living in Jerusalem?"

"His father was Catholic, but his mother was Jewish. He still has relatives here. David's got a lot of money, so he bought a home. His parents are dead now."

"So is David Catholic or Jewish?"

"Half and half."

"Did you tell him that you were bringing me?"

"He's not home. He's in New York."

They arrived at David's home. It was a double story affair and newly built. Yet its white limestone brick blended in with the older structures standing nearby.

Kyle's jeep halted momentarily while he pushed the button of a concealed transmitter under the dash. The wrought iron gates, fashioned in the form of curling snakes, pulled slowly apart.

Elisheba studied the white wall that surrounded the home. It was eight feet high, and she could see electronic sensors at various intervals. Kyle pulled the jeep into the courtyard, and the gates began closing.

"It looks as though his home is fairly secure," she said.

"It is. Usually he has a security guard staying here, but since I've been here, he let the fellow take a bit of a vacation. Someone has to be here because David likes to collect things. His parents were jewelers with stores in Rome and New York. They left him a lot . . . I explained about the scroll and told him I needed a place to keep it safe. He's very excited about it all and will probably be here in a couple of days. Right now he's finishing some work as a stunt man in a movie."

"I thought he was with the SEALS."

"He was but he's retired now, so he's putting his underwater skill to use. Retirement age for a Seal is about the same as it is for a major league ball player—late thirties."

The windows were barred, and the entrance also looked formidable. The two doors were large and black, and the metal surface was covered with the rounded heads of brass rivets, typical of a medieval fortress. In fact, everything about the house looked strong, reinforced, and impregnable. Kyle withdrew a key from his pocket and inserted it into the lock. The dead bolt withdrew, and they stepped inside.

In the foyer, the unfinished form of a muscular man emerged from a piece of Carrara marble. His arms were folded across his chest; the biceps bulged; the veins in his wrist rose to the surface of the skin. Had the white marble been flesh colored there would have been no discrepancies between the sculptured form and that of a human body. Only the torso was finished; the head was still entombed in the rock above. Elisheba believed she recognized the artist, but was skeptical that such a work could be found in a private collection. She stepped closer and saw the signature of Michelangelo.

"If you're looking for renaissance pieces, it helps to have a rich Italian father," Kyle smirked.

She followed him into a hallway which opened into an enormous room that served as a den. Under its ten-foot ceilings, the dark cedar paneling of the walls held hundreds of weapons: broadaxes, scimitars, swords, bayonets, derringers, pistols, knives, bows and arrows—seemingly every type of instrument ever devised for destruction was arranged throughout the room.

In the northern corner, hung the ancient weapons, and then

moving clockwise, they became more modern, until at the corner where the north and west walls touched, the greatest disparity occurred, as swords from the earliest era hung inches away from high-powered rifles.

A large, oak table with four massive legs, fashioned in a corkscrew manner, sat in the middle of the room. Upon it lay the manuscript. Kyle strode to the table, and she followed.

He pointed to a high-back, leather chair, and she sat down, but he remained standing, staring at the brownish parchment in front of him, uncertain where to begin.

"This book contains the writings of Enoch. There's no doubt about that, and the end is near."

"What end?"

"The end of the world."

She pointed to the scroll. "It says that in there?"

Kyle nodded his head.

"I don't think that's anything new, is it? People have been saying that for a long time."

"Yes, but it's sooner than you probably think, and this scroll is going to help to make it happen."

"I know the conditions around the finding of the scroll were all very eerie, and especially the coincidence of Samuel's death . . ." she said.

"Coincidence?"

"I think so, yes."

"It was no coincidence."

Neither of them spoke for a moment, and then Elisheba rose from her chair. "You say this scroll talks about the end of the world?"

"Yes."

"So what does it tell you?"

He paused, unsure of the right words to say. There could be no gentle way. "It will involve Jesus Christ."

She started to laugh. "Did you see his name in the scroll?"

"Yes."

She stopped laughing and turned directly towards him. "Show me." She was so agitated she wasn't aware of a slight trembling in her lower lip, almost imperceptible, but Kyle saw it.

"I can't," he said.

"Why not?"

"I can no longer allow anyone else but me to read it."

"Did the scroll tell you that?"

"Yes."

"How convenient. You've been having a regular conversation with it, haven't you?"

"Don't talk about it that way."

Her eyes flashed. "Am I offending your sensitivities? Am I being sacrilegious about this scroll?"

"You don't understand . . ."

"I understand plenty," she said angrily. "Oh, Kyle. Don't be deluded just because the writing is ancient. You know as well as anyone that there are superstitious writings that tell everything from the right way to pass over the River Styx into the underworld, to how to chant away your infertility or baldness. Are those right just because they were written three or four thousand years ago?" She rose from her chair and stood behind it with a new look of confidence.

"Kyle, don't you realize that Enoch lived long before Jesus? This was obviously done by one of the early Christian groups with the purpose of justifying their beliefs. Don't you see that?" She looked at him with unconcealed pity for having to be the one to break the news.

"Don't you believe in prophecy, Elisheba? Wasn't it Zechariah who said the 'streets of the city shall be full of boys and girls playing.' Jewish boys and girls are in your streets playing again, just as he said. Noah predicted the flood. Why couldn't a man, with God's help, learn Jesus' name?"

"Because Jesus Christ wasn't the Messiah! The Messiah will yet come, and when he does, Israel's enemies will no longer torment her the way the fraud who wrote this scroll did," she said vehemently.

"I tell you now that this book is no forgery. It's as true as your Torah, and it will have a great impact on your people."

"The only impact it could have," she said angrily, "is to incite more hatred for my people. Christians have often looked for reasons to persecute us. Hitler didn't have a difficult time convincing the Germans, because he simply reminded them that they were sending the killers of Christ to the concentration camps.

"The Jew-hater who is responsible for this scroll had a similar motive, but he wasn't content with stirring up a little anti-Semitic response in his own time—oh no! He hated my people so much that he wanted to strike a blow at us from beyond the grave."

"I'm sorry I had anything to do with it." She began walking belligerently towards the manuscript, but Kyle stepped in front of her. "I'm not going to hurt your precious find," she said angrily as she whirled away and approached the north wall of the room where the most ancient weapons were arranged.

"Do you see your friend's weapons? How many of them, do you suppose—starting from the beginning of time," she said as she lifted an ancient hatchet from the wall, "were fashioned to be used against my people?" She felt its sharpness with her thumb, and then raised her eyes to meet Kyle's.

"I wonder if this hasn't been used to hack the limbs off a Jew—perhaps to behead a Jewish child. And now you want to publicize another writing that will awaken the sleeping dogs?"

Kyle strode quickly to her. "That's just it—I'm not going to publicize it."

"How will you ever become a world-famous archaeologist if you don't tell the world what you've found? I find it too hard to believe that you're willing to pass up your chance for archaeological immortality. Aren't you the one who didn't want me to contact the authorities because you were afraid that they might give me the credit?"

"Maybe you'll see me in a different light once you see I'm not going to broadcast this about," Kyle said.

"What will you do with it then?"

"For right now, nothing. I'm still reading it. I'll see what God wants me to do."

"I can't believe you're the same no-nonsense archaeologist that I knew before."

"I'm not the same."

"That's a pity. I found the old Kyle Shepherd to be more interesting."

"Because I believe in the scroll? I'm prepared to give you some additional proof."

"Such as?"

Kyle reached into his back pocket and withdrew a sealed envelope. "Don't open this now. We don't need to say anything more, but read it when you get home."

"OK. I will. It won't change the way I feel, but if you'll keep your word about not publicizing your discovery, I'll read it."

He smiled. "Fair enough. I won't say anything about the scroll, until you tell me to. Call me if you want to discuss the envelope."

She turned towards the door. "Don't wait up for me. Take me home now, please. This place gives me the creeps."

V

An Opening in the Golden Gate

At the entrance to the Dome of the Rock, worshippers and sightseers queued to flock inside, with the women covering their heads and faces as required by Islamic law.

Though this spot had once been the site of Solomon's Temple, and later, during Jesus' time, King Herod's Temple, few Jews were here for it was forbidden since the ground had been desecrated by the presence of gentiles or non-Jews. The faithful Jews could only approach the edge of the grounds to look longingly at the land where they once worshipped.

This site had been fought over for years. Long ago, when a group of Jews who called themselves the Temple Mount Faithful had tried to place a cornerstone for the future temple at the border of the forbidden land, many had died in the fighting, but at the moment there was an uneasy peace on the Temple Mount, although there were some

Jews who wanted even now to tear down the Muslim buildings and replace them with a new temple.

On this morning, a young Englishman entered the Dome of the Rock. He was carrying a tourist map, through the south gate known as Bab el Qibleh. Inside, he was impressed with the spaciousness and the colorful tiles that stretched from floor to ceiling. But his eye was immediately drawn to the center of the chamber where a hand railing kept people back from the very place where the faithful believed Mohammed had ascended to heaven and Abraham had raised his knife over Isaac before the angel of God had stayed his hand.

A group of Americans from Colorado were chuckling as he approached, so he moved around the railing, preferring to remain alone. His trip to Jerusalem was for inspiration, and he didn't need the worldly influences of others, spoiling his mood.

He found a spot where no one else stood by the guardrail and looked down upon the Rock of Abraham. It was larger than he had imagined, stretching fifty-eight feet in length and forty-five in width. Across from him, the Americans' guide pointed at the western corner to a spot, which supposedly bore the fingerprints of the archangel Gabriel, where he had held the rock steady as Mohammed departed to heaven.

Some Palestinian students, standing with their instructor, looked for Mohammed's footprints. Three girls, who were part of that group, were more captivated by the young, dark-haired Englishman than the rock. They didn't know how inaccessible he was, for he had postponed his second year in college in London, to find spiritual fulfillment, and at this moment in his life, girls held no part of his thoughts. He was oblivious to their smiles. When he raised a camera to his eye, they began to giggle, for they thought he was going to snap a picture of them, but, ignoring them, he angled it downward and snapped one of the rocks.

Then the English student heard a rumble below which sounded as if a train were passing in some underground tunnel, but the sound steadily increased until the noise was deafening, and he realized that there was no train but an earthquake; the first scream from the crowd came from one of the Palestinian girls who had flirted with him; the shaking of the building commenced; the Englishman took hold of the hand railing to keep from losing his balance; some began to bolt for the door.

Just as the he released his grip to make a break for the outside, a stocky man wearing a polo shirt slammed into him, sending him sprawling across the tiled floor. Another woman tripped over his legs, causing a chain reaction, which eventually put several people on the floor. Another man stepped hard on his back, knocking the air from him. He struggled to his feet and looked upward to see the dome swaying gently. Dust that had accumulated for centuries was shaken loose and drifted down like curtains of rain. Some fragments of tile on the dome were dislodged and shattered violently on the floor. Many began to scream.

Their terror intermixed with the rumbling groans of stressed rock, fracturing below them, making the whole cacophony of destruction unbearable.

A ceiling tile struck him across his forehead with the force of a fighter's blow. He stumbled momentarily, then caught himself at the railing and leaned on it while his head cleared, then shifted his feet, for there was debris which made it difficult to stand.

Below, the Rock of Abraham pulsated like the back of a giant elephant whose head and legs were buried beneath the ground; it seemed to twist and writhe under the earth's crust, struggling to be set free.

At the moment when the tumult from the earthquake reached its zenith in noise and vibration, a tremendous shattering rent the air and a fissure opened in the south corner of the rock and raced rapidly forward, veering toward the east, so that in a matter of a few seconds the entire floor of the mosque had split in two. At the wall a jagged opening indicated where the fissure had traveled. It sliced through the courtyard past the Chain Cupola, and hurtled toward the confines of the old city wall; there with the force of a missile strike it shattered the ancient brickwork that enclosed the area known as the Golden Gate.

The trembling of the earth ceased. Inside the mosque the tiles no longer fell. The shouts from the city's residents stopped as the stunned people outside the damaged building turned to find loved ones separated during the melee. Here and there cries of joy rent the air as one family member discovered another.

Within the Dome, the Englishman stood above the Rock of Abraham, split in two with powdered rock still spewing from its opening. He turned and followed the crack to the place where it punched through the wall, then stepped outside into the sunlight. Across the courtyard he walked, passing the stunned tourists, many of whom were sitting on the ground in their good clothes, crying or mute from shock.

Twice the Englishman straddled the split in the ground as he squeezed through openings in other walls, and followed its route northeastward. Around him residents of the city slowly gathered to view the destruction.

Although the earthquake had been severe inside the mosque, it was increasingly apparent to him that the vibrations had been limited to that area immediately around the Temple Mount, for the city in general appeared to be unscathed. The steeples and crosses of various churches still soared above the horizon, unhurt.

He passed a young Israeli boy of seven, who had already turned the crack in front of his home into a game as he jumped back and forth.

An old man of eighty who had been taking his daily walk around the mosque with the aid of a gnarled cedar cane, stood ten feet away from the fissure, fearful that it might suddenly grow larger. His mind was trying to adjust to the sudden change in his environment. In fear he recited the Ten Commandments in order and then, having finished, began again at the beginning.

The seismologists were already studying the data generated by their buried detectors, trying to understand a quake which had opened the earth for approximately 250 yards—from the center of the Temple on the Mount, to the eastern border of the old city wall, but had not spread beyond that area.

At the Golden Gate, the Englishman found a heap of jagged, crumbling stones which had minutes before blocked that opening. Many men and women who had stood near the Gate when the shaking began were just recovering their composure enough to talk about what they had seen.

"A crack ran directly up through the middle of the blocks," said one man wearing the black dress of an orthodox Jew, "and from that crack, others shot out, until the wall began to disintegrate. We are lucky to have gotten away from there alive. Why the whole wall didn't collapse while we were standing next to it, I will never know. God saved our lives. I will be a better Jew from this moment on."

The opening of the gate was clearly visible to the Englishman as he approached, still carrying his backpack. The blocks could not have been more cleanly removed had a wrecking crew carefully pried each one out with crowbars. For centuries no one had passed through this spot. Jesus, on the weekend of the Passover in the final week of his life, had ridden through this opening on a donkey while adoring followers draped palm leaves in his path.

The Englishman climbed the rubble under the arch of the Golden Gate until he stood at its peak, looking out at the Kidron Valley, and the rising slopes of the Mount of Olives to the east. He saw a lone eagle riding the currents in the valley below him. Without a flap the bird caught a thermal flow and directed its flight upward toward the Mount of Olives, carrying it over the Garden of Gethsemane. Its shadow sped across an ancient olive tree before it shot vertically up the slope of the mountain. The thermal dissipated and the eagle flapped several times to crest the summit of the mountain where it finally disappeared.

Beyond the pile of rubble that had been the Golden Gate, the fissure continued another ten feet then shriveled to a negligible crack before disappearing completely in the dust. The tombs and stone markers that lay in the Kidron Valley remained untouched, but some mourners who had come to honor their dead were moving away quickly from the spot because they believed that a terrorist bomb had blown up the Golden Gate.

A crippled man, missing his right leg at the knee, remained in the shadows by a corner of the wall to the left of the Englishman. Since his injury in the war of 1967, he had lived a life of devotion to God, and he alone among the Israelis who were gathering around was calm. He wore a slight smile and seemed to be completely at ease, while his eyes searched the heavens in expectation of some marvelous sign, which he believed was imminent.

THAT NIGHT AFTER Elisheba returned to her home, there was a message to call Kyle. She dialed the number to Andreone's home, and Kyle answered. "Hello, Kyle."

"Did you go near the Temple Mount to see the damage from the quake?"

"Yes," she answered. "I was just getting out of class when I heard about it on the radio. They had the roads blocked off, but I was able to park my scooter and take the steps up. Did you see the Dome of the Rock?"

"It's badly damaged. I don't know how they'll repair it. It's remarkable that nobody was hurt during the whole thing."

"Elisheba, do you remember that envelope I gave you last week? Would you mind getting it and bringing it to the phone?"

"All right." She was gone less than a minute when he could hear her fumbling at the receiver. "Here it is."

"Open it and read it to me, please." Her fingers quickly peeled up the flap of the envelope and she withdrew a single sheet of paper folded three times.

She opened it and saw these words: "From the Revelation of Enoch."

She picked up the phone and read aloud: "Though the woman may doubt the truthfulness of the book, she will have evidence from me when the rock covered by the great dome divides in two, and the fissure thereof opens the holy gate." For a moment, nothing was said, and then

Kyle broke the silence.

"So what do you think now?"

"I need to talk to you. I'll be there first thing in the morning."

VI

THE PLACE OF THE SKULL

David Andreone knew that Kyle Shepherd was not in the habit of exaggerating, so when he received a call in his Manhattan apartment and was told to come as quickly as possible, he did just that. He had another movie he was supposed to start, but he called up the producer, who was an old friend, and persuaded him to postpone the underwater scenes, and then caught the next available flight to Jerusalem.

The taxi driver recognized David. A year earlier he given David a ride, and he remembered he was a good tipper. For a taxi driver, the thousands of faces faded quickly into one another, but occasionally a man was so striking in appearance, that he was difficult to forget. David was that kind of man. The driver would not have guessed that David was forty-two. His excellent conditioning gave him a much younger look.

From his sports coat, David withdrew a pair of English handcuffs that he had brought along on the trip to pass the time and slipped them on. He kept the key on the seat by him, just in case he couldn't get out, and began working on them with a small, metal pick. On his right ankle, concealed under a bandage, was a similar pick, which he had hidden for any emergency. He kept his hands low, so the taxi driver couldn't see him and perhaps worry that he was going to be assaulted.

Several minutes passed before he opened them the first time. He was a bit rusty on the procedure, but after once releasing the catch, he was able to duplicate his success very quickly, and within the next few minutes, he snapped and unsnapped the cuffs a number of times.

David noticed a settlement with the statue of a soldier at the entrance—some sort of war memorial. The statue reminded him of an advertisement he had seen on the plane. "I mustn't forget the art show at the Rockefeller Museum," he thought. Art was one of David's passions, and he had developed a deft hand at portraits and the human form in general. Whenever he was in Rome, he set aside time to visit the Sistine Chapel where he would lie on his back on a bench, if the room were not too crowded, and gaze up at Michelangelo's forms.

The driver turned on the radio and David heard for the first time a report of the earthquake. The airport was only a few miles away, and he waited anxiously to see the condition of Jerusalem and his home, and was relieved to find both apparently untouched.

He did not disappoint the driver with his tip. In gratitude, the driver offered to carry the suitcases inside the house, but David refused. The taxi lurched into the flow of traffic to the accompanying blast of an angry horn.

Inside, David threw his arms around his friend and met Elisheba. "This find of yours, Kyle, must really be something. You're not the sort who blows something out of proportion."

David set his bags down and led Kyle and Elisheba from the foyer into the living room. Kyle began the story as they walked, telling first of his search near Qumran. They climbed some stairs and entered a sitting room with a cathedral ceiling. They sat in Louis XV chairs while Kyle continued the story from Samuel's death, stopping momentarily as the emotion gripped his throat. He left nothing out, but softened Elisheba's opposition to the scroll, saying only that she was worried about its possible repercussions.

When Kyle told of the prophecy, which predicted the quake at the Dome of the Rock, he pulled a chair close to his friend and looked directly into his eyes. He spoke of writing the passage beforehand and sealing it in the envelope. He turned to Elisheba who verified his words with a nod. Then she took the letter from her pocket and gave it to David to read while Kyle paused in his account.

"Go on," David said after finishing the letter, even though he continued to hold the paper in front of him, pulling at its edges, as if he were measuring the truthfulness of their story by his touch alone.

"The Eastern Gate is now standing wide open," Kyle said.

"Just as you had predicted in this letter," David added.

"Just as the scroll had predicted," Kyle said. His friend listened intently but not without an upturned eyebrow, that indicated some skepticism.

"If you both weren't so serious, I'd say that you were kidding me."

"It's all true," Kyle said.

"You must realize how all this sounds to someone who has not been involved with this from the beginning. I really don't know what to say. Certainly this episode at the mosque is unexplainable."

David rose from his seat to look out the window. Over the surrounding wall he could see the white buildings of the old city wobbling under the mirage of the hot August sun.

"Well, my curiosity has got me now. Show me your find."

Kyle led the way to the weapons' room. Sitting upon the table where the scroll had lain, was a black, wooden box, long and slender with a handle, which perfectly accommodated the scroll.

"This box was not part of the find. Elisheba hasn't even seen it. I had it made especially for it just to give it some protection." Kyle undid the latches on the lid, and then opened it.

"It certainly doesn't look as old as you say," David said.

"I know. If God can preserve manna in the Ark of the Covenant, I suppose it's no great problem to keep this in such a state," Kyle said.

"I must say that your new-found faith is a little unnerving, when I remember the cocky Kyle Shepherd who nearly came to blows with an umpire during the Arizona State game . . . What I want to know is how do I figure in all of this? You're not going to tell me that the scroll mentions me?"

"No, it doesn't."

"That's a relief. Somehow I would feel like I was under a lot of pressure if the Almighty should single me out," David said.

"He didn't, but you might show up somewhere else."

"If I do," David said," don't tell me unless it's somehow crucial to the scheme of things."

"Do you mean, Kyle," Elisheba said, "that you haven't read it all yet? I thought this was the day that you were going to tell me everything you've learned." She was obviously disappointed.

"I'm not that fast yet, but I'm getting better."

There was silence until David finally broke it: "So why do you need me?"

"The scroll needs to be protected. Of all the people I know, you're the most capable of helping me in that category."

"Protected from what?" David asked.

"We're going to have some trouble. I'm convinced of it. There are those who are opposed to what we might find within the scroll. They would destroy it if they could."

Elisheba looked perplexed. "What are you talking about, Kyle? We're the only ones who know about it. Who would give us trouble?"

"There are those from whom something like this can't be hidden," he said.

"I'm afraid I don't follow you. Who are you worried about?" David asked.

Kyle rose and walked to the wall covered with weapons. "I wanted to talk about this later on with David, after he had the chance to absorb what we had already talked about. But I guess we'll have to cover it now... Who was it that was behind the creation of all these weapons? Who is the author of all evil? He was at the side of the pharaoh's magicians who opposed Moses. He stood at the elbow of Pontius Pilate when he washed his hands of the blood of Christ. He has caused every atrocity in the history of the world, and now we're involved with a record that will contribute to his defeat, and he must be determined to stop us."

"This is pretty heavy stuff," David said. "I didn't think you believed in the devil."

"I do. I always have really."

"Are you saying that he may try to hurt us . . . try to kill us?" Elisheba asked.

"Maybe."

David let out a low whistle. "Like I said—heavy stuff." He walked behind Kyle, then returned to look over his shoulder at the manuscript. "Well, this is sure a new one for me. Terrorists I've dealt with, but I've never tackled something from the unseen world. Are you expecting some sort of attack?"

"It's not clear what's going to happen, but I know this from what I've read—we're not going to get through this without some problems. We just have to be on guard."

"I don't know what kind of abilities you think I have, but when it comes to fighting Old Scratch, himself, I think you're expecting more than I can deliver, but I'll hang around and see if I can be of some assistance. If the earthquake happened as you said, there must be something to it. You believe it, too, Elisheba?"

"I know what I saw today, but I would like to see the passages in the scroll that call Jesus by name," she said resolutely. "I'm not willing to just accept that. It's possible that somebody else has gotten hold of it and messed with it."

"I wish you could see it to satisfy yourself, but that's not allowed.

I'm the only one who can read it now, David. I was telling that to Elisheba before you came."

"But why?" she said angrily. "I helped you find it in the first place. If I hadn't given you that piece of pottery you never would have found that cave. It's as much my find as it is yours."

"You act as though I were calling the shots," Kyle countered.

"Well, aren't you?" she said bitterly.

"Was I calling the shots today at the mosque? Did I really have anything to do with that?" He tried to take her hand but she pulled away.

"Don't be angry with me, Elisheba," he said gently.

Elisheba turned away and left the room quickly.

"All right," David said, "so we wait around until you do some more translating. I'm in the mood for a little rest."

They left the den and went into the kitchen. David insisted on making supper. Elisheba joined them but said very little during the meal. Afterwards, they moved to the living room where David recounted his latest filming experience off the Florida Keys. There was talk of encounters with sharks and a drunken stunt man that David had subdued.

Elisheba listened quietly, but eventually fell asleep on the couch. When she awoke, she could hear the men's voices in the other room. She arose and walked silently through the house, making her way to the den. After pausing at the threshold and listening for any sound that would indicate she had been detected, she closed the door and turned on the light. By itself the light was strong, but reflected from the barrels and blades of the various weapons, it was absolutely dazzling. She winced and closed her eyes for several seconds, and then she squinted and walked unsteadily to the huge table and sat down in front of the box.

For over ten minutes she hesitated, staring at the box and glancing around the room at the weapons. She was thinking of Samuel's death. Once she stretched out her hand, then pulled it back. Rising from the chair, she circled the table completely and then stopped.

"What about my family?" she thought. "If there is truth in this record, I should not keep them from it." The decision was made. She returned to the chair at the table, undid the latch that secured the lid and opened it.

Slowly she unrolled it until the scroll lay full length upon the table. Determinedly she began the search for the Aramaic markings which would translate as "Jesus." Hovering over the withered paper, she found within a minute the symbol for his name. Her breathing stopped and she examined the word more closely, hoping some additional mark would eliminate it from consideration. It was as Kyle had said.

She stood straight and stared at the writing and then quickly bent again, searching more frantically. In a moment his name appeared again—and again! His name was everywhere. The manuscript was about him!

Finally she stopped and her breathing came in deep gasps; tears welled up, and as she hung her head, they dropped to the floor. She was crying for her people—for all of Israel—and not for just her time alone.

She returned the scroll to its box, and walked haltingly away, steadying herself on the doorframe, her vision still clouded. She gathered her things and quietly left the house.

For an hour she walked the road until she hailed a taxi and asked to be driven to a certain spot. The driver, a young man who had lost his thumb while serving with the Israeli army in Lebanon, knew the place she wished to go very well. It was one of the most popular spots in Jerusalem and he had taken many tourists there, but never had he done so at this hour of the morning.

"That spot is not well-lighted at night. I don't know if you are aware of that. Maybe you would rather wait until the morning?" he suggested.

"No . . . I want to go there now," she said curtly.

He sensed her mood and realized that any further suggestions were unwanted, so he said nothing and drove along the road known as

Sultan Suleiman until he neared the Damascus Gate located at the north end of the old city wall. He pulled off on the shoulder and allowed an empty tour bus to pass him. For the moment, they were alone on this ancient thoroughfare. "Do you want me to wait, Miss?" he asked.

"No, thank you," she said as she pressed the money into his hand. He watched her cross the road and disappear into the darkness. She nearly stumbled on a large rock that caused her ankle to buckle. She was not hurt. Her eyes adjusted to the skimpy light from a wisp of a moon. She reached the upper knoll of Calvary. It was all clear to her now. She bent over and pulled the shoes from her feet in respect and walked farther on, shifting the weight from one foot to the other to avoid the sharper rocks. A slight breeze arose, which lifted her hair gently behind her. She stood on the hill and took in the cool scent of the desert air transporting the faint smell desert flowers, and then gazed out at the barren landscape, dotted with dried grass and withered bushes.

"This is what he saw when they brought him to be crucified?" Suddenly she fell to her knees and began to weep bitterly.

VII

INTO THE DESERT

*F*ive women, all widows who had come from Italy, were making their way up the slope of Calvary believing that a sunrise service would be the most spiritual way to conclude their trip to the Holy Land. After saving for years, each had put away enough money to come to Jerusalem on a pilgrimage to see the holy relics and places of their Lord's sinless life. Someone had suggested that their last day should begin with morning prayers on the spot of the crucifixion. Their leader, Angelica Lozada, an attractive woman in her mid 50s, was well aware of the controversies surrounding the sacred sites, but she was convinced that Gordon's Calvary was the real spot of the Savior's crucifixion, and she had recommended that they begin their day there.

The morning sky was still black, though faint orange hues played upon the eastern sky, as she led her friends up the holy hill. Elisheba had fallen asleep at the summit of the hill, and Angelica nearly stepped on her before realizing that she was not simply another rock formation in the meager morning light. Her startled shriek unnerved the women behind her, and they stepped backwards.

"Ci Scusate! Non la vedevamo!" Angelica said hastily in Italian before remembering that they were not in Rome and that English would more likely be recognized. "Excuse us," she said in heavily accented English. "We did not see you there."

"I'm sorry to have upset you," Elisheba said as she stumbled to her feet. The other women gathered around her. They had all worn white blouses and dresses so they might easily distinguish one another in a crowd, and those white garments seemed to hover around Elisheba like disembodied spirits.

"My child, what are you doing here by yourself?" Angelica asked as she took Elisheba by her arm and steadied her.

"I came here . . . to rest," she said haltingly, and the older woman wondered momentarily if the girl had been drinking. She leaned closer to smell the young girl's breath and found no trace of alcohol. Elisheba's mind cleared as she remembered her purpose for being there. Initially she had forgotten where she was. Encompassed by the strange white images, she had become disoriented.

"This is a holy place. I wanted to rest on the spot where He died," Elisheba said, her wits now gathering as she found her voice. She spoke with such sincerity that the women were touched, especially to see devotion in one so young. There was an unspoken feeling that they were with a special girl who shared the same reverence for the spot that they did.

Angelica noticed that Elisheba was shivering and she placed her arm around her, drawing the full material from her sleeve over her shoulders to warm her.

"We, too, have come here to worship Him," she said. "It is comforting to find one as young as you who believes in the savior. Of what faith are you?"

Elisheba felt uneasy. It was a question that caught her off-guard. When she seemed confused, Angelica felt she needed to clarify herself: "Are you a Catholic or a Protestant?"

"No," Elisheba answered quickly, bending over to brush the dirt from her jeans. "I'm not either of those."

Angelica sensed her quandary and felt compelled to reassure her that her religious views were most tolerant when it came to other denominations. "Whatever your Christian church, we would like to know what organization can cause such faith in a girl so young?"

"I am a Jew," Elisheba said boldly.

Though they did not intend for it to happen, a few of the women could not stifle an audible gasp. Angelica cast a stern glance in the direction of the others. "Forgive us. You can understand our surprise."

"I know . . . I am a Jew who has come to believe in Christ. Maybe that means I am no longer Jewish. I don't know what I am anymore. I had hoped to find some answers here. I came here to sort things out . . . to understand Him better."

"And may God be with you in your search to know Him." She patted Elisheba's arm and leaned towards her and kissed her on the cheek.

"Thank you," was Elisheba's embarrassed reply as she pulled away from the women and made her way down Golgotha. The women watched her go in silence and then filed off to pray, while Angelica remained longer, watching the young woman make her way along the highway. She had come to this spot looking for spiritual renewal, and had found it in the words of this young girl. She would join her friends in prayer, even as they were now kneeling a few yards from her, but for her, the living testimony of the Master was in the image of this Jewish girl who had so recently come unto Him. Nowhere had she felt the Lord's presence more strongly than in this brief encounter.

In some ways Angelica had been disappointed by Jerusalem and its commercialism, but now she could feel His spirit burning within her. The ground which had become holy so many centuries before was newly sanctified by Elisheba's presence. Only when Elisheba had hailed a bus, did the older woman turn to join her friends. Her candle of faith had been rekindled and she was filled with gratitude.

ELISHEBA WAS BEGINNING to believe that she had seen the last of Kyle until he called on a Monday morning. Elisheba took the bus to her neighborhood but got out a block from home. When she entered her front door, she moved silently, so as not to disturb her parents and sister.

In her bedroom she removed her sleeping bag from her closet where it lay on the shelf, then gathered together a few clothes and stuffed them in a backpack resting at the foot of her bed. She went to the kitchen and found a fresh, unsliced loaf of bread that her mother had baked the previous night and slid it into her backpack, then surrounded it with several cans of soup and a chocolate bar.

Leaving a note on the table, she told her parents not to worry, but that certain circumstances would cause her to be working in the area of Qumran for the next few days. If they had to contact her, they could find her there. She left the note propped against the menorah on their dining room table.

Stealthily she stole from the house and unlocked the padlock that secured her small Honda motorcycle. She pushed her bike into the shadows down the rock path which led away from her house, then turned to follow the road. It was another block before she dared to mount it and hit the kick-starter. The engine caught on the second try, and she rolled away.

Soon she was traveling over the Derekh Yeriho, or the Jericho Road. It passed alongside the eastern wall of Jerusalem and took her within a stone's throw of Samuel's burial spot. She could not see the place where he lay buried even though she looked for it. Other larger monuments obscured it.

The Mount of Olives stood solemnly at her left. She bore to the right, staying on the route that would carry her to Jericho. If she remained on it long enough, she would go all the way to the ancient city, but less than an hour later she veered hard, towards Qumran.

Good roads would last several more miles before she was forced to travel the more hazardous routes.

She was not sure why she was returning to the area where they found the scroll since that spot was responsible for unsettling her life so drastically. She maybe hoped there might be some answers awaiting her there as to the course she should now pursue. She definitely needed time to be alone, to ponder the events of the past weeks and to search for God's will.

At the very site where she had originally found the pieces of shard and where Kyle had pitched his tent, she also set up hers. She wanted to be in this place not only because of her discovery, but also because of her memories of Kyle. As uncertain as she felt about her future, she was not at all in doubt as to her feelings for him. She loved him, and yet those feelings must be set aside now.

She was hungry, and she found the candy bar in her knapsack and offered a prayer over it before eating. That done, she took a swallow of water from her canteen, which was still cold from the faucet, then replaced the lid. Stepping outside, she looked upward and located the cleft in the rock face, which represented the opening to the cave. She smiled when she remembered how startled Kyle was when she had burst in on him shortly after he had found the jar.

"If the cave were not full of water, I would go there," she thought. "But this is as good a place as any," she said aloud and then knelt on the very place where she first saw the shards lying on the surface. She folded her arms and began to pray.

A half hour later she stood up to rest her back, entered the tent and took another swallow of water, kneeling as she tilted her head back to take in the water in heavy gulps. She couldn't seem to quench her thirst.

She sat on the slick nylon floor. The green skin of the tent was aglow as the rising sun struck it fully, making her feel cool and comfortable, as though she were resting in a tropical forest, basking in the greenish light of its overhead canopy.

Even though she was not certain as to her course of action, her soul had drawn spiritual strength from her extended prayer. Once before had she prayed with such determination and that was during the days when her grandmother was dying. Elisheba was eleven when the heart attack occurred. Desperately, she wanted her to live, but four days later the old woman breathed her last while Elisheba held her hand as she sat next to her grandmother's hospital bed.

It was her grandfather who had convinced her that God would hear and answer her prayers, but on the first crucial test for Elisheba's burgeoning faith, she was dealt a harsh blow, and in some ways she had never recovered. True, she had not given up prayer entirely, but her doubts always seemed to undermine her faith from that moment on. Now, however, for the first time since she was a child, she felt that God was really listening to her again, and within her there was a deep conviction that if she continued to call upon Him, she would know the right thing to do. She felt better. Prayer did work. There was a feeling within her that said, "Continue as you are doing."

Throwing back the flap of the tent, she returned to her spot of prayer and knelt again and continued her supplications. An hour later, she arose suddenly and walked quickly to the tent and knelt in its opening. Her backpack lay just inside, and she felt within it until she found the heavy weight of the Bible. Returning to her spot outside of the tent, she sat with her legs crossed and turned to the New Testament and began reading the first verses in the book of Matthew.

She had read these pages once before as a teenager, but it had been done simply from curiosity. Now that her attitude was different, the words took on an entirely different meaning. She was filled with faith. She read steadily until the sun had passed its zenith, stopping to eat and drink only when necessity required it.

By 3 o'clock her muscles were stiff, and she rose to walk along the cliff face. A cactus had taken root at the base of a large sandstone rock which weighed several tons. There had been other smaller plants in the sandy clay, but this one had grown to the height of her waist, easily the largest of any she had seen. Its longest needles were more than an inch. She stopped and touched her forefinger to one of them, and then applied a slight pressure which caused the needle to puncture her skin. The pain was immediate and sharp, and a shiny, crimson drop quickly enlarged itself at the opening.

After the initial wince of pain, her face remained expressionless and yet, inside, she was imagining what it would be like to have a ring of thorns pressing into her scalp, running their way through the skin on her temples, and she thought of how some of the pain He had suffered had been for her.

The doubts of the past, her skepticism regarding the goodness of life, were all replaced with faith, and she sank to her knees in appreciation.

"Thank you," she said. "Thank you, so very much . . ." But when she tried to say, "for everything you've done," her voice broke and great tears welled in her eyes, and she could not finish. She did not repeat the words. He had understood her.

SHE REMAINED NEAR Qumran for two days, reading periodically, and walking among the rock formations. She did not stay because her faith needed strengthening, but because she wanted to better know the Bible before she returned.

On the afternoon of the third day, she returned slowly to her camp from one of those walks, using a gnarled limb as a cane that she had found in an area devoid of trees. With no sign of any trees, she wondered what had brought it there. She stopped to examine the barkless limb to see if there was any indication of teeth marks. She was still examining it when she heard Tabitha's voice calling her name.

She held the stick to her with both hands in surprise. Why was she so startled? She had intentionally left a note for her family so she could be found if necessary, and it was just like Tabitha to come looking for her, as she had done on other digs. Maybe because she had cloistered herself to meditate on the things of God, any other human voice seemed an intrusion. Elisheba ran to her tent and saw her sister standing there.

Tabitha's face seemed drawn, and Elisheba knew that someone was injured or dead. "What is wrong? Who is hurt?" she asked before her sister could say anything.

"It's Mr. Shepherd. He's been hurt," Tabitha quickly answered.

"What happened to him?"

"He's in the hospital. Someone broke into the house where he was staying with his friend and beat him up. They nearly killed him. He's been in a coma for two days." Elisheba was already packing her equipment.

"No one knows who did it. Mother saw it in the paper and called the hospital." The tent was already lying flat on the ground, and Elisheba began rolling it up into a tight bundle.

"How did you get here?" Elisheba asked even as she tied the bundle on the back of the scooter. "Mother brought me. She's parked over there, behind those boulders."

Elisheba hit the kick-starter, and the motor caught. "Tell her I'm going to the hospital and not to worry. I'll call her tonight and talk to her." A moment later she was on the road, driving as fast as she could to Jerusalem.

VIII

In the Hospital

"Are you a member of the family?" the petite nurse with the slender fingers asked Elisheba.

"No . . . I'm just a good friend." Those fingers touched lightly on the keyboard of the computer terminal and she stared at the monitor, which was angled away from Elisheba. The nurse seemed to be weighing her words. "He's holding his own, I can tell you that. Unfortunately, I'm not allowed to say anymore about it right now.

"The nursing staff has been asked not to give out a lot of information. A Mr. Andreone made that request. He was here earlier, but had to leave. He said he would be back by 11:30 this morning. May I ask your name?"

"It's Elisheba Muir."

"Yes, I have your name as one of those who would be allowed to see Mr. Shepherd. If you'll follow me . . . The police thought that there might still be some threat on his life. He's staying in the security wing. I'll have to accompany you or you'll be stopped by the guards."

A burly guard sat in a seat outside Kyle's door. He questioned the nurse, and then opened the door for them. The nurse entered first and Elisheba followed tentatively, afraid of what she would see.

The top of Kyle's head was wrapped with bandages. She could see the deep bruises on his arms and neck. She pulled a chair towards the headboard and sat closely to him, listening to his steady mouth-breathing. His lips were dry, so she filled a glass at a sink next to his bed, then dipped her fingers in and touched them to his mouth.

She wept to see him as he was, and she was crying when David Andreone opened the door. She turned her head as he moved silently to her side, placing his hands on her shoulders. He was wearing a bandage over his left eyebrow and his eye was purple and swollen. "I've been trying to get hold of you for days."

"I didn't know," she said. "What happened?"

"I don't know really. They got to me while I was asleep. When I woke up, he was like this. I'm usually a pretty light sleeper, but they got past me."

"You said 'they.' How many were there?"

"I don't know, but there must have been more than one to have beaten Kyle like this. However many there were, they didn't leave any evidence behind. The police are completely baffled. I found him lying in the den. I guess he must have surprised them. I thought he was dead. He nearly was . . . He still hasn't made it yet." David sat down.

"I'm so worried about him. He looks awful. Hasn't he said anything since it happened?"

"Nothing, and he was attacked the night you left."

"Look at his arm," David said as he lifted the sleeve of Kyle's hospital gown.

There was a bruise in almost the exact shape of a hand. "Kyle is in good shape, and he's a fine athlete, but somebody really threw him around. Look where that guy, whoever he was, took him by the arm. Part of the wall was damaged and several weapons were jarred to the floor. He was thrown against the wall. That's what caused the concussion. That's how he hit his head."

"What was the reason, David? What did they want?"

"They got the scroll."

Elisheba reeled from the blow. "Oh no!" she said, and then she clutched at her chest with both hands as though she were having a heart attack. Rising from her seat like a sleepwalker with her eyes open, she began to pace.

Stopping at the foot of the bed, she steadied herself, and then ran her right hand through her hair. For a moment she looked as if she had lost her mind, then she closed her eyes and bowed her head. "I don't know why God would allow that to happen after he had saved the record for so long," she said.

"I'm surprised to hear you say that," David said. "I thought you were opposed to the record.

"David, you don't understand. I read the record—not all of it—but enough to see that what Kyle has been saying is true."

"You read the record after Kyle told you not to?"

"I had to find out for myself. If I was going to be involved in all of this, I couldn't go into it with doubts."

David stared at her somberly until Elisheba became unnerved.

"David, why are you looking at me like that?"

"No one was supposed to look at the scroll but Kyle."

"Are you saying that I'm somehow responsible for what happened to him?"

"I didn't say that."

"But the way you were looking at me—you think I'm responsible. I didn't do this to him. Robbers—thugs—they are the ones who are responsible. They were looking for things to steal and your place looks rich, so they broke in and stole some things and saw an old scroll lying on the table. There are a lot of people living in Jerusalem who are aware of the worth of old scrolls. They're worth more than gold—so they carted it off with the other stuff."

"There's one thing wrong with all that," he said coldly.

"What's that?"

"The record was the only thing they took. They passed all the other art pieces."

Elisheba returned to her seat and sat down, looking at Kyle, hoping that his eyes would open. David stayed for a while more, then excused himself and went to the nurses' station. "I'm afraid the young girl you escorted to Mr. Shepherd's room is really upset. Maybe one of you nurses could look in on her."

The nurse with the slender fingers was gone, but a young nurse from Taiwan who had not lost her capacity for sympathy said she would check on Elisheba. "I'm sorry to hear that," she said sincerely. She had not grown callous during her years as a nurse, and she was true to her word, for fifteen minutes after David had departed, she went to Kyle's room and found Elisheba kneeling at his bed. The nurse stayed for a while, and when she had to leave, Elisheba was still on her knees.

His condition did not improve that night or the next day. The doctor warned her that head trauma could cause a number of complications. If he came out of it, it would usually be within the first three or four days. After that time, they entered a whole new dimension of problems.

On the following evening, while Elisheba still maintained a constant vigil in his room, alternating her routine between praying at his bedside and reading the Bible, she heard him moan and saw his hand lift to touch the wrappings around his forehead.

"Elisheba, are you here?" she heard Kyle say.

"I'm here, Kyle. Oh, you're awake. Thank God. Thank God. I love you Kyle. I've wanted to tell you that. I was so afraid you would die without knowing how I felt about you."

"I know you love me," he said in a whisper. "I love you, too. I'm just too tired to tell you how . . ."

Those were the only words he said. Immediately he was asleep again. An hour passed, and she saw him open his eyes, and he searched the room as if he were looking for her, because when he saw her, he smiled and said, "Good. You're here," then he dozed off again for less than a half hour.

"These bandages are too tight," he said at the end of that time. "I never really felt sorry for any of those mummies I've found until now. I hope they were dead before they wrapped them up. This is an awful way to go."

She laughed, but it was really from her relief, and then she took his hand.

"You've been out for over three days."

"Really? Three days? I can't believe it."

"Do you know why you're here and what happened?" she asked.

"As a matter of fact . . . I do know what happened." He did not speak but squinted his eyes together for a long moment, then opened them again as though trying to ease them back into full operation.

"So, Kyle, what happened? Who did this to you?"

His body seemed to be awakening. He acted as though he hadn't heard her question, raising his hands slowly. There was a bruise that circled the knuckles of his right hand. His middle finger appeared to have taken the brunt of the blow. Something flashed across his face, and his tiredness was replaced with worry: "Where's David?" he asked, turning his head quickly to her.

"He's all right. He was here earlier today. He's been here every day. He has a cut and bruise over his eye, but it's nothing like what you've gone through. Will you tell me about it?"

"I will, but get me a drink first, will you, and then call David on the phone and let me talk to him."

"I will . . . Kyle, when you first woke up, I said something . . ."

"I heard what you said, Elisheba. Did you hear me?"

"Yes."

"I told you that I loved you, right?"

"Yes, you did."

"Just as long as we understand each other. Any second thoughts on your part?" he asked.

"No."

"None on mine either . . . Has the doctor been in?"

"He asked me to get him whenever you showed any improvement. I'll call him now."

"No, not yet. Later. Call David first." She did and listened as David answered and then Kyle spoke without any introduction: "David, you've got to do something about that security system. It stinks." There was a long pause, and Elisheba could feel the excitement on the other end and then the mighty shout of joy that caused Kyle to pull the receiver away from his ear.

"Kyle! Kyle! You're awake!" she could hear him say clearly.

"Yes. I'm among the living. I awoke to a beautiful angel in my room."

They talked for a couple of minutes with Kyle responding to questions about his pain, his eyesight and his memory. Then he told David to come to see him as soon as he could, that there were important matters for them to discuss. She heard David say that he would be there within thirty minutes and then Kyle hung up. "Should I get the doctor now?"

"No. I don't want anyone bothering us until we've had a chance to talk."

"All right," she said and then lapsed into silence, waiting for him to begin, but he didn't speak. She was afraid to mention the loss of the manuscript, fearing the emotional impact could be dangerous to him in his weakened physical state. If he asked her about it, she would avoid it, saying that she hadn't been back to David's house since the night she left and wasn't sure of everything that had happened. She wished he had allowed her to call the doctor, so he could force Kyle to rest;

maybe the doctor would order her to leave, and there wouldn't be any opportunities for answering difficult questions.

"I read your note before he came," he said.

"Before who came?"

"The guy who beat me up . . . Guy maybe isn't the right word to describe him. I'd have to go into the animal kingdom to find the right word."

"You can remember him?" she asked in surprise, and he nodded his head.

"Well, I remember his face very well. Don't get me wrong; he was a man, but his face would be hard to describe—wide-eyed, hideous expressions—baring his teeth at one moment and then snarling like a mad dog the next. It was more evil concentrated in one spot than I've ever encountered.

"He was a short guy actually, probably five feet six or seven, and not all that big—maybe 160 pounds. I went to the den, and when I turned around, there he was. He was wearing blue jeans and a black sweatshirt and the sleeves were ripped off at about the elbow.

"I was startled, you know, and at first I just ordered him to leave, and he gave this laugh. It reminded me of a guy I knew who had throat cancer—ragged—wretched—seemed to be coming from deep within his chest. Possessed, I suppose.

"He began walking toward me, stalking me, and yet he didn't have any weapons that I could see, so I made a run to the wall to get a hatchet and he grabbed me before I could reach it . . . There's where he took hold of me." Kyle pointed to the bruise that David had indicated. With one arm he lifted me off the ground and then hit me with his other hand. I don't know what happened after that because I was out. He maybe hit me again."

"David told me that you were apparently thrown against the wall," she said.

"Most likely. I mean he had me in the air over his head, lifting me as if I were one of those plucked chickens hanging in the meat market."

"How did he ever get past the security system?" she asked in disbelief.

"I think he had help."

"From whom?"

"Someone else who does know the layout to David's house," he said, and Elisheba became more confused.

"Who else could have given him help and for what reason?"

Kyle's eyes narrowed. "You might find this a bit roundabout, but to answer who helped him, we must simply answer the question: What was it the thief wanted? What was stolen?"

Elisheba averted her eyes, but she knew it was no good; she would have to answer, and if she didn't, her face would be answer enough. Where was the doctor? Why didn't he come to check on his patient? The turmoil within Kyle seemed to reach a crescendo, and he clasped his hands together and wrung them like a man reliving his past sins. "Who is it that wanted the scroll?"

Elisheba looked up quickly. "How did you know the scroll was stolen?"

"I knew what he was after by the way he looked. Elisheba, he was not the run-of-the-mill thief. He was on somebody else's errand."

"Whose errand?"

"The same being who inspired Judas to sell Jesus for thirty pieces of silver."

She stood and walked to the window and looked out, but in actuality she wasn't seeing anything in front of her. "If he has the scroll now, then I'm the one who is responsible for its loss. I read the scroll when you told me not to."

"You're no more responsible than I am. I guessed that you would read it if I gave you the chance, and I gave it to you."

"What do you mean?"

"I left the door to the weapon room open and the scroll lying out."

"Why?"

"I wanted you to know. I knew how anxious you were that night to see it, and I let you do it. I was wrong to do that. So wrong."

She worried that a big, emotional downturn could be hard on him, so she went to get the doctor. When Dr. Langestein came a moment later, he smiled emphatically to see his patient out of his coma. The doctor was prematurely gray, and his silvered hair, combed back on both sides of his head, gave him an air of distinction. But when he saw how distraught Kyle was, the smile quickly faded. He tried to calm him by being cheery, but Kyle remained inconsolable, and Langestein began to wonder if some neurological damage had been done. He told Elisheba that Kyle would need some rest, and she left the room.

They would not let her in again that night. Soon David arrived and asked to see his friend, but was refused. When he grew persistent, Dr. Langestein was summoned to the nurse's station, and there in subdued tones, so as not to upset others sitting in the waiting room, he explained his position.

"When I heard that he had come to, I was elated, but seeing his emotional state as it is, I'm afraid something is wrong. Perhaps there's some damage. I asked him if there is anybody whom he would like to see. He will not respond. I've given him a shot of Valium, and I insist that he not be disturbed. Let us give him a night's rest, and we'll see how his condition is tomorrow." David nodded his head and thanked him and then took Elisheba by the arm and led her to his car.

The trip began in silence, but when David asked her if Kyle had said anything to her, she told the whole story. She was not finished when they reached her home, and they sat in the car until she was done.

"What do we do now, David?"

"I have no answers. Let's see if a night's rest makes him feel better. He has been through an awful lot." She nodded and then got out of his car. She gave a little wave and walked up the sidewalk to her house.

IX

A Darker Side of Capri

Elisheba arrived at the hospital at 8:00 A.M. on the third day after Kyle awakened from his coma. When she opened the door, she was startled to find his bed empty. Stepping back into the hall, she returned to the nurse's station, and there found the duty nurse studying a chart with an intern.

Elisheba was about to speak when she had a hunch. She strode across the hall to the window and looked down into the enclosed courtyard. There on a wrought iron bench sat Kyle, still wearing his robe and his bandages. She found the stairwell and took the steps two at time, holding the railing on the way.

"Did the doctor say that you could come down here?" she said as she walked up behind him.

"He told me to stretch my legs if I could. Once I got on my feet, I wanted to be out in the sun."

"How are you feeling today?" she asked.

"The headaches have stopped."

"And how about your spirits?"

"They won't be much better until we take steps to recover the scroll."

She sat down by him. "What steps can we take?"

His fingers pushed against the grain of his beard. "I'm not completely in the dark. I have an idea where it might be. The last words I read in the scroll contain the answer. At the time I thought it was some figurative language, but now I see how clear it really was."

She leaned slightly forward. "What did it say? Can you tell me?"

"Yes, I can tell you. In fact I can give it to you word for word, because I studied it so long, trying to figure out what it meant. The passage went like this: 'Disobedience may give power to the Wicked One who for centuries has established his house on the island of the goats below the knee of Caesar. He will rule in the midst of that house, and he will possess these words in the place where the diadems were gathered for God's glory.'"

"So what do you say it means?" she asked.

"The scroll is in Italy," he said.

"What makes you think that?"

"The word Capri means goats in Italian. The words would be taken to the Island of Goats. The scroll said the island would be below the knee of Caesar." He reached to his side and lifted an atlas onto his lap.

"Do you see this picture of Italy? It's shaped like a leg of course and here where the knee would be we find Rome where Caesar ruled, and below that knee is the bay of Naples with the Isle of Capri right out here."

"It seems to fit," she said with a nod. "But Capri is a resort island. I would think it would be on Palermo. Isn't that the home of the mafia?" she questioned.

"Yes, but Capri hasn't been any model of virtue. In Roman times it wasn't much more than one big brothel where rich Roman fathers took their sons to have an experience with a prostitute when they reached their twelfth birthday." Kyle closed the atlas. "I'm convinced this is where we must go."

"In what way convinced?" she asked.

"It's just a feeling that I'm on the right track. A feeling of peace would be the best way to describe it," he said with a shrug of his shoulders.

"I see a problem with that passage as you've interpreted it," Elisheba said as she looked toward the ground not wanting to meet Kyle's eyes.

"What's that?"

"You say that Enoch has called Caesar by name."

"Yes," Kyle said.

And then she lifted her face toward his. "I can't understand how that can be because Enoch lived two or three thousand years before Caesar, so how could he know his name?"

"I guess the question is whether God could have known his name?" Kyle said as he raised his eyebrows.

"Well, yes, I'm not saying God couldn't have known that the leader of Rome would be called Caesar," she said defensively. "He knows everything."

Kyle took her hand. "We're in agreement then. Actually, there's a precedent for this kind of thing. Do you remember that Isaiah lived a couple of hundred years before Cyrus King of Persia, and yet, he called him by name and said that he would be responsible for bringing the Jews back to their homeland and helping them rebuild their temple."

"Isaiah called Cyrus by name?" she asked.

"That he did. Of course, Enoch gave the name thousands of years before, but time really doesn't make any difference with God, does it?"

"No," she said. "I believe in the scroll. You know that. It's just hard for me to understand the kind of detail you're translating."

"You and me both."

A birdbath in the courtyard drew a lark to its edge, where it drank and then warbled its contentment, which rang clearly within the enclosed walls.

"That's nice," Kyle said with the first smile she had seen since before the attack.

"You said, 'The Wicked One will establish his house.' Are we talking about the devil again?" Kyle didn't look away from the nightingale.

"I would say so. Yes."

"You mean," she said, dragging the words out, "that he, the devil, has a place—a house—where he actually stays?"

"He doesn't have to have a roof over his head to get out of the rain. No, I would say 'headquarters' would probably be a better explanation. I believe these are his headquarters, for right now anyway. Maybe they were in Berlin during the '40s . . . I wish I knew what we were looking for. I haven't the slightest idea. But we do know that it was a place where some sort of diadems were 'gathered for God's glory.' It's probably something to do with precious stones.

It was time to voice more of her fears. "How are we going to be able to approach this place without him knowing it?"

"That's a good question. He'll probably know. That doesn't necessarily mean he can prevent us from going."

"You were nearly killed here," she countered.

"Yes. But that was after I was disobedient. I don't plan on making that mistake again, and because of that, I hope to have God's help. Maybe they won't know we're coming. We might have the element of surprise on our side—I don't know. I guess we'll just have to have a little faith, Elisheba. Remember your Moses approached Pharaoh with only a staff."

"You're not Moses."

"Well, I know that. And how rude of you to remind me of my limitations," he said with a smile, "but nonetheless, we are headed to

Egypt—in a figurative sort of way... Well, at least I'm going. You can make your own decision."

"Of course I'm going."

"Good. I can tell you right now we're going to discover a side of Capri that the tourists never see. At least I don't suppose they see it."

"What will you do once you get there?"

"I don't know. It's hard to make plans until we see what we're up against."

"Kyle!" David's voice rang out, echoing momentarily within the courtyard, giving flight to the lark.

David and Elisheba turned simultaneously to see their friend striding quickly across the grassy enclosure. He seemed agitated.

"Have you heard the news?" David asked.

"No. What news?"

"The Prime Minister has just held a press conference. He said that since the Dome of the Rock was so extensively damaged by the quake that there is no other option but to tear it down."

"If they do that," Elisheba said, "there will be war. Even if the mosque is damaged, the Muslims won't allow its total destruction."

"And so many Jews cannot go on the temple mount, how can they tear it down without the ashes of the red heifer?" asked Kyle.

"Wait a minute," David interrupted. "What are we talking about? What are these ashes and what does that have to do with tearing down the Dome of the Rock?"

"There has always been talk about tearing down the Dome of the Rock," Kyle said. "With that out of the way, another temple could be built, but the temple mount has been defiled, and many rabbis, especially on the far right, cannot set foot there, unless they are somehow purified. In ancient Israel a special red heifer was cremated and its ashes were used in a ceremony of purification that allowed people to enter the temple if they had been defiled in any way, but those ashes were lost or hidden when the temple was ransacked."

"Well, from what I understand, an American company is going to do the demolition work," David said."

"That's how they'll handle the problem," Elisheba said.

Kyle rubbed his hands together in some despair. "This is another sign of the times. The end is coming and it's coming quickly. We must hurry and recover the scroll."

"That sounds like a good plan, old buddy," David said, "but the police still don't have a clue as to who took it."

"Kyle thinks he knows where it is," Elisheba said.

"Oh yeah. Where is it?"

"The manuscript is on the Isle of Capri, and we must move now to get it back," Kyle said.

"How do you know that?" David asked.

"I'll explain it to you once we're outside of the hospital, but in fairness, I should warn you that we're going to a dangerous place."

"Really? Sounds fun," David said with a smile.

"I'm not kidding, David," Kyle said seriously.

"I know. I'm not kidding either. I'm happy for a little excitement."

"OK . . . So let's go. Once we're outside, David, if you don't mind, I'll have you call the airport and find out when the next flight leaves for Italy. For right now will you go to my room and gather up my clothes. I know the doctor won't release me this early, so we're going without his permission. Elisheba and I will try to sneak out of here."

They made their way to the parking lot, where they waited for David to come with Kyle's belongings.

TWO DAYS LATER they were winding through the streets of Naples, Italy in a rented, white Fiat. They found a branch of the car rental agency near the Bay of Naples and turned the car in. Instead of waiting for a bus to take them to the water's edge, they opted for walking the last half mile, passing through an open-air market where the head of a swordfish had been lopped off, its torso lying nearby on a wooden bench where a man shaved off steaks with a sharpened meat cleaver. Even now the fish's sword was serving one final purpose, for impaled upon its point, three feet off the ground, was a handful of wax papers that would eventually wrap the rest of its carcass.

Crossing a city park, which was loaded with palm trees, they approached the Bay of Naples, and the temperature dropped as the sea breezes reached them. Stepping through the last row of trees, they saw the bay spreading before them with the land jutting out on their right and left. To the right, expensive villas clung to the hilly countryside; to the left, the Castle Dell'Ovo, weathered by time and battles, sat, with Mount Vesuvius rising ominously in the background.

Directly in front of them, the Isle of Capri rose darkly out of the water like the single hump of a sea serpent. In the blue waters of the Tyrrhenian Sea, fishermen maneuvered their boats towards the shore, bearing their catch, while others pushed off to renew the hunt. A hydrofoil was just picking up speed, lifting a few feet from the blue water as it rode up on its foils, like an airplane struggling to become airborne.

"The best way to make good time," David said, "is to take a hydrofoil." Kyle nodded and David took the lead, walking around the stonewall of the harbor that was only high enough to reach his waist.

Elisheba stumbled slightly on the rough edge of a rock that stuck out from the path, and Kyle caught her hand to keep her from going down. He did not let it go until they stopped in front of the ticket office. David approached the vendor to pay for their passage, and they moved to a bench facing the sea.

When David came with the tickets he said, "I just called my Uncle Stefano and told him we would be there soon. He lives on the other end of the island in the city of Ana Capri. After we land, it's only four miles away."

On the hour a hydrofoil departed for Capri, and twenty minutes later they were boarding one. The white fiberglass hull moved away from the wharf, and for the next minute it plowed through the water just like any other boat, but when the sleek boat had reached a sufficient speed, it noticeably heaved upward, and the outline of its four foils became visible as they elevated the craft in the air. A half an hour later the boat's speed cut back and the craft settled back into the sea to prepare for docking.

Kyle took Elisheba's hand as they walked down the plank. A cable car waiting at the shore lifted them to the town of Capri. From their seats they saw the Bay of Naples beyond and the white spray of another hydrofoil hurtling towards them.

The city of Capri was bustling with tourists. Several shops along the street that followed the hilly terrain of the island had their doors propped open to provide easier access. One middle-aged man with a huge belly, and a flapping shirttail stood outside his shop and did his best to lure his victims within his shop.

David led the way to another car rental agency. He filled out the papers, made the down payment, and the car was theirs. They began the four-mile ride to Ana Capri on the western edge of the island.

"My Uncle Stefano loves this island. That's because his hobby is scuba diving. He taught me how to dive. This was my favorite place to visit while I was growing up. Some of my best memories as a teenager are of here."

The road meandered through the swells and valleys of the island until Ana Capri came into view. It was a bright, happy town with white, marble storefronts, outlined by the blue sea.

There were fewer tourists on the sidewalks than in Capri. David did not stop but downshifted into second gear. He passed a fountain in the square and remembered that it was there when he was twelve that he had first told a girl he loved her. She was two years older, and she had laughed at him.

He resumed his speed until he saw his uncle's driveway on the outskirts of Ana Capri. Built on the face of a cliff, the home was anchored in the rock and looked like a dangerous place to live. Really it was more secure than if it had been sitting on the beach eighty feet below where it would have been in the path of violent waves. After entering home, it was unsettling for Elisheba to stand by the kitchen window to look downward at the lapping waves of the ocean so far below, so she avoided looking out.

Stefano's personality was gregarious, and he was truly happy to see his nephew and his friends. He had stayed on this island, not because he didn't like people, but because it was here that he had made a living, taking tourists on scuba diving adventures. His hair was graying, but the arms that extended from the t-shirt that said "Cannes Films Festival" were knotted with strength and rippled easily. Muscularity seemed to be a natural heritage of David's family tree, and yet Stefano's conditioning was not entirely a gift. His daily routine, even now, was to spend hours scuba diving.

"You see those stairs that cut back and forth over there? That's my boat at the bottom. There it is—a twenty-five footer. The waves do not come in with great force there because I have a natural rock reef at the opening to my little harbor. I named my boat Anna after my wife. It is a new boat, David. I had some good luck awhile back and could buy a new one."

"I'm anxious to see it, Uncle."

Mounted on the walls were over a hundred different fish, some very large like the great white shark, which filled the center wall and was surrounded by smaller fish, which seemed to be huddling around their chosen leader.

From the ceiling dangled a large stingray. Stefano took pleasure in watching his guests admiring his catches.

He sat in his favorite place, a black leather easy chair with a matching hassock for his feet. A German shepherd plopped down next to him and closed his eyes. Stefano's hand fell from the armrest onto the back of the dog and he stroked it gently.

"I call him Vescovo because in Italian the word means 'bishop.' I consider him to be a very spiritual dog—more so than most people. I believe heaven will be filled with such animals and with people who have the kind of loyalty and love that such animals have. Over these past ten years, Vescovo has been my closest companion, especially since my wife died. Anyway, this is our favorite room. He was with me in the boat when I caught many of these fish, and he sat in my workshop when I mounted them. The larger ones were done by a professional. That great white shark, for instance, the walls had to be reinforced to take the weight."

The Great White's multiple rows of white teeth were exposed, and the fleshy eyelids were just beginning to close as they do when the fish is about to strike, a reflex that protects the sensitive eyes from the flailing movements of its dying victim.

"Now, I have spoken enough of myself. David, you said that there was something important you had to do on Capri. What is it?"

"Kyle made a valuable find of an old scroll in a cave near Jerusalem. It was a very remarkable manuscript, and he had already translated parts of it when it was stolen. We have reason to believe that those who took it have transported it to Capri, and that it is somewhere on the island right now . . . Kyle, would you mind telling my uncle about the scroll?"

Kyle began the story at the meeting with Tabitha and finished with the scroll's disappearance.

"On the night that it was stolen, I read some words which indicated that the scroll would be taken to this island and to a place where 'diadems were gathered for God's glory.' Mr. Andreone, do you know of any place where they used to manufacture crowns or worked with precious stones? Is there any historical place on the island that was known for that kind of thing?"

Stefano shook his head. "None that I know of."

"I can imagine how strange all of this must seem, Mr. Andreone. If I hadn't lived it myself, I would be skeptical of such a story, but it's all true, exactly as I have told you, and we must—at all costs—recover the scroll. As I said, the story is difficult to swallow, but David can verify much of the story."

There was a pause as the piercing, brown eyes of the old man stared at Kyle. He had not looked away from Kyle since he began his story, following the narration with the deepest intensity. He even stopped stroking Vescovo as the story progressed.

"I do not need to have David confirm your story. I believe it already, and it is not because I'm a gullible man. I've lived too long for that. But there are a couple of reasons why I think it is true.

"I have lived on this island for over twenty-five years and I have seen and heard things that make me believe what you say. This is a tourist island with a small permanent population, so at any time, a large portion of the island's inhabitants are temporary boarders. People come and go so quickly that it is difficult to know what is happening at any given time. People can disappear and maybe no one is aware that they're missing."

"And are you saying," Kyle said slowly," that some people have disappeared?"

"Yes, I think so. And such disappearances have been going on for a long time." His powerful hand reached over the edge of the chair and once again began stroking Vescovo.

X
❦
WHERE THE DIADEMS WERE GATHERED

Stefano gave a final pat to Vescovo and then sat back in his chair ready to tell what he was thinking.

"David, perhaps you remember the old fisherman, GT, who used to run his nets at the base of my cliff, Giovanni Tempesta. He had a humped back from birth and it was made worse by years of bending over a net. He fished these waters before I was born, and so had his father. Once he said to me, 'There's something wrong on Capri.' 'What do you mean?' I asked. 'Have you noticed,' he said, 'that some people leave Capri much sooner than planned? I'm talking about the tourists,' he said. 'No,' I said, 'I hadn't made many acquaintances with the tourists to be aware when they were leaving.' 'Keep your eyes open,' he said. 'You will begin to notice a number of unusual things on this island. My father said that it has always been so,' he said. 'Those who have been around long enough, who are vigilant, will soon see much that is hard to understand.'"

"A year later, after Giovanni said these words to me, I helped a student who was backpacking through Europe. He was about twenty, I suppose. His name was Olaf Nhisjlld. He was from Sweden with almost white hair. He told me that he was a Catholic and hoped to enter a monastery after traveling the world and seeing its wonders. He said that he wanted to travel through Europe then to America, and when he returned, he planned on enrolling in a monastery he had seen in Florence. But, he was going to keep his options open until he had seen as many monasteries as he could. He was heading south toward Sicily because he had heard there were some beautiful monasteries overlooking the sea. 'If you're going to spend your whole life in a place,' he said, 'you had better choose well.' He was young, but there was no doubt of his faith and determination.

"In Florence on the Ponte Vecchio, the 'old bridge' where so many vendors have their little shops, he found one who sold crucifixes. He chose a rather large one—it was made of silver and was expertly done. The form of the Savior was not one of those distorted kinds that made him look grotesque and unnatural, but made him appear as I've always thought a man would look who had made his living as a carpenter. It was really quite inspiring. I thought that I would like to have it to hang on my wall, but this young fellow—to show his faith I suppose—had attached a silver chain to each end of the cross, and had it hung around his neck. On the back of the cross his name 'Olaf' was inscribed. That's how I remembered his name.

"He stopped here and asked if he might pitch his tent on the ridge over where you saw the flowers growing by the stairs. The land is mine and I gave him permission, and he was so appreciative that he said he wished to do me a favor.

"He was an artist who did caricatures, too, and he showed me some of his work that he kept in a leather satchel. It contained sketches of some world leaders: De Gaulle and Roosevelt and Mussolini—they were well done. They had that humorous touch of a caricature, but he had been quite successful in catching their personalities and the overall look of those men.

"He asked if he could do one of me as payment for allowing him to camp on my land. I told him it wasn't necessary, but he insisted. He said that it would take less than a half hour and wondered if I would have time the following morning. I told him I would, and we both went to bed. When I woke up the next day, he was gone."

Stefano rose and crossed to the corner of his room, which also served as his study. Walking behind his oak desk, he shoved the leather chair under, giving him room to search for something on the bookshelf. "When I went to the spot where he had pitched his tent, I found this. It was leaning up against a rock about a dozen feet from his sleeping bag. That particular rock would have made a nice little seat. I imagine he had been resting there."

Stefano withdrew from the shelf a leather satchel and carried it towards the others, and while doing so, he unzipped it and pulled out its contents—a collection of papers—and handed a portion of them to his nephew, and some to Kyle and Elisheba. They were the artist's sample caricatures of famous people.

"These were his livelihood! He used these samples to get work! They were very important to him, and yet he left them and I never heard from him again."

"Perhaps he forgot them, Uncle?"

"That's a possibility, but there's something else. When I found these I got into my car and drove to Capri to find the young man. I thought that maybe he had some emergency happen in the middle of the night that had forced him to leave so abruptly. Maybe he had gotten sick. I didn't know, but it's a small island and I didn't mind returning these to him if he was leaving.

"The ferries didn't run all night, and I knew the first one hadn't left yet.

"I arrived in time to see the passengers loading. He wasn't there. I thought that maybe he was somewhere in Capri or Ana Capri and was going to board later. I left word at the boarding office for him to call me when he arrived, that I had his drawings. I remembered his name from the cross, but he never checked in for his return passage.

"You know, when he came up missing, the first thing I remembered was the words from Giovanni Tempesta: 'Have you noticed that some people leave Capri much sooner than planned?'

"I made some more inquiries, but I never found anything. There was never a word from him, and his pictures still remain with me."

David whistled long and low. "That is strange. Have there been others?"

Stefano gathered up the drawings and returned them to the bookshelf. "No one that I'm aware of, but when I asked one of the older residents whose family has run a curio shop in Capri for generations, he acted strangely and recommended that I leave that topic alone—that it wasn't good for business.

"One other older resident seemed to hush up when I brought up the subject of this boy's disappearance. But none of the locals have ever been bothered and so there can be no missing person's report, but I think others have disappeared, yet no one is aware because they are just tourists and tourists are here today and gone tomorrow."

Elisheba shifted uneasily. "And you think this has been going on for some time?"

Stefano returned to his easy chair and Vescovo raised his head to receive a stroke as he sat down. "I believe as Giovanni said that 'There is something wrong on Capri.' There is something dark, something sinister, that stretches back for many years which has marred the beauty of this place.

"Since I have become aware of all of this, I have done some research about the history of Capri. It is an ancient resort area. The unchanging beauties of nature lured people throughout history. Its importance in Roman society is well documented. It continues to draw people today even as it has for thousands of years.

"Included in that history is an ancient villa on the northern tip of this island, a large, imposing place with brick walls that enclose it entirely. It was built as a monastery in the second century A.D. The monks who ran it were known for their self-denial. They wore a heavy, coarse, cloth garment, even during the hot summer. They lived there for some time until the plague came. Many of them died all at once. They used the heavy robes of those who died as blankets, and the disease spread very rapidly. Within two months, nearly the whole order had died and those remaining assumed that the plague had somehow been a judgment of God. They disbanded and the building was abandoned for many years because people were superstitious and afraid to enter.

"There is a long period where the history of the villa is lost. The next notable owner was a knight templar who had just returned from the second crusade. History has recorded him as a ruthless individual who went to Jerusalem for the thrill of killing and looting. His murderous tendencies didn't end when he came home, and he was found to have kidnapped and killed several children who lived on the island. The evidence against him mounted, and he was finally beheaded under the orders of the man who eventually became the patron saint of Naples, San Gennaro. The cathedral in Naples still holds Gennaro's bones in a glass case.

"The villa has passed through the hands of a number of owners since then—men and women. They have not distinguished themselves in any way.

"There have been rumors that the villa is a pleasure house and has been for centuries. People have gone there to indulge themselves. It is the only place on the island that could possibly be the place that you are after. Today it is understood that if you want to gamble or enjoy yourself, the Villa di Marco is the place to go. The present-day owner inherited it from his father who brought the roulette tables in."

"And what is his name?" Kyle asked.

"Antonio Primavera. He's about forty-five and handsome—a real lady's man. He's Italian and was born in Naples. His family moved to Rio de Janeiro when he was a youth to run a travel agency, but his father was not successful and went bankrupt, perhaps because he was spending so much time in Rio's nightlife, which is quite excessive from what I understand. It might be called the pleasure capital of the world.

"During these centuries, as the villa passed through the hands of numerous owners, the port at the villa has been extensively used. There were many passages between that villa and the mainland. So regularly were those trips made that for several centuries the various owners of the villa also contracted to bring the mail to the rest of the island. Once radios and telephones came in, the trips stopped."

David arose and walked to the Great White to study the teeth. He stood facing it with his shoulder next to the wall and stroked his forefinger gently over the front teeth, admiring, even as he had done as child, the incredible sharpness. "What would be the purpose of so many regular trips between here and the mainland? They weren't involved in any kind of commercial business that you know of—running pieces of cameos into Naples maybe? Naples has always been famous for those kinds of things."

Stefano rubbed his forehead. "As far as I've been able to tell, they had no commercial business going of any kind."

"I'll bet they were dealing in the world of communication," Kyle said.

Elisheba angled her body towards him. "What do you mean?"

"I mean they were not selling goods, as Stefano has said. I think they were carrying information. It sounds to me that by the time we get to your knight templar the devil had real control in that villa."

Stefano seemed uncertain. "But why would he come here to this island? With so many evil countries in the world, where terrorism is a way of life, why would he—or it—pick this beautiful spot?"

"Maybe because the spot is beautiful. I suppose the devil likes pleasant surroundings. Why set up in a desert when there are places like Capri for the picking? Plus," Kyle continued, "this particular locale has some distinct advantages: number one it is located on a waterway. From here you could sail to the Mediterranean and thus reach many of the main routes to important capitals of the ancient world—Alexandria, Rome, Constantinople, et cetera. The Mediterranean was the access route to the known world during the centuries after the birth of the Lord. Capri would be a perfect jumping off spot to get to any of those areas.

"And number two is the fact that Rome was just up the coast. If the devil is going to make inroads in other places, he must have the hearts of some of the military leaders of the strongest armies. If he was intent on stopping Christianity, he would need a foothold near the Roman army. If you remember, the Romans just about snuffed out the early church. Under Nero they made killing Christians a national pastime."

"I believe," Stefano said, "that he's here and that he has your scroll. What can we do to get it back? I mean, doesn't he already know what we're planning?"

Kyle rubbed his chin. "We've asked ourselves that one. I don't know. Maybe God has prevented him. But if he does know, we can't let that stop us."

"What can I do to help?" Stefano asked.

"Stefano," Kyle began, "we really appreciate your help, but you've told us plenty, and I think we've narrowed the location down. We are dealing with a very dangerous situation. Maybe he hasn't developed a habit of kidnapping and killing locals, but he will if it should suit his purposes. I think we're going to have to go it alone from here."

"Thanks for worrying about me, son, but I would like to be involved. I have a reason for wanting to help you."

"And what's that, Uncle?" David asked.

"I am not naturally a gambler, but there have been times since I have been without my wife that boredom has overtaken me—even on an island this beautiful. I have on a few occasions resorted to gambling at the Villa di Marco.

"One night I was a big winner. My game is cards—twenty-one is my favorite. My new boat was bought with proceeds from that evening at the Villa. I had already won over 12 million lira—about $20,000 in American money, and I turned behind me and placed it all on twenty-seven red on the roulette wheel. I would not have done such a foolish thing had I not been drinking a little. My loneliness has sometimes driven me to that, too.

"Can you imagine how exciting it was when the ball landed on my number? It increased my winnings several times. Antonio Primavera was standing by me during my run of good luck. I could see him growing more and more upset as I continued to win. Even half drunk the way I was, I still remember his red cheeks as he grew angrier. I thought he would get over it, that any gambler naturally takes the first moments of defeat badly. But I was wrong.

"The way to Villa di Marco is along this road. Primavera travels it. Vescovo was lying out by the mailbox, as was his habit. The mailman had taken a liking to him and would occasionally bring a bone from his lunch. I heard him yelping and ran out the door to find his right leg dangling. The veterinarian had to take the rest of it off, as you can see.

"Later I went to the mailbox and saw where the wheels had swerved intentionally from the opposite side of the road to hit my dog. There was a clear impression of the tire tracks in the dirt. I took some plaster of Paris and mixed it with water, then poured it into the tracks of the tire tread. When it hardened, I took them and drove to the Villa di Marco."

Stefano could not restrain his emotion, nor did he try. His teeth clamped and the muscles along his jaws tightened. "There I found a white Mercedes which I knew belonged to Primavera. I checked the tread and found the whitewall was coated with dried blood and hair from Vescovo.

"I have been waiting for a proper moment to repay him for the attack on my innocent dog. I am willing to take whatever risk is necessary."

Kyle closed his eyes and nodded to say that he could understand the man's desire for justice. "Thank you . . . I just wish we had more to go on. Primavera is obviously a wretch, but that doesn't mean he's guilty of running the kind of organization that we're looking for. If we're going to launch some sort of drastic action against him, we need to be absolutely sure.

"I don't see how this old monastery could be the place. The revelation said, 'they will be taken to that island in the place where the diadems were gathered for God's glory.' How a group of monks could be connected with something of the value of diadems, I don't understand . . . I think I'm going to get some rest. Do you have a place I can rest?"

"Certainly. Follow me."

The white tile floor clicked under their heels. David took a seat near the picture window in the kitchen and stared out to sea. There were some storm clouds gathering on the horizon.

An hour passed and Stefano stepped into the kitchen carrying a copy of Gibbon's *The Rise and Fall of the Roman Empire* and laid the book gently on the table. He walked to the window to look at his ship. A twenty-five foot red fishing boat was pulling into his dock.

Stefano recognized it immediately.

"There is the boat of my friend, Luigi Pacchelli. What is he doing here now? This is not the day to go fishing." Stefano turned away from the window toward Elisheba and David.

"We usually go fishing once a week, on Wednesdays. I don't know why he has come a day early, but I will take the steps below and tell him that I have company."

"You don't need to stay around for us, Uncle," David said.

"The sea will always be here. I can fish whenever I want, but my busy nephew is not always a guest. I want to spend time with you. You are not spoiling my plans. As I said, he has come a day early, and so it is his fault. You wait here. There is coffee on the stove and some things to eat in the refrigerator if you want. I'll be back in a few minutes."

He excused himself and left the house. A moment later they saw him making his way rapidly down the stone stairs on the face of the cliff opposite them. He held tightly to the steel railing, barely glancing at the steps as he took them two at a time.

When he turned the corner on the last landing, he called out in a jovial voice, speaking in Italian: "Luigi old friend, are you so anxious to go fishing this week that you have decided to come a day early?" Luigi sat on his haunches, tying the rope from his boat around the mooring post. He shook his head slowly without looking up, and his foot-long beard, that now contained more white hair than black, rubbed on his burly chest and lagged momentarily behind the motion of his head. He was a large man with big arms and a neck that seemed to rise from his torso as a continuation of his shoulders. When he stood up, his 270 pounds settled onto his sturdy legs. He waited as Stefano walked to him and extended his hand, taking it in his customary powerful squeeze.

Stefano saw immediately that something was brewing. "What is wrong, Luigi?"

"I did not come to fish," he said in a deep baritone. "I need to talk to you about something. I thought it was important enough that I should come tonight." His right hand dropped to his protruding stomach and began to rub it just above the navel, as he was wont to do when he was agitated. He was unaware of the nervous habit, but Stefano had learned to read him.

"We must put in a bench on your dock someday, so I don't have to make that climb to your house. That kind of exercise only increases my appetite and then I eat like a horse for the rest of the day. Let us sit in my boat."

He lifted his right leg over the edge of the boat that bobbed in the waves that rebounded within the enclosed harbor. When his entire weight settled once again onto the deck of his boat, it listed slightly to the starboard side. Stefano followed him, and they took seats on the cushioned benches behind the running controls.

"I have found something," Luigi began, "that I knew you would want to know about right away."

A half an hour later, Stefano stepped onto the dock from Luigi's boat, gave his friend a nod of appreciation and ran toward the stairs. At the top landing he stopped to watch the red boat backing out of his harbor. He could see the top of his friend's head, which now had as much skin showing through as hair.

Stefano suddenly wished that he had warned Luigi to be careful—to be on guard the next few days. He had never been concerned about the personal safety of his husky friend, but now he felt there was danger everywhere on the island. Stefano would have shouted a warning had not the rumble from the inboard motor made it impossible for him to be heard. Instead, he raised his arm and waved, which he was not sure was seen, but a moment later Luigi raised his arm and returned the signal, and Stefano felt better, feeling that his friend had somehow understood his unspoken worries and would now be more cautious.

Stefano put his hand over his shirt and felt something within, and his jaw tightened. An unexpected cool breeze touched his face and for the first time he noticed the gathering thunderheads that were rolling in from the west. The advancing breeze was the harbinger of its approach.

From the west he saw a sudden flash, and he began to count under his breath. When he reached eighteen, a deep rumble rolled over Capri, and he knew it was about three miles away and that Luigi could probably make it home before it hit. Glancing downward once more at his friend's boat, he turned his back on the approaching storm and re-entered his house. David and Elisheba were sitting in the kitchen, facing the ocean, just as he had left them. He pulled out a chair from the table and placed it near her.

She smiled. "I'm sorry if you missed an outing with your friend."

"No. That is not the reason why he . . ."

Just then the door opened at the end of the hall, and Kyle came out. He entered the kitchen and smiled, then took the last chair from the table and drew it near his friends.

"Truly God's hand is with us," said Stefano. "In the very moment that we were talking about the Villa di Marco, my good friend, Luigi Pacchelli, was in his boat, next to the villa, using his sonar device to find schools of fish, so that we might have a successful hunt tomorrow. He saw something bright reflecting the sun from the base of the cliff.

For some time he watched it. Whatever it was seemed to be caught on a bush. So when he was ready to leave, he pulled his boat in close to the shore to have a better look. This is what he found." Stefano reached into his shirt and withdrew a silver cross of a most intricate workmanship with a powerful figure of Christ. He turned it over, and there was inscribed the name "Olaf."

"This was dangling from a bush directly under the Villa di Marco. There was blood on it—especially on the backside. Luigi could not read it until he had washed it off in the sea. Immediately he remembered me talking about this boy and headed his boat straight here."

Stefano raised the cross in the air by the chain, allowing it to turn slowly in the flashes of the approaching storm. "Now, Mr. Shepherd, after hearing all of this and seeing this, do you still feel hesitant about going to the Villa di Marco to look for the manuscript?"

Kyle slowly shook his head. "You are right, Mr. Andreone." The first drops of water from the advancing storm began to streak the kitchen window, and the difference between lightning flashes and their accompanying rumbles was now a matter of only a few seconds.

"But I have my own reasons for now being convinced," Kyle said. "Do you remember that the place the scroll would go would be taken where the 'diadems were gathered for God's glory'? I have been going over that translation, and I found this."

Kyle lifted an Aramaic-to-English dictionary to his lap. "I translated the word diadem correctly, but I put a present day meaning on a word that it didn't originally have. If Samuel hadn't died, he would have seen it."

"Seen what?" David blurted out. "What are you talking about?"

"That the word diadem no longer means what it originally meant. Look at this. Diadem also means a 'coarse cloth.' Do you understand? The words could be translated 'in the place where the coarse cloths were gathered for God's glory' . . . Coarse cloths—don't you see that Enoch was talking about the monks and the coarse robes they wore—the monks who first started Villa di Marco? The Book of Enoch is there all right . . . and so is Satan."

The rain increased in intensity and began to coat the window like clear syrup, distorting the flashes that came from deep within the bowels of the storm.

XI

THE VILLA

The brunt of the storm lasted an hour, but the skies did not immediately clear, and a light drizzle fell intermittently for the next two hours. By sunset, the rock cliff opposite Stefano's home spouted numerous tiny waterfalls that shot from the face of the cliff and cascaded all the way to the sea.

Rising from the harbor was a fine mist that had drifted upward on the air currents that rolled in from the Adriatic Sea. The abrupt rock cliff in the path of the sea breezes forced the currents upward, carrying the vapors above the rim of the cliff. The misty air seemed to boil up, as though from a giant cauldron, and the setting sun played upon those mists, producing a small rainbow whose arch stretched backward toward the sea, making it float directly above the harbor. One leg of the rainbow, from the vantage point of the kitchen, seemed to stop above the rock where Olaf had once sat and left his satchel of drawings.

It was 8 P.M. and Stefano stood at the kitchen window transfixed by the phenomenon of the rainbow. Never during his time on Capri had so much water catapulted over the side of his cliff creating such a sight. He wondered about the rainbow that stood over the spot where the young artist had once sat.

Within fifteen minutes the ocean breezes slackened, dissipating the mists, and the rainbow disappeared at the same moment as the sun's rays began to wane.

Stefano was worried about his nephew and the others who were preparing themselves to go to the Villa di Marco. He had given them a plan to reach Antonio Primavera, but there were many risks and now he wished that he had allowed Kyle to take the lead. If his plan should fail and a life should be lost, how would he live with himself?

To carry out his plan, Kyle and Elisheba made a quick trip into Ana Capri to buy some clothes for her. They had returned less than twenty minutes ago, and she was changing now. A moment later Elisheba stepped from her bedroom dressed in a black, satin evening gown with a silky lace border that began at her thighs and stopped above her knees. It emphasized her pretty legs. The material clung to her form, revealing her athletic conditioning.

Kyle entered wearing a black sports coat and gray pants with a matching gray tie.

"I am worried about Elisheba," Stefano said.

"Do not waste time thinking about that," she said hurriedly. "You said that Antonio has a passion for women, and I'm the only woman among us, so the job is mine."

Stefano cleared his throat. "When I've had a chance to really think about this, I realize how foolhardy it is to send you up there alone."

"Yes, but I'm not going to be alone. Kyle will be with me."

"He will be with you, but when you allow yourself to be led to his boat where Luigi says he conducts his romantic evenings, Kyle could be detained within the villa, and then you would be by yourself. I know for a fact that he has several bodyguards. They could stop Kyle from following you, and then what might happen?"

She took her earrings from her purse—rhinestones set in two

teardrops—and tucked her purse under her arm, tilted her head to the side and began putting them on. "It's a risk I'm willing to take. What other alternatives do we have?"

"We three men could go up the north side of the cliff and find a way inside," Stefano said.

"It is steep but we all have some training with rock climbing. David and I did it when he was growing up and, Kyle, too, is an expert at it. I have been there several times. That knowledge would help us. And then we could conduct a search. If we did it later in the evening, the guards will not be as alert—perhaps they would even be drunk."

Kyle stood by listening, hoping that Stefano might concoct a better plan, for he too was worried about Elisheba. "And where would we begin to look?" he asked.

"We would search in any rooms that we could get in. David has some experience with picking locks, and so do I. I don't know where we'll find it—his bedroom, maybe—library perhaps."

Elisheba shook her head. "And what do you think the chances are that three men could roam through that place without being spotted by one of his bodyguards or maybe a security sensor."

"I don't know," Stefano said. "They probably aren't very good, but at least we would stand a better chance than Elisheba, isolating herself with Primavera. I know of one individual at least who has been killed at that place. I suspect there have been many more."

"I believe you're right," Kyle answered.

"So it would be wiser for the three of us to go in than Elisheba," Stefano said with finality and his eyebrows arched for emphasis.

Kyle shook his head. "If that were our only alternative, I would say we must try and hope that God would open the right door to us, and yet, I am a firm believer that we must try the most practical plan. You have said that he likes to take his lady friends on the boat."

Stefano nodded. "That is what Luigi tells me. He has spent even more time there gambling than I have. According to Luigi, Antonio is one of those men who take their pleasure from the number of different women that they can seduce. He has become a bit of a legend in his habit of approaching a new woman every night on the floor of his villa and then leaving with her to go to his boat.

"So persistent is he," Stefano continued, "in this obsession of being with a strange woman that I'm told he ignores women he has already known, refusing to give even the common acknowledgments that one would think should pass between people who have been so intimate. He seems to lose all interest in them."

"Why do women go to him if he treats them that way?" Elisheba asked.

Stefano shrugged his shoulders. "Many of them are strangers to Capri and the villa so they are unfamiliar with his habits, but that, of course, doesn't explain those women who do yield to his desires, knowing what the relationship will be like afterwards. I suppose many believe that they will be the one who finally turns his head permanently. The opulence of his villa is enough of a reward to entice a lot of women to try, even if they become—how do the cowboys in America say it?—'another notch on his gun.'"

"This obsession for women," Kyle said, "might possibly be his Achilles heel. His bodyguards follow him at all other occasions, you say, but during his romantic interludes, while he is on his own dock away from his bodyguards, we can get him. If the villa is as big as you describe it, we must have an idea of the scroll's location."

"It's simply too big to search everywhere," David said. "This all hinges, of course, on whether Elisheba can strike up the kind of relationship with Antonio that will move him to invite her to his yacht."

Kyle nodded. "That's true, but if you were in Antonio Primavera's position of constantly looking for new conquests and a girl like Elisheba came to your house, would you be interested?"

David looked again at Elisheba. "You have a good point there, Kyle."

"But let us be practical," Kyle added, "if, for whatever reason, Elisheba is not able to strike up an acquaintance with him because some other woman has him cornered, or because he's out of town, or staying in his room—whatever—then we'll be forced to sneak into the villa without any idea of the book's location and hope that we can find it."

"Agreed," said David. Then he turned to Elisheba. "Well, are you ready?"

"Yes."

"You're beautiful," Kyle said. "If I were Primavera, I would forget entirely about my gambling operation tonight if you stepped in front of me."

Elisheba smiled. "You're naturally prejudiced in favor of archaeologists."

"Even if I didn't know that you were a budding archaeologist . . ."

"Budding?" she interrupted.

"Nearly in bloom, yes, but with a few petals left to open. Even if I didn't know you, the way you look tonight would definitely catch my attention. Remember though, you're going to have to forget your manners tonight and act a bit forward, if you're going to land him."

She put her hand on her hip in a come-on fashion, cocked her head to the side and gave a slow wink.

"Oh that's good! He doesn't stand a chance." Elisheba looked embarrassed, and her face reddened. Kyle was no longer smiling. "You can't act like that."

"I know," she said.

"I mean it, Elisheba. When you blush, I can see right through you . . . I think you are right, Stefano. This isn't the best plan."

"Stop it, Kyle!" she almost shouted. "I can do this. When I have to be a tramp, I can . . . Now, let's go." Kyle considered it for a moment, then he extended his arm, and she took it.

Within a few minutes they were pulling into the tree-lined driveway of the villa. The parking lot was secluded in a grove of trees, and Kyle stopped the vehicle while a young valet with a pencil mustache, and wearing a white tuxedo, opened Elisheba's door.

A sidewalk made of fitted slabs of lava rock led the last fifty feet to the wall surrounding the villa. On each side of the walk were six oval islands of roses in reds and whites.

Kyle had taken only a few steps when he stopped to look at the flowers. Until that moment he had not noticed that there was a motif for these beds of roses. Now he saw it. The red flowers only served the purpose of providing a rich background for the white flowers, which were always arranged in some shape of a cross. To his left the white roses joined to make a Gothic cross, and to his right they united in a Roman cross, and there a Greek cross, and those symbols were repeated in the other beds.

"Did you notice," he asked, "the shape of the white roses?"

"No, I didn't." She too became observant. "Crosses? Why would a place like this have such a design?"

"I don't know. Since most people knew that this was once a monastery, maybe they're trying to keep up appearances, or perhaps they want to divert suspicion from what really goes on here."

Though the monks had only remained a short time after the building was officially blessed, they had labored for years to build it. The stone was gray limestone, taken from a quarry a hundred yards away. Every rock was painstakingly hauled by six men from the order, first with block and tackle, and then dragged on a skid by mules to the construction site. One monk had helped in the construction of a cathedral in Milan and he put his experience to use on this building, and it was he who suggested the place be called St. Mark's Cathedral. It was said that he brought skills taught to him by Jewish Masons, whose ancestors had worked on Solomon's Temple. The rocks of the villa were similar to the ancient temple, fitting so tightly together that they needed no mortar.

Now the structure remained virtually the same, rising seventy feet above the cliff's edge and measuring over 150 feet on each side; four stone columns supported the overhanging roof that hung above the main entrance, where two large oak doors (replaced several times during the villa's history) rose ten feet high.

Above the doors, carved into the rock, was the eight-foot high image of St. Mark, sitting on a throne with a halo circling his head, writing his gospel on parchment.

Above the saint was a twelve-foot cross of bronze. The original was gilded with gold, but the medieval crusaders, after returning from the holy land, did not leave the gold for long, stripping it away and dividing it up, justifying their actions on the grounds that the monastery had not been favored by God because he had caused the plague to kill its members, so it could not have been a sanctified spot.

A stone wall six feet high made of the same grayish composition as the villa surrounded the building, and on each corner the statue of an angel stood with a drawn sword in his hand. The iron gates were swung open wide, and through them Kyle and Elisheba entered.

On either side of the sidewalk, the motif of the cross continued with the same combination of red and white roses. They climbed the final twelve steps in front of the main portico, passing three cherubs with extended wings who gazed blissfully.

After stepping over an original mosaic floor, depicting the villa when it was first constructed with its name written in Latin at the base, they strolled casually into the main hall that was once used as a chapel.

The pews and penance boxes were long gone leaving a hall now filled with the accessories of gambling.

Hundreds of people stood around roulette wheels, backgammon boards, and myriad card games. Men and women in elegant dress busily placed their bets, or pulled in chips from a winning hand, or grimly watched their chips being swept away.

There was the scent of liquor intermingling with colognes and perfume. Only the constant circulation of the air conditioning system prevented the odors from becoming stifling. For those who had the noses to detect it, there were the slight traces of marijuana smoke.

The slot machines stood in the middle of the room where people deposited money with the left hand and pulled the handles with the right hand, each movement so well rehearsed, that they no longer needed to watch.

At either end of the room hung two huge chandeliers which once graced a French chateaux. Instead of candles, incandescent bulbs in the shape of flames sparkled among the hundreds of pieces of cut glass, lighting the room magnificently.

Midway between those two chandeliers in the very center of the room—for all to see as they glanced up from their games of chance—was a reproduction of the center section of the Sistine Chapel where Michelangelo painted God and Adam. The painting was identical in every manner to the original, especially in the muscular physiques of both Adam and God, as God transferred the power of life. Yet there was something different. Kyle paused to study the painting, as Elisheba approached a cocktail waitress to ask about Antonio Primavera. What was it that was not the same as the original? The face of God was different—there was no beard. But why would the artist have drawn everything else so exactly yet altered the main figure? Something else about the face of God bothered Kyle, but he could not put his finger on it. He was still staring upward when Elisheba returned.

"Do you see anything unusual about that picture?" he asked.

She was too preoccupied with the evening to give it any thought, but she glanced up anyway and gave it a token scrutiny. "It's a copy of the Sistine Chapel," she said quickly.

"I know that, but there's something strange."

She hurriedly looked again and then dropped her gaze to the game tables. "It's a wonderful reproduction, but I'll tell you honestly, Kyle, that I'm not in any mood to discuss art with you tonight. Listen. I just learned that Primavera is at the twenty-one table in the corner of the room. That's his favorite game, I guess. There he is. He's sitting on the bar stool next to the dealer."

Kyle saw a man dressed in a black tuxedo move his hand to his head and stroke his hair twice. There were a couple of dazzling reflections from two large rings on that hand; the nose was slightly aquiline; his cheekbones were high and his jaw descended narrowly to a rather small chin with a slight cleft, and when Kyle saw the cleft, he knew exactly what was wrong with the reproduction of the picture from the Sistine Chapel.

"That's it, Elisheba," he blurted out. "Look at the face of God."

"I already have," she said irritably. "Kyle, will you forget about that painting. Awhile ago we were talking about the risks of this meeting, and now, all you're interested in is some of Primavera's art work."

"Primavera has exchanged God's face for his!" She looked again, but this time, she was more patient in her observation.

Glancing quickly toward the table where Primavera sat, she took in his features and then turned upward toward the ceiling. "You're right. That's him. What an ego . . . Anyway, let's get on with this thing." She touched her necklace, and he noticed that her fingers were trembling. She turned them into a fist to cover her shaking.

"If you feel uneasy," he said, "let's call it off, and we'll try to sneak in through the cliff side."

"Don't be silly. I can do this. Nervous hands are just a sign that I'm getting charged with adrenalin . . . Here we go. I'm ready, as you Americans say, to rock and roll." Elisheba withdrew a compact from her purse, took a quick glance at her makeup, returned it to her purse, then smiled confidently at Kyle and walked toward Primavera's table.

She assumed a slight sway to her hips that made her normally smooth walk provocative; her back remained perfectly straight and her shoulders regally erect. If there were self-doubts before, they seemed to have melted, for now she sauntered as seductively as a cover girl on a Parisian magazine cover.

Kyle noticed the heads turning as she passed, and at one table when a middle-aged banker from Florence with a port wine stain on his right ear craned his neck too obviously, his wife, sitting at his side, disgustedly turned him from Elisheba's sultry promenade by yanking at his black, silk tie. Meanwhile, Kyle walked slowly through the room pretending to be choosing a game of chance, but his attention remained on her.

Primavera sat to the side of the card table, enjoying the high rollers who were losing heavily. The house dealer dealt two more cards to the three men, all brothers from the perfume manufacturing company called La Sera. They were betting with the same fierce competition that had driven them throughout their lives. From childhood they had battled one another in soccer, in drinking, in woman chasing and in their father's business, and now they tested each other again with their gambling.

They all wore mustaches, and since there were several years separating them in age, they looked as though they might be the same man in slightly different stages of his life.

It was this competitive fierceness that had drawn Antonio Primavera to their table. Besides his inordinate desire for different women, Primavera's other passion in life was gambling, and he enjoyed seeing other people wagering big at his tables and then losing. There were those occasions when someone would do well and go home a winner, and he did not begrudge the small winners—they were good advertisement, but he resented those who took a lot of his money as Stefano had done.

For the brothers the bet was now at $5000 and the dealer, a slim Italian with a tight, white, silk shirt who looked more like a Spanish Flamenco dancer than a professional gambler, turned over his hidden card. He had two face cards, a king and a queen, each worth ten points, for a total of twenty.

There were audible groans of disappointment from the oldest brothers, but the youngest sat sullenly, staring blankly ahead, although he, too, had lost. He pushed his chips away without looking at them. It was the eighth hand he had lost. For a moment, he no longer looked like the youngest of the men: the strain of the night emphasized his wrinkles, and his eyes were puffy from the smoke and from worrying about his losses.

Elisheba was only five steps away from Antonio when another girl, a tall Florentine, wearing a white, strapless dress approached.

With her beautiful, black hair hanging to her waist the girl stood near Primavera, pretending to be interested in the brothers' game.

"This is very exciting, isn't it," she said coyly to Antonio.

"Yes, it is. They are all brothers," he responded.

"Oh, really!" she said, happy to have a chance to turn to him and open her eyes in amazement, a look she exaggerated, so he would notice her eyes, for her eyes, even above her hair, were her best asset, and she knew they had effectively disarmed many in the past.

At that instant Elisheba stopped next to them, carrying a glass of pink sherry that she had just found on the edge of a poker table. She stood there, waiting for the opportunity she sought, pretending an interest in the brothers' next hand of cards. The chance came when a cocktail girl, carrying a silver tray of fizzing champagne, came down the aisle of tables, carefully avoiding the patrons who sat with their backs to her. There was plenty of room for the cocktail girl to pass, but Elisheba rocked backward on her right foot and bumped her, causing the tray to falter momentarily, knocking over two of the glasses, and Elisheba, pretending to be startled by the collision jumped forward and emptied the sherry onto the front of the Florentine girl's dress. The Florentine shrieked while the sherry was absorbed, staining her chest pink.

The girl shouted and then snapped her body and head around so quickly to see the wretch who had soiled her dress that her long hair whipped into Antonio's mouth, where some of the strands lodged.

He pulled at his mouth, and Gabriella, for that was the Florentine's name, felt a tug at her scalp and turned to see Antonio picking at his tongue. She jerked her hair away, and then turned to confront Elisheba, cursing her in Italian, because she assumed that the dark-haired girl was of her nationality.

Elisheba feigned embarrassment and apologized, but Gabriella was not pacified. With both the mood and her dress ruined, she knew her opportunity for seduction was gone—as shattered as the glass that crunched under her feet.

She made another crude remark to Elisheba in the Florentine dialect, then snatched her rhinestone-covered purse from the table and stormed away, covering the pink stain on her chest with her purse as she wound through the gamblers.

Elisheba turned to Antonio. "I'm so sorry. Please, forgive me for staining your wife's dress."

"Oh, she wasn't my wife, or my girlfriend. You needn't feel so upset. Overturned glasses in a place like this are simply a fact of life. She shouldn't have been so upset. What she said to you was completely uncalled for."

"I'm glad I didn't catch it, but I suppose I deserved it."

"Not at all," he said. "No one deserves that kind of language, especially when you were doing your best to apologize."

"I did try."

"Yes, you did . . . Would you please sit down?" And he offered her the stool at his side. "My name is Antonio Primavera. I own this place."

"Do you really?"

"Yes, and I'm sorry that you were treated so shabbily here on your first night. I believe this is your first night here at the villa? At least I don't recall seeing you here before, and I doubt that I would have forgotten someone so lovely."

"Thank you. But you're right. I am here for the first time."

"By yourself?" he asked, and she nodded. "Then you will pass this first evening as my guest, and I will be glad to show you around, if you're interested?"

Elisheba smiled her appreciation, as he took her by the arm to stroll among the green tables and roulette wheels. They approached Kyle who stood slightly in their path pretending to be watching a game of backgammon. He looked up as they passed and smiled cordially. She returned the smile and raised her eyebrow slightly, adding an almost imperceptible wink.

XII

❦

Oceanic Persuasion

It was near midnight when Primavera ushered Elisheba from the back of the villa. She had spent the preceding hours watching the gambling, enjoying his collection of art, and listening to him tell about the history of the villa. Having come with some knowledge of the place, she found it interesting to hear his sanitized version. According to Primavera, the villa had been the home of saints since the monks first built it, and he was, though subtly implied, the recent link in that chain of virtue. He opened a single door, and they stepped out into the calm night air.

The back door to the villa was not at all like the fancy double doors and the carved stone railings at the entrance. The rear of the villa was designed totally for security, and the heavy steel door, resting on its heavy hinges, gliding silently with the help of a hydraulic opener, made Elisheba realize how futile it might have been had they tried to enter there.

Antonio reached past the lace of his dress shirt and withdrew a penlight from his inner pocket. He had several similar lights that he kept in his room so he could slip one into his shirt as he dressed for the evening. It had become a habit, just like putting on his tie. So habitual were these late-night walks with a strange woman at his side that carrying a penlight was routine. At one time he thought of having little lights strung along the steps, but he had learned to like the feeling of having women clinging to him, and now he would have it no other way.

A four-foot high mortared wall painted a variety of shades of green to blend in with the vegetation protected them from the sharp drop to their left. Long ago, vines and bushes were added to the natural plants around the stairs to cover the stairs existence as much as possible.

The clicking of Antonio's heels was unusually loud, for he liked to wear steel caps over them, a habit he carried over from his poor childhood when his mother put metal strips on the shoes of her seven children to make them last longer. He liked the attention it brought him as a youngster as he strutted down the backs streets of Naples, and he had never grown tired of what he imagined to be the envious looks of others.

The air was clean and moist, a carryover from last night's rain; and the breeze from the ocean, which had begun as they moved farther down the stairs, was gentle, smelling of salt but also intermixed with the fragrances of the wild flowers growing along the steep slope. Only the mournful cry of a single gull mingled with the clicking of Antonio's heels.

He spoke freely, not knowing that the half dozen drinks which he had offered to Elisheba to put her in the right mood had not been drunk. Again and again she had dumped the alcohol into the potted fern alongside her table, whenever Antonio was distracted. He, on the other hand, had drunk all of his, and though he insisted on holding her arm should she lose her balance, she was actually in a better state to catch him.

"So you had a tutor?" she said.

"Yes. My father did not want to trust the education of his son to the priests and nuns."

"Why didn't your father want the priests or nuns teaching you?"

"Let's not get into that. There's nothing that puts a damper on an interesting evening like a bunch of stuffy talk about religion."

Soon they had descended to the sea. Lying at the end of a thirty-foot dock was a magnificent eighty-foot yacht named "Vasco da Gama." Antonio's harbor had been widened for the craft, which sported a mini-helicopter resting on the stern of the craft.

Ordinarily he would have continued to use the penlight, but he was feeling a bit unstable tonight—he couldn't understand why the girl seemed to have so much of her wits about her—so he decided to use the switch from a green panel box at the beginning of the wharf. Immediately hundreds of little lights turned on around the outer edge of the dock, outlining its exact shape, providing him an extra measure of protection against falling in. Those lights were generally used for occasions when he brought groups to the yacht.

"Oh, that's beautiful!" she exclaimed as the walkway lit up like a miniature landing strip.

"Do you know why I call my ship Vasco da Gama?" he asked as they moved farther across the water.

"No."

"Most students of history remember that he was the first one to make the sea route around the Cape of Africa to India, but there was more to him than that. He had style, and I liked his style. He was a man who knew how to make a point. For instance, when he landed off the shore of Calcutta, he demanded the Samuri to surrender. When they wanted to waste time discussing the matter in a peace conference, he captured a number of traders and fishermen who happened to be handy, hanged them, cut them up into little pieces and put them into a boat which he sent to shore."

"How brutal!"

Antonio laughed. "What seems brutal to you is simply his own particular style. He was effective and got what he wanted, while a lot of weak men couldn't make their way around the coast. He didn't make the trip just for the culture. He was after wealth, and he got it. You decide on your goals and then you go after them."

Generally, Antonio would not have talked about such gruesome things with one of his lady friends, for he was smart enough to know that it wasn't the sort of discussion that would enhance the romantic climate, but he had drunk more than usual in his attempts to soften Elisheba's willpower and his own tongue had loosened in the process.

There was no reason for her to smile to pretend to be amused by his grisly philosophy. The dim light cast by the little lights at their feet could not show her disgust. She forced her voice to sound pleasant, "So is that the way you go after your goals?"

"Definitely. That is a quality I learned from my father. He was the one who brought the gambling to the villa. There were those on the island who opposed him, saying that a holy spot like this should not be used for such activities. Ha ha! A bunch of hypocrites. They fleece the tourists by charging double for their wares, and then they have the nerve to talk about the image of the villa. If they only knew. Gambling is a very tame diversion compared to some of the things that have gone on—and continue to go on."

"What do you mean by that?"

He had said too much, and he scrambled to cover himself. "Oh, nothing really. I mean, whenever you have as many people visiting a place as we do, you're bound to get some thefts or something. These people have money who come to the villa. You saw it lying on the tables tonight. Money draws all kinds, but fortunately, we do a good job of keeping the rabble away."

"Here's some rabble you couldn't keep away," Kyle said from behind, and although Elisheba was expecting it, she was genuinely startled when she heard his voice and her scream was authentic.

As she pulled away from Antonio, a rope looped down around his arms and drew tight; he turned around just as Kyle threw a stiff right, which missed slightly, and caught him just under his left ear, dropping him to his knees. He nearly tumbled off the dock backwards, but Kyle pulled on the rope and kept him from falling. He rocked back onto his behind and there he sat, dazed, while Kyle took the three-quarter inch hemp rope and looped it over his shoulders, tightening it on every completed circle.

When there was fifteen feet of rope left, Kyle tied it off, even as Antonio was starting to struggle. From his pocket Kyle took out a pair of handcuffs and slipped them on Antonio's hands, which stuck out from under the ropes like the appendages of some misshapened creature, and then he pulled Antonio to his feet.

Elisheba was gone from the dock, as prearranged, having run into the underbrush shortly after the rope began coiling around Antonio's chest. If they were wrong and his bodyguards were nearby, it would be safer if she weren't a clear target.

Antonio had recovered his senses and began to talk slowly because there was a searing pain at the base of his jaw. "What is it you want? I did not carry my billfold with me. If you mean to rob me, I have my ring here and my gold watch."

"I'm not going to rob you," Kyle growled more than spoke. "I just want some information. Tell me where you've hidden the Book of Enoch."

"I . . . I don't know what you're talking about," he stammered.

"You do know what I'm talking about. I can see it in your eyes that you do. I didn't think you would willingly tell me, so I've decided on a way to persuade you."

With that, Kyle pushed him into the water. There wasn't time for Antonio to scream; he simply gulped as much air as he could before going under. He believed that Kyle might drown him then and there and was greatly relieved to feel the rope dragging him to the surface—back first. He burst sputteringly into the open and hung limply, suspended out of the water from the waist upward; his head hanging downward and the water running off his nose and chin in a steady torrent. He shook his head to throw the water away from his eyes, which blurred his vision, and then he cursed Kyle.

"You're in no position to be using that kind of language on me,"

Kyle said and with that dunked him again and then hauled him out once more.

"Now what were you saying to me?" he asked but there was no response from Primavera. "I ask you again to tell me where the Book of Enoch is hidden within your villa. It will do you no good to deny it. I have enough proof to know that it is here somewhere."

"You're wasting your time," Antonio bellowed, and Kyle immediately dropped him once more. For several seconds he allowed him to thrash around like a hooked tuna before hauling him out.

"If you want to breathe air, I suggest that you not raise your voice again, or you'll spend more time under water than above it."

Antonio spoke again, but this time his volume was considerably lower. "If you drown me, I won't be able to tell you anything, so how does that help you?"

"Are you really ready to drown for what you know? Does it mean that much to you?" There was no answer from Primavera.

"I know more than you imagine Primavera. I know that you and others who work with you are murderers, and that there isn't anything you haven't done or wouldn't do."

Kyle lowered him into the water again, but this time he did not submerge him. His upper torso was still exposed, and then Kyle wrapped the rope several times around a pylon and tied it off. Turning away, he walked to the end of the pier and picked up a five-gallon bucket, which he had hidden behind another support beam. He returned to Primavera and set the bucket down.

Taking a ladle that was tied to the handle of the bucket, he dipped into a reddish, lumpy liquid and flung the ladle's contents into the water in a semicircle around Primavera.

"Do you know what that stuff is, Primavera?" he asked with a sadistic sneer.

There was no answer.

"It happens to be some very tasty blood and fish parts. Now you might ask, 'Who thinks that stuff is tasty?' and I'd respond, 'Why sharks think that's yummy!' And I just happened to catch sight of a shark a while ago after I had thrown a few gallons of this tasty meal in the water for him. He came in real close, and oh my, was he big! Now, I'm willing to bet that he hasn't gone very far, what with so many delicacies being tossed at him tonight. I'm just going to try and lure him back here again for another treat. And guess what, Primavera? You're the main course!"

Kyle saw Primavera's head snap up. He scanned the water's surface; then his struggling resumed against the ropes and the cuffs on his hands.

"I'd suggest that you not struggle so much, Primavera. You might just pull yourself out of those ropes, and how well do you think you're going to swim with those handcuffs on?" The struggling ceased.

Again and again the water rippled around Primavera as Kyle whipped the ladle in an arc above him, dispersing the bloody stew. When he had emptied most of the bucket, he stood up and stared out at the point of the harbor.

"There he is. I didn't think that he had gone very far. It's just as I thought—it's a great white."

"You're bluffing," Primavera said. "There aren't any great whites in these waters."

"Oh, that's where you're wrong, Primavera. There aren't many of them around, but we've definitely got one coming this way, and he's picked up the scent of that blood. You forget that the oceans are connected and occasionally you'll find a marine animal in a place you didn't expect, and fortunately for me—unfortunately for you—one has made its way here. I'll admit I'm quite surprised. I would have been satisfied with a blue shark or a hammerhead, but in this bright moonlight I can tell that I've hit the jackpot."

"You're trying to frighten me, so I'll..." Primavera had caught sight of a dorsal fin slicing the water directly towards him, two hundred feet away.

"I take it that you can see it, too," Kyle chuckled. "Sharks have the most uncanny sense of smell. That big fellow might have been a mile or two away, and he followed the scent right here, licking his chops the whole way! Absolutely amazing! It's the kind of thing that National Geographic Specials are made of." Primavera began to struggle again, this time more furiously than ever.

"You're not going to leave me here until it kills me? Don't let it kill me!"

"I'd gladly pull you up right now if you'd tell me what I want to know. So, servant of the devil, if you don't want to join your master in hell on this very day, you had better come across."

"I am a rich man. I will gladly give you a fortune if you pull me out."

"It's getting closer!" The great white, which had been turning slightly from left to right, as though it were trying to pick up the signal, now began a slow but steady course towards Primavera.

"He seems to have zeroed in on your thrashing around," Kyle said. "I told you should have remained more calm. With all the blood in the water, it was having a hard time pinpointing us, but now it looks as though it's going completely by the vibrations you're giving it."

Primavera became dead still. The shark was only a hundred feet away now, but was narrowing the distance more rapidly.

He turned his head slowly upward, so he could see Kyle, hoping to find some hint that his attacker didn't intend to leave him suspended there, that there was some compassion in the man which would not allow him to carry through on so grisly a deed; but he saw only a resolute stare and a tightly set jaw.

"Impossible!" Primavera said in a breathy gasp. "Someone who has come for the Book of Enoch could not stoop to murder to get it back!"

Kyle's faith soared within him. "How do you know what kind of people would come after the Book? What you're saying is God would not have his servants do this. Did you forget about Jonah? I'd say that shark is big enough to swallow you if God wants, but you're running a risk that he won't chew on you a little before he does."

The shark was fifty feet away now and bearing down on Primavera's half-submerged body. Its speed was still not great. The front of its snout broke the surface and the frightened man could see the moonlight glistening off its sleek frame like the nose of a torpedo. He could see its right eye—it was wide open—and it was locked on him. There was no need now for chasing the scent of blood or monitoring the vibrations through the water. Primavera knew that he had been seen.

For an instant he remembered the screams of another man, who was killed at the villa. His men had remarked how similar the man's voice was to his own, and when they killed him, he couldn't help wonder if his own screams would sound as his.

At thirty feet Primavera could see the reflection of the moon slightly illuminating some of the teeth from the already gaping mouth; its eye remained fixed; it was the eye of a predator whose only feeling was tied to the emptiness of its stomach and the constant urge to fill the void. It saw him as only a temporary fix for its ravenous appetite.

Primavera's terror was great. For an instant longer he hesitated as the wake of the shark fanned out on each side of him with the hideous snout at its apex moving directly towards him. And then he knew what he must do! It was obvious what he must do! Why hadn't he acted sooner? He must preserve himself now and worry about any repercussions later.

"I will tell you!" he shouted. "I know where it is! I will tell you!"

"Tell me now, and I will pull you up," Kyle shouted.

"It is in the catacombs under the villa! It is in the master chamber on the hill!"

"How do I get to the catacombs?"

"Go through the scriptorium! Through the Garden of Eden! Save me! Save me!" Kyle quickly grabbed the rope with both hands, bent his legs, and pulled upward as the rope rubbed across the rough edge of the boards on the dock, dragging Primavera out of the water, so only his feet were still submerged at the ankles; meanwhile, the shark had narrowed the distance to within eighteen feet.

Kyle took another grip on the rope to pull again, but his hands met the dampened rope where Primavera had gone under the water, and it slipped through his left hand, flailing the skin off his palm, causing the rope to play out until it caught where it was tied on the pylon, leaving Primavera waist deep in the water again.

A deep moan of abject terror swelled up from the base of Primavera's throat and when he opened his mouth, his cry was agonizingly painful, like a distraught mind from an insane asylum, and he closed his eyes.

Kyle ignored the pain in his hand and grabbed the rope again, this time preparing himself for the dampened portion, and with two violent thrusts, Primavera was three feet above the water, spinning slowly on the rope with his head eye-level to the dock. When he realized that he could still be saved, he was reanimated and he struggled to reach his manacled hands up from beneath the ropes that held them at his side, but could get them no higher than his breastbone and his wild thrashing forced Kyle to simply hold tight with bold hands without attempting another pull on the rope.

"Stop moving!" he shouted at Primavera, but the man was too much beside himself to hear or understand how he was thwarting Kyle's efforts. Holding the man's entire weight with his left hand as the rope rested on the exact spot where the skin was flayed, coating it red from the blood seeping through from the exposed tissues, he grabbed it farther down with his right hand and pulled up savagely, and Primavera, now fainting with fear, flopped unconscious onto the dock.

In his effort to throw Primavera onto the dock, Kyle's own body was yanked toward the water's edge; his foot struck a wet spot on the plank, and he slipped forward; for an instant he stood nearly upright with his arms making circles, trying to regain his balance, but his momentum was too great, and he toppled over with his feet still frantically working to find a toehold. He struck the side of the great white and careened to its side only a foot away from the massive jaws.

XIII

Unwanted Ally

The great fish no longer moved in the water; its mouth remained slightly open, as it was when it first broke the surface. Kyle's collision had changed its direction, and it floated face to face with a wood support column. It remained rigid, staring into the pylon, as if it were considering an attack—but there was no movement.

Kyle, who had disappeared below the surface, now bobbed up sputtering, for the blow on the shark to his rib cage knocked the air from him, and he had swallowed some water.

Instead of fleeing from the shark, whose torso was an arm's length away, he kicked once and reached forward to take hold of the dorsal fin, then pulled himself onto its slick back.

The fish sagged slightly under his weight but did not arch itself to snap at the interloper. There was no retaliation as Kyle struggled higher onto its back, using the dorsal fin as a handhold.

Suddenly a scuba diver surfaced next to him. For a moment the diver seemed confused, then he recognized Kyle and took off his mask. It was David.

"Kyle! What happened? Did it work?"

At that instant Stefano broke the surface. "What's going on?" he said, as he removed his mask.

Kyle tried several times to talk, but he had not yet regained his breath. Once again he labored to speak: "I got . . . I got . . . the information."

"What happened to him?" Stefano asked David, indicating Kyle.

"He fell on the shark," came Elisheba's voice as she ran up the dock.

"And on me," David added.

Elisheba was concerned. "Kyle, are you hurt?"

"I'm all right," Kyle said weakly. "I just knocked . . . the air . . . out of me."

"Where is Primavera?" Stefano demanded. "You mean I ruined my shark and he wasn't even here?"

"He's right here," said Elisheba, as she pointed to the still form at her feet.

David used the pylon to hoist himself up until he could swing his hand over to grab hold of the dock, then taking hold with the other hand, he pulled himself eye level with the dock. "What happened to him? Did he have a heart attack?"

"No. He's still breathing," Elisheba said as she stood close to him and watched his chest heave.

"I guess he fainted," Kyle said as he gave the shark a pat and then pushed off and took hold of David's back, using it like a tree trunk which he scaled until he too could reach the dock. Grabbing the edge of the plank with both hands, he pulled himself up and sat for a moment to catch his breath with the water running off him, pudding on the boards beneath his legs.

David dropped back into the water.

"He fainted, huh?" Stefano said beaming. "And you guys doubted how believable my shark would look!"

"So did you learn anything about the scroll, Kyle?" David said.

"Yes, what about the book?" Stefano added.

Kyle smiled at the old man, whose body seemed so youthful, and whose outlandish plan had worked so well. "Yes, he told me."

"So where is it?" David said.

"We go through the Garden of Eden."

"You mean that's still around?" Stefano said.

"Let's get him out of here, and then I'll tell you," Kyle said.

Kyle moved to his knees and began to use the rest of the rope to pinion Primavera's arms to his side. He wrapped it around his legs, and then took out a wet handkerchief from his pocket and stuffed it into his mouth, pausing to assure himself that the unconscious man was getting sufficient air through his nose.

"Would you two carry him down to his boat," Kyle said to the other men, "and place him in his bed. Elisheba needs to tell me everything she learned while she was in the villa. Maybe you can even draw me a map?"

"Let's talk about it," she said, while David and Stefano pulled themselves out of the water. Less fit men would have been forced to remove their tanks first, but this was the sort of thing they had done for years as a sort of silent competition between them, so there were no words said as they both sprang from the water, using the pylon once more as a support, then taking hold of the dock to pull themselves upward. David saw that he was beating his uncle slightly, so he intentionally slowed his upward lift and timed it so they were on the dock at the same time.

Primavera lay motionless as David knelt by him and slid his arms under his back and legs, then stood up, lifting him. Meanwhile, Kyle and Elisheba took cover in a grassy area among the heavy vegetation.

"You did it," he said. "You were absolutely wonderful." She

acknowledged his compliment with a smile. "So did you see anything like a scriptorium while you were in there?"

"I did. Primavera showed me some books that he was proud of."

She began by telling him of their walk after leaving the game room, emphasizing how complicated the layout was. "Then we descended some stairs and we stepped into the scriptorium. It was huge. It must take the whole bottom layer of the villa. The ceiling was thirty feet over our heads. The outer wall was circular, and there were bookcases all over. It's a huge place.

"Do you remember anything there that could have stood for the Garden of Eden? Any paintings of woods or maybe some sculptures that could represent Adam and Eve?"

"I saw some paintings, but nothing like that . . . There were some more paintings."

"Where?"

"On the ceiling. The ceiling was rounded and the whole thing was covered with an ancient map of the world."

"I don't see how that can help us. We're looking for an opening that will take us down."

Kyle saw Stefano and David climbing over the edge of the yacht and onto the dock after having left Primavera tied up somewhere inside. Still wearing their wet suits and flippers they walked awkwardly toward them.

"They're coming. We'll have to go, so tell me now how to get into the scriptorium from the back of the villa."

"I'll show you. It's too complicated."

"And have you go back in there? No way!"

"No, I can't give you specific directions. We went through several corridors, each with passages leading off them, but I think I might be able to retrace my steps if I went back in," she said.

"You need to go with Stefano to his place. That was the original plan."

"I don't think you can find the scriptorium without my help."

"We'll do the best we can. If it occupies the lower floor, we ought to be able to stumble our way in there somehow."

"The place is complete confusion. You need my help."

"No."

"Look, Kyle, I was with you when you first found it; I was there when Samuel died; I was called just as much as you were to protect it. I was also the one who went against God and read it when I wasn't supposed to, so if someone should be sticking her neck out to get it back, it should be me, so let me go. Our best chance is with me leading the way."

"And if you should die in there, and I should get out, will you tell me how I could live with myself?"

"You're tough, Kyle. You'll cope."

"What's the problem?" David asked.

"If Kyle would take me along, you guys would have the best chance for success, but he's too stubborn."

Kyle stood. "Call it anything you want." He turned to David. "How about Primavera?"

"We put him in his stateroom, and then Stefano switched on his stereo and hit the switch that repeats the music, then we locked the door after us, so if anybody comes investigating, they'll have to pound on the door over the music. They'll probably think twice before interrupting what they believe is a passionate evening."

David handed Kyle a small radio. "These are the best. We should be able to keep in contact no matter where we find ourselves in there. At least, I hope we can. When you flip that switch, they're voice activated, so you don't have to worry about holding any buttons in. Just talk, and I'll hear you."

"OK, good. Did you bring his clothes?" Kyle asked.

David held up a plastic sack. "Here they are. What are you going to do with them?"

"I might have to wear them. We'll see how it goes," Kyle said. Then he turned to Stefano. "Will you make sure she gets home safely?"

"Yes."

Kyle looked at Elisheba whose eyes remained averted, and then he said, "Let's go," and began walking up the path.

Stefano threw his arms around his nephew, and they parted company. Elisheba rose and took David's hands in hers.

"Good luck," she said.

"Thank you."

"Tell Kyle I love him, and that I'm sorry. He knows that already. Just tell him that I love him." He put his hand on her shoulder.

"He knows that, too, but I'll tell him anyway." David tugged at the shoulder strap that supported the black leather bag at his side, which contained his special tools. Then he turned on his heels and hurried up the path.

"Did you check Primavera's pockets?" Kyle said after David had relayed Elisheba's message. David felt in his own back pocket and withdrew a set of keys and a security card. He held it out so Kyle could see them. David replaced the card and keys, then felt at his shoulder holster—the .38 was there. He checked it often during missions, a habit he had picked up years earlier.

They slowed their pace as they approached the black metal door, hesitating for a moment to be certain a security guard wasn't present. A single bulb within a white globe hung above the door brightly illuminating that area—there was no one. Edging forward again so quietly that their darkened forms seemed to be gliding over ice instead of the coarse granite stairs, the men drew nearer to the door. At twenty feet they went into a crouch, remaining in the darkness of an olive tree whose branches overhung the walk.

"Did you notice the symbol on the door?" David asked. Kyle peered around a branch to look. It was a pentagram. "The sign of the devil," he whispered.

Both sat for several seconds, studying the opening. "Did Elisheba say anything about this area being lighted?" David said.

Kyle shook his head. "She said it was dark and that Primavera used a little flashlight. Somebody has turned it on, or some timer activated it. Maybe it turns on automatically."

David took out a miniature pair of binoculars from his black pouch and held them to his eyes. "There's a camera above it."

"There is?"

"Yup. It's by the roof, protected by the overhang, just to the left of that gargoyle in the corner. The camera is angled at the doorway."

Then David turned his binoculars on the door. "I see the opening for the security card, too, so it's a good thing that we've got it. It looks like we're going to need Primavera's clothes. I won't fit in them, so it looks like you'll have to go for it."

"Give me the bag with his tuxedo," Kyle said in a whisper. He pulled out the black coat, the pants, the cummerbund, then the ruffled shirt, and he placed the tie on top of the pile. He took his shoes off, and then sat down on the steps where he pulled off his black pants and sports coat, stripping down to his underwear. Soon he was wearing the tuxedo. He wrapped his own clothes in a ball and hid them behind the olive tree.

"So I'll act as if I'm drunk?" Kyle asked.

"That's right. If you get the door open, try to turn that light off. When you get it, I'll make a run for it, but we don't dare leave it off too long. They might send somebody down to replace the bulb or something, and we'll end up running into them. I can make it inside within five seconds, so you turn it back on as soon as I'm inside."

"OK," Kyle said. "But what if the light is on a timer and there's no switch for it inside the door?"

"If there's no switch to shut the light off, open the door again and break it with your shoe. The door swings inside, so they shouldn't see you opening it, not with the camera where it is. I doubt there's a microphone there, we'll just have to hope they don't pick it up."

Kyle smiled. "OK. Sounds like you've done this kind of thing before."

"Here," David said, "take the pass card and that set of keys." David dug them out his pocket and placed them in Kyle's hand. "Good luck."

"Thanks."

Kyle stepped from behind the olive tree and walked deliberately toward the door, slightly straying from a straight course to indicate Primavera's drunken condition. He kept his head down, as though he were concentrating on every step, and those mannerisms allowed him to avert his face from the camera.

Inside the villa, in the electronic nerve center for the building, several operators were watching a variety of TV monitors that were linked to the cameras which were hidden all around the villa.

Remote sensors were concealed around the foliage in the gardens and in the rose beds. Optic fibers ran through artificial stems to flowers of silk. Virtually every inch of the grounds could be watched—but the back had been left nearly unguarded except for the single camera. Primavera had given that order for two reasons: first of all, he did not believe that the back side of the villa with its windowless construction and its camouflaged staircase was a source of concern for security; and secondly—and more importantly—he did not want his romantic episodes watched by his workers.

Giovanni Inverno, a twenty-five-year-old art student dropout from the University of Naples, sat at the control station with twenty monitors in front of him. He was wearing a set of headphones. He was supposed to be listening to a speech from the United Nations General Assembly, but at the moment he was listening to a soccer game between Italy and Germany.

The Italians were down by a goal and were on foreign soil, but they had been staging some aggressive offensive action within the last five minutes and were threatening to score. Giovanni had to be very careful that he did not begin to yell in the middle of the control room, or his superior, or perhaps one of the other two men who were manning their own jobs in chairs nearby, might call him on it. He had been warned before about listening to soccer events instead of properly monitoring calls.

It was during the climax of the game that he noticed the screen from the camera-feed at the back of the villa just as Kyle ascended the last steps before the security door. He noticed the slight stagger of the man and made a move to speak to Carlos, his friend, sitting at his left, so they could watch the screen together in case they might actually see Primavera fall. He reconsidered the action and decided that his humorless supervisor with the rimless glasses and the bushy sideburns might reprimand him, so he said nothing and watched for himself.

On the screen Giovanni watched Kyle withdraw the security card and run it through the reader, and then try the door unsuccessfully. Again Kyle ran the card through with the same results. Giovanni laughed in amusement. Primavera was obviously so drunk that he had forgotten how to use it.

Just then, from across the room, his supervisor took off his glasses and put them in his front pocket. That was a sign that he would be leaving for a while. It was his habit. A moment later he did leave.

"Hey, Carlos," Giovanni whispered. His friend turned. Though Carlos was eight years his senior and a more dedicated employee, he too longed for some diversion from the constant monitoring.

"What is it?" Carlos whispered back.

"Primavera is drunk. He can't remember how to use the security card."

"Really?" Carlos looked at the monitor covering the back door. He saw Kyle standing there fumbling at the opening and pulling at the handle at the same time. Finally, he stepped back and looked at the card as though he were having trouble seeing it.

"Why don't you help him out?" Carlos asked.

"Do you think I should?" questioned Giovanni. "What if he's insulted?"

"Speak diplomatically to him," Carlos suggested. "Maybe the consigliere will reward you by raising your rank to a security level one."

Giovanni liked the possibility and reached across the control panel and activated his microphone.

"Consigliere?" he said to Kyle who was genuinely startled by the unexpected voice coming from out of nowhere. Fortunately, he had the presence of mind, after an initial lurch of surprise, to regain his air of drunkenness. Kyle realized the voice was coming from a nearby speaker and he responded to it in a deep baritone that he hoped would pass for Primavera's drunken voice. Again he was surprised, but this time by the closeness of his voice to that of Primavera's as he remembered hearing it at the gaming tables.

"What is it?" he asked.

"Consigliere, if you remember, the card must be run on both sides to open the door," Giovanni said.

Kyle said nothing more but passed the card through the opening in one direction and then flipped it over to the other side and repeated the movement.

Within the door he heard the metallic click of the deadbolt withdrawing, and when he pushed on the doorknob, it opened inwardly, under the controlled pull of some silent hydraulic system. Kyle saw that the door was half a foot thick and was glad they were not forced to enter in any other way.

The door slowly opened to its full width and then began closing again at the same velocity. There would be no time to get David in.

His hand raked along the wall looking for a switch, but found nothing. Throwing his shoulder against the door, it suddenly reversed directions, still moving under the silent force of the hydraulics. Again he raked the wall with his hand, looking for the switch, and his fingernails pulled loose some of the mortar that held the limestone blocks.

He sprang to the other wall and found the switch and turned off the outside light. Pulling on the door, he felt its direction reverse once more. It was fortunate that he had changed its course, for a moment later David shot through the opening but caught part of it with his shoulder, causing the door to once more begin to open.

After David spun to the side against the wall, he straightened himself up and began rubbing his shoulder, and at the same time Kyle reached for the light switch, finding not one but two. He realized the extra one must be for the hall they were in. Since he wasn't sure which one was the outside light and because he was anxious to have it off, he flipped both switches simultaneously, immediately plummeting them into darkness while turning the outside light on again.

An instant later another figure burst through the door, careening off the wall, and rebounding into Kyle, who fell upon his assailant with all his weight. They dropped heavily to the floor where Kyle tried to wrap his hands around his attacker's throat to smother any cries of help.

In the Control Center Giovanni suddenly shouted out, "Did you see that?" Carlos turned to him. "What's wrong?"

"The screen went dark for a moment," Giovanni said, "and then it came back on, and I saw the back of someone as he was rushing in. He kind of dove through the door, and I saw the feet." Giovanni and Carlos swiveled their chairs around so they, too, could see the screen.

"Are you sure it wasn't Primavera stepping back out to pick up something that he had dropped?" Carlos said.

"Who turned on the light then?" Giovanni demanded. "The light just came on when the man was rushing through the door."

"That does sound unusual," Carlos said. "I think you better call Security One."

Giovanni punched a button on the console and lifted his eyes to a darkened monitor to his right. The stark image of Hans Lichner stared back at him.

Hans was a blond-haired German, 38-years-old, with light blue eyes that looked as if they would be more at home within the skull of a bird of prey—emotionless, pitiless eyes—regarding Giovanni not as another human but a mechanical object.

"What's wrong?" he said brusquely. Giovanni immediately felt uncomfortable and his tongue tightened. He was used to his ungracious harshness, but he had never gotten used to the whitish, dead skin that covered the left side of Lichner's face, remnants of an awful burn. After a few haltering attempts, Giovanni explained what he had seen.

Hans didn't pause after Giovanni's last words. "I will go to that area myself and check it out." The image on the screen disappeared, and Giovanni was relieved.

Meanwhile, Kyle struggled for only an instant with his assailant before his hands became entangled in long hair. He recognized the outline of the face under his hands, and whispering fiercely he said, "Elisheba, are you crazy? What are you doing here?"

XIV

666

*E*lisheba pushed Kyle away and then struggled to her feet. "I'm here to help you. I'm your best hope for locating the catacombs. I helped find the book, and I have a right to be here as well as you men."

"We made a plan, and it doesn't include you being here!"

"No," she said vehemently, "you made a plan and just expected me to follow it, even if it wasn't the best plan. The best plan is to allow me—who has already been in there—to try and help you find your way to the stairs, but you didn't consider that because you've got this macho idea about protecting me. Well, I don't want to be protected. I want to take my chances like the rest of you. Now, I'm going in. You can come with me if you want, or wait outside until I return with the scroll."

She spun angrily away, rubbing her right ribs now that her back was to them, covering the action, for she had taken a severe blow as Kyle fell upon her. Her side and shoulder both hurt badly. She was afraid that one or more of her ribs were broken, but she would say nothing now that she was inside. She didn't want them using that as a reason for sending her out again.

"Elisheba," David whispered. She stopped, expecting him to offer some resistance.

"There was a camera outside that back entrance. Did you know about that?"

"No, I didn't," she said, suddenly subdued. "Is that why you turned the light off?"

"Yes, it is," David whispered as he stopped next to her.

She tried to allow her right arm to dangle naturally at her side and ignore the pain.

Kyle shook his head. "Do you see the situation we might be in now? If anyone saw you, we're probably not going to make it very far."

"I didn't think about that."

"Well, you should have."

"Look," David said forcefully, "we don't have time to discuss this. Let's get out of here." They moved down the hall as he led the way.

"I'm sorry about the camera," she whispered. "I looked for them when I was with Primavera. I didn't see that one."

"It's past. Forget about it," Kyle said. "Let's keep our eyes open for any others."

Her arm and side still ached badly. "I asked Primavera about cameras, indicating that I might want to be romantic, but he said there wouldn't be any surveillance after we left the main casino."

Kyle didn't turn his head to speak to her. "You didn't expect him to tell you the truth, did you?"

Another hall intersected the one they were in. David kept his eyes riveted there, waiting for someone to respond to the problem they had as they entered.

"Let me take the lead," she said from behind. Both men halted and let her pass, and they turned to the right.

In the next hall, they were greeted by another fortified black door, again bearing the sign of the pentagram. She glided silently by, walking slightly more hunched than before from the pain, but neither man noticed. They all moved noiselessly, passing like shadows.

Kyle touched the rocks and was surprised at their coldness for this time of year. Elisheba remained in the lead. Had she been walking alongside the others, they might have seen her lips moving in her own silent prayers: "God of Abraham, Isaac, and Jacob—God of the Lord Jesus—forgive me for putting our lives in danger."

She felt another wave of pain in her side. "Oh Father in heaven," she thought, "help me. Maybe I should have gone back out once I realized that I was hurt, but now I can't. Please help me to get through this."

Kyle might have seen her occasional shudder of pain if he had been watching her closely, but his attention was directed at the lights hanging from the wall on either side of him, fifteen feet apart, made of brass. Once torches had hung there to show the way. The brass arms survived the looters of various ages only because they were so deeply anchored in the stone.

Above each brass holder burned a single bulb, enclosed within an irregular translucent fixture. Initially, he thought they were merely spherical glass coverings, but two points rose from the top to break the clean line. He studied another light as he passed and saw that the glass covering the bulb was actually in the shape of the head of a goat—another demonic sign representing the horns of the devil.

At that moment, Elisheba stepped into a small chapel on their left. She stopped abruptly and studied it, and then entered, confident that this was the room she was looking for. The men followed after her.

At the back of the chapel stood a marble altar and behind it rose a six-foot cedar cross, once transported from the forests of Lebanon.

The men were perplexed because the room obviously had no other entrance or exit. "What are you doing?" Kyle asked.

"I know what I'm doing," she said. "There's another way out of here. It leads into the scriptorium. There's a way to trigger it."

David turned toward the hallway and peeked around the corner. There was no sign of anyone. Then he leaned toward Kyle and whispered: "Did you get a look at the lights?" Kyle nodded.

Kyle walked to Elisheba. "Elisheba, what are you looking for?" he asked.

She waved him to silence. "Let me concentrate. I know it's right here." Kyle looked at the cross rising from the altar. Upon it hung a wooden image of Christ with his head leaning on his left shoulder.

"Give me some idea what you're looking for," he said.

"We came up right here," she said but as she tried to point, she suddenly crumpled forward in pain, catching herself on the cross. Both men rushed to her side.

"What's wrong, Elisheba?" Kyle asked anxiously as he put his arm around her waist and began to pull her upright, but his strong grip hurt her more and she let out a gasp of pain that made him release her.

"I . . . I hurt my side when we fell to the floor," she said with eyes closed, "I just need to walk it off."

Kyle helped her up gently from the altar, while her hand touched her side. He lifted her chin towards him, and saw that her face was sweating.

"The breath was knocked out of me, and I haven't recovered yet," she said. "I'll be all right. There's a tile at our feet that must be lifted up. We came up from below and exited into the hall from this chapel. Look for a way to raise it!" she demanded.

David moved first, dropping down on his knees, where he began rubbing his hands on the floor. Kyle watched her a moment longer, then dropped to his knees, too, and began searching the floor.

"Primavera barely pushed on the tile from below and it rose," she said.

There was a pattern on the marble tile of hundreds of interlocking circles, and David's hands searched those patterns. Suddenly his fingernail snagged something. "I think I've got it!" he said, and he pried up with his finger a metallic ring that blended in perfectly with the floor.

Kyle stood away from the spot, while David took hold of it with his middle finger. He pulled and a section of floor three feet on the side and hinged at the area closest to the altar began to open slowly like a door.

As the marble slab approached the vertical, they could see the counterweight and the pulley system below which was lifting it. When the door reached its upward limit, it bounced backward slightly and then stabilized.

Circular stairs wound downward with a metal bar acting as a handrail. A light below illuminated the next level. Elisheba did not wait for the others but stepped between them and took the stairs. David kept the rear and when only his head remained above the hole, he reached upward and pulled the floor over them.

The corridor below was slightly cooler and was made of the same gray limestone, but the ceiling was not quite so high; the same goat motif continued in the brass lights.

Elisheba tried to recognize something that would indicate the right direction. She was feeling light-headed from her injury, which was hindering her judgment. The pain coupled with the circular descent was disorienting her.

"God of my fathers, please help me to remember the way," she thought, and she paused momentarily, staring down both ends of the hall, which were identical in their construction, each running fifty feet before being intersected with another hall, and there were no windows, pictures or anything else to differentiate them.

She leaned back against the staircase, waiting a final instant for God to manifest the way—she felt nothing. Indecision would lead them nowhere, so she turned to her right and took four steps with the men at her heels. Suddenly she stopped and looked in the opposite direction. "Let's go this way instead," she said aloud.

No sooner had they passed out of the hall, than the false floor under the altar began to rise again, and in an instant two men, dressed in the black uniforms of Security One moved noisily down the spiral staircase. One of the men was Hans Lichner. His blue eyes scanned the hall quickly for Mr. Primavera. If he was the one that the controller had seen going into the back of the villa, Lichner knew that it was his custom to return to his study after being with one of his lady friends. It was early for him to return from his yacht, but perhaps the woman for the evening was not to his liking.

For a moment Lichner looked in the direction that the three people had just taken, knowing that was the way to the scriptorium. Mr. Primavera would often send a servant there to retrieve a book and carry it to his study. He might have gone to pick out his own book tonight. He did that on occasion. The other direction led to his private quarters.

If Primavera had come back early tonight, he might well have gone to the scriptorium himself. There was much of the evening left to fill. Sometimes he passed the entire evening among the old books, if no woman in the casino had caught his fancy enough to invite onto the yacht. But that was rare, and tonight he had found a woman, and she was quite beautiful.

Lichner remembered admiring her himself. Maybe they had quarreled and it was the woman who had tried to rush in after Primavera had entered. Most likely he and the woman had returned early from the yacht, and he was probably taking her to his study right now.

Hans turned and walked in the direction of the study with his subordinate following closely behind. We might as well play the odds and follow his regular route, he thought, and then smiled. One thing you learn about working in a casino—you always play the odds.

Down the opposite hall the three people moved stealthily, measuring every footstep, hoping to avoid a stumble, or a scuffing of shoes. They had turned twice more since being disoriented under the altar, and this last hall was not lighted. They felt for a switch but could find none.

Seventy feet in front of her was another doorway. "There it is," Elisheba whispered. "Just beyond that are the stairs descending into the scriptorium."

But someone was walking ahead of them. His back was towards them, and they could easily hear the shuffling of his sandals, ascending the steps, leading into the scriptorium. Instantly Kyle and David flattened themselves against the wall while Elisheba hesitated where she stood. Reacting instinctively, David's forearm shot forward, catching her at her waist, pinning her against the wall. Immediately afterwards the form of a hooded figure appeared in the doorway.

David's blow caught Elisheba exactly on her hurt side, and she couldn't restrain a slight moan that carried to the ears of the hooded figure. Elisheba put her hand over her mouth to prevent any further sounds, but the damage had already been done, for though the man had nearly cleared the door, they could see the back of his robe suddenly stop, obviously alerted by the sound from the hallway. He pivoted and stepped into the door's opening and stared into the blackness.

"Who's there?" came a man's voice that was not frightened, but suspicious.

He spoke again: "Hans, is that you?" The man was well aware of the Chief Security Officer's penchant for moving around the villa as furtively as he could, often stepping out from a hiding place as someone passed near. No one liked the games he played, but they passed it off as in keeping with his training. Was he playing some of his games now?

In that moment of hesitation, David leaped into action. As the hooded figure felt for a light switch, he ran forward, like a cheetah breaking from cover; his swift feet remained remarkably silent. Kyle watched him sprint with a detached fascination, considering there would momentarily be a violent confrontation.

The priest found the switch and reached to turn it on. At the instant his hand flipped the switch, David was upon him, and the priest saw nothing more than a black blur. He let out a brief, but loud gasp, before the rocketing fist struck him squarely on the left cheek, sprawling him backwards.

The unconscious figure might have toppled down the stairs, but David's momentum was in the same direction, giving him the chance to grab him by the robe, so he could lower him to the ground.

David motioned Kyle to join him, and then switched off the hall lights. He turned to the form lying motionless at his feet. The cowl was still covering his face within the shadows of the dim light. Bending over, he grabbed the man by his wrists and hoisted him in the air, placing him on his shoulder, then took the stairs into the scriptorium. The shelves of books loomed into view along with the high circular ceiling displaying the map of the world.

Easing his head into the room slowly, David looked for others. As far as his limited vision could tell the room was empty. Stepping inside, he turned to his left and stealthily moved to a poorly lit corner of the room where two shelves met. A gap between them provided an obscure spot to hide the man.

David lowered the body to the ground, and for the first time he saw the man's face. His eyes were blackened as well as his lips with makeup or maybe ashes. The exposed chest was hairless, as though it had been shaved, and on it were three numbers. David had seen those numbers in relation to the occult, especially in Columbia and Rio de Janeiro. Kyle and Elisheba stepped through the doorway and stood next to their friend as he continued to kneel. Standing up, they could see the monk's exposed chest.

"666," Kyle said out loud. "If there ever was a place to find an anti-Christ from the Book of Revelation, this is it."

David removed the man's sash and tied his hands behind his back, then from the black pouch at his waist, David took out a pre-cut, three-foot length of black nylon cord, tied his feet, gagged his mouth and stuffed him in the corner.

Meanwhile Kyle gazed around at the huge room they had entered. "We're in the scriptorium," he said. "We've made it."

"I'm sorry about the noise in the hall," Elisheba said. "My hip is so sore, and you hit it David."

David surveyed the room. "I'm sorry."

Kyle looked closely at Elisheba. "How are you now?"

"I can walk, and I'll keep my mouth shut. There will be no more sounds from me. I promise."

"Wait here for a moment," David said. Then he moved farther into the old library and disappeared behind some shelves.

Kyle put his arm around Elisheba's waist, and she leaned her head on his shoulder and closed her eyes for a moment. For an instant she imagined herself in Jerusalem again, and the fear that gripped her chest began to subside, but she was jarred back in reality by the sound of David's voice, as he returned from his quick reconnaissance.

"As far as I can tell, there's no one here, but as I said, I can't see much. So far, I haven't found any stairs going down or seen any pictures that could stand for the Garden of Eden. The library is big with bookshelves scattered all over. There are no long aisles. I can only see a dozen feet in front of me at any time."

Kyle nodded. "It's just as you warned us, Elisheba. These scriptoriums are often as mysterious as the mysteries they are supposed to unravel. Let's go."

David shook his head. "I wish we had more to go on. This place is incredibly chaotic. You can get caught between shelves of books and have a hard time getting yourself out. Make sure your earpiece is in and your radio on, Kyle. If you have to say anything do so quickly, or they'll have time to lock on our signal. If you're brief, we should be off the air before they're aware of it. It looks like you'll have to stick with Kyle, Elisheba, since we don't have any way to communicate.

"Why don't I just use my radio," she said as she pulled one from her pocket. "It's your spare. I hope you don't mind me using it?"

David smiled at her. "No. I'm glad you've got it. Put them all on channel four. Be short and to the point."

They scattered, and the others soon found David was not exaggerating. The bookshelves made it easy to become disoriented. They were not laid out in right angles. They twisted and turned for no apparent reason.

A minute later Kyle stood in an open space. Why there were no shelves in that area, he couldn't tell. From where he stood, he could see most of the ceiling. It was a huge, oval-shaped dome, completely covered with a painting of the medieval world, not an accurate map of the earth, but ancient man's belief of how the earth looked.

In the center was the city of Jerusalem. Kyle could make out the walls of the city and see the Latin spelling. This map, as in so many mariners' maps of the time period, had relied on the Biblical passage in Ezekiel: "Jerusalem is the center thereof" referring to the world. On the outer perimeter of the ceiling were the walls that suggested the limits of mankind's knowledge.

He stepped into another row of books, and followed them as far as he could. When that aisle ran into a dead end, he looked for a way out, but was forced to retrace every step he had just made. He began what he thought was another rack nearby but soon found that they intermixed with the racks he had just searched. For five more minutes he looked, frustrated at the time wasted with so little area actually covered. Surely there must be some sort of a pattern to this place, he thought. He didn't have time to go in circles.

"Help me understand it, God!" he said as he launched into another aisle of books.

XIV

Searching for the Garden of Eden

Hans Lichner hesitated a moment in front of the dark green metal door that led to Primavera's quarters, considering the propriety of his knocking. He knew there was a risk that his superior could be irritated at such an interruption, especially if the girl was with him, but surely he would appreciate Han's thorough investigation of the matter after he explained the peculiarities at the back entrance.

Accompanying Hans was a Welshman named Iago, who had dark hair and a broad nose and thick lips. His father chose the Welsh form of James in naming him Iago because he had a fascination for the character in Shakespeare's Othello who relentlessly went after his enemies. He hoped that his own son would show some of that same ruthlessness, and in that wish he had not been disappointed.

"He might be grateful after I've explained," Hans thought, "but what will he be like until I do? Will he even give me a chance to explain?"

Hans had seen him verbally lash another subordinate. He remembered occasions during the last years when some workers' performances were substandard—a few were no longer around at breakfast—vanishing in the night. A place that knows cruelty can sometimes turn on its own, if performances did not match Primavera's expectations. It was unfortunate that they had not overtaken him while he was returning to his quarters. Hans could have been spared this decision.

Iago was familiar with Lichner's decisive actions, and he wondered why his commander didn't immediately knock. This waiting caused Iago to lift his normally impassive eyes from the floor to meet Lichner's as if to say, "Are you having a hard time making a decision?" Hans understood the glance and waited no more. He gave three hard raps and then stepped back and waited for the door to open.

When no response came, he knocked again and once more assumed a crisp, military posture. Finally he relaxed, and withdrew from his shirt pocket his communicator, which was only slightly bigger than a credit card. He pushed twice in the area designated with a red triangle and its outer edge took on a luminous, green glow.

"Control Center, this is Security One, Hans speaking. Is Master Primavera wearing his communicator this evening?"

"Negative," came the reply.

Hans cursed. Although the communicators were small and could easily fit into Primavera's pocket, Hans had not yet been able to convince him to keep it on him constantly. Within the last year they had revolutionized communications throughout the world, but Primavera felt inept around electronic gear, and he avoided wearing the communicator, though it was simple to use.

"We are still investigating the suspicious incident at the western entrance that happened earlier. We're outside the consigliere's room and there's no response to our knock, so I want you to ring his intercom."

There was a pause, and Hans spoke again. This time it reflected his frustration. "Will you acknowledge my request and do what I say, or do I issue you a citation for insubordination?"

"Commander Lichner," came the rather shaken response from Giovanni, "I am willing to follow your orders, but at the same time I'm recalling a recent meeting with the Security Force and the Control Center at which you were not in attendance, where we were told not to contact Master Primavera after he had left the casino with his guests unless it was an emergency."

"I am well aware of that policy—I authorized it, so ring the Master's room, or you'll answer personally to me."

"Yes, Sir," came the terse reply.

Lichner could hear nothing from Primavera's room. It was soundproof. Fifteen seconds passed as he held the communicator in front of his face, squeezing it between his thumb and forefinger, slightly waving it back and forth in a nervous rhythm. Finally, he could hear the background ambience of the Control Room.

"There is no answer, Commander Lichner."

There was no hesitation now. "Then patch me into the communicators of all the members of the Security Force."

If he was wrong, this would be a good practice exercise. Certainly there was enough evidence to indicate the validity of a complete sweep of the Villa. He could justify his actions if he were called upon to do so.

"You're go, Commander," came the reply in his earpiece from Giovanni.

"This is Commander Lichner speaking. Do any of you know the whereabouts of Master Primavera? If any of you have seen him within the last half hour, identify yourselves and let me know his position." There was silence.

Lichner wanted to be sure that the Control Center had correctly patched him, so he zeroed in on one of his men who had been assigned the casino for the entire night.

"Maurizio, are you sure Master Primavera hasn't returned to the Casino since he left with the girl?"

Maurizio's voice was smooth and collected. "I've been scanning the monitors continuously, Commander. I can assure you he has not been here."

"Then none of you have seen him? All right, I'm initiating a Code Beta. Code Beta. I'm ordering all members of the Security Force One to immediately conduct a sweep of the villa. You know your areas. We have a possible break-in at the western entrance. The facts are still vague. I'm ordering a search of the stairs leading to the ocean on the western side by Athan, Jeeves, and Kyriakos. That's Athan, Jeeves, and Kyriakos. You should continue to the Master's yacht, and radio me immediately whether you find him or not. If he's there, apologize for the intrusion, and tell him I'll explain the whole situation later.

"I do not wish to alarm the patrons within the casino, so, Maurizio, scrutinize the area intensely with the cameras. Make sure he isn't seated at some table and blocked from the cameras by some woman's hairdo or something. If you're in doubt, go make a visual check yourself. Again, if anyone should see Master Primavera, he is to radio me immediately. If you do find anyone within any of our unauthorized areas, hold him for interrogation if at all possible, but don't allow the integrity of the villa to be compromised. Go to work."

Lichner replaced his radio and took out his gun. Iago pulled his. Lichner's weapon was a .38 German luger that he had taken as a memento from a captured CIA agent. It looked archaic compared to Iago's laser pistol, but Lichner had not been converted to the new weapons. Both could kill, but he liked the sound of the explosion of the shell and the resulting effect when the lead-tipped bullet flattened out as it made its way through a man's body, creating an exit hole that you could put your fist into. He had seen people surrender just by seeing the horrendous wounds their comrades had suffered.

The lasers cauterized the hole as they punched through, leaving virtually no blood, and only a small, blackened hole. How could an opponent be intimidated with no blood? He would keep his luger. He nodded his head and they turned and walked abreast down the corridor still carrying their weapons.

SOME CONCEALED NEON bulbs on the perimeter of the ceiling provided indirect lighting within the scriptorium. The map of the world was clearly distinguished. Kyle, Elisheba and David used their flashlights sparingly, flipping them on only when the shadows within a row of shelves prevented them from seeing distinctly.

David, walking as quickly as he could—some moments actually sprinting—had just completed a circuit of the room, looking for paintings or statues that might provide the symbolic reference to the Garden of Eden.

There were no statues but many paintings, only a half dozen of which could be interpreted to somehow stand for the Garden of Eden. He stopped to analyze the frames of several which had pastoral or wood settings, looking behind them for a sign of a secret panel with his flashlight. When he found nothing, he moved on until he was at his starting point again without a trace of the stairs.

Elisheba, although having had no more success than David, was still confident. She was feeling better, and the pain at her side was barely noticeable. To her, she had experienced a miracle, and that having come after all her thoughts of unworthiness. It made her feel yet accepted of God, giving her hope that they could succeed.

Kyle scanned the racks frantically, but he was becoming discouraged; there were so many books and the layout so haphazard that time was going fast. In their haste, he knew that it was possible that they had already skipped over it. How much longer could the three of them possibly be in there without being discovered?

Although their goal was obvious—to find the stairwell—he kept wrestling with the organizational layout of the place. In other medieval libraries he had seen, there had been some kind of a system: all the math books, or language books, or philosophy books were stacked together; or the books were lumped together by author, but he had noticed the same author located on two different shelves. Here everything seemed helter skelter.

He moved in a section of manuscripts and folios that were written in Latin, French, German, and Italian, and on a shelf under those diverse offerings was a shelf containing books written in the ancient dialects of Italy: Latin, Florentine, Tuscanese—the dialects that flourished before Garibaldi united the diverse sections of Italy.

He saw a pine-green book that was written in the Neapolitan dialect with its typical Spanish influence. It was some treatise on biology. On the shelf below those were books in Latin. The majority of this bookcase dealt with Italian works, but what did the motley assortment of French, Latin and German books have to do with the others?

Suddenly, he had an idea, and to confirm it he looked upward to the map. Directly above him was the boot of Italy. Quickly he looked to the books in front of him and pulled one from the shelf that was in the French language.

It was written in Brindisi on the eastern coast of Italy. He grabbed another book in German. It was written in Rome. Every book he studied was written somewhere in Italy, even though the authors might not have been native Italians.

He ran from that bookcase, dodging his way among the book shelves, continually glancing upward to get his bearings from the map. When he saw that he was under France, he lurched to a halt. He ripped a book from its shelf and flipped open the cover. He could find no indication of the land of its creation, but in the second book it was clearly labeled as France, as were the third and fourth and fifth. The sixth book was also unmarked as far as he could tell, but the next two were both written in France. H e saw, as he examined the shelf, that the books gradually became older, with the books on the bottom shelves entirely written in Latin and ancient dialects.

He stepped quickly to the east as indicated on the map and found books written in German and the tongues that served as its ancient underpinnings. Directly above him on the map was the land of Germany.

So the whole room was organized according to the original place where any given book had been written. One simply needed to know what country had spawned the book and then position himself under that area on the map and the bookshelves held the writings produced in that place. The shelves themselves, like the rings of a tree, dated the books by stacking them in chronological order; the older books were on the lower shelves.

That also explained why some shelves were so much higher than others; where the literary output had been greater, it took more shelves to accommodate the increasing number of books.

Kyle could tell that the bookcases were generally laid out according to the outline of the countries, but this was not strictly adhered to, for some countries' output was more prodigious than others, and so their borders necessarily encroached on the more meager writings of other areas.

He had an idea and he strode away quickly through the books of what are now the modern nations of Poland and Romania. The shelves bore the languages and histories of the various countries that had once flourished on those parts of the earth but had been swept away by politics or wars. The racks were closer together and would have made the passing of two browsers in the ancient library difficult, but Kyle moved easily, slowed only by the need to find his bearings from the ceiling. Continuing his general southeasterly direction, he turned the corner past the last shelf representing Bulgaria, and stepped into a small reading area where a diminutive blue table stood. It could accommodate only one person. Under it stood a blue, three-legged stool. The floor was also blue, having changed from the dark brown tile. This represented the Black Sea, although its proportions were nothing close to the dimensions of the map; here Kyle assumed they had maintained the integrity of the map by indicating the water, but had made some concessions to accuracy to accommodate the large number of books.

Passing through the area of what would be modern-day Turkey, he saw that on the map the place was labeled as "Land of the Hittites." Just as he was about to leave Turkey's section of books, he came upon another reading area done in blue, this one representing the Mediterranean Sea. There were several small reading stations, and over one of those cubicles he saw Elisheba. Kyle silently stepped into the blue area of the sea and walked towards her.

He saw her glance up quickly as she caught his movement from the corner of her eye. Without speaking, he motioned her to follow, which she immediately did. Her eyebrows lowered and bunched up in suspense, but Kyle remained silent, preferring to give a wink. When she drew close, she spoke softly: "Have you found it?"

"No," he whispered back, "but I think I know the general area." She fell in behind him, and he stepped easily along the blue tile floor to what would have been the eastern edge of the Mediterranean.

Other bookcases confronted him and he entered into the area of the Mid-East.

He turned his head toward Elisheba and spoke in a hush: "I think we'll find the staircase somewhere among these shelves."

"What makes you think so?" she asked while searching. He saw a book with two lions' heads butting, a typical symbol found on Assyrian artifacts, and he knew that was too far north.

"Let's go this way," he said, "I've learned that the monks placed the books under the country they were written in. The map is the key. Now the question is where was the Garden of Eden located, according to the people who made this map?"

"It was in the Mideast," she answered.

"That's why we're here, but can we pinpoint the spot any further? As I remember," he went on, "the Garden of Eden was believed to be located near where the Tigris and Euphrates Rivers joined, which might put it at the southern part of modern-day Iraq."

"Yes, but the rivers start in Turkey. You keep looking here," she said.

Glancing upward, she found the area that stood for modern-day Turkey. She disappeared behind a rack of books, moving in a northeasterly direction in relationship to the map. Sometimes she was blocked.

Kyle walked among the shelves, studying the books on the lower level carefully, looking for any indication of a passageway through the floor.

"Surely it must be here!" he thought.

Suddenly Elisheba appeared at his side, her breathing heavy with excitement: "I've found it!" she blurted out. "It's located in the racks of Turkey."

Kyle lifted his communicator to his mouth. "David, we've got it. Look at the map. We're right under where the light is shining." Immediately Kyle pointed his flashlight towards the ceiling. Its rays shone out, illuminating Turkey. He held it on that spot as he followed Elisheba, averting his eyes from her form to make sure his beam was holding steadily on Turkey. Periodically, he was forced to raise the flashlight above his head and step back away from a taller shelf to keep it from blocking his light.

She walked between two rows of books. Another shelf intersected them but didn't completely block off access as the left bookcase continued on.

Through the remaining gap that was so narrow, Kyle was constrained to turn his shoulders sideways to fit through. In that position, he sidled his way along. It only continued for three feet before a chamber opened up, replete with vegetation of all kinds, and from these walls the ancient stairway descended.

Here the books were gone, replaced by an arboretum; the myriad flowers, plants and small bushes were completely surrounding the stairwell. The plants were attached to the backside of bookcases, which formed the walls of the room, and at the top of the bookcases were the fluorescent lights—hidden from the outside—all angling downward towards the flowers.

A powerful fragrance, somewhat oppressive in its combined mixtures of sweet smells, permeated the air, for the flowers represented many species. Their colors were spectacular—golds, yellows, lavenders, brilliant reds, soft blues. Protruding directly above the arch over the stairwell were a dozen flowers known as Bird of Paradise, and on their long stems the flowers, which looked like birds from the depths of the Amazon, seemed to hover like a flock ready to attack anyone foolhardy enough to descend.

Kyle checked to see if his light was still shining on the area of Turkey, then turned to Elisheba who was staring into the pit with some dread. "This is it. It's certainly different from any basement entrance I've ever seen," he said with a slight smile. "Making it this far is a pretty good sign, I'd say."

"Maybe we've been allowed to make it this far," she said. She looked up to the map. "Why doesn't David hurry?"

The stairs were of white marble, and in remarkably good shape, and a slight updraft crawled along them with a chilling breeze.

Elisheba shone her flashlight into the blackness. There were twelve more stairs past the place that they could be seen from the ceiling lights, and then they ended.

They heard someone at the entrance to the corridor and turned to see David walking sideways past the narrowest section. Elisheba pressed herself close to the books so he could pass.

"Good work," David said through a big grin. "This would have been tough to spot. In fact, I think I already went past it once."

"The overhead map was the key," said Kyle. "I'll explain later."

"This whole place just seemed like one big mess to me. So let's get going," David said.

Kyle took the first careful step on the stairs, then extended his hand for Elisheba's. She edged past David who was in her way, and stepped next to Kyle. Kyle hesitated for a moment, and she was afraid that he knew something that he wasn't saying. "What is it?" she asked.

"Nothing," he said but he was thinking if hell had an opening, they had just walked into it. He led the way, and they began their descent.

"Knowing what we do about this place, why would these stairs stand for the Garden of Eden?" Elisheba asked. "Why make any reference to God or Adam or Eve?"

Kyle smiled pallidly and then swallowed. "If you remember, there was also a snake in that garden."

Without releasing the grip on her hand, he took the steps, turning his light on as the darkness rose from below them. David followed, spending more time looking up, holding his pistol, guarding their rear, than he did looking down, for he was certain that an attack might happen at any moment.

XV

THE HEART OF EVIL

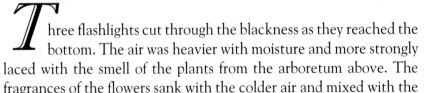

*T*hree flashlights cut through the blackness as they reached the bottom. The air was heavier with moisture and more strongly laced with the smell of the plants from the arboretum above. The fragrances of the flowers sank with the colder air and mixed with the stagnant air from within the catacomb, compelling Elisheba to breathe through her mouth.

The room was circular, thirty feet in diameter with an eight-foot ceiling. Directly in front of them was the opening of the catacomb, and leading into it, a double doorway, flanked by two Corinthian columns, supporting an onyx slab that formed a little roof. The onyx caught the rays of her flashlight, reflecting some brilliant bursts of white. The floor was a mosaic. Kyle turned his light to it while David's beam searched the walls for more openings. Elisheba shone her light on the portico that led into the catacombs, and she seemed mesmerized by the darkness beyond.

David, having finished his scrutiny of the wall, moved toward the main portico. He turned to see Kyle still studying the picture in the mosaic and was irritated again at the lost time because of Kyle's curiosity. "C'mon, Kyle."

"Whether we find the scroll or not might depend some on how well we can understand this place. We might even be able to avoid some dangers."

David turned his back on Kyle and faced the stairs, waiting. "Look at this picture," Kyle said.

Elisheba joined him. On the floor was a circular image. At the foreground of the picture stood a hill supporting three crosses, and behind it in the background stretched a city wall.

"It's Jerusalem," she said. "And that's Calvary. But why have that image here, unless it was done by the monks?"

Kyle shook his head. "No. The monks didn't make it. Look at this Latin inscription at the base. Can you read it?"

Slowly she read the words. "ON THIS HILL I VANQUISHED MY ENEMY. I KILLED JESUS CHRIST."

Elisheba gasped, and Kyle felt her tighten the grip on his hand. The full impact of the villa—its significance in the agony of the human race, the torturing of the innocent, the murdering of children, the defiling of women, the letting of blood in all ages through war, through greed, through cruelty—all of this she suddenly saw; all of these evils and more, she knew, could be traced in some way to the being who commanded here.

David motioned for them to move, but she hung back. Her courage had suffered a setback. Kyle stepped forward, still holding her hand, but she didn't move, and he turned to face her. She did not wait for him to speak. "Kyle, I'm afraid." She looked at the opening into the catacombs as the grave itself.

"Elisheba, don't let this inscription frighten you, for it's a lie," he said forcefully.

"A lie?"

"Well, look what it says" and he turned the flashlight downward again. 'HERE I VANQUISHED MY ENEMY . . .' He didn't vanquish Jesus. Our very presence here is proof of that."

"Yes," she said. "You're right." Her courage returned and she stepped forward with Kyle, deliberately walking on the inscription. When they reached the portico, they did not hesitate but stepped through. David waited to see if they were being followed. When he was satisfied they weren't, he stepped into the catacombs.

They walked slowly at first. There were no Christian symbols etched into the walls, the kind that were so prevalent in other Christian cemeteries—the sign of the fish, for instance. The Greek word for fish was i-ch-th-u-s, and those letters formed the initials for the phrase, "Iesous Christos theou uios soter—Jesus Christ, Son of God, Savior. In other catacombs such symbols often began at the very entrances, but not here.

They had walked less than a hundred feet before seeing that the tunnel dead-ended. Immediately to the left another opening appeared. David saw it first, and the beam from his flashlight took the lead in breaking the blackness beyond.

Elisheba was the first to enter this small room, less than twenty feet on the side. For the first time they saw a loculus, a sealed chamber where a body had been buried. The opening was plastered shut, but from the indentation it was clear where it had been cut into the wall.

The men followed as she walked to the center of the room where another circular mosaic lay in the floor. None noticed it until she stood over it and felt the raised letters with her foot. The inscription was in Latin, and Kyle read it:

"HERE LIE THE BONES OF PAUL"

"Does this mean the Apostle Paul?" Elisheba asked.

"It could be," Kyle said. "He was supposed to have been beheaded on the Appian Way in Rome. That's not far from here."

"But why?" David asked. "Why put an inscription in the floor like this?"

Kyle shone his light around the room again. "You must remember the mentality of the creator of all this. He reckons his success by mortal victories—death and pain—those he enjoys. His goal is to defeat God. Paul did a lot to stop him. To have his body is a victory to him."

"So this is kind of a trophy room?" David said.

"Yeah, you could say that."

Kyle took Elisheba's hand and led her from the room, and they stepped into another long tunnel. There were other burial chambers. The loculi were not opened. The bodies were Christians, for the signs of the fish were now everywhere present.

"So this really was a Christian cemetery," he said. "Maybe that's why the monks decided to build here. Maybe they're buried here . . . Elisheba, do you want to stop and rest a while?" Kyle asked.

"No," she said, although she would really have liked to, but she was determined not to slow them down. An opportunity to rest did come less than a minute later when the tunnel abruptly branched into two. Their flashlights could not pierce the blackness far enough to clarify the correct route.

David glanced both ways. "Which way, Kyle?"

"I don't know. Let's scout them quickly. You take this one," he said while pointing to the left," and I'll go this way. Elisheba, do you want to come with me?"

"No. I'll wait here. Just try not to be gone too long. I'm going to sit down here, if you'll help me, Kyle." And he took her by the hands and lowered her till she was sitting with her back against the wall.

"Let's hurry!" David said as he darted into the darkness. Kyle waited a moment longer.

"Are you sure you don't want to walk with me? You can take your time."

"No. We don't have time. I'd rather wait here. Hurry, Kyle, or David will be back," she said, and she extended her hand and patted his knee. "I'm better here. I can use the rest." She tipped her head back and managed a wan smile. He smiled back, but it went unnoticed in the darkness.

"If you're sure you won't be too frightened," he said. "What's there to be frightened about?" she said with a straight face. He laughed, and she did, too. He patted the top of her head and as she turned her face towards him, his palm gently found her cheek.

"I'll be back in a few minutes," he said and walked away quickly.

She turned off her flashlight to conserve the batteries, but the darkness left her uncomfortable, and she turned it back on. She rested her head on her knees and moved her light back and forth between the two corridors, waiting for them to return.

Kyle saw more unopened loculi with their accompanying fish symbols, and there were other drawings—an anchor, a dove, a peacock drawn in a reddish pigment, now faded pink. As an archaeologist he was fascinated, and he forced himself to keep up his pace.

While looking at the writings on the wall, he failed to see a stone object suspended from the ceiling, directly in his path. He struck it in full stride on his forehead, knocking him to his right. As he fell forward, his arms shot out instinctively to protect himself, and he crashed into the middle of a loculus whose protective seal had weakened through the years by water seepage. In one piece it split open and dropped inward on the bones of the two skeletons buried within.

Kyle fell to his knees, and his body pitched forward, stopping his face from crashing into the rock. The sensation of blacking out still buzzed within him.

His head cleared, and the strength returned to his knees, and he drew himself upward. Inside he saw two skeletons lying close together, the one with the arm around the other. He did not know that the larger skeleton was a mother, whose arm was draped over the body of her daughter, placed there in death by the grieving father who had also suspended the stone cross from the ceiling that his head had struck.

Kyle stood and saw the cross for the first time. It was made of a marble that was pure white. There was blood running down his face from a one inch gash at his hairline. He was angry with himself for not concentrating on the business at hand. David was right about him wasting time studying things, and now he had paid for it.

He turned to the broken wall of the loculus. If anyone came this way before they got out, he might suspect their presence, so Kyle took hold of the main piece of the plastered section, which was still largely intact, resting atop the two skeletons and pulled it back in place. It dropped into its original position neatly. Only a piece at the corner in the shape of a small rectangle was still missing, but that would escape detection, unless one looked closely.

He stepped around the cross and continued down the corridor. Somewhere ahead he could hear the sound of water dropping to the floor, and his beam caught the puddle at his feet. The water disappeared into a crack in the corner of the cave.

He forced himself to keep his flashlight away from the loculi. There was no time for that, especially after he had struck his head. He wasn't sure how much time he had passed on his knees while recovering his senses, but he feared he might have been there for several minutes. Perhaps David had already returned from his search, had found the chamber, and was waiting for him to return. What had been a fast walk on his part, now turned into a trot.

Eighty feet farther the tunnel stopped abruptly but was intersected by another. He looked to the left and saw stairs leading downward. This was what he was looking for.

He turned around and retraced his route quickly. He heard the dripping water and sidestepped it on a dead run. His light was held high this time, not distracted with the figures on the wall, and he saw the cross hanging from the ceiling well in advance, giving it a wide birth as he rushed by. David was kneeling by Elisheba when he arrived. He stood and stepped toward him.

"Did you find anything, Kyle?" And then David's light caught the blood on his face. "What happened?"

"It's nothing to worry about," Kyle said breathlessly. "I just bumped my head. It's not bad. There's a lot of blood from a head wound. You know how it is. How's Elisheba?"

"Did you find anything?" David persisted.

"Yes. I'll tell you about it. Is she all right?"

"The same, I guess," David answered. "It's hard to say. I don't know if she's faking so we don't call it off right now, but she says she can walk and that the rest did her good . . . So what did you see?"

"I found some stairs. I didn't follow them. I was worried about her."

"Kyle?" Elisheba asked, "Did you find it?"

He took another swipe at the blood on his face with his shirt sleeve before moving to her side and kneeling. He had not gotten all the blood, but the darkness concealed it. "Yes, I did. Are you ready to walk?"

"Yes."

He pulled her up and she flashed the light on his face just as another heavy drop of blood rolled down from his cut.

"Kyle? What happened?" she asked, obviously agitated.

"I was careless, but it's nothing. Let's go. The catacombs continue this way."

David joined him and together they put their arms around her as she walked between them.

"How did you cut yourself?" she persisted.

"I bumped my head," he answered.

"Were you playing the archaeologist again?" David asked.

"Yea, I guess I was."

"Then it serves you right."

"You saw nothing, David?" Kyle asked.

"My tunnel just dead ended. I only went about three hundred feet. There were plenty of burial chambers, but that's all."

"You needn't hold me," Elisheba said. "I can walk now."

Kyle kept his arm around her anyway, but David was glad to be free to turn around and cover their back. He did so immediately and the cave behind them lit up. He had a strong feeling that their element of secrecy was over. The extra time they had taken because of Elisheba's injury, the search in the scriptorium, and the seconds lost here and there as they dawdled their way through these catacombs would come back to haunt them. It was so frustrating to him to move so slowly in a location that offered no quick outlet for escape.

During his assignments with the SEALS, getting in and out was usually done in a matter of a few minutes. Sabotage missions against enemy boats in the Persian Gulf had always provided him with the cover of the ocean, and it had been possible to swim off in any direction after planting a charge or taking the clandestine photographs before maneuvering his way back to the rendezvous vessel. But here they would have to exit the same way they came, and he hated the feeling of being trapped with no options.

When they passed the cross, Kyle stepped around it without releasing his grip on Elisheba. He stole a glance at the loculus he had broken open and was relieved to see that its crack was barely distinguishable. They passed the area where the water yet seeped so slowly. Elisheba didn't seem to notice it, and her feet trudged through the puddle; she was slightly startled to find her feet in water. Then they turned the corner towards the stairway.

The stairs were twelve feet wide and made of granite blocks which swung into a circular staircase after the first thirty steps; gradually they turned to the right and then the turn became sharper as it took on a spiral configuration. Down they went, winding around and around, so far down that Kyle was convinced that they had gone below sea level.

Once before while on the Amazon, his canoe was caught by the pull of a whirlpool that gradually sucked him in from its outer boundaries towards the violently spinning center. He had not thought of that experience for years, and now he had a similar feeling of entrapment as the circular motion of the stairs grew tighter.

Finally, the stairs stopped in front of a short corridor that was less than twenty feet long. Beyond was another room that was well lit.

David motioned for them to wait as he checked it out. The opening into the chamber was without a door and was encased with black molding, a foot wide, carved with olive leaves and branches.

David stood to the left of the doorway, his gun held upward next to his cheek, listening. Slowly he eased his head into the room and scanned the length of the chamber. For sometime he looked.

"Why is he taking so long?" Elisheba whispered. Finally he turned around towards them and rested with his back against the wall staring strangely ahead before motioning them on.

Kyle led Elisheba quickly across the last few steps and stopped beside David, who remained silent. "What is it?" Kyle asked.

"You'll recognize it." He nodded toward the room, and then stepped inside. Taking Elisheba by the arm, Kyle led her within.

In front of them was the opening to a gigantic cave, incredibly circular in shape, almost as though it had been cut from the rock. The ceiling was a dome but considerably larger than that which spanned the scriptorium, stretching over two hundred feet across, and eighty feet above them. On the walls covering the entire room was a mural, and on the walls by them, through which they were passing, was a painting of the Damascus Gate and extending from it a mural that depicted the old city wall of Jerusalem; the barren land to the north of the city; the mountains in the far background—all meticulously portrayed.

Lying in the middle of this huge room, surrounded by the mural, was an actual hill, and rising from the crest of that hill was a wooden cross. Eight spotlights shone from recesses in the ceiling, bathing the cross in bright light from every angle.

"Is it possible that this . . ." Kyle began, but he didn't finish. He stepped forward and turned to study the wall behind him. He scanned the entire room looking for any openings where someone might be watching. He could not see the whole room at once because of the hill, but that which he could see indicated they were alone within this macabre diorama.

"David, would you check the outer edge of this room and see if there's another opening?"

David set off on a run around the right side of the hill and was gone in a few seconds. Kyle looked again at the ceiling, checking for cameras or some other place where they might be watched.

"Do you think the book is in here?" she asked.

"I don't know. Did you notice the markings on the hill?"

"Yes. They're exactly the same as Calvary," she said.

"That's right. This hill is an exact replica."

Kyle left her side and walked closer. "This part is artificial," he said.

"You mean it's not even rock?"

"No. Looks like fiberglass," he said as he dug at a portion with his fingernail.

"Why would they go to all this work?" she asked, but before he could respond, David ran up, breathing heavily.

"There are no other openings that I can find," he said.

"Let's climb this hill," Kyle said.

"I don't like this place," David added quickly. "If we go up there we're sitting ducks. I've been in a number of tight places in my time, but this is spooky. Did you notice that all the rocks aren't real?"

"We noticed," Elisheba said.

"Why go to all this work," David said, "to make a fake hill and a fake cross? Can you imagine what it must have taken to cut this place out of the rock?"

"The being that has caused this has had a long time to work on it," Kyle said. "We haven't come this far without checking it out completely." He strode forward. When his foot touched the place where the ground began to climb, the others were behind him, and he paused to allow Elisheba to catch up, and they began the ascent.

More and more of the mural that they could not see before now came into view. It continued with the same authentic detail of the land to the north of the city, meanwhile the cross loomed ever larger. It rose from the very center of the hill, but it did not look like the cross before which most Christian churches worshipped. Instead it was shaped like a capital T.

Kyle was expecting to see a smooth cross of polished wood, after such an elaborate setting, but as he got closer he could see that it was not as he imagined at a distance; the wood was pitted in several places where it had been carved and notched, and there were areas where it was dark with stain. There were holes in the areas where the extended hands of the condemned would have reached.

Everywhere the hill seemed real, even to the bushes and grasses that were so typical of Calvary, but there was a spot which they now approached which was obviously manmade. It was another one of the mosaics, circular in formation just as the others they had seen, but there was no picture on this one, only a large black circle with a message written with small pieces of white rock. Kyle translated.

"FROM THIS VERY TREE I SLEW MY GREAT ENEMY."

XVI

Hiding among the Dead

"But I have seen pieces of the cross in different churches," David said. "I thought that was found a long time ago and divided up."

"I don't think so," Kyle answered. "Constantine's mother was supposed to have located it in the third century, but that's only so much speculation. I think this is it. The devil isn't fooled by fakes like we are. He's after the real thing. We've already seen how far he'll go to recognize his victories. What greater monument could he possibly have than this one?"

"Look, Kyle!" Elisheba suddenly shouted out, as she pointed to the ground at the base of the cross. So intent had they been on the cross and the inscription that they failed to notice the Book of Enoch lying at the foot of the cross upon a red velvet cloth. They quickly moved to it, and Kyle, without hesitation, picked it up. He was too full of emotion to speak, but simply clutched it to his breast.

Elisheba reached out to comfort him, and then she turned her attention to the cross and touched it. It was rough as she slid her fingers over it. She couldn't reach the crossbeam, but she did find a hole in the vertical section near her waist where the crucified could have been impaled and felt it with her hand.

"We have it again," Kyle cried out.

"But will you be able to keep it?" said a voice from below them. They turned to see Lichner entering the room with a contingent of Security One men. "You would be wise to drop your gun now."

David let his weapon fall by his feet. Hans passed through the Damascus Gate. Thirteen men all dressed in the black garb of Security One followed him. Each man carried a weapon; some held handguns; others entered with rifles. They were all similar in shape because Hans had a fetish for choosing what he considered the ideal man. Each weighed between 210 and 230 pounds; each man was over six feet—but no higher than six foot three; and lastly, each had a certain menacing look, indicating he was capable of inflicting pain without any remorse.

These men were no automatons, not simply unfeeling soldiers who took orders. They obviously possessed an intelligence that relished acts of cruelty and were capable of creatively fulfilling their assignments.

"Circle the hill!" Hans yelled loudly, and they dispersed in two directions as they burst through the opening, running around the perimeter of the hill until it was sealed off, stopping equidistant from one another. With their circle complete, they raised their weapons at the three who remained standing at the base of the cross.

"Do not fire until I give the command!" Hans yelled so his voice filled the chamber, and then he smiled and slowly circled the artificial Golgotha so he might draw closer to the cross and the area where the intruders stood.

"I see you have the book. You must be the archaeologist—Shepherd is the name, is it not—the one who first found the scroll? And you others are some of his misguided friends. Oh yes, I know about you. Who else could have known of the scroll's presence? You must obviously feel that you are on some sort of an errand—a mission—perhaps—to recover it. Who sent you?'

There was no answer from those standing near the cross.

"You are silent now, but I have a feeling your voices will echo in pain through the walls of this fortress before this day is done. These men will see to that. They're experts in what they do. The secrets of torture have been preserved here.

"Now, I will not ask you who sent you, because I already know," Hans continued. "It was our Master's great enemy, the same one he killed on this cross—it was Jesus Christ. Only he could have helped you find this place, so far from the spot where we first took the scroll."

Kyle took a step towards Hans. "You're right. Jesus has led us here to recover the book."

"Recover the book?" Lichner said in mock derision, and then he burst into laughter, and the men nearby joined him. "To recover the book! Do you mean to take it from us?" His laugh echoed gratingly from the curved walls. "You fools! Do you see how wrong you were? Don't you realize that this Jesus has made another mistake? You are standing on his biggest blunder of all—the very hill from which our Master killed him. Now from the next world he continues to delude people today as he did when that cross was fresh with his blood."

"We are not deluded," Kyle said forcefully. "You have the book only because of our disobedience, not because anyone is more powerful than the Lord."

"Do not speak disrespectfully of our Master within these walls, or the girl will die the most painfully of all . . . Your Jesus has been trying for some time to make people believe in him, but I want you to remember what happened when he was alive."

"He did not fail," Kyle interrupted. "His kingdom has been growing. It continues to grow."

"His kingdom?" Hans answered contemptuously. "Surely I would have thought that an archaeologist like you would have a better understanding of the history of the world than you obviously do. The world is ruled by Satan . . ."

"Not all!" shouted Kyle.

"The vast majority of this world tends to serve our Master. Those who don't are simply ignoring the facts. They hang on to promises given by your Jesus which will not come true. Don't you see that he already tried to set up his kingdom, and he was destroyed . . . as you will be destroyed today? Now, set the scroll back under the cross where it belongs as another token of our Master's superiority over yours."

Kyle held firm. At the same moment David cast his eyes downward to his gun, so he could know exactly where the handle was. He would need to pick up the gun as quickly as possible without any fumbling. Once these men began shooting, the three of them could drop to the ground out of the line of fire. Of course there would be little hope once they stormed the hill. With the gun, he could possibly kill the first ones over the rise, but getting to their weapons, once he had killed them, seemed remote. It was a possibility, and his thinking was in that mode now, where he was measuring the options that could prolong their lives, if only for a few seconds more.

Hans spoke again: "Surely you don't value the scroll so little that you are willing to take a chance that it will be damaged by your stubbornness?"

His words were true. Kyle did not want to take chances with it. If they were to be shot now, there was no reason to sacrifice the book. Perhaps God would send others more worthy of its recovery. He turned slowly and walked back to the base of the cross, then gently laid it down and returned to the others.

"I thought you would see it my way," Lichner gloated. "Truly the act of a bona fide archaeologist. You have that innate sense of the importance of antiquities. We, too, have a similar sense. You have already been in the chamber where you have seen how lovingly we have preserved the remains of others who believed in your Jesus. They were leaders of your idiotic movement. You saw their final, pitiful end."

"They will live again," Kyle said.

"We have their bones!" Hans shouted. "Can't you see the facts?"

"They will live again," Kyle repeated.

"You hold to your stupid traditions just as your kind has been doing since Jesus was first crucified on this tree. There is no hope for such ignorance. You were sent here by Jesus, but where is he now? Why doesn't he save you? I ask you: Why doesn't he save you? I'll tell you why: he doesn't dare come here, for here our Master rules without..."

Suddenly Hans stopped and turned his head as though he were listening to someone. He bowed his head slightly, and when he raised it, he spoke to his subordinates.

"Men! We are to have a rare privilege. Satan has elected to destroy these intruders himself." Hans closed his eyes and raised his arms over his head. "Be it according to your will!" he shouted.

No sooner had he spoken the words than a black mist materialized from nowhere and surrounded the three on the hill, making their forms slightly less distinguishable than before; simultaneously they felt severe pains in their chest, as though the muscle and skin were being pulled to a center point over their hearts; they dropped to their knees and clutched at their breasts and cried out in awful agony; Hans smiled broadly and looked at his men in great satisfaction, but at the moment the trio fell to the ground, a light appeared directly over their heads and the mist dissipated from the center outward.

At the first sign of the light their pain instantly ceased. They stood on their feet again as a fireball some twenty feet above them formed in midair, which continued to grow in intensity. Hans, who had become even more excited at the first sighting of the luminous glow, believing it to be a wonderful manifestation of his master's power, now took a step back, when he saw his captives rise from their knees, obviously no longer in pain.

The light grew more intense and expanded until the three were enclosed, but there was no pain, no heat, and they could still see each other. In that state, David bent over and picked up his gun.

Though the light within the cloud was not harsh for them, the men surrounding the hill were blinded by its intensity. It pierced through their eyelids as though they weren't closed; as if the sun itself had been transported within the room and its light magnified, making the men cry out; they clasped their forearms in front of their eyes and crumpled to the floor. Lichner tried to shield his eyes and look toward the hill, but it was impossible.

"Don't let them escape," he yelled. "Shoot at them! Take your guns and shoot at them!" He unstrapped the luger at his side and fired wildly at what he hoped was the top of the hill. In reality, he was off the mark. His steel jacketed shells struck the ceiling around the room in several places, exploding pieces of rock, showering it down upon a number of men who were already terrified by his echoing gun.

The cascading rock careened off the floor and grazed one stunned guard. In his abject terror he believed he was being shot at and he fumbled for his weapon, then squeezed off several rounds, but he did not aim at what he thought was the top of the hill. Believing the shot was fired from behind him, he swung his weapon around and fired several rounds in that direction. One of the security guards was killed outright; another guard was hit in the collarbone and knocked down. When the injured man found his gun, he stood and shot, drawing others into the melee as he fired wildly. Seconds later dead and injured men lay about the room.

"We're leaving with the scroll," Kyle shouted. He had no trouble in finding his way to the base of the cross, where he picked the scroll up, clutched it to his chest, and then retraced his steps to the others who were still on their knees. "Don't be afraid. Stand up and follow me," he said with authority.

Elisheba rose quickly but David hesitated. It was so against his training to stand upright with so many guns going off around him. "David, join us," Kyle repeated.

Warily David stood and hustled after them. They could see the ground around their feet but the light blocked out the sight of the rest of the room. The firing continued on all sides, but they walked erect with only David bending quickly when he believed a shot had come close to them. They reached the bottom of the hill and stepped through the opening into the mural from where they had entered. It was then that the light faded.

The moans from the wounded continued to echo awfully around the chamber. It was apparent to all still alive that the intense light had subsided, but no one could immediately open his eyes, though each tried—none more determinedly than Lichner. His squinting eyes watered as though they were severely sunburned. Through narrow slits, he could see the top of the hill was vacant.

"Stand up!" he yelled even as the tears streamed down his face from trying to force his eyes open. "They're getting away. Take your guns and follow them."

He wiped his eyes on his black shirt sleeve, and then surveyed the carnage from the frenzied shooting of his men. Iago, who had not been injured, stood over one of those who had been struck in the hip. The injured man was in terrible pain and begged for help. "What about these men, Captain Lichner? Bjorn may bleed to death if someone doesn't help him quickly," said the Welshman.

"We will radio for help for those who have been hurt, but we can't take time ourselves." When he perceived that some were hesitating, he spoke angrily: "Don't you understand that those people have left this chamber with the scroll? Our own futures depend on how well we pursue them."

"But Captain," Iago protested, "you saw what happen here. We were not dealing with only three people. Just as it seemed that they were to die, some power saved them."

"Whose power was it?" Lichner asked derisively.

"I don't know," replied the Welshman, "You said that we were to be honored with a display of our Master's power as he killed them himself, but they were not killed!"

"Perhaps it is a test given to us by Satan to see how willing we are to protect his interests. We have lost some men, but whose fault was it—our own! Instead of firing reasonably, we panicked, and turned our guns on ourselves. Now those people we were supposed to stop are making a mockery of us. I believe our Master produced the light himself to see how we would respond, and our nerve was not up to it, or perhaps these people brought in some device that we're not aware of yet, and they were able to frighten us. We're better than that."

Lichner turned to the others who were circling around them. "Don't suppose that this light was some power from Jesus Christ. That's exactly what those three would like you to think. We are standing near the cross that killed him. That's how little power he has. Don't be deceived! There is only one ultimate power, and we are his men."

Lichner took out the card from his pocket. "Control Center. This is Captain Lichner."

"Yes, Captain," came the reply.

"There are three people making their way through the catacombs. I want all remaining men of Security One to enter the catacombs and prevent them from exiting through the old library. Relay that message to all my men."

"Let's move," Kyle said as he led the way into the tunnels. He hadn't realized how the stairs had provided better ventilation, removing some of the musty odors trapped within the cold damp walls, so just when he needed more air for his exertions, the catacombs gave him less.

As much as possible they ran, and when Kyle's strength began to wane, David grabbed the scroll and carried it. Soon they reached the area where the water covered the floor, and Elisheba splashed through it. She alerted David, and he watched his footing as he went through so he wouldn't go down.

"All this light," David said, "makes us too easy to shoot at. Both of you turn yours off, and I'll keep my light in my hand, like this, and cover it with my fingers, just so we have enough to see."

Elisheba and Kyle turned their flashlights off, and David stepped into the lead, but they were forced to move more slowly with the rationed light.

"Stop," whispered David.

His suggestion to extinguish the lights had been an inspired one, for in front of them he had caught the faint glow from several lights reflecting off the walls a long way away, even though they still could hear no movement of approaching feet.

"What should we do, Kyle?" Elisheba asked.

"There's certainly no going back the other way," Kyle said.

David turned off his flashlight, and they considered their options in the darkness. "Do you have any ideas, David?" Kyle asked.

"I've got my gun. If we made it back down to the hill, we could get some cover, and I could hold them off awhile there.

"That wouldn't buy us much time," Kyle said.

"No, not much," replied David.

"I've got an idea. Follow me," Kyle said. "I think I know where we can hide. Let me use my light, and you keep yours off. We've got to run."

David caught up with him. "We've been through this area, Kyle. There's no place to hide, and you're heading right toward them."

An instant later, Kyle's light caught the cross that his head had struck.

"Here, hold this," he said to David as he handed him the scroll. He walked past the cross and then, turning to the wall where he had broken the seal to the loculus, he slipped his fingers into a couple of openings under the crack in the broken piece of wall and then lifted it out with both hands. The skeletons stared back as if in mute disapproval.

Kyle pushed the bones together. "Get in," he said.

Elisheba lifted her leg up and stepped in. Kyle took the scroll from David and dumped it into her arms. David entered next and seated himself on top of one of the skulls and drew his legs underneath him.

"Hold this," Kyle whispered to David and handed him the broken piece of wall. Kyle pulled himself into the loculus and between them they slipped it back in place.

Soon they could hear the sound of many footsteps echoing within the walls of the cave, and from within their enclosure they could see the light from the approaching flashlights through the broken outline of the wall.

Twelve men and two women, all dressed in the black uniforms of Security One, approached with Antonio Primavera in the lead. Each of Primavera's soldiers was carrying a handgun or rifle.

Elisheba sat on the thigh bones of the skeletons, tucking her legs beneath her to give enough room for the two men. She leaned back and placed her head against the rock, as the tromping of the feet grew louder. Her mouth was dry, and she found it hard to swallow. She started to tip to the side and put her hand out to catch herself, placing her hand directly upon the long skinny fingers of the larger skeleton. She pulled her hand back quickly, and there was a slight rattling from the bones. She froze, thinking they had heard her, but the movement of so many feet had covered the sound.

David had his pistol in his hand. He knew that if they saw the break in the wall the people coming towards him were not the kind to show mercy. If they began to shoot at the loculus, he had already chosen the small hole where he could stick the barrel of his gun and begin firing. With the sound of so many feet, he was bound to catch a few before they finished him off.

His curiosity moved him to look between the cracks in the wall, and he caught sight of Primavera and the stony faces of his devoted followers. Suddenly Primavera stopped and put his arm up to halt the others. Elisheba pressed her hands together and prayed, while David moved the gun nearer the hole in the wall.

"Something is here," Primavera said. There was nothing but silence that followed his announcement, and then his single footsteps were heard as he advanced a little farther by himself. "Look at this cross hanging down," he said. "It's so white that it is easy to see that there is some blood on it right here. Here where it smeared, it has dried, but you see this drop is still fresh. Certainly not the blood of ages."

Primavera smiled. "Someone has run into it. Possibly because they heard us coming. Which means that they are trapped between us and Lichner's group."

They moved into the darkness and the sound of the footsteps receded. A minute later the broken piece of wall was lowered silently to the floor. Kyle and David got out at the same time, and Kyle helped Elisheba down.

"Take the scroll, will you, David?" Kyle said while he took Elisheba's hand. Using only one flashlight, they moved onward.

Retracing their steps, they exited from under the portico and into the foyer, passing over the mosaic, then ascended the stairs that led into the scriptorium. Looking upward, Kyle found his bearings and pointed the way they should go. David took the lead now with his gun in his hand.

They entered the tunnels again at the spot where David had knocked out the guard and within a few minutes were climbing the small circular stairs under the altar. David pushed at the tile in the trap floor, and the counter balance lifted it. Stepping through the opening, he knelt next to the stairwell and reached for the scroll as Kyle boosted it up; he pulled it through and set it on the altar, then returned to take his friend's arm and Elisheba's.

Finally they made it to the west entrance where Kyle had injured Elisheba. When the security door had opened enough, the three of them ran out.

From out in the harbor the vessel of David's uncle appeared with his Great White lashed to the side of the boat. For some time he had kept his ship just beyond a point of jutting rock, lying in wait for the return of the others. Since Elisheba had run away from him, he had not dared leave, though their original plan was to have Kyle and David return to his home on their own. And then he saw their three forms burst from the villa and confirmed their identities with his binoculars. He watched as they made their way down the stairs, fearing a sniper's bullet would drop one of them. When they reached the halfway mark, he started his engine and made a run for the wharf.

Just as they reached the bottom of the hill and scampered across the wooden planks, Stefano pulled up to the harbor. Elisheba hopped in first, then Kyle and David leaped from the planks and landed inside the fiberglass hull. Stefano was already hitting the throttle as the men jumped in. He turned the wheel hard to the left, rolling the boat over on its left side; it shot away from the wharf, making a tight circle in the still waters of the harbor, sending an arcing wave towards the shoreline.

Once the craft was headed seaward again, Stefano gave it the rest of the throttle and the front end lifted out of the water, exposing twelve feet of the hull. By the time they were shooting through the opening in the small bay, they were doing thirty knots.

They sat on the cushioned seats which circled the interior of the boat, all except Stefano who stood behind the steering wheel. Each person looked toward the villa, even Stefano, for he glanced over his shoulder as often as possible while his boat skipped like a shell over the ocean.

He followed the coastline of Capri and was soon out of sight of any gunfire. Stefano turned to look at the scroll and let out a long, hardy laugh. "We've gone into hell and taken back what was rightfully ours," he said.

Soon they were back at Stefano's home. As Kyle sat at the kitchen table with the scroll on the table, Elisheba stood up to leave the room.

"You can stay in here while I translate," he said.

"No," she said. "I don't want to be tempted to read anything."

She went outside and stood on the edge of the cliff. For over an hour she remained there, even after the ocean breeze had begun to chill her. She pulled her collar up and folded her arms to trap some heat.

Looking toward the opposite edge of the cliff's rim towards Stefano's house, she saw Kyle sitting in the light at the table, hunched over the manuscript, studying it carefully.

XVII

THE EARTH REELS

*I*n August earthquakes rocked the world. There was no spot that didn't feel it in some measure. Many people were killed by falling debris, while others were consumed by fire that came from within the core of the earth. Although scattered reports said that the fire actually came from above, those reports were quickly discounted by scientists who said that the earth had simply unleashed firestorms from its interior that had traveled upward and outward from the core, only to have its super heated rock fall back to earth again, sometimes miles from its origin.

The ocean was whipped up by the seismic activity beneath its surface, generating huge tidal waves that swept many coasts on every continent. Large tankers and cruise ships were struck and sometimes capsized. In some shipping lanes lifeboats, jammed with people, dotted the currents.

Birds everywhere were jarred from their nests, and the suffocating dust and gases that rose from below the earth's crust made them take flight, and in some locales the ground was shadowed from the millions of wings flapping above. Birds that naturally had no affinity and were even enemies now flew side by side as one group.

In Africa, the fear of the animals momentarily suspended the natural predatory instincts and meat eaters ran in huge packs along with zebras, wildebeests, and gazelles. From the moment the shaking began, animals of all species had begun to run, trying to evade a terror they could not outrun.

Within hours after the first quakes, the sky over major landmasses darkened from the ash and debris emitted during the rumblings, as air currents gradually pushed it over the face of the planet. Over major metropolitan areas, there was darkness with survivors searching for the injured with lights, though it was the middle of the day.

All of the shaking occurred within forty-five minutes. But even after the trembling subsided, huge waves pounded the shoreline and did so for many hours, as waves spawned in the remotest parts of the ocean raced inward. As the waves decreased, sailors from all regions noticed another phenomenon: millions of sea creatures, frightened by the jarrings on the ocean floor and the sudden release of heat, swam upwards. Other organisms were caught in the frightening upsurge, driving them to the surface as well. So there was an incredible mixture of marine life—squids, porpoises, sharks, sea lions, manta rays, whales, and many unidentified species, fomenting the water.

IN AMERICA THE roads were broken up, leaving the transportation system shut down. Panic set in after a week when grocery stores were depleted. In many major cities there was widespread looting and anarchy reigned as the power grid throughout the Americas was destroyed. When batteries finally ran down, the inhabitants were left to live much the way their forefathers had survived in the 1800s.

Nearly every part of the globe experienced some shaking, but the Middle East was left unharmed. The Arab countries believed that Allah had finally shown his approval of them and their worship of the one true God. Western scientists said that the quakes throughout the world had placed stresses under the ground in the Mediterranean areas that would soon yield to those pressures with their own repercussions. The leaders of those countries explained the warnings away as more Western propaganda. In Israel, another kind of shaking was about to occur, not of the ground but of their political and religious beliefs, and it had to do with the discovery at Qumran.

ONE MONTH HAD elapsed since the recovery of the scroll in Israel. In Jerusalem at the Temple Institute a special conference was in progress, convened by a group known as the Temple Mount Faithful. Their assembly hall comfortably accommodated the fifteen hundred members who had united to discuss what they could do to help rebuild the temple that was destroyed by the Romans in 70 A.D.

At one time only Jewish militants were a part of the Temple Mount Faithful and their numbers were less than a hundred, but gradually the cause had become popular even with the more conservative branches of Judaism, and now the society numbered in the hundreds of thousands.

Three times a day their prayers voiced the plea that the restoration of the temple would come quickly: "May it be thy will Lord God, God of our fathers, that the temple be rebuilt speedily in our days." Even the top rabbis of the Ashkenazi and Sephardi branches of Judaism had joined the movement, offering their experience in a joint effort of support.

There were obstacles in rebuilding the temple. Even though the site was now available because of the earthquake that destroyed the Dome of the Rock and other buildings within the old city, it was forbidden for an orthodox Jew to walk upon the temple mount without being purified.

Only a purified Jewish worker could begin erecting the temple, and the ceremony to perform the purification could no longer be performed. Once the Jewish priests could have used the ashes of the red heifer, which had been cremated for such a purpose, but the ashes were taken from the temple, along with the tablets of the Ten Commandments and the Ark of the Covenant and hidden away before the Babylonians could desecrate them. The final resting place of all these holy objects had been lost.

Even with those difficulties, the faithful continued with their plans in the hope that at some time a way of purifying the Jewish laborers would be found so the temple could be built. Exact measurements of the original temple had been fed into a computer so the architectural plans would be available when the time arrived.

Those very plans were being projected on a large screen on the stage of the auditorium by Rabbi Webberman when there was the sound of a slight disturbance at the back of the room, and Elisheba's voice could be heard trying to convince a security guard that she and the two men who accompanied her had actually been given an invitation, and although their clothes were dirty and tattered, they must be allowed the right to sit with the rest of the Temple Faithful.

Rabbi Webberman paused in his discourse. "Is there a problem in the back?" he said.

The guard, whose subdued voice had not carried through the auditorium before then, now spoke up. "Only that these three people don't have an invitation for the conference, Rabbi Webberman, although they say that they were given one," said the embarrassed guard.

Kyle had not recognized the voice of the rabbi during the commotion, but upon hearing his name, he yelled out: "Rabbi Webberman, I am Kyle Shepherd. We worked together on a display of terra cotta figures at the Rockefeller Institute two years ago. Do you remember me?"

"I do indeed, Mr. Shepherd. Guard, you may allow these people to enter. I commend you for stopping them if they did not have an invitation, but I can vouch for Mr. Shepherd and his friends."

The three people moved down the aisle as the audience turned their heads. Clutched to Kyle's chest was something wrapped in a red blanket. Their clothes were indeed dirty and bore the sweat rings of those who had been laboring in the oppressive August heat. David wore a white sweat band around his forehead made from a terry cloth towel that was now more brown than white. They did not take the first seats available but walked quickly toward the front so as to be near the speaker. Kyle smiled at some people he recognized.

"I hope you will forgive me, Rabbi Webberman, but we have just made a find within the last couple of hours of something of immense importance to the people at this conference. I know that this is the final session, and that you have an interaction with the audience. We wish to participate even though we aren't dressed for the occasion. When the time comes, what we have to say will be of real importance."

"If that is the case, Mr. Shepherd, we would very much enjoy having you speak to us now," Webberman said.

"I'll wait until the end of the program," Kyle said as he began to seat himself on the front row with the others joining him.

"That will not be necessary. I am the last speaker, and I have essentially finished my speech," the rabbi said as he moved away from the screen and condensed the telescopic pointer he was using into a wand again. "Why don't you take the podium now and we'll bring up the house lights. Besides, everyone will be so anxious to hear you that I might have some trouble holding their attention."

There was polite laughter from the audience as the Rabbi moved toward his seat behind the podium. Shielding his eyes with his hand so he could see towards the back of the auditorium and the technician running the light booth, he said, "Will you bring up the house lights, please?"

Kyle arose to climb the stairs to the dais, and he motioned David and Elisheba to join him. Waiting for a moment by the podium until his friends were settled, Kyle stepped in front of the microphone and set his bundle down.

"Ladies and gentlemen, members of the Temple Mount Faithful, I apologize for interrupting your conference," Kyle said. "This was not planned, but we have come across something that I felt needed to be heard at this conference, for I attended your meeting last year and was aware that during your final session you hold a forum discussion where members of the audience interact with the speakers. It was our intention to be present for that portion of the program. However, I can say without hesitation that what we have to present will more than compensate for our inadequate appearance." There was another subdued chuckle.

"Last year," Kyle went on, "you talked of reconstructing the temple. Because of the earthquake, the site for the temple is now available, but Jewish workers cannot set foot there because there has been no way to purify them. There is an answer to that problem, and it lies in something that we uncovered not more than three hours ago in a cave along the old road from Jericho to the city of Secacah."

At the mention of the city of Secacah, Rabbi Webberman suddenly sat up and slid forward to the edge of his seat. Until that moment a slight smile had played across his mouth because he was amused at his old friend's appearance and his dramatic entrance into the conference to announce what the rabbi believed would be some fact about the original construction of the old temple—something that would help them, in time, to reproduce it more accurately. But he suddenly knew that Kyle's find was much more important than that.

"Anciently," Kyle continued, "your Levite priests performed a ceremony to provide the nation of Israel with a purification rite. I know I am speaking to many who are well aware of this information, but for those who are not, your great lawgiver, Moses, took a red heifer as described in chapter nineteen of Numbers and sacrificed it and cremated it. Its ashes were then sprinkled into water whose drops could purify a house where a person had died, and where a wedding needed to take place. The holy temple, or its sacred ground, could be purified if it came in contact with unbelievers—as it has in our own time."

It was this mention of the temple that made Rabbi Webberman suddenly clasp his hands together, almost as if he were saying a prayer, and yet his eyes remained open.

Kyle continued. "The ashes were held within two containers. The inner bowl, made out of a special clay, was set within a larger bronze bowl. When the ashes were nearly used up, another red heifer was found. It was sacrificed and its body placed into the flames along with the clay bowl that held the ashes from the first cow. This bowl was made in such a way that the heat of the fire would cause it to disintegrate, so the ashes of the cow that Moses offered intermingled with the next cow. It was after the seventh cow that the ashes were taken from the temple and hidden."

The Rabbi stood up and walked towards Kyle until he was three paces from the red blanket, and he stared at it wide-eyed, as though having suddenly lost his senses.

From the audience, most did not guess the import of Kyle's message, but seeing one of their distinguished colleagues so excited by the stranger's words, they too were caught up in a buzz of rising excitement. Some scholars rose to their feet in the midst of the audience.

"Others have searched for it," Kyle said, "but the exact location of the city of Secacah has been doubtful, and the cave where it was hidden even less known, even though, according to the copper scroll that was discovered in 1947, the find would be made in a cave between two columns on the road from Jericho to Secacah. We have discovered the cave. My colleagues and I bring to you today—" he pulled the blanket away revealing a clay vessel—"the ashes of the red heifer!"

The audience gasped. The rabbi stepped up to the vase in amazement. He, himself, had once given a paper at a conference about these very ashes. He studied the jar closely and saw the image of a cow painted on the front and knew that it corresponded to the description found in the historical documents.

For a moment the audience saw the rabbi converse excitedly with the unkempt archaeologist. For those who didn't understand the significance of the find, there were frantic conversations, each trying to grasp its import; hurried explanations were given, and then the uninitiated also became agitated.

Finally the rabbi drew near the microphone and his voice was full of emotion. There were those near the front who could see the spotlights reflecting off his tears.

"I know this man very well. He is a good friend of mine and a good friend of Israel. His integrity is beyond question. I have just asked him some of the details of the find. I know the area. It does fall within the facts given by the copper scroll, which talks of the ashes. More important than that are the correct markings that should be upon the authentic jar. I can tell you from my own studies that this jar matches the description in every detail. God has heard our prayers! We have the ashes of the Red heifer! We can begin building the Temple!"

If the conference attendees had suddenly heard a peal of thunder accentuating the rabbi's words, there could have not been greater excitement. There were shouts of joy and loud applause while everyone jumped to their feet. Some people moved into the aisles and pressed their way toward the stage. The rabbi moved to the stage and held up both hands to stop them from ascending the dais. The security guards positioned themselves at the base of the stairs, while one moved to Kyle's side on the dais.

Kyle handed the vase to the rabbi who carried it reverently to the front of the stage as the conference broke into thunderous applause, and when he took it firmly in both hands and held it out in front of him, turning to all sides of the room so none could miss seeing it, there was no voice in the entire hall that wasn't cheering loudly.

FROM THAT MEETING the news raced throughout Israel that God had bared his arm and provided a way to rebuild the temple. Rabbis performed the ceremony of purification for a small army of Jewish workers who readied themselves to begin the construction. But permission was not given.

At the Knesset, the leaders debated the threat to Israel's security if they should begin the construction of the temple. "Certainly there will be war if we set one foot on that ground," one politician said in mirroring the emotions of many. "If we are going to drag our nation into war by constructing a new temple, then we ought to let the people decide if it is worth it. There should be a vote, and the majority will decide."

Another politician said that they should "fear God more than man. We should perform our duty and give the money to begin construction of the temple. Moses did not always go to the people to see what a majority of them wanted to do before he gave them God's laws." Within seconds someone was shouting that he wasn't Moses, which somewhat subdued the speaker.

Eventually the decision was left to the people. In a referendum, a vast majority of the Israeli people sided with the Temple Mount Faithful and gave their leadership the mandate to finance the building. Since the days of Israel's poverty and bondage were over, it was agreed that no effort or expense should be spared in the workmanship of the new temple. They would make a building that would be more opulent than the Temple of Solomon. God had sustained them in reclaiming their homeland, and the building would reflect their gratitude.

On the day that the construction was to begin, a small army of Jewish workers assembled themselves at the northern boundary of the Temple Mount where they awaited the ranks of the Levitical priesthood who would lead them onto the temple complex itself. Overhead there was a constant drone from a battery of military helicopters patrolling the area.

On the Mount of Olives west of the Dome, Captain Fischel stood on a recently installed platform that gave him a clear panorama of Jerusalem and the surrounding area. With him on the concrete platform was a subordinate, and together they surveyed the area.

Around them, each bearing a weapon, were Israeli soldiers under Captain Fischel's command. Scattered across the Mount of Olives were several other platforms, each platform representing another company whose sole responsibility was to protect the area.

Across the Kidron Valley from where Captain Fischel stood, the Jewish workers, who had volunteered for the purification rites that would allow them to walk on the Temple Mount, stood in a line as though they were part of the military personnel who were so intensely trying to protect them.

Each of the workers wore a special forest green uniform, making him look as though he was on a re-forestation project. The group was uncommonly quiet for so many men. The sacredness of their cause had silenced them.

A young man, Moshe, with deep-set eyes, and still in his twenties, stood silently next to the other men. He had once wanted more than anything else to be a pilot in the Israeli Air Force, a job that would have made him a hero in his home town of Gibeon. It was the pilots, more revered than doctors, who protected the country from border to border. It was the Air Force that had made the difference in battle during the precarious years of Israel's existence. For his whole life, no other goal had had such an impact on him, but he did not pass the stringent physical fitness exam, and the Air Force would not accept him.

Heartbroken, he turned his interests towards the Temple Mount Faithful and became one of their most ardent members. If God had not wanted him to fly above the ground to protect the physical habitations of his countrymen, perhaps he wanted him to work on an effort that would help protect them spiritually, which, in the analysis of eternity, would be more beneficial.

On that dramatic day when Kyle and his friends had entered the conference room bearing the ashes of the red heifer, Moshe was in the audience at the front of the auditorium. When the discovery was unveiled and the Rabbi proclaimed its importance, Moshe committed himself to be one of those who would one day be purified to step on the ground where the temple of his ancestors had been built. This day was the realization of that promise.

The wind was so calm that Moshe saw the down from a bird fall directly in front of him without moving to the left or right. He looked upward to find its source . . . there was nothing. The sky was an absolutely clear blue, without the specks of any distant birds.

From among the ranks he heard a voice shout that the rabbis were coming. He turned to see them, making the last stairs from the lower city. The ancient temple site was built on an elevated portion of Jerusalem; it was Mount Moriah, the place where Abraham had come to offer his son Isaac.

Over five hundred rabbis moved toward the opening in the southern wall. As they approached, Moshe and the men around him moved back to allow them to pass. The expressions on the rabbis' faces as they passed were varied: some were extremely somber; others could no longer suppress their supreme joy at being among those who would walk upon the sacred ground of their forefathers. Silently they entered through the southern entrance.

One of their leaders, a rabbi from the Ashkenazi branch, stepped aside and allowed his fellow rabbis to pass through onto the very ground where no orthodox Jew had been allowed to pass for centuries. He was a vigorous man with a sable beard and a voice that carried like the roar of a lion. Turning toward the hundreds of men, including Moshe, who stood waiting for instructions, he held his hands in the air to stop them from following the rabbis.

"Israelites!" he shouted as the last of the religious orders stepped onto the Temple Mount, "we are here to begin what our fathers, and their fathers before them, for centuries have looked forward to with great joy. You are here to help raise the temple where our God may come to speak to us. Wondrous are His ways!

"If we serve Him well during our work, He will honor us with His presence, for He will not deny the offering of those who love Him so much. The Rabbis have stepped first upon the Mount because it is their right as natural heirs to the priesthood. Those with hand tools may follow me now and you can begin the work that you were assigned."

Just then, three military helicopters from the Israeli Air Force flew past the northern boundary of the Temple Mount. At the same time, far above them, two Israeli jets streaked across the sky, leaving their tracks like the runners of a sled across a frozen blue lake. The rabbi paused in his discourse and he, as well as the men, watched the flight of the aircraft. When the noise subsided, he spoke again.

"You are all aware of the risks in the task that we have undertaken.

There is great danger in being here today, even though our army is all about.

"The United Nations has condemned our action. The World Court has ruled against us. We do not expect the confirmation of the world. We have never had it. The only confirmation is the one that God gives us. Didn't He lead us here? Isn't this the place where the Lord appeared to King David on the threshing floor of Araunah, the Jebusite? And when his son Solomon built the first temple, it was here. And when the Temple of Zerubbabel was erected in its place, it was done here. And when Herod worked hand-in-hand with our own priests to build a more elaborate building that bore his own name, it was built here. Our last temple will be here as well!"

A mighty shout arose from the combined voices of all the workers. His eyes filled with tears. Then came the signal from the head rabbi, and he turned again to his men.

"The time has come. Remember, we walk on holy ground. Let your thoughts be worthy of those who are in the service of God. Your children and their children will honor your names as the ones who restored this holy spot to Jerusalem." With that, the rabbi turned towards the opening in the wall and led the workers onto Mount Moriah. Moshe was one who couldn't restrain his emotions. He lifted his shoulder and wiped his eyes on his clothing.

No sooner had they all entered than a jet helicopter suddenly came roaring in from the west, flying fast over the ancient city, not yet over the Temple Mount, but hurtling directly for it. It was the speed that drew the rabbi's attention to it, for there had been helicopters flying over the area for the last several weeks in preparation for this day.

He saw two other helicopters converging rapidly on both sides, and he looked quickly around the grounds for some sign of terrorist activity. At the same time, the two legitimate Israeli aircraft converging on the flanks of the intruder began firing.

"It's an attack!" the rabbi shouted as he waved his arms. "Take cover!"

Inside the center helicopter, the terrorist squeezed the trigger and the strafing began. His twin fifty caliber machine guns mounted at the front of the helicopter peppered the courtyard, but the warning from the rabbi had come soon enough, and the scattering men did not provide one large mass of the enemy that the attacker could concentrate upon. Some were knocked down by spraying fragments of rock, but they bounced back to their feet, clutching an arm or a forehead, and continued their scramble for cover.

Before the enemy craft could pull up in his rapid flight, the bullets from one of the two Israeli 'copters found their mark, shattering the blades on the jet turbine, propelling them into the fuel tank, causing the whole craft to explode in a ball of white heat. The momentum of the dropping wreckage carried it over the temple wall and down into the Kidron Valley where it landed near the Ha-Ofel road.

From the Mount of Olives, just above the smoldering wreckage, a bush serving as camouflage for a shallow cave that had been cut into the mountain months earlier was removed and the shaft of a hand-held rocket launcher protruded from within the crevice. Another terrorist, who had hidden himself there for the last month, moved forward and the rocket launcher's tip jutted out still farther.

Through his scope he found the figure of the head rabbi who was conducting the construction. Once he fired the missile, he could control its direction. If the head rabbi should suddenly start to run, he could keep the cross hairs on him and the missile, tracking the laser beam, would follow his moving form. He clicked off the safety and took aim again.

Farther south on the Mount of Olives Captain Fischel scoured the hillside with his binoculars. If the helicopter that had just crashed several hundred yards below and to the north of him was the vanguard of the opposition's attack to stop the temple's construction, then another assault might be imminent.

It was then that Fischel saw the jutting tip of a hand-held missile, and he reacted so quickly that he startled the soldier standing at his side.

"What is it?" the other man yelled. But Fischel did not stop to answer; he snatched a machine gun from his side and whipped it into position, but before he could find his target in the scope, the Muslim warrior sent the missile rocketing across the gulf of the Kidron Valley. At the same instant, Fischel squeezed the trigger, throwing a barrage of bullets towards the protruding launcher whose scope was holding steady on the figure of the head rabbi.

One bullet nicked the launcher, jolting it to the right; the missile followed the path of the invisible beam that was directing it, causing it to veer far to the right of the city.

Fischel threw the sergeant the machine gun. "If you see anything sticking out of the side of the hill below that rock overhang, shoot it!"

He jumped on his motorcycle and hit the kick starter which jolted the motor into activity; he twisted the throttle hard, turning his back knobby tire into a blur, causing it to spew a torrent of mud and grass from under the back fender. Suddenly the tire caught some buried rock, accelerating it so wickedly that his bent arms were straightened from the thrust, and for a moment he was just holding on.

With the angry buzz of a chain saw, the bike streaked forward, with Fischel straining his back and neck upward trying to read the lay of the terrain.

He avoided a series of boulders by driving above them, then what he thought would be a gentle rise turned out to be a natural ramp which hurled him into the air, instinctively bringing him to his feet on the pegs to absorb the landing.

The clandestine cave was less than a hundred yards away now, and he could see that the launcher had been rearmed and was again jutting from the opening.

He heard the burst from the machine gun from behind him and saw the ground kick up all around the cave. Although no slug had found its mark on the launcher, the flying dirt from the bullets seemed to stall the attacker's aim, giving Fischel a chance to pull the gun from his side.

Veering to the left, he drove past the cave's opening from thirty feet away, giving him time to place six slugs into the darkness. He aimed at the space just at the end of the launcher. His aim was effective for the weapon dropped from sight.

Fischel turned toward his encampment and the sergeant he knew was watching with the binoculars, and gave the thumbs-up sign. On the Temple Mount the workers huddled under portions of the buildings and wall for fifteen minutes, still unsure that the offensive was over.

Half an hour passed on the Temple Mount before three Israeli soldiers appeared and approached the rabbi who had spoken to the workers before. They conferred for a minute and then the rabbi shouted to all the men scattered throughout the complex: "Men of Israel. Our soldiers have been victorious. The attack against us has been repulsed. Our soldiers will protect us now while we serve the Lord of Heaven. Let us go to work!" The men rose and shouted together.

That night Israeli television carried the story along with taped footage of the terrorist assault. All Israel rejoiced in their good fortune, while Arab leaders throughout the Mideast and the entire world condemned the construction of the temple, vowing to continue their war on all fronts.

XVIII

AT THE RIVER JORDAN

The day after the attack on the Temple Mount, Kyle went to the largest electronics store in Jerusalem and purchased a number of outdoor speakers and bought the most powerful amplifier he could buy. To those he added a generator to provide the power, and this system he began to mount on his jeep. It was while he was busy bolting the equipment in place from inside the jeep that Elisheba pulled up on her scooter. She was still nervous from yesterday's battle, and she glanced around and in the skies too, as though their mere presence outside was unsafe. When she finally took a good look at the jeep and all the modifications that Kyle had made, she was shocked.

"Kyle, what in the world are you doing?"

"My old radio just isn't carrying over the street noise anymore so I thought I'd boost it a bit," he answered, and then he laughed when he saw that she had actually believed him.

"Seriously, Kyle, what are you doing? I'd like to know. You've got something in mind, and it must be important. Why would you need four speakers of that size?"

"When the time comes, you'll understand the reason why," he said.

"Oh, I see. It's something from the scroll."

"That's right."

She was afraid to pry when it came to the scroll. "So it's something important then."

He pulled the ratchet wrench from the bolt. "It's very important. I'd say it ranks right up there with finding the ashes. But as I said, when you see me start to use this system, you'll know what it's all about. Until then I . . ."

"I know. You're not free to tell me about it. I understand. But that still doesn't stop me from being curious."

"Just be patient."

"I will, Kyle. I have no other choice."

He smiled and returned to bolting down the speaker.

She fidgeted a bit. "I came over here to tell you something."

"What's that?"

"I think I should be baptized."

He stopped working again. "When did you come to that decision?"

"I've been thinking about it for a long time. It's the right thing to do, isn't it?"

"Yes," he said, as he hopped out of the jeep and stood facing her, "but what about your family?"

"It will be tough on them, but it's something that I've got to do. Didn't Jesus say that he had come to 'to set mother against daughter.' I guess I'm an example of that. I'm willing to accept the consequences. I just don't know who should baptize me. Who do you suggest?"

"I know just the man," Kyle said. "His name is Peter Larsen. He lives here in Jerusalem. He's a great man—a true believer. He meets every Sunday with others who believe the same way he does. I know he'll want to talk with you. I'll call him and make the appointment."

Kyle did call Peter, and Peter in turn made contact with Elisheba, and they made plans to meet. For over two hours they sat at an outdoor café, and he probed her beliefs, and taught her, and afterwards she was to tell Kyle that it was one of the most spiritual experiences of her life. Kyle replied, "I told you that he was a true believer."

Elisheba met with Peter twice more before the day her baptism was set. At the final meeting, she told him she had a definite place in mind where she wanted to be baptized. She said it wasn't in the city, so they'd have to do a little traveling. When he heard of her choice, he was delighted.

It was a Saturday afternoon when she and Peter and Kyle rode out of Jerusalem in Kyle's jeep. For over thirty kilometers they headed east to the Jordan River, the place that Elisheba had requested. From the moment that Peter had said that her baptism must be done by immersion, just as the Lord had been baptized, she knew that she wanted to go to the spot where he had once stood.

They pulled the jeep off the road alongside a clump of bushes that were growing beside the river. Flowing nearby were the narrow waters of the Jordan. Elisheba jumped out quickly and ran to the gouged out bank etched by the waters movement and used one hand to hold onto a clump of grass as she climbed down the steep embankment.

She sat on her haunches at the water's edge while her white dress fell around her legs and touched the ground on all sides. The brownish green water moved slowly by her, following its erratic course through the lowest valley on earth, heading resolutely toward the Dead Sea.

Floating in the current was the fleshy leaf of a cactus, a sabra, that grew so prodigiously throughout the region. So much was the sabra identified with Israel that those born within the country were called Sabras. Half submerged, it looked like the severed tongue of some giant lizard.

Cupping her hand, she let it fill with water and brought it to her cheek where she splashed it, letting its coolness roll down her neck.

Looking up the river, she saw where it twisted from sight. Downriver it flowed longer in a straight line before suddenly veering to the left, disappearing behind the thick vegetation competing for space in the moist ground near the water's edge.

Soon the men joined her. Peter stepped into the water first. Elisheba removed her sandals and took his hand as he led her deeper into the water. The current was slightly slower there, having lost a little of its speed in the sharp bend immediately upriver from them, so it was not difficult walking, even when the water reached their waists. Fifteen feet from shore they stopped, and Peter took her hands and after uttering a prayer, baptized her.

That afternoon in the café off the Via Dolorosa where Peter and Elisheba had held their lessons, they celebrated her baptism. She was radiant with joy, and remarked twice during the conversation that she had never been so happy.

"You're feeling the Spirit of God, Elisheba," Peter said, "as he puts his stamp of approval on your actions."

"Yes, I believe it."

Shortly after finishing the meal, Peter excused himself. "I hope you won't think I'm running off. Tomorrow is the Sabbath and I'm in charge of the services. I still have a talk to prepare."

"You can count on us being there to hear it," Kyle said.

"All the more reason for me to prepare well. We start at 10 A.M. I'll see you then. Oh, by the way, the meal is on me. That's my last little gift on your special day, Elisheba. Congratulations!"

"Thank you," she said as she reached over to hug him as he stood next to her chair, and then he was gone.

"I have a gift for you, too," Kyle said, as he withdrew something from his pocket. Whatever it was, he held it in his closed fist in front of her face.

"What is it, Kyle?"

"Put your hand out and I'll give it to you."

She held her open hand under his, and slowly he uncurled his pinky and the other fingers up his hand until a diamond ring dropped into her palm.

Elisheba's hand began to shake, and she looked at Kyle to see if he were somehow kidding. His smile was of love and not of jest. He lifted his eyebrows as if to say, "Well, are you going to take it or not?"

"Oh, Kyle! You mean it! You really mean it!"

"Sure I mean it. I'm not the kind of guy to kid about something like this. I'm too old to mess around with your emotions. Of course, that's something you have to take into consideration before you put it on. I'm a lot older than you. They say that women outlast the men. You run a risk of being a widow for a long time."

Without another hesitation she slipped the ring onto her left hand. "I don't care about that. I love you. That's all that matters. I'd much rather live forty years with you than fifty-five with any other man."

"That's the right answer," he said as he leaned across the table and gave her a kiss that brought her to her feet, and the waiter that was just approaching with vanilla ice creams that Peter had ordered as he left was forced to stand by, holding the platter as the kiss stretched out. The patrons sitting at the other tables began to giggle. Elisheba lifted her ring finger even as she continued the kiss and pointed at it with her right hand which brought applause from everyone, including the waiter who had to set his tray down before he could join in.

Within a month of her baptism, she and Kyle were married. So it wouldn't be too hot, she scheduled the wedding at dawn in David's back yard. None of her family came, but she expected that, knowing how deeply her father had opposed her conversion to Christianity.

Although Kyle had no immediate family nearby, there were many friends among the archaeological community and they were in attendance. Rabbi Webberman from the Temple Mount Society was there, and so was Samuel Bernstein's widow. At Elisheba's request, Peter married them.

David was there, of course, and served as Kyle's best man. With his arm interlocked with Elisheba's, David led her through the well-wishers, over the ground that was covered with a strip of red carpet. Wearing a white tuxedo with a golden cummerbund, he walked slowly, matching her steps.

Remembering David's size from their days as roommates, Kyle had ordered the tuxedo, and he had it in his car when he picked his friend up at the airport, just a few hours before the wedding. Generally the tuxedo fit David fine, but there was a little tightness across the chest. Pumping iron had increased his size there.

Peter officiated at a brief ceremony, making reference to Paul's words in the New Testament about being yoked equally together as husband and wife. He referred to the couple's recent accomplishments. At the end, they kissed and their friends gathered around. David kissed Elisheba and gave her a hug, unknowingly lifting her off the ground in the process.

Afterwards, at the bottom of the hill, Kyle excused himself from the others and found Peter who had asked to talk to him. Reaching into his pocket, Peter withdrew a slip of paper.

"Here is the person you should call when you arrive in America ten days from now. His name is Jon Dawson. The day after you land, you'll be giving your first speech about the scroll and the things that you've learned. Here's the plane ticket. Jon is a wonderful guy. He'll put you up in his home. Oh, have you reconsidered about taking Elisheba?"

"No, I still think it might be dangerous. The devil will try to prevent me, and he might enlist the aid of Primavera or someone like him. You see it's known around the world that the ashes of the red heifer have been found, and that I was the one that pointed out where they were with the help of the scroll. When I tell people that according to the scroll the judgment is coming, there will be a lot of repenting going on. The devil is completely opposed to that. I'm a threat to his kingdom and how many people, in the final analysis, he'll drag to hell."

"I understand. I'm sure it will be a hard adjustment for you to leave so soon after your marriage."

"Yes. Well, we live in desperate times. It wasn't easy going into the villa either, but we did what we had to do."

"At that first lecture," Peter said, "you'll be speaking to a group of approximately three thousand in a high school auditorium that we've rented for the occasion. We were going to have you speak in one of our churches, but the number of people who wanted to come soon outgrew our capacity to seat them. Of course, that's just the first of several meetings, and Jon will have your itinerary when you arrive."

"I understand."

"Plans are still being made as to where and to whom you will speak. Ideally, you need some air time, and I know that he has at least one talk show lined up for you."

"I'll speak anywhere I have to."

Peter smiled. "I know you will. That's why God has called you. He has certainly given you a wonderful wife to support you during this time."

Kyle put his arm around his friend. "That he has."

THE DAY AFTER their marriage, Kyle and Elisheba moved into an apartment close to the Temple Mount where they could watch its construction. Each day after breakfast they climbed the stairs that led there, passing by the many security people who were stationed all around, who recognized them immediately. The couple had become celebrities throughout Jerusalem since their picture, along with David's, had appeared in newspapers and magazines as they held the urn of the sacred ashes.

Special badges were issued which allowed them to watch from scaffolding. Of course, they were not allowed direct access to the grounds, but the four-story-high platform gave them a good vantage point.

It was only a week later when Elisheba took Kyle to the airport to catch his plane. He tried to dwell on his return because talk of his departure upset her. In the last day before he was to leave, she had grown inconsolable.

Elisheba cried all the way to the airport. Even though he told her he didn't believe the trip would take that long, he could not give her a definite date when he would return, and that ambiguity bothered her greatly. She believed he was in danger, for she could not forget her fright in the villa.

"You won't put yourself in danger, will you, Kyle?" she said as she wiped a tear with her handkerchief.

"Don't worry. I'm not going to the villa."

Still she cried, but at that moment she remembered the jeep that Kyle had modified, which sat in the parking terrace under their apartment complex. Suddenly she felt much better. She realized there was something yet he had to do. He would return.

He was relieved to see her smile just as the announcement came to board the airplane. Giving her a final hug, he walked up the ramp. After finding his seat next to the window, he looked for her inside the terminal and saw her waving. Both their hearts were lighter as the plane taxied toward the runway, and when his plane lifted off, she was already resigned to being without him for a while, but the assurance he would come back made all the difference.

Kyle left on Friday, and he called the following Friday night.

"Any luck at the dig in Secacah?" he asked her. Having found the ashes there, they agreed that she would keep looking for anything else. The plates of the Ten Commandments and the Ark of the Covenant were still to be found, and they should be near the spot where the ashes were located.

"Nothing yet," she said. "There's not a sign that we're close to anything."

"Too bad."

"So what are you going to do next?" she asked.

"I've got several meetings in California this next week. These friends of Peter's are opening some doors for me. I'll be in Oregon after that." There was no immediate response on the other end.

"So when am I going to see you again?" she said.

"Well, I'll come home after Oregon. I can tell you that."

"I should hope so. I miss you."

"It wouldn't be this way if I could make it any different. You know that."

"I know," she said.

"But in the meantime keep working at Secacah. You'll be less lonely."

"OK."

"Is David still out of town?" he asked.

"Yes. For at least another week."

"You've got enough to pay Jacob haven't you?"

"I do, yes."

"How's he working out?"

"He's a pleasant man, and a good worker. We've been riding to the dig together. The three college students are doing fine, too."

"Good," he said. "You know how much I love you, and how hard this trip is on me, too, don't you?"

"I know. I just wish I could be with you," she said, and he heard her stifle a sob. "But I don't want you worrying about me. I'll be all right. Jacob is a good man, and Peter calls me almost daily to make sure that I'm OK. He and his wife come by and pick me up for church, but it's not the same as having you around. You know what I miss so much?"

"What's that?"

"Cooking for you. I enjoyed that so much. You were always so complimentary. I loved cooking for you. It made me happy."

"Well, when you get really lonely, cook me something, then you can just put it in the freezer, and I'll eat it when I come home, and I'll compliment you up one side and down the other."

"It's too long to wait," she said sadly.

During the first three weeks while he was gone, she arose early to climb the hill and check on the construction of the temple, then returning to her apartment, she waited for Jacob to come and pick her up in his jeep. Together they made the half-hour ride to Secacah.

XIX

The Martyrs

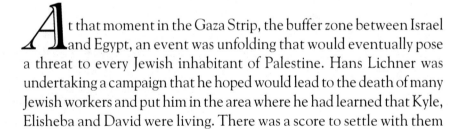

At that moment in the Gaza Strip, the buffer zone between Israel and Egypt, an event was unfolding that would eventually pose a threat to every Jewish inhabitant of Palestine. Hans Lichner was undertaking a campaign that he hoped would lead to the death of many Jewish workers and put him in the area where he had learned that Kyle, Elisheba and David were living. There was a score to settle with them as well.

He began his preparation in the Villa by studying maps and three dimensional models of Jerusalem and the neighboring countryside. He became familiar with the Mount of Olives, from where his attack would be staged, so even in his dreams he scrambled over the terrain that he would eventually be seeing.

When his training was finished, he dyed his hair and eyebrows black and put on makeup that gave him a Mid-Eastern look; then he boarded a plane and flew to Egypt. Two days later, undercover of night, he boarded another transport plane, supposedly part of an Egyptian paratrooper exercise, whose purpose was to practice jumps alongside the Egyptian/Israeli border.

There were over a hundred men involved in the exercise, all of whom were wearing camouflage green and makeup. A soldier recognized that Lichner was not part of their group, but when he began to question him, the commanding officer sitting nearby silenced him with an order to concentrate on his mission. Others who were sitting nearby quickly understood the stranger was off-limits.

In the cockpit, the pilot was uneasy. Just before taking off, he had been briefed on some new flight plans, and he didn't like what the upper-echelon brass had planned for him; instead of skirting the Israeli border, which of itself was an unpleasant act, they actually wanted him to fly over Israeli air space! The fools! It was easy enough for them to sit at their secluded desks and made a decision that might coast his life and the lives of anyone else on the plane. It was easy to be brave when death was no possibility.

Whenever these nighttime exploits were conducted, the pilot knew a call was sent to the Israeli air command, informing them that the Egyptian maneuvers would take place near the Jewish border. Then if Israeli radar surveillance picked up a plane straying into their airspace, they wouldn't shoot the intruder down. The Egyptian pilot knew it was always risky. Israel was justifiably paranoid about every Muslim in the world calling for their blood, and now his asinine commanders wanted him to provoke them. They were probably trying to measure the Israelis' response time during an encroachment on their borders—as if they didn't know what it would be already.

Then the pilot had a thought that made his hands tremble. He pulled at his thin, black mustache nervously. Suppose there was more to this than he had imagined. Maybe they weren't just trying to measure how quickly the Israelis could respond to a breach of one of their borders, but were actually trying to start a confrontation and his plane was the bait they were throwing to the sharks to get them to strike!

The plane approached the jump area, and the soldiers rose to attach their hooks to the jump line. Lichner, however, did not rise with the others. The sliding door was pulled back, and the commanding officer stood next to it. The red jump light flashed on, and he motioned the first man out of the plane, who was immediately followed by another and another.

When the plane was empty except for the officer, and a subordinate—who was filling out the forms for the night's activities—and Lichner, the plane veered northeasterly and assumed a route heading toward the city of Gaza. They held a course that kept the Mediterranean only four kilometers to their left, so if there was a sudden Israeli response before they could drop their passenger, they could swing out over the neutral space of the Mediterranean. And when they had flown along the coast for twenty kilometers, the pilot, following his instructions, suddenly veered inland away from Gaza and assumed a course toward the small hamlet of Seana. They were certainly being seen now. The confrontation with the jet fighters was inevitable as long as they stayed on this course; in fact, their audacity at flying so far inland might still be met with some belligerent actions from Israeli jets even if they should now turn and head out over the Mediterranean, but still they continued onward.

There was a modern road that passed just to the west of Seana and it was there that the pilot intended to deliver Lichner. From there he would be someone else's problem. Already the pilot was praying to Allah that he wouldn't be required to give his life tonight.

"Two kilometers," his co-pilot said to him, indicating the distance they would yet need to travel. The pilot frantically searched the skies for the sleek hulls of the American-made, Israeli planes. From the northwest he saw the first exhausts from the fighters. There was no longer anytime to wait. He pushed the button on his console that activated the red jump light in the cargo bay, and Lichner's face was basked in the bloody light. Instantly he arose and without attaching any cords to the pull wire overhead he leaped into black space, freefalling for over forty seconds before pulling the rip cord; out popped a black chute that kept him nearly invisible against the sky.

Above him he could see his transport plane turning in the direction of Gaza. Below him he could not see the highway by Seana where the rendezvous would happen. The overcast sky prevented the reflection of the moon on any portion of the road, and yet it should be somewhere beneath him. He strained for the lights of a car, but there was total blackness. Perhaps the pilot had panicked and sent him out prematurely, believing they had gone as far as they could. In any case, he would find the highway if he headed due east.

Lichner hoped his contact had not somehow been detained. If he was left stranded, Jerusalem was a long way off. True, he could stop a car, if any traveled along this isolated stretch, and take it over, but that would mean killing the passengers, and he was not anxious to start that kind of activity. If he had to begin killing now, there was a possibility that the real focus of his mission would be thwarted.

Lichner found the pocket over his left breast, undid the velcro catch and stuck his thumb and middle finger in carefully until he found the transmitter. His forefinger found the starting switch and flipped it on, and a red light pulsated on the top of the device. If his contact was out there, he should be picking up that signal. It would still be up to Lichner to make it to the road, but once he did, he should eventually be found.

Objects on the ground began to take shape. He could discern the black clusters of thorny bushes indigenous to the area. It would not do to land in a clump of those, nor did he want to careen off the jagged edge of some boulders. With less than five hundred feet to go, the moment for making a quick decision among this rocky terrain was at hand. He saw an opening between two rock ledges which were a couple of meters in height, and running parallel to each other like a natural hand-ball court. The floor between the rock ledges looked smooth, indicating few, if any, bushes growing there.

He pulled hard on his control cords which swung him around in a complete circle and slowed his vertical drop; then maneuvering his chute to the left to keep him from straddling the rock wall, he lined up his position and at the last moment yanked hard on both cords, flattening out his vertical fall so he landed by running a few steps.

He released his cords and stowed his chute in a cleft in the rock wall, which was concealed by some of the thorn bushes. He checked his transmitter to see if it was still flashing. It was. Shutting it off accidentally now would send the wrong signal to the man who was waiting to pick him up.

He took out a compass and oriented himself. To head directly east, he needed to climb the rock wall in front of him. To his side there was a section that provided a natural ramp which he easily scaled without having to search for a handhold.

At the top of the rock wall he could make out the white shapes of houses three hundred meters to the west. There wasn't supposed to be any housing around here. He wondered if the pilot had made some gross miscalculation. And then he reconsidered and remembered how quickly new housing was springing up all around Israel as waves of immigrants poured in. With the government's generous offer of free land for those who were willing to homestead it, a tract like the one he was looking at with about a dozen homes could be put up in a week's time. Turning right, he headed due east. Within twenty-three minutes he found the highway. A single pair of headlights moved slowly down the road as he approached, and he could hear the distinct shifting of a truck's gears.

He felt for his transmitting device and flipped it off, but only for five seconds, which he marked by observing his watch, then he restarted it and the red light pulsed dimly once more. That cessation of the signal for exactly five seconds was the signal for his future partner to pull back onto the road from whatever area in which he had secreted himself north of Lichner's location, and drive southwesterly until they met.

In the night Lichner would be able to identify the pickup vehicle, for among the headlights would be a single fog light, mounted beneath them. Within five minutes he saw the telltale yellowish glow, and he stepped into its path. The vehicle braked in front of him; it was a covered three-quarter ton truck, red in color with the logo that said, "Elishua's Tapestry Cleaning" on the side, and under the writing was a Persian rug with a picture of the Taj Mahal suspended in midair on a giant carpet.

Lichner walked quickly to the passenger side and let himself in. The driver whipped the truck around in the middle of the road and began the return route to his home in Jerusalem.

The driver was Elead Tfilah, a Jew who had secretly converted to Islam, and that was the value of his help in this operation. He was known in Jerusalem as a Jew, but at the age of twenty-one, he was given a copy of the Koran and was converted.

Because he still lived in a Jewish community, he couldn't afford the loss of business from the Jews who would shun him if they knew that he was no longer one of them. For centuries his family had cleaned the sacred furnishings of the holy buildings around Jerusalem—churches, mosques, synagogues—they all had tapestries or chairs or rugs that needed to be cleaned.

Sometime during the seventeenth century, one of his ancestors had discovered a solvent that worked wonderfully on such delicate items, and though some had tried to pressure various members of the Tfilah clan for a list of the ingredients, none had succumbed to the pressure and promises of financial reward. Somewhere in the life of every Tfilah boy, to whom the business was passed along, a solemn oath was administered by his father and grandfathers to never reveal the secret of the solvent, which was so marvelous that it left absolutely no mark on any fabric after it evaporated, and there were few stains that would not disappear under its influence.

When the demolition work began on the Dome of the Rock, Elead had decided that he must make a stand for his Muslim beliefs. He passed word along to other Muslims that he had access to the Mount of Olives through his work, and that he was willing to risk his life to retaliate against those who were desecrating the holy site. Eventually, the plan for sneaking Lichner into the country and placing him on the Mount of Olives where he could attack the Jewish workers was proposed and accepted.

Thirty-kilometers outside Jerusalem, Elead pulled the truck off the road. He checked the mirrors, and when he was certain that no one was nearby, he gave the signal for both men to leave the truck.

At the back of the vehicle Elead got down on his knees next to what seemed to be a spare fuel tank. He touched a hidden catch at the side of the tank and the back section sprang open. The tank itself seemed well used, with gasoline and grime covering the outside, but the inside was shiny clean.

Lichner surveyed his secret chamber. There were a half dozen holes in the base of the tank to provide air holes for him. He would have to bend his legs, but there was room enough for that, and he could still place his backpack with his rifle alongside of him. Still he didn't relish the thought of being cramped inside such a spot. They were a half hour from Elead's house, and the trip would be unpleasant.

"Isn't it a bit premature for me to get in now?" Lichner asked.

"You will find," Elead said, "that Jewish patrols will begin very soon. They are out in groups around the entire countryside within a thirty-kilometer range of Jerusalem. It would be best that you hide yourself now, in case any of those soldiers feel suspicious about us and decides to search the vehicle."

Lichner said no more but placed his backpack inside the empty gas tank, and crawled in and drew his legs alongside him, while Elead closed the hatch. Inside there was a little light from the holes below him, and he could see some fist-sized pieces of rock lying in the dust. When the truck began rolling again, Lichner's head jarred against the gas tank until he used his knapsack as a cushion.

The truck was stopped once before they actually entered the old walls of the city, but the soldier was familiar with Elead's occupation and he did not conduct a thorough search of the vehicle, using the dogs or the artificial sniffing devices, devices which could be even more reliable than the dogs. He did, as required by his orders, make Elead open the cargo bay, which was loaded only with a few rolled rugs. Afterwards, the soldier motioned Elead on into the city.

They drove to his small shop in the Jewish Quarter, and Elead backed the truck up to the loading dock at the back of his store. He stepped out of the truck and walked to the front of the vehicle to see if anyone was coming along the sidewalk. Finding the way was clear, he returned and undid the hatch on the fake gas tank.

They entered his small apartment which was attached to his business, and Elead showed his guest a cot placed in the corner of the room. Lichner took off his boots but did not bother removing his clothes, and then he lay down. He felt emotionally drained and was asleep in five minutes.

It was two days before the next step in their plan could be taken. Part of Elead's cleaning route was the Church of the Magdalene on the Mount of Olives. Three times a year he was asked to pick up carpets, chairs or tapestries that were in need of cleaning. One week ago he went to the church and carried away for cleaning several entrance way carpets and one valuable tapestry that hung in the baptistery. This was the day they were to be returned.

Lichner climbed into the tank, dressed in a blue work shirt like Elead's with a logo of the flying carpet over his shirt pocket. The plan was that Lichner would pretend to be a handicapped relative of Elead from America who could not talk. Because Elead had so many friends who knew his family intimately around his shop, they decided it would be easier to avoid questions if Lichner once again hid inside the gas tank until they reached the church.

Lichner was more comfortable this time because his head rested on a towel, which he had borrowed from Elead. Lying next to him again was the black case that held his rifle plus the pound of Semtex, the explosive of choice by terrorists. Semtex had been responsible for downing many commercial aircraft. Because it was not metal, Semtex didn't show up on an airport's x-ray machine, making it easier to smuggle aboard.

Twice they were stopped by military patrol units before beginning their ascent of the Mount of Olives. These officers were more careful now that the truck was approaching a militarily sensitive area. The dogs were used in both cases but the gasoline-coated tank successfully covered any odor of Lichner. Each time, he lay in the tank, barely breathing. At the moment the truck stopped, he covered the breathing holes by his head, too, with a piece of plastic, in case the snouts of the dogs poked through those holes. One dog's back rubbed against the tank, and he became very nervous, believing the animal was trying to point him out, but it wasn't so. There was, in fact, a little hesitation by the German shepherd around the tank, but the dog couldn't be sure, and the gasoline was so powerfully covering the smells that the dog made no fuss.

The soldier who was supposed to be watching the German shepherd might have noticed its slightly erratic behavior, but he was familiar with Elead's truck and his route among the religious edifices, and his disciplined nature had been dulled by the monotonous work of searching vehicles day after day. He should really have been relieved some time ago, but his superiors had more pressing matters, and the soldier had been forgotten. He waved Elead on.

Lichner felt the truck swing wide and then heard the downshifting of gears as it started the climb towards the Russian Orthodox Church of Mary Magdalene with its seven onion spires. These golden spheres clustered around the roof; the largest one, located in the very center, shone the most brilliantly, for the early morning sun had already bathed it.

Within a few minutes the truck pulled into the courtyard, and Elead hopped out. He walked to the back end and opened the cargo doors to help block the view in case anyone was watching from somewhere in the church. And then, with his foot, he touched the latch on the side of the false gas tank and the hatch dropped opened. Lichner climbed out, but he left his gun case within the tank.

Together they mounted the truck and grabbed the tapestry, which was wrapped in brown paper, leaving behind the two entrance rugs. As they picked it up, a priest appeared at the back of the truck and smiled up at them appreciatively.

"You said that you would have it done today, and you have kept your word. That is something very hard to find in today's business world," the priest said. "You couldn't have picked a better time to return it, for we are expecting visitors tomorrow from Moscow, and we would like the church to be at its very best." Lichner stepped down first from the truck, carrying his half of the burden.

"Are they coming to check out how you guys are doing here at your church?" Elead said.

"Yes," answered the priest still smiling. "Although they are a little early this year. I believe they are anxious to see the changes on the Temple Mount. We have a wonderful view from up here and a rather limited one lately with all the military activity. You probably had your share of problems in getting here."

"I'll say," said Elead. "I'm stopped at least twice every time and sometimes four times if I have to travel farther up to the Church of the Ascension."

"Who is your partner?" the priest asked Elead.

"He is a cousin from the United States," he responded. "He has come to stay with me for a while. Unfortunately, he cannot talk." Elead turned away from Lichner as though he meant to exclude him from the conversation. "He had an industrial accident in New York. A beam fell from a crane and struck him on the side of the head. It nearly killed him and now he doesn't think as well as he used to. He can hardly speak and has a lot of trouble remembering anything. He is a religious man and hopes that the holy city of Jerusalem might have a miracle for him."

The priest looked sad. He turned towards Lichner and spoke in English. "So you are from the United States?" Lichner nodded his head. "I will pray today and throughout the remainder of the week for you. I will pray that your prayers will be answered and you will receive help while you are in Jerusalem. On this mountain there have been a number of miracles that have happened. I will pray that you might be another of those miracles."

"Thank you," Lichner replied in English, feigning a slowness of thought.

The two men lifted the carpet to their shoulders and followed the priest inside. As they passed a spiral stairway, Elead pointed at it, indicating those steps as the ones Lichner needed to take to complete his mission.

In another room the men set their carpet down. Elead sent Lichner back to the truck for the tool box, pretending that the hooks in the wall upon which they were to support the tapestry were too weak to be trusted. At the truck Lichner unhooked the latch on the gas tank and pulled out his gun case, and then reentered the church, found the spiral staircase, and took the steps two at a time until he entered the circular, observation room of the onion spire.

He stood at the window that faced westward towards the holy mountain and felt his soul boil with rage to see the spot bare of the Dome of the Rock and rising in its place the walls of the hated Jewish temple. Kneeling, he placed the black suitcase on the floor next to the opening of the stairs and undid the latches. There lay a rifle in four sections—a barrel, the stock, the scope, and a silencer—all lying in the pre-molded, foam rubber patterns. He screwed the barrel into the stock, then took the two-foot long black scope and snapped it into place, and finally he applied the silencer. Then placing the weapon in his lap, he checked the safety and popped in a clip of thirty shells. Along the stock was a group of buttons and above it a small LCD screen. Lichner typed in a "500," which stood for the number of meters between him and his target. He pushed the "enter" button and on the diminutive screen appeared "ACCEPTED." Next he programmed the angle of trajectory, which was not severe because the Temple Mount was only slightly below him.

From somewhere beneath in the church, he thought he heard someone. Leaning his weapon against the side of the wall, he leaned over the stairwell and peered downward—nothing. There was no time to waste. He returned to his weapon, shouldered it, crouched by the window on both knees, and stuck the barrel out the opening, then placed his eye up to the scope. He placed the cross hairs on a wrecking ball suspended sixty feet in the air from a crane. The forefinger of his right hand found the button along the right hand side of the stock near the chamber, and he pushed it. In the scope appeared the word

"CALIBRATING." There was a pause of two seconds and the word" READY" replaced the previous message.

His forefinger found the safety button and he released it. He directed the cross hairs downward until they fell upon a Jewish worker who was mixing mortar.

"What are you doing?" came the passionate question from behind him. It was the same priest who had met them in the courtyard. Without really weighing the consequences, Lichner swung his weapon around quickly and squeezed off a round into the man's chest, and the muffled explosion dissipated quickly and without great volume.

The priest did not immediately realize that he had been hit, although he had heard the explosion. In the next instant he understood that he had been shot, but believed it to be a slight wound. He felt himself falling backward along the circular stairs. He extended his hand to catch himself on the railing, where he could rest awhile, but instead of stopping, his body crumpled downward, and around him it grew darker, making him wonder who had covered the window at the bottom of the stairs.

"I just need to rest," he said to himself. "Thankfully, I have not been seriously hit, because I don't feel bad. He has grazed me along my side. It's made it warm there in that spot, and it itches a little."

He lay on the steps and his legs were higher than his head, and he thought, "I can't believe that's my body. It's twisted, and yet I don't feel very bad. I must have fallen slowly enough that I really didn't notice." It was then that he saw that the light was returning to the room. "Whoever blocked the window earlier must have uncovered it now because the sun is shining in right on me," he thought. "Maybe they'll see that I've been wounded. I hope so, because I don't think I can stand up unless someone helps me."

The brilliance of the light grew, and he kept his eyes open to see its origin, for he couldn't remember that window ever being so bright. The brilliance intensified, and as it did, his soul filled with joy, making him believe that it really was a most extraordinary day, that he was happy to be alive, and that he completely forgave the man who had tried to kill him. Staring at the light gave him no feelings of discomfort, and he could face it directly, which he did, wearing an expression of contentment. When he exhaled for the last time, his eyes remained open, looking serenely ahead.

Lichner had not moved since squeezing the trigger. He recognized the man as the priest who had led them in, the one who was so caring for his feigned handicaps.

"I will pray today and throughout the remainder of the week for you," he had said to him in the courtyard, and there was no doubt as to his sincerity.

"Perhaps he was praying for me even as he was climbing those steps," Lichner thought to himself, and then he leaned the rifle against the window, and crawled to the stairwell and looked over the edge. There in a heap was the body with the eyes open.

Another priest passed through the room below, carrying a candle on a holder. The light fell on the face of the fallen priest and the man gasped. At first he thought the priest on the steps had tripped, but then he saw the blood, and as he held the candle nearer, the chest wound was obvious. Terrified, he quickly hurried out to report his hideous discovery.

Lichner stared blankly at the far corner of the wall, and then as if aroused by an unheard voice, he sprang to action again, lifted himself to his knees, and moved quickly to the window where he grabbed the rifle in a fluid movement and raised it over the ledge of the window. He could not see everyone who was working at the Temple Mount, for the city wall on its eastern boundary hid many who were working on the ground. However, there was an opening in the Golden Gate originating from the tremor that had damaged the Dome of the Rock, and portions of the wall on each side of the gate were missing, providing a gaping hole through which he could see many workers scattered around the northern portion of the temple. In addition, there were men working atop the rising edifice of the temple who would be easy targets. He would aim there second, for when the firing began, they would be the slowest in finding cover.

On the ground, Abraham Rosenfeld was pushing a wheelbarrow loaded with mortar destined for some stairs in the Court of the Gentiles. He was uncomfortable for he was twenty-five pounds overweight, plus he was wearing one of the lightweight bullet-proof vests that everyone was supposed to wear, although he had seen a number of men slip theirs off even before the sun rose as high as it was now. Only his promise to his wife, who feared daily for his safety, to keep the vest on made him wear it today.

There was no breeze, and the beads of sweat clustered together on his brow and cheeks where they eventually formed into larger drops that suddenly rolled down the front of his face. After one followed the curve of his lip into his mouth, leaving a salty residue, he stopped to wipe his face with his handkerchief. It was that cessation in movement that singled him out to Lichner.

The cross hairs of the scope were placed on the area to the left of Abraham's sternum and the trigger squeezed. In an instant the bullet flew across the Kidron Valley and struck him, knocking him hard to the ground on his back, where his head collided with a half-submerged rock.

Unconscious, he lay there as others became aware of his condition. For the handful of men who first saw him go down, most believed that he had slipped, but there were those who were constantly thinking attack who feared the worst, and they were already taking cover. One who assumed the worst, but who counted Abraham as one of his friends, darted to his side and rolled him on his back, even while searching for wounds.

While he was kneeling, Lichner placed the cross hairs on the upper portion of the man's back—at the place where it should penetrate his heart—and squeezed the trigger again. An instant later the bullet struck with such force that the shirt stretched over the protective vest, shredded around his back in strips, and the worker was knocked completely over Abraham's body.

For the dozen men who had initially gathered around, there was no doubt as to what was happening, and they scattered in all directions.

Lichner did not worry about the moving targets for there were other men who stood nearby who were not aware of the danger. He started to move the gun to the right, when he noticed Abraham sit up. Lichner was certain the shot had been on the mark. Through the scope he studied the chest area—there was no blood.

"They've got vests on!" he said out loud. "Let's see what a head shot does." Those men who had witnessed the first attack were now yelling wildly and waving their arms from behind whatever protection they had found, and others were dashing frantically for cover; meanwhile, Lichner worked at keeping Abraham's head in the middle of his sights, for his head continued to waver back and forth. Though the shot had not penetrated the vest, the blow to his chest area had been considerable, breaking two ribs, but it was the blow to his head after striking the ground which caused him to rock erratically, making it difficult for the gunman to draw a bead on him.

If Lichner's compulsion for finishing jobs had not now dictated his actions, he might have let Abraham go and concentrated on other stationary targets. Even the worker who was struck in the back was pulled to safety, but Lichner again pulled the trigger, while trying to follow Abraham's bobbing head. He incorrectly anticipated a movement that didn't happen and saw the ground behind his victim's head pulverize into a cloud of dust.

The incident with the priest had upset Lichner more than he had imagined. His judgment was faulty, and he was taking too much time in between shots, wasting time on a target that was difficult. By this time, he should have already fired a dozen rounds and should have had an equal number of bodies to show for it.

Abraham's senses finally cleared, but there was a trickle of blood to verify his head injury. He heard the shouts of his fellow workers and realized his danger. He turned on his side and began rolling as quickly as he could. Lichner rapidly squeezed off three shots, two of which missed completely—though one struck so closely to Abraham's face that his mouth and eyes were filled with dirt. He did not stop his rolling, until the third bullet caught his thigh muscle, passing through the tissue and emerging again, before burying into the ground.

For an instant, his motion was paralyzed, and in that state, Lichner might have finished him off, but below Lichner came the voice of his partner. "Lichner! We must leave right away! A truck is coming loaded with Israeli soldiers!" The discovery of the priest's body earlier had shortened the amount of time he had to complete his mission.

In frustration, Lichner snapped his head back to the scope—Abraham had rolled his way to the protection of the wall. Lichner turned the gun to the top of the temple and looked for bodies there. The screaming from the ground sent everyone scrambling for cover. A few stragglers were making their way across the support beams for the roof. Without taking careful aim, Lichner fired a dozen more shots at anything that moved. Whether he had actually hit anyone, he could not tell. One man seemed to fall off the far edge.

"Lichner!" came Elead's voice from below. Lichner shouldered his weapon and ran down the stairs, leaping over the body of the dead priest. Both men ran out of the church; Elead bounded into the cab while Lichner undid the latch, dropping the fake wall on the gas tank, and slid his rifle in butt first. He climbed in with his head facing the rear end of the truck; he slammed the covering back into place, concealing himself and pounded twice on the gas tank—the signal to leave. He felt the transmission being thrown into gear; the truck jumped forward and raced down the steep incline of the Mount of Olives.

The road cut back and just as they made the turn, Elead saw two military trucks. At a hundred meters, the trucks stopped and a dozen men climbed out carrying weapons and hurried next to the road bank to keep themselves out of the line of fire. Elead slowed the truck and stopped completely, twenty-five meters away. Lieutenant Fishel, who had earlier stopped the terrorist on the Mount of Olives, walked quickly toward Elead, crouching near the ground, using the embankment to protect him from the sniper that was firing above them. He called the names of a half dozen men who fell in behind him and together they crawled toward the truck, while Elead sat behind the wheel with the sweat beading on his upper lip.

"What is the problem?" he asked as the soldiers drew near but remained hidden from the view of the Church of Mary Magdalene by the bushes growing alongside the road.

"We've had some firing from somewhere here on the mountain," said the lieutenant after recognizing Elead and his truck as frequent visitors on the Mount of Olives. "Did you hear or see anything?"

"No," Elead responded.

"I'm afraid I'm going to have to search your truck," said the lieutenant. "Please, pull it over against the side of the road here, behind those bushes, so we're out of the line of fire."

"Have you got a sniper?" asked Elead and the lieutenant nodded. Elead put the truck in low and drove where he was requested, then swinging his door open, he dropped to the ground and walked to the back. He undid the double doors and pulled them back slowly on their large hinges. Then he stepped aside for the inspection.

The lieutenant motioned a young soldier, who was always anxious to respond to his commander's request. He moved obediently, an ideal soldier whom the lieutenant had taken a fancy to. In fact, the young boy reminded him of his younger brother, killed long ago during a terrorist raid near the Lebanon border. There was no place to hide other than the rolled rug, so the young solder began at the length of it and pushed down with his foot periodically until he had checked it out. He turned to his commanding officer who motioned him to come down.

"You're free to go," the lieutenant said to Elead. Nodding gratefully, Elead closed the doors and climbed back into the truck. Lingering behind while his soldiers returned to their transports under cover, the lieutenant scanned the hillside for any sign of the sniper. He walked up the road where there was an open view, keeping his body inside his last bit of cover.

The report said that the sniper might be hiding in some vegetation just above the Church of the Magdalene, and with his binoculars he studied the area. Turning to the transport trucks, he saw that they were loaded and motioned them on.

Elead was nervous and did not clutch well as he attempted to get the truck moving; his foot slipped clumsily from the pedal, making the truck lurch forward. Lichner's body slid several inches inside the slick tank and his head bumped the hatch at the back, knocking it open. At that moment the lieutenant glanced at the retreating truck and saw Lichner's form, his face protruding from the spare tank, and the barrel of his rifle. Dropping his binoculars, he jerked his gun from its holster and fired a shot above the vehicle.

The transport trucks were just passing Elead's vehicle and the lead driver had no idea why the officer was firing his gun. He pulled so quickly to the side of the road that several men inside were thrown to the floor.

Elead gunned his truck and raced down the road, while Lichner wrestled to get his rifle into place. The first man out of the transport was the young officer who had searched the vehicle. He was perplexed as to the commotion and spun around, hearing the lieutenant's command to stop the truck. He was just dropping his rifle from the sling on his shoulder when Lichner fired, killing him instantly with his first shot.

The young soldier was wearing a vest, too, but Lichner was head-hunting now. The lieutenant leaned against the side of the transport truck and emptied his clip into the back of the receding truck, but the bullets from Lichner's rifle pinned him down, and he could not take accurate aim. Other soldiers joined in firing their weapons, but they believed the enemy was inside the truck, and they riddled the doors and the cargo bay with holes.

"Aim at the gas tank!" shouted the lieutenant. "He's inside the tank!" Another man was hit and spun around in a complete circle before crashing to the ground.

The truck was out of range by now, and the lieutenant ordered the trucks to turn around in the narrow road. While they were changing directions, the lieutenant looked after the two men who were shot.

Both were dead. The young soldier, whom he had taken under wing, lay still at the edge of the road, his face hideously red. In a fury, the lieutenant boarded the lead truck, shouting the driver onward, and, yanking the microphone from the radio within the truck, he called ahead and described the renegade truck and Lichner's position under the truck.

Elead was terrified, but he believed it was possible to escape if he could get within the city walls where he might duck into a side street, abandon his truck and get away on foot. He pushed the pedal to the floor. His calf muscle ached with the strain of pressing so hard against the floorboard.

They turned south on the Ha-Ofel road, at the base of the eastern wall of the temple, and sped through the Kidron Valley; the troops monitoring their movement could have opened fire on them anywhere along the route, but a roadblock had been laid just where the road rounded the southeastern edge of the Temple Mount. Waiting for the truck there were tire shredders, placed by a squad of solders who were now hiding along the road, some behind tombstones.

Inside was the fake gas tank, Lichner was appraising the situation much more realistically than Elead. He knew that there was no escape route, and he had resigned himself to death, but it was the form that it would come in that tormented him. He waited at every moment for an explosion or a bazooka blast that would blow the truck to smithereens.

"Perhaps they would not try such an attack," he tried to reassure himself. "These are holy grounds, where many dead have been buried. Perhaps there is a funeral going on right now where people could be hurt."

The army was doing as much as it could in the brief moments they had to secure the area to remove any civilians. Some who were walking among the tombstones along the Ha-Ofel road in Elead's path were herded away by the soldiers and forced to take cover behind a convoy truck. Others were ordered to hide behind some tombstones. From the opposite direction, a jeep was placed across the road near the Dung Gate and all traffic was stopped.

A group of tourists stood on a hill nearby, where they had climbed the grassy knoll to touch the southeast corner of the old city wall. There were six couples, husbands and wives. For years they planned this trip, and now they were seeing the outer wall of the city and recording it with their video cameras. For the last ten minutes, the Americans had followed the wall. They were light-hearted and there was much laughter as the women had all relieved the men of their cameras and were taking pictures of them. Finally, they tired of the joke and, still giggling, passed the cameras back to their husbands. At that moment, Elead's truck made the bend, its inside wheels almost leaving the pavement. The six couples heard the screech of tires and turned as one to see the speeding truck. The woman, who had first yielded her camera to her husband, pointed at the red truck with the flying carpet and told her husband to quickly get a picture of the reckless vehicle. Some of the other men also trained their video cameras on the racing truck.

No sooner had the taping begun than the truck ran over the shredders, and there were the quick, loud bangs of exploding tires. Elead hit the brakes and the truck began to waver; he overcorrected and the swerving increased until the vehicle rolled, to within fifty meters of where the tourists were standing.

Elead climbed out of his truck, his face bleeding at the bridge of his nose where he had struck the steering wheel. He started to run, and several soldiers who were emerging from their hiding areas, shouted at him to stop. He thought that if he could only get to the Dung Gate and get inside the city, there would still be a chance for survival.

He had not run more than ten seconds when a single shot brought him down, and he fell forward with his hands at his sides, making no attempt to break his fall. The women among the tourists screamed and drew near their husbands.

Racing down the Ha-Ofel came the lieutenant in his transport truck. The soldiers who had just shot and killed Elead were not aware of the gas tank, and the lieutenant knew that he needed to act fast, before the assassin opened up on those who might be gathering around the truck. He hopped from the truck with his pistol drawn while the soldiers poured from the back. They ran towards him, but he raised his hand and stopped them. Lichner, who was momentarily knocked unconscious by the rolling of the truck, pushed open the back hatch, and slowly pulled himself out until he was kneeling on the ground. He stayed there for a moment while his head cleared, then stood up. For the first time, he saw the lieutenant and the others standing nearby. He looked back toward the tank and saw the protruding barrel of the rifle and wondered if he could take one more of them with him before he died, but gave it up as foolhardy.

He hoped that some of the workers he had shot at on the Temple Mount were dead. At least he could take consolation in the death of the soldiers a minute earlier. The lieutenant was thinking about those soldiers as Lichner faced him, knowing that if he arrested this terrorist, he probably would be taken to a prisoner-of war-camp and maybe exchanged for the next Jewish fighter pilot whose plane went down behind enemy lines. The thought that this man might possibly walk free again someday was more than he could endure.

Lichner raised his hands and walked toward the lieutenant who watched him coldly. Somewhere at the back of the lieutenant's neck he felt a charge of pure emotion that seemed to spill into his blood and heat it to the boiling point.

"This criminal is pleased with what he has done!" he thought. "He knows he will soon be in a camp with some of his own kind, bragging of the lives he had taken today!" He raised his gun and fired three quick shots into the Lichner's chest whose eyes widened as much from the surprise of the soldier's action from the pain of the bullets striking him.

The soldiers behind the lieutenant were stunned; one yelled the lieutenant's name in horror at the cold-blooded nature of the deed. But there were those who sympathized with the action and shouted with joy to see the murderer of their friends so quickly dispatched. Meanwhile, the video cameras of the Americans continued to grind, recording the execution. They did not see Lichner's weapon that was hidden in the gas tank, and they knew nothing of the killings that had taken place earlier. The Americans were outraged and when they were finally spotted and driven back into the city to their hotel, one man took his tape and passed it on to a network correspondent who had a room in the same building.

Less than two days after the deaths on the Ha-Ofel Road, the Muslim world was fomenting itself into a terrible rage. The pictures of the deaths of the two men continued to be played on television again and again, and the commentaries accentuated the cold-blooded nature of the crimes, indicating in some accounts that they were run off the road, and then brutally shot. The commentators said that both men were Muslim, although Lichner was not, and that a possible motivation for the killing was the illegal nature of being found in a restricted area on the Mount of Olives, and for that they had been ruthlessly killed.

Somehow the rumor mill in the Mid-East, fueled by the Arab satellite channel, Al-Jazeera, which failed to report the death of the priest in its coverage of the events, had decided the two men had been on the Mount of Olives because of their devout feelings in wishing to see the holy place where their sacred mosque had once stood. Soon the status of the men had risen to that of religious martyrs, slaughtered for their profound faith.

XX

Under Attack

Terrorists' attacks increased throughout Israel: bombs exploding aboard loaded buses, gun fire spraying in the middle of crowded streets, innocent families being gunned down in parks—the tension became extreme. Within a month of the deaths on the Ha-Ofel Road, Egypt launched the first full-blown attack.

Elisheba was working at the dig in Secacah where the ashes of the red heifer had been found. She wouldn't allow the threat of renewed fighting to keep her from finding the rest of the temple items: the staff of Moses, the Ark of the Covenant and the shewbread must be found and placed in the new temple. She was with Jacob and other workers when the air attack came. A squadron of Israeli jet fighters flying directly overhead, streaked towards the southeast. In the other direction came their enemies. The clash occurred just at the edge of the Dead Sea and within moments the first dogfights ensued—twisting, dodging, running, pursuing—the combatants maneuvered adeptly in the sky like so many enraged swallows. Here and there the waters of the Dead Sea erupted as a damaged plane plummeted into its depths, sending up huge plumes of water. Elisheba and the others watched in rapt amazement, shading their eyes with their hands, as the planes and missiles streaked across the sky like an incredible video arcade game played from horizon to horizon.

An Israeli F-16 took a blast in its engine. Shrapnel ripped through the plane; one fragment pierced the canopy; another piece caught the twenty-one-year-old pilot in his side, knocking him momentarily unconscious. As he slumped forward, he leaned against the controls, turning the nose of the plane downward. The cold air rushing in from the hole revived him, and he awoke to find his seat coated with blood and his plane plummeting towards the brackish waters of the Dead Sea. He tried to take the wheel with both hands, but his right arm wouldn't respond; a piece of metal had lodged itself in his shoulder, cutting a crucial nerve.

With his left hand he took the controls, but they responded sluggishly; a hydraulic line was severed, and the reddish fluid darkened the lower hull like a lethal wound in the giant bird. Gradually the pilot pulled the nose of the plane upward, slowly altering its plunge into an upturning arc; but the earth was coming too fast, and the pilot could not yet see the blue sky of the horizon. Saving the plane was not possible. Even if he could avert the initial impact, there would be no returning to base.

He checked his shoulder harness, felt the chin strap on his helmet and hit the eject button. With an explosion the seat catapulted into the rushing air that struck him with the force of a heavyweight's blow; that, coupled with the loss of blood, made him black out again. As he foresaw, the arc of the jet was not sufficient to save the plane, and it crashed just beyond the tent where Elisheba and the men sat, sending them diving to the earth as a fireball rocked the ground and a repercussive wave of heat and wind tore the canvas tarp from its moorings.

Elisheba was stunned momentarily, and then jumped to her feet. To her right was the burning wreckage; overhead she saw the still form of the descending pilot, suspended from the billowing chute. She was close enough to see his head slumped on his chest. Then in horror she saw that the breeze was carrying the pilot in the direction of the burning plane.

She sprinted after him, yelling to the others as she went. "You men, help me! Help me!" she yelled at the top of her lungs and without breaking stride. Within seconds the seat, still holding the pilot, landed on top of the tail section, which was burning savagely from the jet fuel that had splattered over it. The seat with its limp cargo bounced to the side, thudding hard on the ground just outside of the flames.

With its burden released and now played upon by the convection currents generated from the flames, the chute spun to the side and collapsed on the ground away from the fire. Meanwhile, the pilot, still enclosed in his seat, lay near the intense heat of the flaming wreckage.

Elisheba ran up and grabbed the nylon chute and tried to pull him from the fire, but the combined weight of the body plus the flight seat was too much. She lost her footing and went down on her back, only to spring up again to grapple with the cords once more.

The men joined her, grasping the chute wherever they could find a handhold. The chair began to slide across the ground, gouging a furrow in its wake.

Quickly they gathered around the fallen figure while Elisheba undid the buckles that held him to his seat, and Jacob removed his helmet. His flight suit was smoking along his elbow and shoulder, which had had the greatest contact with the heat from the flames. Thankfully his face was not burned. She saw the blood splattered down his arm and side, and, examining his suit, found a tear in the garment from which the blood pulsated.

"Put him in Jacob's jeep! We're taking him to Jerusalem!" she yelled over the sound of the dogfights above, and she made the first move at lifting the pilot herself. The others hastened to help in carrying the body. At the jeep, she leaped in and slid the seat back as far as possible.

"I'll take him," Jacob said and he shifted his arms up the wounded man's body until he held the entire burden, then leaning over, he placed him inside over Elisheba's lap so she could staunch the flow of blood. Then he hopped in the driver's side and the jeep sped down the road.

THEY CAME BY land and air, and the Israelis met their attack, flying the Joint Strike Fighter, made in America. With their vertical take-off capability, the Jewish pilots sprang from the ground, meeting the enemy as soon as radar picked up any movement in the skies surrounding Israel, pursuing their jets at supersonic speed.

On the ground the Egyptians sent 500 vehicles. Leading the way were 100 M1A1 tanks from the United States, followed by 300 Russian tanks and 100 armored personnel carriers. Because Egypt had been the best armed of all the Arab countries for years, they asked for and got the honor of leading the initiative against the Zionist infidels. Together the fighting units rushed towards the northern edge of the Suez Canal. Satellite reconnaissance had seen them from the outset. By the time the push towards the canal had begun, 400 Israeli tanks—top of the line Abrams—were already advancing toward the same location.

Although the Sinai Peninsula was returned to Egypt as part of the Camp David agreements, Israeli leaders vowed that they would not allow the Egyptians military forces to cross the canal, viewing that waterway as an important barrier, which could prevent the quick deployment of enemy vehicles across Israel.

The Israelis were already crossing the Egyptian border, sprinting over the Sinai. The amassing of Egyptian troops since the killings on the Ha-Ofel Road were provocation enough. The lesson of the '73 war had been learned well. In that instance they had waited too long, hoping to swing world opinion their way as they waited to be attacked, but that strategy cost them dearly in fatalities, finally exposing the Jewish military machine as vulnerable.

But it soon became apparent that there was more to the Egyptian strategy than just a straight forward attack at the northern part of the canal, because ten kilometers south of the main unit, another force of 400 tanks appeared from out of Egypt and began a drive toward the canal. Moving, as they were, just south of the larger force, they were in position to attempt to cross the canal, or they could move quickly to the north and join the ranks of their comrades, bolstering their forces.

To counter that threat the Israelis sent a second battalion of 300 tanks rushing westward with an arrival point directly across from the second Egyptian unit. Though they threatened a crossing, unmanned drones, so important to the surveillance capacity of the military, confirmed that an Egyptian crossing was impossible. A pontoon bridge had to first be erected, and no support vehicles capable of carrying a portable bridge were traveling with the second unit. In the larger detachment to the north, however, there were several such vehicles, if enough protective cover could be provided to allow them to form the bridge.

While monitoring a drone, the Israeli Command noticed another development twenty kilometers to the south of the second Egyptian unit: a dozen trucks were seen to be moving toward the canal. If these trucks did contain a portable bridge, the Egyptian's second unit might suddenly veer southward, making a break for it, hoping the bridge would be ready by the time they arrived. If such a move wasn't countered, they could quickly be over the canal and on their way towards Jerusalem.

The Command radioed the potential threat to the Israeli second unit. They understood that there might be a dash towards the south, and if it turned into a race, they must not allow the Egyptians to arrive first. Of course, they realized that the gathering trucks in the south might be a diversion intended to draw away some of their forces, while the Egyptians' second unit suddenly sped to the north to join their comrades in a crossing there. And so, like chess masters, the Egyptian and Israeli command centers moved their pawns.

Overhead, the aerial fight continued—twenty-five minutes had passed since the first shot was fired—a long time in jet combat. Across the West Desert billowed the black clouds of those planes already destroyed. Here and there blossomed the parachutes of pilots who, having escaped the cockpits of their damaged planes, were now floating dangerously downward.

Even as the Egyptian F-16s were being pursued, they took advantage of the parachuting Israeli pilots who floated into their path, firing at them. Some of the bodies were limp, their heads tilted downward onto their chests, as they floated toward the desert floor.

On command, the second Egyptian force veered northward as if to unite with the main division, and immediately the Israelis took steps to parry the tactic by turning their own machines northward. Minutes later those same Egyptian tanks just as quickly veered southward, making what seemed to be a mad dash for the transport trucks, which had abruptly picked up speed, rushing headlong toward the canal to erect the pontoon bridge.

The second Israel unit reversed their directions, too, and pushed their tanks at their greatest speed, gobbling up the distance between them and their opponents, thundering along on the opposite side of the canal only a few kilometers away, gradually overtaking them and pulling ahead. Those at the Israeli Command Center saw that the Egyptian ruse had failed. It was clear they would beat the Egyptians to the rendezvous point where they could blast the pontoon bridge out of the water before any vehicles cold cross.

The real worry continued to be the action in the north where the Egyptians' main force was obviously going to try and fight their way across the canal by driving back any resistance. In this kind of combat, the American and Russian tanks they were driving would prove more than capable. Loaded with the latest electronic gadgetry and armor piercing shells, long ago installed in the tanks from the West, they felt they could go toe to toe with any military force. Only the tank-killing helicopters, the Apaches and their counterparts, could stop them from achieving their objectives. Those flying killers could release a missile from miles away, and the newer American copters could shoot behind a mountain or ridge and watch on radar as the missile was guided by satellite tracking systems into the enemy without ever being in danger of taking fire themselves. To avoid these savage machines, the

Egyptians were counting on their air force and their own helicopters to keep the Israeli dogs at bay.

Some fifteen kilometers behind the advancing Egyptian tanks, hundreds of thousands of Egyptian soldiers were assembling. There they waited for the break in Israel's defense that would allow them to cross over the Suez on the same bridges use by their tank divisions. Then they could begin to reclaim all the land lost during the conflict of 1967—land taken by their enemies before their soldiers had even been born. Their fathers and grandfathers had instilled in their bones the necessity of one day reclaiming the land that was robbed from them.

The Israeli tanks sped southward, opening a distance of over a half-kilometer between them and their enemies on the opposite side of the Suez. Intelligence reported the trucks in the south had begun unloading the segments of bridge and had even linked some together on the western side of the canal. At the speed the Israeli tanks were traveling they would easily arrive before the bridge was completed.

It was at that moment that ten of the Egyptian tanks suddenly slowed from the battalion and pulled to the side as the rest of the tanks, although slowing slightly, continued ahead. Their movements were met with very little suspicion. Those watching through the eyes of the drones believed the heat and the terrain, and perhaps the inexperience of the troops were somehow causing some of the vehicles to falter.

The tanks that had been left behind slowly ground to a halt, black smoking belching from several of the machines. It seemed clear that they were disabled and so the drone that was following them was redeployed farther north where several squadrons of planes from Syria and Jordan were entering Israeli air space to aid the failing Egyptian force.

Some of the soldiers exited the tanks and began to look at the vehicles as though they were attempting to fix them. Then suddenly they jumped back in their tanks and barreled toward the canal, where, at the spot they were approaching, was only 200 feet across—as narrow as they could have picked. One by one the Egyptian vehicles ground to a halt with a deep rumble.

None of the Israeli command noticed that the ten tanks, which had lagged behind, differed from the other tanks. Their cannons, although the same length as their counterparts, were not functional, a detail impossible to see even from a drone. The rest of the vehicle bore the aspect of a tank—there were the tracks on each side with the steel shoes and the driving sprockets on the ends—but the hatch portion was bulkier, fully as long as the tracks themselves. They were also wider by a meter.

Explosive bolts detonated on all ten vehicles simultaneously, and the false cannons dropped away. At the same time there was the hum of hydraulics from within the vehicles and two metal plates resting on the top began to move apart, one towards the front and the other towards the back. In less than one minute each vehicle had extended its surface area above it over twenty-two feet, like a metal canopy. Hydraulic lifts appeared from within the vehicles like the arms of an octopus, supporting the farthest edges of the metal canopy.

Four soldiers from each unit, dressed in sand colored fatigues, making them more difficult to spot from the air, suddenly emerged and waited for the next action. The transmissions of the vehicles were thrown in gear, and they maneuvered into place so the pieces of metal highway could be united together. The soldiers climbed onto the tracks to secure all of the individual platforms into one large one, 222 feet long, by dropping short rods through the overlapping holes. There was some maneuvering to line up the individual holes, but this was an exercise that had been rehearsed repeatedly in the last months, all within enclosed airplane hangers.

The remaining Egyptian tanks lumbered onward at a speed that made the Israelis believe they were still trying to reach the pontoon bridge, but slow enough to keep more tanks from dropping out of formation. Or maybe they had slowed down in an effort to give their disabled vehicles some time to make repairs before rejoining them. Still the Israeli unit surged southward towards the floating bridge.

Meanwhile, the coupling was completed. The driver in the lead vehicle gave the command, and as one giant centipede it crawled toward the canal, and upon reaching the water's edge, there was no hesitation as it glided in.

The shell of each vehicle was essentially a large pontoon, giving buoyancy to the bridge resting on its back. With its tracks now useless, they ceased to turn, but a propeller, protected by a recess on the under carriage, dropped downward and began to turn. This action coupled with the thrust of each of the remaining vehicles still on land pushed it ahead.

One by one the vehicles slipped into the water, and the entire structure quickly spanned the 200 feet of water. Just as the tracks of the last vehicle were sinking in the water, the tracks of the lead vehicle crawled ashore on the eastern banks of the canal. There was a hum of hydraulics as both ends of the bridge anchored themselves. Underwater, telescoping poles with stabilizing feet emerged from the underbellies of the machines, descending to the bottom of the canal, where they seated themselves on the floor. Four supports came from each tank, holding the units in place, preparing them to take the weight that would soon thunder across them.

INITIALLY THERE HAD been relief at the Jewish headquarters when they saw the apparently disabled tanks drop out of formation, believing there would simply be ten fewer tanks to contend with. Stopped along the edge of the canal the way they were, they seemed harmless. Having set their trap, the Egyptians radioed the secret code to the tanks. Abruptly, the tanks pivoted on the desert floor, sending up a billowing cloud of dust, till they had reversed their direction, the cloud itself acting as a cover for their maneuver.

Finally, the Israeli command saw the deception and radioed word to their units that were now several kilometers ahead of their opponents that they should turn around. As a group they countered the Egyptians with their own 180-degree turn, retracing their own tracks.

In the north the first Egyptian unit all at once abandoned any pretense at crossing. Their convoy made a ninety degree turn to the right and sped off toward the second unit in the south and their hastily laid bridge. The Israeli front lines that had readied their cannons, preparing to annihilate those who would first cross the canal, were caught with their mouths open. The standoff they had been expecting was suddenly nonexistent. Then the word passed through thousands of headphones simultaneously, ordering them to give pursuit.

It was then that the jet squadron from Jordan arrived at the canal. Their air force split in two, half flying northward to harass the Israeli battalion, still laboring to make up the distance between them and the first Egyptian unit, and the other half broke off as a single entity, going in the opposite direction to pick off the tanks coming from that direction.

Inside the Israeli tank division, the movement on the desert floor was flattened out by the advanced suspension systems of their superior vehicles. At that moment, bristling within their headphones came the clear message from headquarters that the Jordanian planes were zeroing in on them.

"They will be within range within two minutes," said the usually cool voice that was now edged with some anxiety. "Take evasive action and defend yourselves." On the newer tanks, the unmanned, anti-aircraft guns spun around facing the north, guided by satellite systems, they were already taking a bead on the incoming planes. For the older models that still required a soldier to pull the trigger, the men climbed the short ladders which led to the outside guns, banging against the interior in their haste to make the top, sometimes losing their footing, as they struggled to open the hatch and until finally, they grasped the handle of their machine gun. Some had not yet emerged when the first jets struck, launching their Hellfire II missiles.

Despite the signal jamming effort thrown up around the Israeli tanks to counter the smart missiles homing in on them, one rocket made a direct hit on the second tank in the pack, sending pieces of it skyward in a white, flaming ball. The jamming was having an effect for the lead tank had been the real target. Another command crackled in their headphones, ordering the tanks to spread out. A moment later another Hellcat pulverized the ground twenty feet from the nearest tank that was only shaken by the explosion. Affected even more was the trailing tank which swerved to avoid the crater, but caught part of the hole with its right track, throwing men from their seats and across their instrument panels.

The Egyptian Air Force, whose job it had been in the battle plan to keep the majority of Israeli planes occupied while the Jordanian and Syrian planes attacked, were at this time completely routed. The victory freed Jewish fighter planes to come to the aid of their land forces, which they did in a swarming pack like hornets shaken loose from their hive. The incoming Jordanian planes were the first to feel their wrath. Never had the Sinai Peninsula been bombarded with so much destruction. The cacophony of bombs, missiles, exploding tanks and hurtling jets reverberated throughout the mountains of Palestine.

Two hundred and twenty kilometers to the southeast, a group of Bedouins, who had brought their camels to drink on Saudi Arabia's side of the Gulf of Aqabah, were startled by the low flying jets just launched by their country. The camels bawled and pulled at their tethers while dozens of animals, which were not tied, scattered in all directions. The planes, which streaked to give battle to the Israelis, had been purchased from the United States with the stipulation that they would never be used against the Jewish state, but all promises and treaties were abandoned in the turmoil of battle.

There was a chance that such action could mean a severing of friendly relations with the United States, but for the new leader of Saudi Arabia, it was time to rejoin the ranks of his brother nations. He was willing to risk any embargoes of technology from the West to punish Israel for what it had done at the holy spot where the Dome of the Rock had once stood.

The Saudi planes did not go towards the Sinai. Their flight plan was civilian targets in Israel along the coast of the Mediterranean Sea. It was simple: if the Israeli force prevailed too quickly against the Egyptian Air Force without suffering a predetermined number of casualties, then the Saudis would draw them away by moving on their cities along the coast, avoiding the holy city of Jerusalem, forcing the Israeli planes to pursue them to the north, freeing up the tanks for the Suez crossing.

As they tracked the Saudi planes, the Jewish commanders soon realized that that part of the enemy force was not veering to the west, but were continuing northward toward possible civilian targets. That left them no choice but to pull two thirds of their planes out of the dogfights over the Sinai Peninsula and send them in hot pursuit after the civilian threat, which at the moment seemed destined for Beersheba.

Twenty kilometers from that destination, the Saudis veered hard away from Beersheba, flying almost directly westward toward the city of Kirya Gat. Years before it had been a wasteland, but it had become a sanctuary to a wave of immigrants pouring into the area. Several other cities were targeted, but Kirya Gat took the first blow with air to ground missiles. A grain storage facility and a tractor supply outlet were struck first, blowing up as though they were loaded with dynamite. Several more missiles struck in the downtown complex, driving people to cover.

The squadron continued westward toward the beautiful resort town of Ashkelon, lying on the coast of the Mediterranean. The lead planes could already see its white, sandy beaches when the first missiles were launched at some of the prominent buildings. They collapsed in rubble as the momentum of the planes carried them over the sea, banking hard to return to rake them again.

Picnickers who were barbecuing and resting in their lawn chairs at the national park at the northern edge of the beach were shattered from their reverie. A father out with his five, young daughters herded them toward shelter with his arms outstretched around them like a mother hen with her brood, forcing them to take refuge behind the base of one of the monumental Roman statues as the Saudis rocketed by so close to the ground that it was impossible for the girls to hear their sisters screaming.

Several Mig-21s let loose with a barrage from their twin-barrel 23mm guns which strafed the park, shooting through the trees at a man and his wife who were running hand in hand. They were dead before they hit the ground, while sheared branches and leaves tumbled downward, shrouding their bodies in a blanket of green. The planes covered the air space above the park at mach 1 firing all the while. They riddled the huge blocks of the 3500-year-old Hyksos city wall that enclosed the entire area, peppering it with holes from their guns and cannons. Once more they flew over the city, firing at everything that moved, killing some who were fleeing the burning buildings.

After finishing their second run, the Saudis saw the advancing squadron of Israeli fighters on their radar screens, streaking towards them. This was according to the plan—to draw away the Israelis jets from the action around the canal and then engage them until sufficient time had been given for a massive crossing. Still, there were many of the Saudi pilots who were wishing even now that this direct confrontation could have been avoided. It was clear from the number of Israeli planes that the Egyptian forces—even with their training in the newest of planes—had not been as successful as they had hoped. The sun reflecting off the Jewish planes was a frightening sight indeed.

The Israelis spread out quickly, constantly communicating as they singled out their targets. For the Saudis, much had changed since their enemies had dominated the skies over the Mid-East. Now, they believed they were their equals, and with Allah's help the battle would tip in their favor. There was no turning to run, but only a determination to fight with a courage that would make them heroes in their homeland or, if required, in the world to come.

At the Suez Canal the Egyptian tanks arrived first and began crossing the bridge, rumbling over the water one after another. Quickly they spread out in all directions, forming a semicircle. As other tanks joined them, they filled in the gaps, stopping with their cannons pointed outward, ready to provide a cover for their comrades who would yet come.

From the north came the first signs of the Israeli tanks, hundreds of engines straining against the drag of the desert sand as they pushed their units onward. The Egyptians tracked them on their monitors, waiting for them to come within range of their big guns. The United States Global Hawk flying at miles overhead could see the bombardment about to begin and radioed the Israeli Command Center with the facts, and so, nearly at the same time, the tanks from both sides opened fire. The on-board computers in the Israeli tanks immediately began evasive action, protecting their crew from direct hits, as much as possible, while at the same time throwing out a barrage of shells from their 120mm cannons.

A group of forty Egyptian Fah-240 armored vehicles had already rumbled across the bridge and turned southward with their 4-wheel drive capability moving them quickly over the bridge and out of fire from their own men, where they could take a position to attack the Jewish vehicles that were rapidly approaching.

Following the armored vehicles were twenty Chinese Type 90 tanks, each weighing forty-eight tons. The portable bridge strained against the earth sides on each bank of the Suez Canal where it was anchored as several vehicles added their combined weight during the crossing. They turned northward instead, taking the battle to the enemy division coming from that direction, and still the bridge continued to rattle as the vehicles surged over it.

One driver among those Chinese tanks, negotiating his way over the narrow span, felt his nerves fray at the sight of an F-16 coming directly at him, knowing that a missile could be released at any moment. For too long he looked upward before realizing in horror that his tank was suddenly overturning. His tracks had wandered over the edge of the ramp, allowing it to drop into the canal. It sank very fast. A minute later the head of a soldier bobbed in the canal, gasping for breath, but the driver never surfaced.

In a string of remarkable shots by the Israelis, nine Egyptian tanks took direct hits, one just as it was leaving the bridge, and its burning debris clogged the passageway, making it impossible for the vehicles behind it to continue. The entire crossing ground to a halt, leaving the tanks stopped on the bridge in a precarious position—sitting ducks where they couldn't even defend themselves, for they were told that the bridge was not capable of holding a tank recoiling from a cannon shot.

The tank immediately behind the wreckage swung its gun over the water to protect it as it rammed the burning vehicle, butting the obstruction forward, hoping to push it into the canal. The wreckage slid for a ways, then caught on something and rolled on top of the tank that was pushing it. For an instance the flaming mass of metal balanced on its hatch and gun, then tumbled into the canal.

Another tank on the bridge was hit. The missile struck so solidly that the portion of the tank that wasn't immediately blown away, rolled over into the water, leaving the pathway unobstructed.

Lumbering down the western side of the canal came the vehicles of the Egyptian first unit. They could see the cloud of black smoke that rose from around the bridge. In the north on the Israeli side of the canal the dust cloud from their tanks drifted upward, and soon the two clouds intermingled, throwing up a haze over the bluish green of the canal.

It was clear the Egyptian tanks of the second unit would all traverse the bridge before the larger unit arrived, and those units that had already gone across were filling in the vacant space in the semicircle of defense.

On command many of them swung towards the north and began firing at their enemies approaching on the eastern side. The amount of shells thrown up by such a large contingent was a fearsome sight as they pounded the position somewhere far in front of them, hoping to slow their adversary until the eastern side of the canal was filled with more Egyptian tanks than Israelis.

When that bombardment began, the Israelis turned their own cannons on the enemy on both sides of the canal and returned the fire while still on the run. There was a concerted attempt to blow up the bridge, but the submerged pontoon vehicles provided very little target for tanks so far away, and the Israeli Air Force had successfully been kept at bay, which under a lesser attack, could have easily taken it out. Consequently the bridge remained intact and the first Egyptian unit, although slowed by the fire from behind them, approached the installation and began the perilous crossing.

Rushing from the south came the Egyptian trucks with the sections of portable bridge that were used as a decoy. They pulled near to the main crossing where their tanks were rolling across—many traveling too rapidly on such a narrow bridge, fear of the attacking Israelis having clouded their judgment.

One hundred and fifty men jumped from several vehicles and began pulling the conventional pontoon bridge from within the hatches of the trucks, dragging it to the ground, then maneuvering it to the water's edge. One by one they hooked them together like so many segments of a giant worm, extending it over the water. Working so close to the other bridge, they came under heavy fire, and as they concluded their labors, numerous men floated face down. But the second bridge was finished and another row of tanks rumbled across.

The constant artillery pounding kept the Jewish tanks at bay, allowing their adversaries time to swarm over both bridges. Over 300 tanks had filled the ever-widening semicircle, throwing up a virtual wall of shells and ground-to-air missiles at incoming Israeli planes. That cover had kept the two bridges intact and had now placed enough of them on Jewish territory that they could began the next phase of the attack. On a sudden they broke across the Sinai toward Israel's heartland with no intention of stopping once they reached Jerusalem. If all continued as planned, the Holy Land by sunset would again reside in Muslim hands. Trying to halt that advance was a pack of Israeli killer drones, firing air-to-ground missiles at the invading tanks.

A Jewish detachment of tanks left the ranks of their main squadron and pursued the marauding Egyptians. It was their commander's hope that they could slow down their enemies until they were joined by reinforcements. The enemy tanks in front of him were many more than he commanded, but he would do his best and he was praying that the God of Abraham, Isaac and Jacob would yet perform another miracle on this patch of ground where his forefathers had so long ago wandered before entering the Promised Land. Today they desperately needed such a miracle if they were going to maintain the land that they believed He had given to them so long ago.

At the same time the air battle over Ashkelon was providing a portion of that miracle. The rigorous selection process that years earlier had chosen the Jewish pilots was now paying off. Having picked the best and the brightest among their Jewish youth had translated into a superior performance in the skies over their homeland, for the Saudis now found themselves outnumbered. Once the tide had turned, it flowed very rapidly. A Saudi plane under the pursuit of two Israeli fighters stood very little chance of escape.

Within the national park alone, seven Saudi planes lay smoldering, each having left a violent gouge in the earth when its end had come. One crashed into the huge blocks of the Hyksos wall and punched a hole through it. On the white beach a little ways away, the sand, saturated with jet fuel, was burning, and in the middle of the flames protruded a charred Saudi jet. Two hundred yards out on the rolling waves of the Mediterranean, a parachute bobbed on the surface like some gigantic jelly fish, but there was no sign of the pilot, who had been a poor swimmer.

Here and there around the countryside lay the scattered wreckage of so many planes, and the majority belonged to the Saudis. The successful Jewish force now turned their attention to the Egyptian tanks rolling across the Sinai, already twenty-five kilometers past the bridge crossing. In minutes the Jewish planes had skirted the edge of the Mediterranean and streaked over the Sinai Peninsula.

At the sight of those jets, the Egyptians soldiers in the tanks—some so confident they were riding with their hatches open and their heads exposed—believed the planes to be the Saudis, returning to soften up the land in front of them as they rolled on toward Tel Aviv. The invaders had not grasped that their enemies were descending upon them. The Egyptian Command, though aware of it, had withheld that knowledge so their men would not hesitate in obeying the command to press ahead.

When the onslaught came, there was no cover for the tanks among the barren sand and rocks. Cannons and machine guns were fired from every tank. Ground-to-air missiles, intended for a bombardment of Tel Aviv, were used now. The battle raged for another twenty minutes, until the majority of the Israeli jets were forced to break off to return for fuel. Still, the Egyptian vanguard of tanks and armored troops carriers pushed on across the countryside.

All the while, at the Suez Canal the crossing continued, helped now by the addition of a third and fourth bridge. Like army ants swarming toward the untouched vegetation of a new land, the vehicles invaded the eastern side of the canal, joined now by units from other countries who had sent many of their own men and weapons to hide secretly in Egypt, so they could be part of the invasion when the time was right. Having crossed one of the four bridges, they fanned out, rolling across the Sinai toward an Israeli city. They would drive them out of their habitations or kill them.

XXI

FLIGHT TO JERUSALEM

J acob kept the pedal to the floor on the straightaway, removing his foot only when the turns threatened to overturn the vehicle.
   Elisheba sat in the back seat, but leaned forward to monitor the life signs of the pilot. He was breathing steadily, but was still unconscious. A burned piece of skin had pulled away from around his neck directly under his chin.

   The pilot had a pleasant face, round, with small lips that seemed to turn slightly upward at the corners as though they were used to smiling. His eyelashes were long and dark. His face was smooth, but she could see that he was capable of a heavy beard, for the pores were dark. His nose was perfectly straight like some Etruscan statue, but it had been singed along its right side.

   She turned her attention to the wound in his side. It was impossible to tell how bad it was with his uniform so covered with blood. "Do you have your knife, Jacob?" she asked, and without letting his eyes leave the road, he leaned on his left hip, pulled it from the front pocket of his jeans and gave it to her. It had only one blade, which she quickly unfolded. Taking hold of the bloody flight suit under the pilot's injured side, she sawed back and forth, cutting through the material, exposing his rib cage from his armpit to his waist.

The wound was not as big as she expected, more like the end of her finger, but the blood was still flowing. She knew she would have to stop it if he were to survive the next half hour on the road. She looked around the back of the seat for a towel or a rag to use as a compress, but there was nothing. She turned again to the pilot and used the knife to cut away a strip of his flight uniform, which she folded into a pad. After applying pressure for several minutes, she saw the blood on his side had dried from the breeze with no sign of fresh bleeding.

"How's he doing?" Jacob asked while stealing a quick glance at the wounded man.

"I think I've got the bleeding stopped," she answered. The jet fighters streaked past them. In between those deafening moments of man-made thunder, there was relative peace, which allowed Jacob and Elisheba to hear something else which had previously been indiscernible—there were occasional whistling sounds that seemed to begin at one part of the horizon and cover the whole expanse of the heavens very rapidly, until they had faded away.

"What is that?" Elisheba asked after hearing two such sounds. "Are they missiles?" Before he could respond, there was an explosion on the hillside three kilometers away on their left. A yellowish cloud erupted from the explosion and began to slowly billow upward.

Jacob braked the jeep so quickly that Elisheba was forced to throw her arm over the chest of the pilot to keep him from pitching forward into the dash. The jeep pulled to the shoulder of the road, bouncing and lurching from side to side as it skidded to a stop.

"I can't believe it," Jacob said. "It's not possible that those animals would do such a thing!"

"What is it?" she asked, so distracted by his distress that she momentarily relaxed her pressure on the wound and some fresh blood rolled out from under her fingertips.

"It's chemical warfare," he shouted from anger and fear. "They're using a super cannon." He reached in the back on the floorboard and grabbed the box that held the two gas masks and handed her one.

"That stuff could kill us in less than a minute."

She remembered the pilot and pulled the mask away from her face. "What about him?"

"We only have two gas masks," he said. "He might die anyway, Elisheba. The smart thing to do is to try and keep ourselves alive."

She took her mask off. "I'll put my mask on him. I can't sit back and watch him die."

"Neither can I. Here. Take my mask. If I start to go under, you better be ready to grab the wheel. If I feel anything, I'll try to get my foot on the brake and slow us down before I go out. But you get hold of this wheel." She nodded her head stiffly as he yanked the jeep back onto the road.

Elisheba considered what she had done. Jacob was her friend and a family man with children to support. This pilot probably wasn't married. It would be better that he died than Jacob. She pulled her mask away to tell Jacob that she had changed her mind. "Jacob!" she shouted over the wind.

"Put that mask back on!" he yelled angrily.

Fortunately, a breeze was moving the cloud in a westerly direction—away from them. He pointed at the explosion. "The wind is helping us on that one, but if one hits to the east, we'll be driving into it."

Jacob wondered about the condition of Route One. It ran parallel to the road they were using as it hugged the Dead Sea, but eventually it veered westward toward Jerusalem, crossing their path less than two kilometers ahead of them. They would have to take it.

A moment later, he crested a hill and saw the road in front of them. A blue car was moving rapidly towards Jerusalem.

"So the road to Jerusalem has escaped destruction," he thought, "at least on this segment." They flew past the Muslim shrine known as the Nebi, standing erect, as yet untouched by this conflict, but the battle was very close. The existence of this shrine, like many holy places, was in peril.

Route One intersected their path, and he slowed enough to make the left turn onto the highway. Elisheba cradled the pilot's head in her arm for a moment to keep him from pitching to the right. Just as they rounded the corner, they saw the strike of another binary shell to the northwest, less than a kilometer away. Jacob applied the brakes forcefully and pulled to the shoulder of the road.

"Can we make it past before the wind blows it across the road?" Elisheba asked.

"I don't know," he answered, while he looked for some indicator of the wind.

There were so few things that grew. If only there were a tree standing between them and the explosion, he could gauge it.

From the south came the rumble of an approaching jet flying perilously close to the landscape. Elisheba turned first to see it streaking across the barren plain, heading toward them. It was a very old jet, bought decades ago, and saved for the time when it could be used against Israel.

"Jacob!" she screamed, but his hand had already made the move toward the shifter, jamming it in reverse, popping the clutch so all four wheels of his jeep simultaneously spun in backwards, forcing Elisheba to drop the bloody compress and simply hold onto the pilot. The jeep fishtailed off the road just as two piercing rows of bullets left a line of craters across both highways.

In the air, the Libyan pilot cursed his poor aim, but his speed had already carried him to another target—a blue Ford sedan. There was no veering or sudden stops this time. He smiled at the image of the unsuspecting driver who believed he had nearly made it to the safety of Jerusalem's walls, only to be pounced upon here.

The pilot bit his upper lip, as he did whenever firing, and saw the tracer bullets of his antiquated jet chew up the road behind the car, overtaking it in an instant, ripping through the trunk, roof and hood and sending it careening into the ditch, where it veered off the rock embankment and overturned, rolling twice before coming to rest on its top.

The enemy pilot glanced over his shoulder to watch his handiwork. He had a smile on his face, but it didn't remain for long. He had pushed his luck by pursuing cars this close to Jerusalem. A host of Israeli planes, American-made F-15s, each carrying four sidewinder missiles, were protecting the holy city. Two swooped down on the Libyan craft, and although he pulled the plane quickly to the right, two missiles struck him at nearly the same time. The pilot had desperately groped for his ejection controls, but failed to activate them before he was obliterated.

Jacob hunted the skies for another jet, but the immediate danger was the chemical cloud drifting toward the road. Maybe they could beat its arrival. The safer way would be Route One until it intersected with Route 90, which led to Jericho. Most likely Jericho would not be a prime target during this war. It was then that a binary bomb struck on Route One, less than half a kilometer east of them. The road to Jericho was out. Jerusalem was their only chance now.

He slammed the shifter into first, turned sharply to the left and pulled onto the main highway again. The cloud that threatened to block their way towards Jerusalem was spreading faster than he had initially estimated. The wind was pushing the toxic cloud in front of it like some gigantic amoeba stalking the countryside. If they did not make it in time, he would have to try and hold his breath, but would he be able to keep his eyes open? Not likely. These kinds of gases attacked the tissue like fire. Skirting the edge was improbable for the area ahead on Route One wouldn't allow him to leave the highway to any significant degree.

At that moment the bombardment escalated. Three other explosions occurred in quick succession, farther toward Jerusalem—two on the northern side of the road and the other to the south. Jacob knew that more than one big cannon had to be involved for them to hit so rapidly.

Jacob thought of his family. "I wonder if my wife and children are safe? My wife has worked so much with the children, they would know what to do." But then he remembered how his twelve-year-old boy Peter liked to play soccer and would often roam the streets looking for a neighborhood game in progress when no one was available near his home. "Maybe he was too far away to make it home," he worried. "And yet he is bright and fast. Certainly, once he knew there was an attack he would know to go home. But then again, if the gas entered the city quickly . . . Oh God," he prayed under his lips, "please, protect my family."

Approaching on their right was the blue car, an Alfa Romeo, resting on its top with one of its wheels still turning. Jacob could not withhold the wish that the person had died, for what could he do to help, then regretted the thought as cowardly. What if there were a whole family inside with injured children?

He pulled the jeep off the shoulder of the road, and ran to the car. The driver was obviously dead, suspended upside down fastened in his seat belt, still wearing his gas mask. He moved to the other side of the vehicle, looking towards the sky—the bulk of the cloud was no more than fifty meters away, but the invisible vanguard might be much closer.

The door would not open, bent within its frame. He stood back and kicked hard at the side window, causing the already broken glass to haze over in a thousand cracks. Another kick caved it in and the third blow from his heel punched a hole through. He kicked once more, spraying fractured pieces of the glass over the body of the driver, where some of the pieces lodged in his black hair.

Instantly, Jacob pulled at the mask, felt the straps catch on the man's chin, then pulled them away from the back of the head; he had the mask in his hands and for an instant he fumbled with it—was the caustic smell in his nostrils the advancing gas or the remnants of the accident? Finally, he had it over his head and the rubber straps locked in place over his nose and mouth. Taking one more quick glance in the back of the car for any other riders, he raced back to the jeep. The air around them became murky as the gas wafted over them. He put the jeep in gear and once more sped down Route One towards Jerusalem.

They moved past the crest of the Red Ascent and saw the lethal clouds of many explosions around them—perhaps thirty or forty. The vapors of some shells had struck sometime before and spread until they united into one huge haze. Other clouds remained tight and compact, indicating a short time had elapsed since their detonation.

Four kilometers farther, they passed the apartment complex of Ma'aleh Adumim. Tragedy was all about. Children who had been playing in the level areas outside the row of apartments had not all made it to cover. No, nor had some of the mothers who ran from their homes in panic to find their children while failing to bring the gas masks. About the ground lay the dead—some mothers and children still holding hands. Their jeep followed a sharp turn, opening to them the view of a small Roman Catholic Church near where Lazarus was raised from the dead. A portion of the building's wall had crumbled.

The Jericho Road turned abruptly north just outside of Jerusalem. Driving on the edge of the Kidron Valley, they could see the golden walls of the temple still standing, rising above the walls of the city. They made a sharp turn onto the Ha-Ofel and followed it, entering in at Zion's gate on the southern portion of the old wall where all obstructions had been removed to allow easy passage for those seeking shelter.

There they saw a contingent of soldiers and a large hospital tent bearing the insignia of the Red Cross, set up in a spot in the sacred city where they had hoped their enemies would not bomb. Stopping the jeep in front of the tent, they were met immediately by four men who lifted the wounded pilot from his seat. They carried him in without a word of thanks and that was the last Elisheba and Jacob saw of him. Desperate times had strained common courtesies as people concentrated on surviving. Jacob pushed down on the gas and the jeep lurched forward among the wounded still being carried in on stretchers.

XXII

Among the Faithful

On the same day as the battle, Kyle was in New York, speaking to a group of men and women. All of them had been invited through the grapevine of believers to hear his words. They sat spiritually enraptured by his plain, conversational style as he talked of things he had experienced while recovering the scroll and shared the knowledge he had gained during its translation. They all understood that they were expected to pass his words on, to help in the preparation of that which was to come.

As he drew to the end of his presentation, there was a knock at the door. He was interrupted by one of the organizers of the meeting, a thin woman with kind eyes, who said a man whose name was David urgently needed to speak to him. They planned on having lunch together after his meeting, but something obviously had come up.

"It's begun," David said as Kyle stepped into the hall. "There's an all-out assault against Israel right now."

"I thought I would have a little more time," Kyle said.

"So, what are you going to do?"

"I've got to get back to Elisheba, and there's something else I need to do. But first I must tell these people in here that I've got to go."

"Listen," David said. "I have a car. We'll go to the airport."

Kyle stepped back into the room, explained the situation, and encouraged them to spread the word. Minutes later he climbed into David's red Porsche, and his friend whipped them into the traffic.

"You can just drop me off at the airport, you know, David."

"I know, but I'm going with you," David said while gripping the steering wheel firmly with both hands.

"I think you're making a reckless decision."

"That's pretty much the way I've conducted my whole life," David said. "I might as well stick to the pattern. But how are we going to get there? There won't be any planes flying anywhere in the Mid-East."

"We'll have to get as close as we can," Kyle said.

THE PLANES WERE stacked over Leonardo Da Vinci Airport at Rome with all the flights diverted from the Mid-East. Kyle and David's plane circled for forty minutes before receiving permission to land. They went to a phone, and David made a call.

He stepped from the phone booth. "Maurizio will sell the seaplane, but we'll have to drive to Tivoli to meet him."

They rented a car and drove out of the airport, passing the statue of Leonardo da Vinci balancing a spiral device on his finger.

"How far away is this Tivoli?" Kyle asked.

David swung the Ferrari around a slower moving car and pulled in front it. "Oh, twenty-five miles, as I remember. We'll be there in less than an hour. We could do much better but much of the road is curved, so we can't open this baby up. Have you ever been to Tivoli Gardens?" Kyle shook his head. "That's where Maurizio is today. He's a photographer, working with a model in the gardens."

The road twisted as David had said. The countryside was beautifully green from the storms traveling inward off the Mediterranean, but Kyle was in no mood to appreciate it.

Soon Tivoli was in front of them, a city built on the edge of steep cliffs, and perpetual waterfalls crashed on the rocks below. A brisk breeze created swirling mists along the rock face, pushing the cascading water into heavy curtains that drifted slowly upward, concealing a portion of the bluff.

They motored through the narrow streets—streets designed for small carts and wagons centuries earlier, but now contending with cars and buses.

Souvenir stores were abundant even before they reached the gardens, and there were the familiar street kids who moved toward the car like swarming barracuda whenever they realized a tourist had entered their domain, hoping they could catch their prey at a stoplight and convince them to buy something.

The lights were in the Americans' favor. David soon parked the car, and they entered the gardens. Passing the wall of a hundred fountains and then veering to the left, they found Maurizio, kneeling at the pool of the Oval Fountain, trying to make his model relax. Maurizio was a heavy man, of nearly 250 pounds, much of which was centered in his stomach, thus preventing him from getting too close to anyone.

His model was a Corsican, a brown-skinned beauty, with coal black hair and thin lips, but at the moment her lips were shaking from the cold as she stood dripping in her white bikini. Maurizio was trying to coax her to wet her body in the fountain again, so he could take a picture of her lying on the ledge, but she refused.

"You are a model. A model is an actress. You must pretend that you are enjoying yourself—that you are Eve in your own Garden of Eden."

"Is that really going to make her warm, Maurizio?" David said as they approached.

"Oh! My good friend! How nice it is to see you." They embraced and kissed on each cheek. Introductions were made, and the model took advantage of the break to grab a beach towel to warm herself. Her actions had nothing to do with modesty, for she was not so inclined.

"So, David, you have finally decided to buy my seaplane. Was it your uncle who convinced you?" Maurizio asked with raised eyebrows.

"Not really, but he will be excited when he learns I have it."

While they worked out the arrangements and the check was being signed, the Corsican girl intentionally stepped close to Kyle, but he did no more than smile curtly. She was disappointed when he showed no interest.

After the final handshake, Maurizio gave directions to the lake where the seaplane was moored. David was familiar with the spot so the directions were short. They shook hands again and left so quickly that the model suddenly felt inadequate standing there in her bikini, wondering if there were something about the way that Maurizio had applied the lipstick that made her less than desirable. She never regained her confidence, and half an hour later the day's shooting session was called off.

Kyle and David entered the city of Terni, lying in the most picturesque of spots, a beautiful azure lake at its doorstep and surrounded by rugged mountains. A marina jutted from the shore, and there among the various boats floated the black seaplane.

Kyle loaded their bags into the hull while David conferred with two officials who stood on the bank and examined the bill of sale. They were leery of someone other than Maurizio taking charge of the plane, but everything seemed to be in order. They allowed David to join his partner, but one of the men rushed through a hurried phone call to Maurizio, who was lounging disgustedly in his apartment after the fiasco of the day's photo session. He confirmed the sale and thanked the official for his consideration.

The plane moved easily through the water making a slight wake, sending up a mist that covered the picture window of the lodge where the two officials were watching its departure, now considerably more at ease. When the craft was well clear of the shore and any snags lurking in the shallow depths, David pulled back on the throttle and the lake reverberated with the angry blare of roaring pistons; the plane skimmed gracefully over the surface and the pontoons lifted from the water; the wings bent slightly as the plane's weight transferred to them; suddenly the wake ceased and they were airborne.

They crossed the Italian peninsula leaving the mainland at the city of Brindisi. Tipping the plane slightly to give a better view of the city, David looked for a narrow road that led into the city and ended at the harbor. There it was—the Appian Way—the ancient thoroughfare which began in Rome and traversed the whole of the country before ending here at the sea. He had been on it many times with his parents and his uncle. The sight of it made him nostalgic, and he suddenly felt sad.

Ahead of them were the Mediterranean and several hours of flying before they were over Israel.

XXIII

Back to Israel

Normally, the seaplane, the Blackbird, could never had violated Israeli air space, but the clash that had commenced over the Dead Sea had spread across the entire country, and even in the most obscure parts of Israel it was possible to look upward and see the battle raging. Those in the Israeli air command were doing their best to send their remaining forces against any new wave that crossed their boundaries, but at times they had to sit helplessly when more enemy planes were spotted because all of their planes were engaged. It was during one of those frantic moments that the Blackbird approached the coast. Although it was detected on radar, it was correctly analyzed as a non-military plane and ignored for the moment.

Initially Kyle and David planned on setting the plane down in the Mediterranean, but the advance enemy flotilla had stationed itself off the coast and was shelling Tel Aviv and other towns. Israeli ships were returning the fire, and the water in between the warring factions churned with flying shrapnel. If they set down, they were certain to take a hit, so the decision was made to go inland.

The Blackbird broke over the border ten miles north of the destroyed city of Ashkelon and changed course slightly to a more northeasterly direction, heading towards Secacah. It was possible that Elisheba and the others were still there; they could set the plane down in the Dead Sea and then hike the short distance to Secacah.

Barely ten miles into the interior an Iraqi fighter with an Israeli jet on his tail shot past them, then cut in front of the Blackbird in an obvious attempt to use them as a shield. The pilot of the Israeli craft, who had already fired the last of his missiles, had placed his finger on the trigger to his two 30 millimeter cannons, and the unexpected evasive maneuver caught him by surprise, inadvertently sending a barrage across the Blackbird before he could release his finger. Something struck the plane, causing a shattering of glass. In a reflex action, the men ducked their heads to cover their faces, just as the Israeli jet rocketed past them. When they sat up, they wiped the pieces of glass from their hair and shoulders and surveyed the damage.

Kyle felt his forehead. There was a stinging sensation and his palm and fingers came away streaked with blood from three small cuts.

David had not escaped unharmed either; a nick on the top of his ear forced him to use his handkerchief as a compress, which he held in place with one hand while steering with the other.

After checking themselves out, they turned to the rest of the plane. It was David who first saw the fuel dripping from the wings.

"We've got problems," he announced.

"Where?"

"There, in our fuel tanks."

From the wings came a steady stream of reddish fuel, whipped backwards by the wind, and the density of the spray made it clear that they were losing it at a rapid rate.

"It's riddled with holes," David said. "We're lucky to still be in one piece." For the next minute neither man said anything as David studied his dash.

Finally he shook his head. "I can see my fuel gauge indicator actually dropping. We're not going to make it to the Dead Sea."

"Can we turn it around?" Kyle asked.

"It's just as far to the west as it is the east. We can't make it either way. It looks as though we're going to get a chance to use these parachutes after all. Kyle, in that compartment in front of you, I've packed two gas masks. If we're going to be on the ground, we'd better be ready for it. Tie one to the straps on your harness, and then fasten one on me. You'll have to take the scroll from the box and tie it on the front of you with those pieces of Velcro."

Kyle did as he was told, and while he worked, David searched the ground. He thought he recognized the place below them as the Ela Plain, scene of Goliath's battle with David the shepherd. Once his parents had taken him there. Now flying above that very spot, it seemed a strange fortune that placed him here under these circumstances, fighting his own Goliath.

David swung his elbow hard against another break in the glass at his side, punching a hole through it with the first blow, then pushing outward at the remaining pieces until he had cleared enough away to look towards the north. Yes, there was the Forest of Martyrs—six million trees—one for each victim of the holocaust. He knew where he was.

He looked at their fuel. "We can't make the Dead Sea," he said. "We'll get as close to Jerusalem as we can and then bail out."

Kyle wasn't happy at the prospect, but he nodded his head, so David banked the plane to the left, passing over Bet Shemesh. There were buildings smoking on the ground. He checked his fuel gauge again. The needle was hovering over empty.

"How far is it?" Kyle asked.

"Less than twelve miles now," David said, and at the moment he finished the statement, the plane's right engine coughed. Twenty seconds later the left engine did the same, and then like two asthma patients, allergic to the same thing, they began to wheeze. Eventually their lungs gave out with the right engine shutting down first, and then the other feathering to a stop. The silence was eerie after hours of flying.

"Get near the door," David shouted. "I'm going to stay with this as long as I can, so I don't send it into some subdivision. You'll have to jump before me. Don't pull the cord until you've counted to three—and make it a slow count! Remember that you can control the chute to some extent by pulling on the main cords."

The plane was dropping steadily. David could see Jerusalem some seven miles away, sitting on the crest of the hill. He pointed the nose directly at it and concentrated his sensations on the gentle movement of the plane as it contacted different air currents, trying to ride the ones that seemed to buoy them up, hoping to extend their glide pattern even farther over the hill country of Judah, with its ravines and rugged mountains.

"You must remember to bend your legs when you hit," David said. "Your knees must be bent slightly or you'll damage something. I have a feeling there won't be many ambulance services available today, if we get into any trouble."

"Should I throw the door open?" Kyle yelled.

"Not yet. We don't want any extra drag. Maybe we can squeeze another two or three hundred yards out of this baby. But do it quickly when the time is right. I've got to stay with it as long as I can."

The plane dropped more quickly as its air speed lagged, and David turned the plane gently to the right. The Valley of Rephaim would provide them with the most level ground. Ahead loomed a slightly mountainous ridge, but his altimeter showed that he was still well above that.

"I think we can make it into the Rephaim Valley, but it's going to be close. I'd say it's time to pop the escape hatch, Kyle."

Twisting the handle, Kyle threw the door open, and it banged against its hinges. He was surprised to see how quickly the ground was rising up to claim them.

"This is going to be closer than I like," David said as he gauged the distance of the rising peaks and picked an opening to guide the plane through. "You've got a good grip on the rip cord?"

"Yes."

"Good. There won't be much time to find it."

With less than a thousand feet to go, the plane had dropped too low, making the last ridge impossible to scale.

"It's no good, Kyle!" David shouted as he banked the plane hard to the right. "Jump now!"

The floor of the plane tilted hard, and Kyle began to slip, then he threw himself through the opening, leaping out as far as he could. His feet came up, and his head dropped backward, turning his eyes toward the belly of the plane, making it appear to fall away from him. Jerking at the ripcord, he felt the rush of nylon past his head—felt the jerk around his waist and chest as the chute snapped his fall. He drifted downward while watching the plane, waiting for his friend to exit.

The Blackbird continued its steep bank, and David sat at the controls, moving it away from the ridgeline, realizing he would not be able to wait until the plane had completely righted itself before bailing out.

He began his exit by rising to his feet, keeping his left hand on the controls, maintaining the steep arc that turned the ship away from the ragged ravines and tamarisk bushes. He knew he had cut it too close. Moving to the side of his seat, he braced his knee against Kyle's seat to keep his balance.

The belly of the ship was no more than 100 feet from the hills, passing by him in a blur through the open hatch. He was afraid that when he let go of the controls the plane would pitch to the left as it pulled out of its arc, throwing it into the rocks. Glancing at the opening, he measured his next step. Should he slip and crash into the interior wall of the plane, those moments before he could scramble out could be critical—there might not be time to recover.

Hastily he pushed away from the seat and in a clean movement half fell, half jumped through the doorway with his foot catching the edge at the last moment, allowing him to kick off like a platform diver. While somersaulting, he found the ripcord and yanked; the chute billowed, barely breaking his fall before he careened off the edge of a ravine and slid to the bottom.

A moment later the wing of the Blackbird gouged into the ground and the plane cartwheeled completely over before ripping through a stand of tamarisk bushes, shearing them off. The crash echoed throughout the hills as the metal shredded apart in a hundred pieces, and yet there were no flames. The empty tanks had provided no fuel to create the ship's funeral pyre.

David's left hip was bruised, and he struggled to his feet, trying to distract his nervous system from the pain by rubbing the area. In fact the entire left side of his body was scraped as he slid down the embankment. The elbow on his shirt-sleeve was ripped open and its outer edges were dappled in the red of his blood. His hands were likewise bruised and cut where they had absorbed so much of the force of the landing.

Quickly he concealed his chute under a large piece of flat shale close at hand, then climbed the embankment and searched for Kyle. He saw nothing. He yelled his name, but there was no answer.

On the far slope of the hill, where the remnants of the Blackbird were strewn, he used the debris as a marker to get his bearings, then began walking in the opposite direction. At the next rise he yelled again and was relieved to hear Kyle answer. "Yell again," David said," so I can find you." Just then Kyle appeared on the knoll of a hill two hundred yards away. "Here I am."

"Are you all right?" David said.

"I've hurt my arm," was Kyle's reply, and David could see now that he was holding his right arm. David found him sitting on a boulder at the bottom of the ravine.

"It's not broken," David said after examining it. "I'll make a sling for you."

Taking out his pocketknife, David cut a strip from Kyle's parachute, then helped Kyle position his injured arm inside, draping the ends of the parachute over his shoulder and tying it off in the back. "How does it feel?"

"It's throbbing a bit, but I can make it."

"I'd say we're about four or five miles away in this direction," David said.

They turned toward Jerusalem and soon saw the gold flashing from the spires of the temple.

XXIV

The Two Witnesses

During a lull in the attacks, the streets of Jerusalem filled with people, wearing or at least carrying gas masks as they tried to purchase bottled water and medicines for the wounded. All knew that it was dangerous to be out in the open, but the urgency of their own individual problems drove them to take the risk. Some were there representing more than themselves, for there was a spirit of concern for others and one's neighbor that had settled over the land. In a line at a store that was still dispensing items, a woman wearing a head scarf stood carrying a cloth bag that she hoped to fill with cans of baby's milk, for she had a baby and so did her neighbor, and both women were not able to sufficiently nurse their children during this time of stress, and so today she was looking for milk for their little ones.

In the same line two soldiers, one thin, the other thick and muscled. The more athletic looking of the two had hoped, before the war, to one day represent Israel in the Olympics in the hammer throw. Now they were together, on a lunch break, trying to find some food for their families. They themselves had food to eat, because the government had mandated the food first going to those who were trying to defend the country, but their families were not given that same priority, and they were without.

As the soldiers stood in the line, they were trying to discreetly feed themselves from rations stashed in their pockets. The thin soldier was finding it very difficult, for a twelve-year-old boy had become aware that the men were eating, and he couldn't prevent himself from staring.

It was in that same line that a man, still in his twenties, wearing a soiled, white shirt stood. Ezra had come to buy drinking water for him and his mother. He rested his weight mostly on his right leg for his left had been injured during the recent attacks. The bulge around his knee was from the bandage his mother had applied, which again was showing crimson through his pant leg. It needed to be seen by a doctor, but such wounds were not even considered for attention with the much more serious injuries to be attended to among the people.

Standing next to him was a Palestinian man of the same age as Ezra. Long ago the Jewish parliament had by law divided the Jews and the Palestinians. Only the wall built between them had slowed the suicide bombers that had killed Jewish civilians and the reprisals by the Israeli army, leaving so many Palestinians dead.

The Palestinian standing next to Ezra was there illegally. If he could have, he would have been wired with a bomb. Israel's bomb detection devices had become so sophisticated that he was unable to slip one into the Jewish state. But he did have a knife. In the next instant that knife was used as Ezra dropped to the ground, mortally wounded from the blade that had penetrated his chest. The Palestinian first pretended that he was shocked as everyone else and then used the mounting chaos in the line to make his escape.

The mother who had come for milk dropped to his side. She screamed when she saw the knife sticking from his sternum. The two soldiers quickly brought their machine guns up ready to defend themselves and the others while trying to pick out who might have been the attacker among the thronging bodies. Another woman knelt next to the injured man.

"I'm a nurse. Don't pull the knife out. It could cause him to bleed to death before we can get help." She swallowed hard. "He looks bad. I'm afraid the blade made it to his heart."

Among those who gathered around came two men who were wearing rough outer clothing, which was tied around their waists with a sash. They were older men, in their late fifties.

"We can help him," said one of the men who looked Swedish yet spoke perfect Hebrew.

It was as much their manner as the words they said that made the nurse relinquish her spot next to the victim, for they spoke with authority, leaving little doubt they could indeed help the poor man. As she stood up she said, "Who has a phone? Somebody call an ambulance."

"I have a phone," said someone from the crowd. "I'm calling now."

"That won't be necessary," said the other of the two men. He spoke calmly with a smile, as if there were nothing to be alarmed about at all. His hair was curly and dark except where there was silver at his temples.

"What do you mean?" said the nurse. "This man will certainly have to be transported to a hospital."

Even while she was talking, the two men had rolled the man on his back. Then the white haired man took hold of the knife and pulled it out. At the same time they laid their hands on his head, closed their eyes and bowed their heads. The darker haired man spoke, but because of the confusion, he could not be heard by all. Suddenly the injured man opened his eyes and with the help of the two strangers sat up. Then to everyone's amazement except those who had performed the miracle, he got to his feet. Carefully, the wounded man felt his chest. Then he pressed harder but felt no discomfort.

When the crowd realized what had been done, they were as shocked as when they first saw him with the knife still in him. Terrorists' attacks they had grown up with, but they had never seen anything like this.

"What you have seen today," said the white haired man, "was done through the power of Jesus Christ. He was killed in this city, but he lives, and he will return very soon. We are his messengers."

"Remember what you have seen," said the other man, "and tell others." Then they walked quickly through the stunned people and were soon lost among the gathering crowd.

AT THE SECACAH dig Elisheba and the others had again returned in spite of the threat of war. The possibility of discovering more of the temple treasures overrode their concerns for safety. She was on her knees, protected by pads, swinging at hard dirt wall with a hand pick that was yielding only stubbornly to his efforts. Next to her sat Elead, a student from the university. "Do you see Elead? They have continued to fill in with dirt in this direction. There is rock here to this side and rock over here, but this is an opening where someone has packed this clay."

"How deep is it?" Elead asked.

"There's no way of knowing. We'll just have to keep working at it."

From behind her was the sound of someone approaching. She stopped swinging long enough to recognize Jacob, squatting down as he walked so he wouldn't hit his head. "Elisheba, I have just heard on the radio that there was a terrorist attack."

"When did they ever stop," she said as she raised the pick again.

"The radio said that the person who was stabbed was healed by two men.

"She stopped her pick in mid-swing and looked at him. "The two witnesses have appeared?"

"I think so," Jacob said.

"What are you talking about?" Elead asked.

"My husband told Jacob and me about them before he left for America. He said according to the scroll, they would make themselves known very soon. He said that they have been around for some time now, doing their work secretly, but soon they would make an appearance."

Elead seemed no more certain now what she was talking about than before he asked the question. "Who are they? What do you mean doing their work?"

She dropped the pick at her side and sat down on the cave floor with her back against the wall. "They were sent by God to help our country in our time of need. It was prophesied that they would come."

"Witnesses to what?" Elead asked.

"The end," she answered.

He seemed upset with the answer. "Then why am I working out here? I should be enjoying myself."

She reached over and patted him on the shoulder. "Maybe you should, Elead. But for us, our work cannot be shirked. You know that. The temple treasures should be very close to where we're sitting—the staff of Moses, the Ark of the Covenant, and the manna that God preserved—they're all just beyond this last wall, if I've correctly understood the words from the scroll. Can you imagine how that would strengthen our people if we should present those things to them while the whole world is turning against them? It would help them to know that His hand is with them. We can't take time to enjoy ourselves."

"I know, Elisheba. Oh, how I know it," he said wearily as he picked up his shovel and disappeared through the tunnel."

She turned to Jacob who was smiling at her. "Thanks for the news, Jacob. Keep the radio on, will you?"

"I will," he said, as he followed Elead out through the opening.

She raised her pick again and struck the wall another blow. On her second swing the end of the pick broke through. She pulled it back and hit furiously at the spot, widening the size of the hole. When she had enlarged it to the size of a plate, she grabbed a flashlight and shone the light into the chamber as she brought her face as close to the hole as she could. Her eyes widened in amazement, and she let out a gasp out of excitement.

❧ ❧ ❧

IN THE NORTHERN part of Israel, near the border with Syria, eight children were playing by their parents in a Jewish settlement. On a nearby mountain less than a hundred yards away, five Hamas raiders skulked among the rocks trying to get closer to those children and the parents who were supervising them. They carried with them a machine gun and a hand-held rocket launcher. When they had descended as close as they could without revealing their position, they quietly went about setting up their gun.

Over two hundred yards away, a man stationed on his roof with binoculars caught sight of the terrorists and began to yell, pointing at the rocks where the attackers were concealed. His cry had come to late to warn the children and adults who were too far out in the open.

It was at that moment that the gale swept across the mountainside with great fury, buffeting the intruders, and pushing at them so fiercely that the gunner could not keep his sites on his intended targets. In an instant the wind had escalated to near hurricane strength, and just as the trigger was pulled on the machine gun, the barrel was pulled upward, spraying the bullets high above the heads of the intended victims and the Jewish adults scrambling to gather them up.

At the same time as the bullets hit the roofs of the homes beyond the children, the terrorist with the rocket launcher braced himself against a rock and with the aid of his companion who tried to steady his shoulders he put the children in the cross-hairs of his weapon. The wind did not subside but intensified at that moment, causing the rocket to be hurtled violently to the left, where it exploded among the rocks. At that same moment the machine gun was ripped from the hands of the assassin and spun through the air like a propeller breaking away from a plane. It smashed against a huge, yellow boulder sending pieces of metal flying like an exploding grenade.

Then, as fast as the wind had come up, it suddenly died. It was that sudden cessation of the wind that made the blood of the Hamas attackers run cold. They could understand a sudden desert storm, dust devils had been a part of their lives, but when it ended at the moment of the destruction of their weapons, they sensed something uncanny had occurred.

They stood up looking at the sky, which did not offer the slightest hint of a cloud, then turned to each other, staring in disbelief. Where had the storm come from? It was then that one of them, looking further up the rocks, saw the two men who were dressed in rough cloth, standing on the outcropping of a rock. After what he had just experienced, the sight of these individuals unnerved him greatly and he fell to the ground, crying out in fear.

The others turned toward the area where the fallen man had pointed. Together they saw the two witnesses, while those watching from the settlement also caught sight of the two men dressed in sackcloth. The white-haired man lifted his hand and once more, and the wind began to blow, pushing the five men across the rocks and down the hill, herding them onto a barren piece of ground. There they lay, unable to rise from the bruising they had taken against the rocks. Seeing the Jewish security racing from the building with drawn weapons, the witness moved his hands again and the wind ceased.

The terrorists put their hands in the air in surrender even as they gazed upward at the men who seemed to have controlled the very elements against them. The two witnesses stepped backward from the pinnacle where they stood and disappeared into the cleft of the mountain.

XXV

THE FINAL LESSON

The death toll in Jerusalem was extensive. In one place, deadly gas caught a funeral procession, and the bodies of over two hundred people lay everywhere by the Jaffa Gate. The shell struck so close to the mourners that only those who were walking at the forefront of the procession were able to dash through the opening in the wall before the advancing gas trapped them. Some who were able to run through the opening died along the streets within the Jewish Quarter, others at the steps of locked doors. Together Jacob and Elisheba walked among the bodies, looking for any sign of life.

Just entering the city was a caravan of troop carriers, returning from the front. They were the advance contingent of thousands of other soldiers who were retreating and now positioning themselves to face the juggernaut of their advancing enemies. This division was heading for the Temple Mount, determined to keep the spot from being desecrated. The military caravan stopped, and the soldiers exited the transport vehicles to help with the removal of the dead at the Jaffa Gate.

The return of the soldiers was an ominous sign. It meant the Israeli army was on the retreat. With new forebodings, Elisheba watched the soldiers carrying the bodies to a barren patch of land on the other side of the road where they gently laid the victims before returning for others.

Then Elisheba saw two men in civilian clothing working among the dead. Even after she recognized Kyle's form, she stood speechless, unable to mesh the sensory information her eyes gave her with her belief that he was still in America. Was she seeing a double of her husband? Suddenly she shrieked his name in happiness and rushed toward him. Kyle turned in the direction of the scream, which he thought was the distress of a woman finding a loved one among the dead. When he saw her, his face burst into a radiant smile. "Elisheba!" he shouted.

He had only taken a few steps towards her when she crashed into him, throwing her arms around his waist, driving him a step backwards. He held her within his arms, then lifted her gently off the ground and turned slowly with her. She cried and rubbed his back, as though trying to confirm the reality of what yet seemed so impossible.

She spoke her first words with her head still buried in his chest. "How did you get here?"

"We flew." She pulled away to look at him. David drew nearer and she touched his shoulder. "It's so good to see both of you! But how could you have flown? There are no flights here."

"David had a plane," he said and then smiled grimly. "I'm using the right verb tense when I say 'had.' He had it and lost it all within the same day."

She pulled away from Kyle to put her arms around David.

"Thank you for being such a good friend."

"Oh, you just made the loss of the plane worth it," David said. "But I wanted to come, too. I mean, this is where all the action is. I'd be jealous if you guys were here by yourselves while the whole world is trying to beat you up."

"David, I would like you to meet Jacob," Elisheba said. The two men shook hands, and then Kyle stepped forward and threw his arms around Jacob.

"I asked you to watch over my wife, and you did. Thank you. Thank you, very much."

"She is a difficult woman to supervise," Jacob said.

Kyle laughed and patted his friend's elbow. "Believe me, no one could know how true those words are any more than I do. But you've managed to survive."

Elisheba asked about the plane crash, and they recounted the flight.

"We came across these soldiers who are helping here," Kyle said, "about three miles away. They gave us a lift."

"Jacob is worried about his family," Elisheba said. "He needs to drop us off, so he can get home. I have been dependent on him since you took our jeep, Kyle. Where in the world is it?"

"I'll tell you soon," Kyle answered.

They all climbed into Jacob's jeep and drove to David's home, passing other military vehicles. Many people came to their windows to watch the movement of the troops. Younger children watched from their balconies hanging on the railings like monkeys. They were excited to the see the soldiers, but the older children and adults knew the direction they were heading, and it was an omen of more tragic things to come. Jacob pulled up next to David's home. With a handshake and their thanks he departed.

Once inside, Elisheba took Kyle by the hand as David led the way into his office. Without a word David began turning the numbers on his walk-in wall safe. "What are we doing?" Kyle asked.

"You'll see," Elisheba said. David finished the combination and turned the handle as he pulled the heavy door open. He swung it wide enough that Kyle could see a wooden staff lying on the inside shelf on a piece of red velvet cloth. It was worn with use, rounded on both ends after forty years of wandering in the Sinai wilderness, a little over five feet long and made of dark gopher wood.

"It can't be," he said excitedly.

"It is," Elisheba said as all three walked inside the safe. Kyle approached the staff slowly, almost unable to breathe.

"The staff of Moses," he said softly.

"Yes," she said as she gently removed it from its spot and put it in his hands. Once before the Israelites were under attack and this helped to save them," Elisheba said as she put her arm around Kyle and watched his face as he studied it.

"It was where we thought, where the scroll had indicated?" he asked.

"Right there," she said.

"And the rest of the temple artifacts—the Ark of the Covenant, the shewbread . . ."

"It's all there—the temple gold. We put the dirt back in front of the opening to hide it and brought only this with us. We figured it was better kept there."

"I agree," Kyle said.

"We haven't said anything yet," Elisheba said. "The people don't know. I told Jacob that it would be better if you made the announcement. I didn't think they would believe us."

"You're probably right," Kyle said. "We'll contact the television stations right away, and see if we can get the word out. With as bad as things are, it might help to raise the spirits of the people to know that we have the staff that parted the Red Sea."

DURING THE REST of that day and all through the night the survivors from other cities poured into Jerusalem. One city after another had fallen to the blitzkrieg movement of their enemies: Ashkelon, Gaza, Rishon Lezion, Beersheba, Tel Aviv—all were under occupation. The soldiers landed in Palestine and swarmed the countryside like invading army ants, destroying everything in their path. All inhabitants, regardless of age or sex, who had survived the air strikes and could not escape, were killed. The Jewish enemies were not taking prisoners. It was a return to the cruelty of the holocaust, which had never died.

Together Kyle, Elisheba and David sat in front of their television and heard the announcement about the finding of the staff of Moses. That was the last story of the night. The lead stories were dedicated to the terrible things that had happened throughout Israel during the day. Sadly they watched the destruction as described by the announcer: "Israel's ground forces are now concentrated within the area of this circle as determined by a radius of eight miles. Many of the troops have arrived here as a result of a hasty retreat from throughout Israel to provide the strongest protection for the millions of citizens who are gathering here. On the roads outside of Jerusalem, you see the thousands of cars that have been abandoned, so their owners could continue their march to the city. Here is the way it looked about four hours ago in front of the Natural History Museum. A tent city has grown up rapidly on those grounds. Overflow areas that are also accommodating refugees include the grounds at the Knesset, the Israel Museum, and the Monastery of the Cross, and it's expected that the grounds of those buildings and other grassy spots throughout the city will be taken by morning."

The announcer was right. Early the next day, all of the streets and yards of Jerusalem were filled with the exiles from the surrounding country. David's yard, too, was filled, and the three of them did what they could to comfort and care for the dispossessed.

XXVI

Armageddon

Within the next hours the eight-mile radius of defense was pushed inward on a number of sides, as the enemy divisions fiercely drove the Jews toward their Jerusalem. In no place was the attack more fearsome, nor the loss of ground more rapid, than south of Jerusalem. Bethlehem, lying only four miles away, was overrun, and the city was sacked and burned.

At the Church of the Nativity, the traditional site of Christ's birth, eighty-seven men and women from among the Armenians, Greeks, and Roman Catholics, who were caretakers of the building, barricaded themselves within, believing that they could not allow the holy sanctuary to fall into the invaders' hands without some sort of defense. With remarkable courage they talked of giving their lives as a testament against those who would destroy their cherished spot.

Within the courtyard, which measured more than 230 feet long, the valiant knelt and prayed. Around their necks, dangled the gas masks, which they fully believed would give them their first line of defense. Their second line they were leaving to God, for they carried no weapons. Outside them they could hear the sounds of tanks rumbling past the building.

At a sign from their leader, a young Armenian zealot named Enrico, who had convinced them that this was the right thing to do, the priests left the courtyard and their praying and dispersed throughout the church, to continue their prayers on their knees at different locations until the danger was passed, determining that by their very bodies they would act as living shields against those who sought to enter to destroy.

In the nave and aisles of the church they knelt and prayed, some praying next to one of the forty-four columns which supported the ceiling.

Under the main altar a dozen men descended the stairs to the grotto to the traditional place of Jesus' birth. Two more men were stationed by the doors that were the main entrance to the church. The calling of these men as sentinels was dangerous: they would be the first to encounter the intruders, explaining why they had remained here while the rest of the city's inhabitants had fled. As spokesmen, they hoped to reason with the soldiers, who had already demonstrated by their violence that they were not prone to listen.

Through the rest of Bethlehem, incendiary squads torched the buildings. The odor of smoke seeped into the church of the Nativity, causing some sporadic coughing, but generally it served to help intensify the prayers of the righteous, making them realize how close they were to the flames.

The priest leader walked toward the sole entrance of the church where the two men stood watch. At his side hobbled an older man wearing the robes of the Greek Orthodox Church, who glanced attentively at his leader, waiting for any order that he might need to quickly fulfill. Generally, the several churches who claimed a portion of the building often squabbled over the right as to who would clean certain areas, but today, those quests for power were laid aside as they united in a holy cause. The skill and leadership of the Armenian priest were easily recognized and by acclamation the holy men chose him as their leader.

Enrico suddenly stopped and looked toward the western corner of the building where there had once been another entrance. In the stonework it was still possible to see the outline of the original opening. For a few seconds he stared at that spot. The older man believed his leader was looking at Brother Bartholomew who was kneeling in that area. "Would you like me to go Brother Enrico?"

"No," he said in a half daze. Suddenly his eyes cleared, and he turned to his companion. "Brother Jacob, do you know the painting that is in my office to the right of my desk?"

"Yes, I know it," responded the older man.

"Go there now and bring it here, please. Take Brother Bartholomew with you, and have him bring the easel that's in the corner of the room. Place the easel to the right of the stairs leading to the main altar and put the picture on it, so that anyone passing through there must see it. Hurry! There's not a moment to lose."

Enrico walked towards the main entrance as the old man left hurriedly to run his errand. At one time the church possessed two portals, but one was closed centuries before. Now only a smaller entrance remained where his two sentinels huddled fearfully, listening for outside movement. When he was yet a dozen paces away, a heavy pounding from the butt of a rifle jarred the peace of the church, followed by an angry voice:

"I demand that all people within this building immediately evacuate. If you do not, you will be burned with its contents!"

"I will speak with them," said Enrico. He motioned for the other man to help him pull out the crossbeam that locked the two doors in place. When it was nearly out, he said, "Let them not disturb your tranquility. Remember the example of our Master."

As the doors swung open, Enrico with his cowl up stepped forward to meet a dozen men carrying rifles. "Surely you do not intend to burn down one of the most holy spots in all of Christianity?" he asked.

The captain in charge stepped forward, ignoring the priest's question. "Are you the only person inside?" he said gruffly. "No. There are eighty-seven men and women of God who are kneeling throughout the church, praying that you will spare it."

"If I were them, I would start praying about saving their own lives. We are burning everything in the city except Muslim structures. Everyone who is in there will need to be prepared to identify himself. Any Jews will be summarily executed . . . is this the only entrance into the church?"

"Yes," said Enrico.

The captain turned to two men wearing flame-throwing gear. "Follow me inside. You four soldiers come with me, too. Have the safety off your weapons. If they're any sudden movements, shoot them."

"Sir," said Enrico respectfully, "as you know, the army that has entered Israel is a mixture of all religions. There are Christians who are fighting on your side. If you destroy this building, are you not worried about antagonizing your fellow soldiers?"

"We are all handling our assignments as we sit fit. I was told to burn anything that was Jewish. I'm simply fulfilling my orders."

The priest bowed his head. "But that is my point, Sir. This church is not Jewish. It is Christian."

The captain took a step closer to the priest. "To whose honor was this church built?" he asked.

The priest raised his eyes to meet the captains. "It was built to honor the birthplace of Jesus Christ."

"Correct me if I am wrong, holy man, but wasn't your Jesus a Jewish rabbi? While I am in charge of my unit, I will not let a building stand that was built to honor a Jew . . . You soldiers go inside first. If you meet any kind of resistance, open fire. We'll be in a minute to torch the place."

"Please! I beg of you . . ." began the priest but the captain struck him with a backhand that knocked him backward and to the ground. Sitting up, he touched the corner of his mouth, which was already numb, and saw the blood on the end of his fingertips.

The captain and those carrying the flamethrowers entered the doors. Enrico rose to his feet and followed them. The captain's voice could already be heard echoing through the basilica:

"I will give each person within this building five minutes to evacuate or you will burn with it . . . Get to your feet now and move outside."

None of the priests had moved but continued to pray with heads bowed. Turning to his men, the captain said, "If they refuse to obey, do not withhold the flames from them."

From behind him Enrico spoke. "Captain . . . these men pray to the one God. He may be known by many names depending on what church one enters, but we could call him Allah."

The captain continued moving through the church. "Do not try to deceive me, priest. Allah is the Muslim god. You are trying to appeal to our sentiments by calling him a name that we respect."

"I call him Allah because that is one of his names. I believe in that name as much as any other."

"This building," the captain said contemptuously, "was not built to honor Allah. It was built to honor Jesus—a Jew. For that reason, I will burn it to the ground."

"Sir, we pray to God here. One of his children who was born on this spot is also honored, but we pray to God. There is only one God."

The captain by this time had reached the three steps in front of the Altar of the Magi. He began to ascend but paused on the second step. The painting resting on the easel had caught his eye. He stepped downward and turned towards it, as the men with the flamethrowers halted behind him. In the background came the voices of the yelling soldiers, ordering an immediate evacuation. For several moments the captain studied the painting. The inner court of the great mosque at Mecca filled the picture. Muslim pilgrims walked around the Kaaba, the spot that contained the sacred black stone. Twice today the captain had knelt to pray towards that stone.

The captain stepped to the side and examined the frame. "The dust has been wiped off here on the corners where somebody has carried it. You have recently moved this here. You have taken it from some place else and set it here, trying to influence us not to burn this building."

"... Yes."

"Where did you get this picture?"

Enrico stepped closer to his side. "It was a gift from the Muslim community. It has been hanging in my office here in the church. I have had it for more than ten years."

"I will see your office," answered the captain. He turned to a man bearing a weapon. "Shoulder your rifle and carefully carry this picture and follow us."

Leading the way through the church, the priest stopped at a door and unlocked it while the captain and the man bearing the picture waited. Then stepping inside, the captain surveyed the room, and walked to the southern wall. A nail jutted outward from the plaster and below it was the slight outline where a picture had hung. "Give me the painting," he commanded the subordinate, who handed it over. The captain turned to the wall and centered it on the nail.

"It seems to exactly fit the outline on the wall," he said to the Enrico.

"It should," Enrico said quietly, "that's where it has been hanging."

The captain turned to the solider. "Any building that bears such a beautiful painting of the Great Mosque must be given special consideration. Tell the men to cease the evacuation and allow the people to reenter their building. This place is not to be destroyed."

The solider saluted and left the room. The captain turned to look at the painting once more. "I have never been to Mecca myself. Just this morning I promised Allah that if he would preserve me during this battle that I would go next year. He must want this building spared very much."

The captain walked quickly out of the room. For a moment the priest stood motionless then left the room and returned to the main altar where the men and women who had already learned that the building was to saved were already gathering.

There were many in tears and men and women pressed around Enrico to touch his shoulder or kiss his cheek. He told them to thank

God instead and many dropped to their knees around the main altar and prayed then and there.

Brother Bartholomew took his hand and kissed it. In all the years that the church had been jointly operated by the different denominations there was never such an outpouring of love and unity as at this moment.

"How was this done?" someone said from the crowd.

"This is a miracle! A miracle!" others said.

"Brother Enrico convinced them to leave us unharmed," Bartholomew testified.

"Jesus was here among us to prevent the destruction."

"Praise God!"

Enrico walked back among the columns towards the western wall as the last nun knelt beside the altar. He stopped and stared again at the spot where there had once been another entrance. Above that walled up spot, many centuries ago, another painting had hung, a painting of the magi visiting the infant Jesus. That painting no longer existed, but he remembered the story in the moment that he saw Brother Bartholomew kneeling in that area.

In 614 A.D. when the ancient Iraqis, called Persians, entered the church, bent on destroying it, they saw the painting and noticed that the Magi wore Persian costumes. Impressed, they too left the building unharmed. Today, God had inspired him to preserve the building in a similar manner. Next to that wall, below where the picture once hung, Enrico knelt on his knees and offered up his thanks.

When word reached the rest of the world that the Church of the Nativity had nearly been burned and chemical warfare had been directed at Israel, there was great pressure applied to the invading armies to agree to a ceasefire. Ambassadors from the warring parties met at the U.N. where the United States and Britain tried and succeeded in brokering a peace, one that was indeed fragile and one that few diplomats believed would hold for long.

XXVII

THE FINAL ASSAULT

During the ceasefire, the temple continued to rise rapidly. Though Herod's Temple had taken decades to complete, work on the new temple rushed to completion with the use of huge earthmovers, cranes and pneumatic tools. Anciently, the foundation blocks, some of which were more than thirty feet long, took weeks to cut and transport from the quarries, but now teams of workers cut blocks simultaneously and lifted them in place within the same day.

Near the Temple Mount, there was relative calm. Few people were allowed nearby because of the tight security. Kyle and Elisheba, however, were given favored status to climb the observation deck. They were overjoyed to watch as an exact replica of the old temple took form, exact even to the huge bronze columns that were placed on either side of the entrance and the gilded plates that covered the exterior, making the front of the new temple difficult to look at in the daytime for its brilliance, just as the old one had been. Like a well-orchestrated production, the activity on the Mount produced drastic changes on a daily basis.

❦ ❦ ❦

IN DOWNTOWN JERUSALEM a food and water station had been established to help those in need. Many waited in lines. Off to the side some chairs were set up for those who, for whatever reason, were too feeble or injured to stand.

It was there that Daniel Muir sat, looking straight ahead through sightless eyes, his face tranquil as one who had learned to accept his handicap and the kindness of others. To his side Tabitha waited in line to get the supplies that their family so desperately needed, glancing often towards her father to make sure that he was all right. Her mother was in another line in another part of the city where medicine was being dispersed, trying to find some antibiotics for an ailing gash on her shoulder where a collapsing wall had struck her. Tabitha, who was better able to support her father should he stumble, was watching over him as he had had once watched over her when she was a child.

At that moment the people around Daniel began to stir with excitement. Tabitha was too far away to ask what was happening, so he strained to hear some word from a nearby conversation that would explain the commotion. He knew there was no danger, or the people would have been more alarmed or would have fled away, and yet they were definitely agitated for some reason. Here and there he caught a phrase or word.

"Do you see them?"

"Why are they here?"

"Did you hear what they did earlier?"

To Daniel's relief, he heard his daughter's voice.

"Father!"

"What it is Tabitha?" What's happening?" he asked.

"They're standing in the middle of the street. They're coming towards us," she said in awe.

"Who is? Who is coming?" he asked.

"It is the two men they call the Witnesses—the ones that we've been hearing about on the television and radio. They are . . ."

And suddenly they were there, standing next to the blind man and his daughter. The commotion from the surrounding people subsided as they waited to in anticipation.

"Tabitha, we know of your sacrifice, "said the white haired man. "You have done a great thing for you father,"

Her voice was uncertain, shocked at what they said. "How do you know me? And how do you know about my father?"

"Whatever we know," said the other "has been given us of God. This day you shall receive a blessing for your faithfulness. Do not be afraid, Daniel."

And then the two men laid their hands on top of his head and uttered a prayer that only Daniel and Tabitha could hear completely. When they lifted their hands, he felt a strange warmth, beginning at the crown of his head that settled down through the middle of his skull and seemed to pass through his whole body, but no spot seemed warmer than in his eyes and the sockets that surrounded them. The darkness that he had known for so long, all at once began to dissipate, and in its place came an ever brightening light, which started with a pin point of brilliance and gradually grew larger and larger.

Those looking on saw his face fill excitement. "Tabitha, I can see! I can see! Praise God!"

He turned to his daughter and found her hand without fumbling, and pulled her closer to him. He took her face in both of his hands and looked with great emotion into her eyes. "My dear daughter, I can see you again! You are such a lovely woman. The last time I saw you, you were a child."

"Yes, Daddy," she sobbed.

The white-haired witness lifted both of his arms to silence the commotion of the crowd. "People of Israel, your God has bared his arm today in your very presence. This was done in the name of Jesus Christ. We are here to help. He has also called others. When the time comes, you will follow His servants through the opening in the mountain."

"Here us, Oh Israel!" said the second witness. "You must go through the mountain when the time has come. It is your way to protection."

At that moment three members of Hamas who had sneaked among the crowd, opened fire with their handguns. The crowd screamed as the two witnesses collapsed to the ground, and then scattered to save their own lives. Daniel led his daughter to a side street, and then returned to look carefully around the corner. There he saw the still bodies of the men who had given him sight, lying among the overturned chairs. He waited a minute and then when he could wait no more, carefully stepped back into the plaza as he motioned for his daughter to stay where she was.

"No, Father, don't go. The killers can still be there. Please, don't go."

"How can I stay here when the men who gave me my sight back my be bleeding to death out there. I must do what I can." Slowly he crept into the square, searching the buildings for the sign of any threat. Many had come to their windows by now, making it more difficult to pick out the killers, but still Daniel continued forward. He had only gone several paces when a shot struck the street next to him, sending a small piece of pavement into his right foot.

"Father!" screamed Tabitha, fearing the bullet had struck him.

He lurched to the side as he shifted the weight away from his injured foot to the other, and that movement saved his life for the next shot struck where he would have been. At that moment a police officer who had been supervising the food line squeezed off several rounds at the window where the killer was shooting. Those shots backed the shooter away long enough for Daniel to retreat to where his daughter waited. He tumbled into her arms as she broke his fall, still shaking from the fear that he was already wounded. When he showed her the spot on his foot where he was struck, she could see no blood. Pulling his shoe off, she felt his foot, but nothing moist transferred to her hand.

"There's no blood, Father."

"That's good. It hurts right here. Something struck me here, but it did not penetrate the skin. "

"You mustn't try to go out there again," she said.

"I know," he said quickly. "We will have to left the authorities take charge, those who have some way of protecting themselves."

Ten minutes later a siren disturbed Jerusalem's tranquility as yet another ambulance made its way through the city. For some time Tabitha and Daniel could hear it coming, and then it turned onto the street where they were still lying. The vehicle swung out into the square and where it was immediately fired upon. Without stopping, the driver whipped the vehicle around, returning on the same street they had just come. All other efforts to remove the bodies were met with a similar response. It was clear that there were many gunmen who were holed up in the buildings surrounding the square. Eventually, no one dared to venture towards the two men who remained on the ground motionless.

Two hours later a news helicopter hovered high overhead, braving the possibility that it might draw fire, so that the story of the witnesses could be told. Over the next hours that helicopter and others transmitted images of the bodies around the world. With those images came the protests of many who said that it was a crime against humanity to leave the bodies of such good men to deteriorate in the summer sun. The response from Israel was that no armored vehicle could be taken from the front to help in the removal of any of the dead. The living had to be protected first and then the dead would be seen to. And so for three days the bodies of the two witnesses lay on the Via Dolorsa, the street of sorrows where Jesus Christ had carried his cross to Golgotha with no one daring to give them proper burial.

Across the Mid-East the opponents of Israel rejoiced in the death of the two men who had dominated the headlines for so long. Men and women and their children danced in the streets, raised their drinks upward and shouted praises to heaven for helping in the destruction of those who had been highly esteemed by the Israelites. Spontaneous parties took place across the world where Israel was hated, for it was thought the two men represented the technological edge that Israel held over her neighbors, and the inability to stop these two symbols of her power had been humiliating in the extreme. Now that they were gone, it seemed that the end of the hated Jewish state was nearly at hand.

ONLY AN HOUR after the deaths of the two witnesses, an aerial dogfight between a Saudi plane and an Israeli jet, each blaming the other for provoking the incident, began the final assault. When eyewitnesses first saw the encounter, the Saudi jet was pursuing the Israeli across the Sinai, both planes hurtling rapidly toward the desert floor, the Saudi pilot struggling desperately to lock onto his enemy who flew in front of him. The Jewish pilot had turned the chase into a game of nerves by heading his plane directly towards the ground, daring his opponent to stay on his tail while he was locked in a death plunge. The Saudi lost confidence and pulled backward on his stick, pulling his plane upward and to the right. The Israeli jet should have collided with the ground, but the Saudi pilot saw no telltale plume of destruction.

"Did he land?" the Saudi pilot wondered. No, he was still flying, but the distance between his craft and the rough desert floor was unbelievably close. Suddenly, the Israeli pulled upward and toward the Saudi who was streaking away to the west, the Israeli renewing the pursuit—with the prey now having become the predator.

Within hours of that dogfight, each side had again scrambled its military into action. The biggest sign of the renewal of the war occurred in the northern part of Israel: a series of transport planes broke the peace of the sky with a hideous drone. Together, they converged on the Jezreel Valley between Haifa and Megiddo. Over three hundred planes—huge deep-belly crafts—the flying whales of the sky, each carrying hundreds of soldiers—cut through the atmosphere.

This attack was the culmination of years of planning by an alliance of Israel's enemies. The planes departed from airstrips within Turkey, Syria, Iraq, Iran and a large strip near the shore of the Black Sea, filled with Arab soldiers from each of those countries and other nations as well. Within minutes, a massive airdrop was underway and thousands of billowing chutes with their human cargoes drifted towards the Jezreel Valley, while the lumbering transport ships, scrambled away at full speed, hoping to get away before the Israeli jets could retaliate.

Soon the soldiers were on the ground digging with their miniature shovels, each working at the feverish pace of those who believed their lives depended on how deep they could go. The ground was fertile and soft, not at all like the Sinai that many had experienced in the first battle.

The special uniforms of the soldiers were already changing, chameleon-like, adapting to their surroundings. In the darkness of the transport planes, they took on a blackish hue, but now the light-sensitive fibers were adapting once again, mimicking the ground cover where the soldiers tore at the earth.

At the base of the Hill of Moreh, where an immense field had recently been harvested and was now plowed under, the uniforms of the soldiers were turning a dark brown; in another field, adjacent to it where a crop of wheat was moving in syncopation to a light breeze, the soldiers uniforms were more golden. On the slopes of the Hill of Moreh where soldiers were burrowing between thick clusters of cacti, their uniforms had turned a light green.

Everyone, both men and women, wore helmets of impact-resistant Kevlar, designed to protect their lungs from toxic chemicals. Baffles were positioned over the ears, designed to ward off the damaging effects of powerful blasts. Near the mouth, a slender microphone dangled. It was attached to a short-range radiotelephone. For communication nearby, the same microphone was attached to a small speaker located near the throat, giving every man a slightly metallic-sounding voice. A pair of infrared goggles rested over the eyes, giving every soldier the capability of seeing in the night with as much clarity as though it were day. Although each soldier was exerting himself strenuously, a miniaturized refrigeration unit hidden over the chest kept each individual cool, automatically sensing the heat output as he first dug and then rested, cooling the uniform in proportion to his needs.

Twelve kilometers to the west from the Hill of Moreh, on the western side of the valley, soldiers were digging tunnels on the spot where so many battles had been fought through the ages—at the very base of the ancient city of Megiddo.

A group left the shelter of the tunnel and broke into the open on the top of Mount Megiddo, running among the ruins to the western side of the mound, taking a vantage point from where they could see across the Jezreel Valley. Before them, they saw tens of thousands of men already on the ground with their numbers increasing at every moment, and all seemed to be digging in.

Earth-moving equipment floated downward under clusters of chutes and at those places where they had already landed and been freed from the ropes of their parachutes, the diesel engines belched black smoke as they tore large swaths in the dark earth to more speedily provide cover.

The soldiers were excited to stand upon the heights of Megiddo and see the whole operation unfolding before them. None were aware of the prophecies of this spot and their own part in fulfilling them. The place where they stood—Mount Megiddo—was known anciently as "Har Megiddo," but John, the Apostle, had made it one word when he spoke of it as Armageddon—the ultimate battlefield.

THREE DAYS AFTER the deaths of the two witnesses and the renewal of the fighting, David's yard was again filled with refugees from throughout Israel, many carrying children who were too young to understand the danger but sensed the insecurity from their anxious parents.

Elisheba moved among the families distributing pieces of candy to the children and other food to the adults, trying to calm them. She escorted an expectant mother inside the home and placed her in David's bedroom.

A soldier, with a bad shrapnel wound in his thigh, who had limped his way in from the front was placed in the kitchen upon a sleeping bag while a medical student worked to extract the fragment.

Kyle and David found Elisheba in the yard comforting a little girl who was separated from her family. "I need to talk to you," Kyle said.

She turned toward him and saw that he was carrying the staff of Moses. Turning to a family huddled against the wall, Elisheba indicated the little girl needed to be tended, and the father did his best to console her. Then she turned back to Kyle. "What is it? Why do you have the staff?" she asked.

"You tell her, David."

"Just now on the television . . ." he spoke as though he wasn't sure how to say it, "the two witnesses are gone."

"They're gone?" she asked. "Do you mean that somebody has taken their bodies?"

"No. That's not what I mean," David said. "They stood up. They are alive."

"How can that be? Did you see it yourself?" she asked.

"We both saw it," said Kyle. "They're showing the video tape again and again. They just rose and walked away from that street where they've been lying."

"It must be some kind of a hoax. They've been there for over three days."

"It's no hoax, Elisheba," David said. "It was really them."

"I've been expecting it," Kyle said. "There is a passage in the New Testament . . ."

Kyle stopped in mid-sentence. It was at that moment that the shaking began. Only a slight tremble at first that gradually increased, and accompany it was a rumble that seemed to come from below them and around them. The trees in David's yard began to shake although there was no wind.

"It's the earthquake that was predicted to come after their resurrection. These are the signs that I've been waiting for." Kyle took Elisheba by the arm and led her to the gate. "There's one last thing I have to do, and I need the staff of Moses to help me," he said.

"Does this involve your jeep?" David asked.

"Yes," he said. "I'll take you where I've hidden it."

"But, Kyle," she said, "you won't be able to drive through these streets with so many people."

"The jeep is not within the city walls. Follow me."

Soon they were walking quickly on the Ha-Ofel Road, heading toward the Mount of Olives, making their way through the tens of thousands who had sought safety within the city.

"Can you tell me now what this is all about?" Elisheba said.

"I'm to tell no one until the time comes," Kyle said.

They left the road and dropped down into the Kidron Valley, then began the climb up the Mount of Olives.

This area was open to the strafing from Saudi and Syrian jets, and they divided their glances between the skies and the mountainside. Turning to the north, they walked carefully around the ancient tombstones, only a short distance from Samuel's grave.

A new mausoleum had made its appearance on the hillside, a stone structure, composed of slabs of hewn granite with two carved stone doors sealing it off. It was ten feet wide and fifteen feet long, sitting just above the road. To this structure Kyle led the others.

"Ordinarily," Kyle said, "I couldn't have built something like this, but the officials in charge of that department are a bit preoccupied. I knew it would be hard to drive through the city when this moment arrived."

Kyle withdrew a transmitter from his pocket and pointed it at the bronze doors. There was a slight mechanical click from inside, and the two doors began pulling apart, revealing the altered jeep. The ceiling was large enough to accommodate the speakers that protruded from the jeep.

"This is some garage," David said.

Kyle slipped through the opening and climbed inside the vehicle. "I wasn't actually told to build this, but it seemed like a good idea."

David got in the back and Kyle handed him the staff. Then He and Elisheba climbed in and Kyle started the motor. The jeep lurched

Ashes of the Red Heifer

forward and onto the rocky ground of the Mount of Olives. They followed the slope until it joined the next road, then turned right in front of a group of nuns making a hurried pilgrimage to the Chapel of the Ascension at the top of the mount to pray for peace.

The road cut back across the slopes until it united with the main road that circled the old city. Here it was known as Derekh Yeriho, but the name changed many times as it circled the castellated wall. They passed the Lion's Gate, and turned the corner at the northeast section of the city near the Rockefeller Museum.

Soon the crush of the refugees became so great that they could drive no farther. In the distance the artillery thundered, much louder than it was even an hour ago.

Above, the aerial fights persisted. There the story of the losing battle was told dramatically for everyone to see. Even the children were aware that the number of Israeli jets was much less than before. Their pilots had become the prey. When one of their jets streaked across the sky, it was generally being pursued—not by one or two enemy craft, but by five and six. Israel's planes—outnumbered as they were—had virtually lost the capacity to go on the offensive. Now they struggled for survival with the odds overwhelmingly against them. The skies offered an immediate appraisal of the country's position, which added to the survivors' gloom.

On the Temple Mount, tens of thousands of troops from the front lines waited for their last stand. Though there were many civilians who wanted to die there, the shortage of space made it impossible, so only fighting men were granted access.

Within twenty minutes there was not one Israeli jet passing over the city. The air force was completely vanquished, and with its demise, the army was now helpless. Enemy planes that had been engaged in the dogfights were now free to turn their guns on the army, which had run out of ammunition in most places. Never in the history of the world did soldiers of war die at such an awful rate. Battalions of men who could fight no longer, who had thrown down their weapons and were ready to submit as prisoners were mowed down with automatic weapons while jets dropped explosives in their midst.

The eight-mile ring of defense had collapsed, and the soldiers of the opposing nations, bent on Israel's complete annihilation, closed in on the city.

XXVIII

DEATH OF A FRIEND

Northeast of the Rockefeller Museum, advance soldiers from the attacking armies sneaked into the upper level of an apartment building which the residents had left for the safety of a fortified basement. Because the building provided a clear view to the huge crowds around the perimeter of the old city, the soldiers chose it.

They stormed their way to the top floor and moved to the windows looking towards the northern part of the city. They broke the windowpanes and began shooting.

Kyle and the others were in the line of fire, for they had parked the jeep at the northeast corner of the Old Wall to help three different victims, two adults and a child. Elisheba was working desperately to save the life of a four-year-old girl who had a severely injured hand.

David's position was more in the open when the shells began kicking up the rocks and dirt around him. He picked up the elderly woman he had been tending, who was bleeding severely from a wound in her stomach, and, cradling her like a child, ran toward the jeep, hoping to use it for cover. Ten steps away a bullet caught him in his back, piercing his body, and exiting under his right rib cage. He fell to the ground with his burden.

Elisheba saw him hit and screamed out to Kyle. She passed the injured child to the child's teenage brother and showed him where to the hold the compress, then looked to see how exposed she was to the sniper's fire. A single tree provided cover, so she stood up.

"Don't move, Elisheba," Kyle yelled. He, with others, was pinned down behind some grapevines covering a wood fence. He rose from his belly to his knees, then placed his feet under him. Like an Olympic runner sprinting out of the blocks, he lunged forward, starting out low to the ground. Clenching his fists, he pumped his arms in rhythm to his legs and sprinted directly toward David before changing course, hoping to make himself a more difficult target.

He leaped over a young man lying prostrate in the dirt, too afraid to move, and reversed directions once again, this time placing himself on a course directly toward David. He did not hear the sound of the rifle shot, but he recognized the buzz of the spiraling bullet as another one sailed over his head. Stopping over his friend, he bent down quickly, taking him under the armpits and dragging him over the ground until they were behind the jeep.

Stepping out into the line of fire once more, he returned to the injured woman and dragged her next to David. A young man suddenly dove for cover beside him. "How is my Grandmother?" he asked worriedly.

"I don't know," Kyle said. "Tear your shirt into two pieces and see if you can stop the bleeding. This is the exit wound here. You'll have to plug it in two places."

Turning to his friend, Kyle pulled him onto his lap. David's eyes were open.

He spoke slowly. "You know," he said with great effort, "I've never been shot before. All the guns I was around . . . this is the first time . . . It kind of feels like that time you hit me in the back in batting practice . . . except it hurts more."

His eyes moved past Kyle's face, as though someone were drawing near. Kyle turned, expecting to see Elisheba, but there was no one there. David smiled and said, "I'm glad you came." His eyes became absolutely still, his mouth relaxing, his breath exhaling slowly, his lungs failing to draw air in again. Kyle touched his friend's cheek and sobbed, and then closed the eyelids and lowered him to the ground.

Even while he crouched by the body, some bullets struck the jeep, and others exploded into the old wall behind him. He crawled to the front bumper and saw Elisheba still crouching behind the tree. "Stay there!" he shouted to her.

"How is David?" she yelled back. He was expecting the question and began to pull his head in as soon as she opened her mouth, pretending not to hear her.

He felt a slight rumbling. Turning quickly, he crawled on his knees to the back of the Jeep and looked to the east. His fists clenched tightly together, and his forearms began to shake with excitement as the adrenalin pumped into him. Though it was late in the day and the sun was setting in the opposite horizon, the sky in the east was glowing brighter and brighter.

The shaking frightened the snipers from the apartment house, and they ran from the building towards the north. There was a shout from those who saw them leaving, but the shaking of the ground left all too afraid to pursue them. With the threat from the snipers gone, Elisheba ran to the jeep. "How's David?" she asked.

"He didn't make it," Kyle answered.

She covered her face, then slowly pulled her fingers away and turned towards where he was still lying on his back.

"No . . . No. It can't be," she cried.

Kyle took her in his arms and supported her, although he was crying no less than she. "We must finish what we set out to do," he said. "His mission is over. Ours isn't."

The shaking gradually increased in intensity and so did the light in the east. Some feared the worst, and one husky-throated man yelled out, "It's an atomic bomb! They're setting off atomic bombs to kill us all. That's why the ground is shaking!"

"You're wrong!" shouted Kyle. "Don't be afraid. It is part of a plan to help you. The light has nothing to do with the shaking."

Elisheba cried out, "After all that has happened, with so many trying to kill us, and now to have an earthquake. Even God seems to hate us."

"Do not despair," Kyle said to her and those around him. "This earthquake is not to hurt the city nor its inhabitants. It is sent to help them."

"Help them?" she cried. "How can more destruction help them?"

"This quake is not causing more destruction. It is making a way for safety."

At that moment the rumbling stopped. Kyle turned to Elisheba and spoke excitedly. "The sign is being given. Get in the jeep quickly!" Still sobbing, she did as she was told, stumbling in her grief. He took her by the arm, and helped her in, then walked to the back of the vehicle and turned on the generator. The motor whirred, and the meter showed it was kicking out the necessary amps. He turned on the amplifier and the transmitter, then ran to the driver's seat and hopped in.

"Feel under your seat," he said, "and put on the ear protectors." They both found the devices and placed them over their heads. Reaching in the back seat, he grabbed the staff of Moses and set it on the seat beside him so it was standing upright from the jeep.

Reaching under the dash, he found the microphone resting in its holder and lifted it to his mouth, then pushed the button which activated it, and though he had not yet said a word, he could hear the speakers kick on, reacting to the handling of the microphone. And then, like the public address announcer in a football or basketball arena, his voice boomed out and simultaneously was transmitted through the communicator band. At first, he spoke quietly to prepare the people near him.

"Citizens of Israel. My name is Kyle Shepherd. I am the man who found the ashes of the red heifer. The stick that I am holding is the holy staff of Moses. I've been sent here to help you. I am broadcasting on communicator band 63. Please tell those who are too far away to hear me to turn to that channel. What I have to say is vital for your survival. The light that some of you have already seen in the east means that help has been sent to protect you from your enemies. They are closing in at this moment, but there is a way to escape to the east. The light you see is part of a special project to split a passage way through the Mount of Olives. I'm a scientist and I know what I'm talking about. Every other way of retreat has been cut off. You cannot go to the north, west or south. The enemy is waiting for you there. Follow the staff as your forefathers did and live!

"Go to the east, down through the Kidron Valley. A passageway is already being made. That is the nature of the rumbling you feel. Please pass this message on. Some will not be able to hear my voice. Safety is through the Mount of Olives. I repeat: Safety is through the Mount of Olives."

He put the jeep in gear and moved slowly down the road toward the west. "Go to the east. A passageway has been opened through the Mount of Olives. Your enemies are coming from every other direction to destroy you. Go to the east." The road cleared for them as they made their way around the Old City, and people began picking up their children in an exodus towards the east.

Even though the talk of a passageway through the Mount of Olives seemed incredible, people hoped that it could be true, that somehow their government had made some preparations of which they were unaware.

Periodically, Kyle repeated his message, and eventually he and Elisheba approached the Damascus Gate. "There is a passage way through the mountains," he said as the jeep drew abreast of the large doors. "The earthquake has caused a passage through the mountain ... All of you should begin moving towards the east. Here you will soon be trapped." His voice carried within the city among those jamming the streets there, but people by the thousands were monitoring his message on their communicators. Others would not move, believing that the safest place yet was near the sacred and ancient buildings of Jerusalem.

Passing the Damascus Gate, they rolled slowly through the people crowding the Hatzanhanim Road. By the New Gate, a group of twenty soldiers, who had recently been at the front and told to fall back within the city limits, stood in the road and refused to move as Kyle and Elisheba approached.

A soldier who had suffered a superficial head wound and was still wearing the bandage around his brow, drew close to Kyle. Some who had begun to move toward the east upon hearing Kyle's message, now stopped to see the outcome of this encounter.

"What is this talk about a passageway?" the soldier asked. "We've received no word on anything like that, and we would have been informed."

"Nonetheless," Kyle said, "there is a passageway. This last earthquake opened up a crevice in the Mount of Olives. I'm Kyle Shepherd, an archaeologist. You might know me as the one who discovered the Scroll of Enoch."

"Whatever your name or title, you're not authorized to start a general migration of the people. Put that stick down. You need to stop broadcasting your message until we receive authorization for such an evacuation. You might cause these people to panic."

"The opening in the mountain is a recent event. It happened just within the last few minutes. God has his hand in this to provide a way for His people to escape to the east. I am holding onto the staff that Moses used to go through the Red Sea. In the same way your people will be saved by going through the mountain today. A crevice has actually been formed in the side of the Mount of Olives right now."

The soldier turned and looked at the other soldiers knowingly, then rotated his eyes upward as though Kyle were a madman. "We can use God's help. There's no questioning that, but until He gives us orders, you are to say no more about it. Now, give me that stick and get out of the vehicle."

Kyle complied, and the captain took the staff from him, but before he could say another word, the man's eyes suddenly closed and he fell unconscious into the arms of his friends, while Kyle caught the rod before it struck the ground.

Suddenly fear overcame the other soldiers, and they made no protest as Kyle and Elisheba entered the jeep again and resumed their broadcast. "There is a place," Kyle said into the microphone, "prepared for you in the east. Follow the staff of Moses which I hold in my hand."

As one body, the onlookers began moving in that direction—including the soldiers who waved the others on to greater speed—and the word spread rapidly throughout the city.

"There is no reason to run," Kyle said. "You have time. Your enemies are still some distance from Jerusalem, but they are advancing, and you should move steadily towards the Mount of Olives." The crowd parted in front of them on the road, allowing them to move faster.

Eventually, the jeep turned the northeast corner of the Old Wall and headed south. Driving past the Jaffa Gate, Kyle did not cease to warn them. The episode with the three soldiers had preceded them, and the crowd listened attentively as they passed, then followed. They rounded another corner of the wall, turning due east toward the Mount of Olives.

At that moment, the word was given from the commanding officer of the enemy forces, which reached the headphones of all the soldiers that they were to rush the city and destroy every living thing. From the combined voices of millions of men, an awful scream shattered the air, as they rushed forward to satisfy their lust for blood. The horrifying sound froze the inhabitants of Jerusalem in their tracks as they looked in the far distance at the tightening circle of their enemies. The eastward migration toward the Mount of Olives took on real urgency, and the people began to run.

The jeep turned the last corner of the Old Wall, and Kyle and Elisheba saw the opening in the Mount of Olives for the first time. Starting in the Kidron Valley to the north of Absalom's tomb, continuing upward along the north side of the Church of the Ascension, it was as wide as a six-lane highway, and thousands were already pouring through the great crevice. To the others he spoke. "Descend and begin the climb." Those who were hesitating, stepped downward into the Kidron Valley and then began ascending the Mount of Olives.

Spying a slight knoll that would give him a clear view of the people, he drove the jeep up the incline so its nose pointed eastward, and there he and Elisheba watched the people flow by.

She looked nervously at the advancing armies, still several thousand feet away. "Kyle, they're coming."

"We'll wait for them to go in," he said.

The floor of the remarkable passageway led steadily up, but not at the extreme angle as that of the hill itself, so with a little exertion the masses walked forward. Older people who had tired edged their way against the sides of the walls and let those moving faster go by. Many of the injured, who were not capable of walking, were carried on stretchers. Two teenage brothers carried their younger sister on a blanket stretched between two broomsticks.

Those approaching the midway point in the chasm began to notice a lone man standing directly above them on a rock outcropping at the very peak of the Mount of Olives. He was bearded, and he was dressed in red robes, and he stood watching the progress of the people.

XXIX

On Earth Again

For the enemy soldiers, the distance was short between them and the helpless Jews. Again they united their voices into a spontaneous shout of excitement, and it was heard on the far side of the Mount of Olives.

Several thousand people still remained outside the protection of the pass, and some at the back tried to push their way through the crowd, fearing that they would be in the rear when the soldiers reached them.

"Don't shove!" Kyle yelled. "People will be hurt if you lose your heads."

The last people were crowding into the pass when Kyle pulled the jeep forward into the valley, but before it had cleared the edge of the hill a bullet struck him in the back, and his arm jerked forward, knocking the shifter out of gear. Elisheba screamed as he slumped over the steering wheel. She tried to turn the wheel under his limp body, but to no avail. The jeep accelerated down the hill, and they shot over a rise that sent them flying. She held onto the dash with her right hand while grasping Kyle by his shirt collar, and for a moment was actually standing on her feet. He pitched to the side and would have fallen out of the jeep had she not caught him. She grabbed the steering wheel and fought to put her foot on the brake, but his foot was under the brake pedal; stomping her foot down over his, she managed to apply enough pressure that the vehicle began to slow, and she brought it under control.

The bullets were still flying around her, and the windshield was struck, punching a hole through it. Reaching her foot across the shifter, she lifted his legs away from the pedals with her foot, and then pulled him away from the steering wheel by his arm. Climbing over him, she dropped into the driver's seat, found the clutch with her right foot and depressed it, then ground the gears back into first. Transferring her foot to the gas, she drove the jeep up the other side of the valley into the opening and stopped.

The last of the Jews had made it within the immediate safety of the pass, but in another minute they would be easy targets for the first soldiers who were pumped with adrenalin at the thought of renewing the slaughter. As they ran toward the retreating Israeli nation, they spontaneously united their voices in an uncontrollable shout of excitement, which was heard on the far side of the Mount of Olives, where the majority of the Jews were now huddling.

The bullets riddled the farthest walls within the chasm, sending chips of rock flying. One struck the windshield again, completely blowing it away, leaving only jagged edges of glass around the frame. For the first time she looked Kyle in the face. A shudder rocked her body. His eyes were open, staring blankly ahead. He was dead. She sobbed and pulled his head close to her breast, for some time sitting in shock before she realized that the shouting of the enemy army was bringing them closer to her.

From the Kidron Valley, she could hear the noise of the enemy as they shouted and ran over the ground. Laying Kyle's head back, she jumped from the jeep and hugged the wall towards the opening, as the bullets by the hundreds continued to chip at the exposed rock wall opposite her. Below her she could see the first soldiers beginning the climb from the floor of the Kidron valley toward them.

They were less than 120 feet away, and yet the remaining Jews were still moving within the Mount of Olives. In a matter of minutes they would be trapped, standing helplessly, as the guns opened up on them.

It was then that the first piece of hail hit. It struck the opening of the cave and shattered, while its flaming remnants scattered across the floor. Other pieces struck the ground rapidly, spreading tongues of flame wherever the fragments splattered. They fell in fist-sized lumps of the texture of glowing igneous rock, still red with heat, and casting her eyes upwards towards the source, she saw the sky had assumed a crimson hue. In the Kidron Valley that same bloody aura colored the terrified faces of the soldiers who had not yet been knocked to the ground.

Elisheba ran to the jeep and pulled Kyle towards her, covering his head with her head and arm, the roar of the falling rocks escalating, while she waited with her eyes closed, anticipating the first stones that would strike them. But they did not come, and gradually she turned her head to the side and looked at the chasm around her—no stones had fallen where they were. The Jews in front of her, who were clutching their loved ones to their breasts, were also discovering that they were untouched.

From the mouth of the cave westward the hail fell. Beyond that point, even within the pass, nothing happened. Where the Jews had covered the slopes of the mountain, no one was injured, although from their vantage point they could see the skies apparently on fire.

Among the armies of the invaders, the hail struck with lethal blows, slicing its way through helmets and protective coverings, and igniting the clothing. At every solid blow a soldier fell. Those who were not immediately hit yelled and cried in terror, and tried to cover themselves with the bodies of those who had already died. But the hail increased in its fury, and the fiery pieces that were thrown off as they struck the ground, soon had the entire ground burning, driving many out from under the bodies they had tried to crawl under for protection.

Enemy tanks appeared in the mouth of the valley where the people had taken refuge, and though the firestorm raged to the west of the Mount of Olives, these vehicles were in the area that, as of yet, remained untouched. By the hundreds, the tanks rolled into position, only allowing sufficient distance between them and those vehicles in front so their cannons could be fired.

Although all the tanks were not positioned, the order was given to begin firing, and the crews within loaded the shells into the chambers. On the hillsides, the people met the arrival of the tanks with differing degrees of faith. There were those who began to climb the Mount of Offense, or another slope enclosing the valley, hoping to reach safety. Families and friends gathered together, and many held hands and prayed.

The firestorm that continued to pelt the army, suddenly shifted eastward, swinging past the southernmost edge of the Mount of Offense and into the tanks, and yet northward, on the hillside, the people were untouched. What had been fist-sized pieces of hail took on greater size, and within seconds, they came crashing from the heavens the size of bowling balls, whose great speeds jarred the interiors with mind-rattling noise that prohibited communication with one another.

The fiery boulders struck the ground with tremendous violence, spraying sulfur and flames into the air as if the tanks were in the middle of fireworks that had prematurely ignited on the ground. Within minutes the tanks were buried, while the flames danced along the tops of the rocks. On the hillsides, the Jews sat in stunned silence as the shower of hailstones waned, with the last few boulders crashing into the pile.

After watching the last pieces of hail, Elisheba stepped back into the pass to return to Kyle's body. As she did so, she heard various voices in the crowd shouting for the people to look upward to the top of the Mount of Olives. She turned around and scanned the hillside, but the crowd had all risen, and since she was standing in a slight depression, her view was blocked. Stepping onto a boulder, she looked upward again and saw, descending from the top of the mountain, a crowd of people—perhaps two hundred in number—a mixture of men and women.

They had moved less than a hundred meters from the summit when they stopped.

She had a clear view of them now and could plainly see that these people were dressed in white robes. As if on command, they suddenly knelt to the ground, leaving one person in their ranks still standing—a bearded man wearing red garments. Elisheba did not know, but others in the crowd recognized him as the same individual who had stood upon the rocky ledge and watched quietly as the people passed below him.

This man walked through his followers, looking from side to side at the people who stood or sat on each side of him, seeming to take note of the children especially, whom he smiled at, as though reassuring them that their time of terror had passed.

"It is the deliverer!" Someone shouted not far from her.

"The Messiah has come," another voice said.

For the next several minutes He descended, and through the crowd the word passed that the God of their forefathers was in their midst. Then He reached the bottom of the steps in the valley where so many people were crowded tightly together. He stopped to talk to a group of elderly people, both men and women, whose faces showed the weariness of the climb through the pass, and the terror of the destruction of their enemies, and yet in His presence their faces emanated joy and tranquility. Elisheba could see an older man, splattered with mud, asking Him a question. She could not near the question nor the answer, but immediately all those round about Him put their faces to the ground in humility. The Man then turned and looked out over the multitude, and when He spoke His voice, though quiet and meek, was heard by everyone, piercing not only their ears but their hearts as well. "I have been asked where I received the wounds in my hands and my feet . . . They are those with which I was wounded in the house of my friends . . . I am Jesus Christ . . . I gave my life on a cross not far from here because of the unbelief of your fathers . . . Will you believe in me now?"

Through the gasps people fell to their knees and put their heads to the ground. "Heaven and earth are become one this day, for my people have at last humble hearts to receive me. This is a day of rejoicing for the righteous—and not for you only, but for those who have slept." A bright light in the east in the last moments since He had begun descending the Mount of Olives had increased in intensity until it filled the whole sky. Pointing to the light, Jesus said, "The righteous spirits of those who have slept are coming to reclaim their bodies and to greet the faithful. The multitude glanced upward and saw that the great light emanated from millions of spirits moving through the sky, and while they watched, Jesus ascended from the hill right in front of their eyes, and as He rose His body began to glow with the brilliance of His glory, so that it outshone the luster of all the righteous with whom He was uniting. And as the spirits moved through the atmosphere, they suddenly dispersed, each moving rapidly to that area where the last remnants of their bodies were preserved. To cemeteries throughout the world, to the ocean for the bodies of those who had died at sea, to jungles, and deserts, to the four corners of the world; in an instant the light of the righteous spirits spread, and there the bodies reformed. For even those bodies where nothing seemed to remain, the elements were still existent. At the command of the Great Jehovah the genetic material again began to replicate so that bones formed; sinews reattached and the flesh appeared once again on the structure; the hair returned to each follicle so not even one was lost. The spirits entered into their bodies and felt a fullness of joy at regaining that which had been from them so long absent.

These resurrected bodies, wearing sparkling white robes, next longed after their children and spouses who had tarried on earth and had survived the destruction. Even before they arrived to the home or tent where their loved ones were anxiously waiting, their desire to be with them was so great that their children, and righteous wives and husbands were lifted off the ground to meet them in the clouds.

Accompanying the celestial display of lights was music, a choir singing. It was a song that Elisheba had never heard before, but the song seemed familiar. Among the Israelites, tens of thousands were suddenly lifted skyward to meet their returning loved ones. Sometimes the reunion of husband and wife happened so close to the ground that those still remaining could hear the shouts of joy and love as they threw their arms around each other after the long separation.

When Elisheba understood what was happening, she turned toward the pass and began to run, sliding to a halt as she rounded the corner, extending her hand toward the rock wall to prevent her from falling. At the mouth of the canyon the jeep remained as she had left it. Though far from the jeep, because of the brilliance of the ethereal lights glowing in the atmosphere, she could clearly see Kyle's body still lying in the seat with his face heavenward. Walking slowly at first, then breaking into a full run, she covered the distance, barely taking her eyes from the still form, only doing so long enough to keep from stumbling. The walls, rushing past her, danced with the illumination from the glory of His coming, and the voices from the celestial choir reverberated throughout the chasm.

When she reached the jeep, she stopped, afraid really to go farther, afraid that what she hoped would somehow not take place. And yet at that moment, a white light formed around Kyle's body and penetrated into his tissues. At the beginning his body seemed to simply absorb the light, but as the seconds passed it started to glow outwardly. The skin turned translucent, and for an instant she could see deep into his organs and his skeleton, as though her eyes had become x-rays. Then his density altered and the internal glimpse disappeared. His skin and features were touched with the handsomeness of youth, for though the body still was Kyle's, it was younger—it was his body in its prime.

From above, she saw a light descending and within that light was his spirit, brilliant in glory, and yet she recognized it as him. When it reached the body, it did not hesitate but entered in, and a moment later Kyle's eyes opened and he sat up and smiled at her. In the final fusion of body and light, there was a flash of brilliance, and his mortal clothes were changed into the white robes of eternity.

He swung his feet from the jeep and walked to her and offered his arms for an embrace. With a sob, she stepped into them and felt his love in a way that had never been possible before. What he was feeling was magnified through his perfect body, making it a direct conduit of communication to her heart, giving her the impression that they had united into one spirit. "Elisheba, I'm here again with you," he said in almost unbelief. "This time it is forever."

At that moment, while he still held her in his arms, the power of Jesus permeated the whole earth seeking the righteous living. Many who had been caught up were changed at that moment, while in the sky, others, such as Elisheba, who had remained on earth for the reunion of their loved ones, were changed there, and in another flash of light like the one that had welded Kyle's spirit eternally with his resurrected body, her body was changed in the twinkling of an eye to immortality. There was no pain but an incredibly exhilarating sensation at the moment when her spirit was lodged inside its new temple—immediate communication with God's spirit, with His love, were now part of her makeup. For a moment, she held her hands up and studied them intently. The form was still the same, but they were different. She felt her face and then touched the white robes covering her. She smiled and thought the words, "No one could have ever known how it would be until it happened." Kyle smile and nodded; then took her by her left hand and walked her to the entrance of the pass.

Above the layer of hailstones, the righteous dead who had been buried in the Kidron, or killed recently in the battle, or died on this spot of ground throughout all the centuries milled about, speaking with others they had known in mortality or some they had met while they were spirits. From the people gathered near the opening, David stepped forward, smiling broadly. "Long time, no see," he said as he threw his arms around both his friends.

Jesus lowered his arms. For a moment He stood looking out among those He had just healed, and then bowed His head as if in prayer. When He lifted it again, those closest to Him could see the tears that trickled down His cheeks. "Kyle and Elisheba and David," he said with the same gentle but penetrating voice that allowed all to hear, "come to me."

Together the three people stood and began moving through the crowd, which parted to let them pass, and holding hands, they ascended the hillside. Their eyes remained fixed on Jesus until they had drawn close to him, then Kyle lowered his head, and he was overcome with emotion and began to cry. Elisheba shifted her hand around his waist to support and lead him while she looked ahead, seeing for both of them, her face radiant with joy, her eyes never leaving the eyes of the Master.

They stopped in front of Him, two steps below where He stood. Kyle, whose eyes were still lowered, saw only His feet and sandals, and without looking up, knelt to the ground. Elisheba and David knelt with him, bowing their heads. Jesus extended His hand and touched them on the tops of their head.

"Look at me," He said gently. Together they lifted their heads and looked into His loving face.

"Well done my beloved friends."